Memories for Tomorrow

DIANE GREENWOOD MUIR

This is a work of fiction. Names, characters, places, brands, media, and incidents are either the product of the author's imagination or are used fictitiously. The author acknowledges the trademarked status and trademark owners of various products referenced in this work of fiction, which have been used without permission. The publication / use of these trademarks is not authorized, associated with, or sponsored by the trademark owners.

Cover Design Photography: Maxim M. Muir

ISBN-13: 978-1542309486
ISBN-10: 1542309484

Don't miss any of the books in
Diane Greenwood Muir's

Bellingwood Series

All Roads Lead Home – Bellingwood #1
A Big Life in a Small Town – Bellingwood #2
Treasure Uncovered – Bellingwood #3
Secrets and Revelations – Bellingwood #4
Life Between the Lines – Bellingwood #5
Room at the Inn – Bellingwood #5.5
A Season of Change – Bellingwood #6
Tomorrow's Promises – Bellingwood #7
Through the Storm – Bellingwood #8
A Perfect Honeymoon – Bellingwood #8.5
Pages of the Past – Bellingwood #9
The River Rolls On – Bellingwood #10
Look Always Forward – Bellingwood #11
Out of the Shadows – Bellingwood #12
Home for the Holidays – Bellingwood #12.5
Unexpected Riches – Bellingwood #13
Reflecting Love's Charms – Bellingwood #14
Capture the Moments – Bellingwood #15
Memories for Tomorrow – Bellingwood #16
All I Want for Christmas – Bellingwood #16.5

A short story based
on the Biblical Book of Ruth (Kindle only)
Abiding Love

CONTENTS

ACKNOWLEDGMENTS

In the midst of chaos and upheaval throughout the world, the one place I find peace is in the community that surrounds these Bellingwood books. There are people who show up there and leave notes for me and for each other. The things I learn about everyone reminds me how terrific this world really is. Spend time with us at facebook.com/pollygiller.

The beautiful photographs that grace the covers of the Bellingwood books are shot by my husband, Maxim Muir. While I might do the actual work, it's only because of Rebecca Bauman's eye for color and design that these photos turn into covers.

When I think about the number of people who are part of my life and who help me get from book to book, my heart fills, often so much that my eyes leak.

My beta readers are more than just readers. They edit, find continuity problems, point out unnecessary words / phrases / thoughts, catch strange grammar and are such a necessary part of my process. Without them, I'd be lost.

Thank you to these amazing people: Carol Greenwood, Tracy Kesterson Simpson, Alice Stewart, Fran Neff, Max Muir, Edna Fleming, Linda Baker, Linda Watson, and Nancy Quist. And to Judy Tew who cleans things up after I do a final edit.

My life is extraordinary because I get to do what I love to do. Thank you for making it possible.

CHAPTER ONE

The incessant noise was enough to drive a sane person crazy, but Polly refused to complain. Those machines working – ripping, tearing, sanding, cutting - meant that day by day they were closer to finishing rooms on the main floor. For the last month, though, it had seemed like everything that could possibly interrupt the progress at the Bell House erupted. Jerry Allen's heart attack in early August meant that Doug Randall and Billy Endicott covered his other work. Of course, she and Henry told them to go. Their house could wait.

Liam Hoffman had encountered so many issues with the plumbing that he'd walked off the site one day threatening never to return. That might have happened after he was doused with sewage a second time. He did return the next morning, but with large equipment that ripped Polly's beautiful front yard to shreds. The old pipes came out and he laid new from the house to the street.

While he was at it, he brought brand new line in from the city water. At least their plumbing would last for another hundred years. Hoffman guaranteed that it was done correctly this time.

He never wanted to see the sewer line at Bell House again.

He finished that last week. For the last few days he'd been running pipe through walls in the kitchen, back porch, and the back bathroom. Polly had been appalled at the idea that this immense house only had one bathroom on the main floor, so they'd knocked out walls and built in a second bathroom at the other end of the house. Hoffman moaned and groaned about pulling pipe that far, but Henry told her to just stay quiet and let him do his job. He was working on that this morning and Polly was doing her very best to keep her head down. It wasn't easy since both were in the basement.

Polly planned to go through each crate of china in the old moonshiner's office. If it was all only china, she wanted an inventory before deciding whether to keep it. She also needed to pull down and inventory each of the tally boards on the walls.

She nearly jumped out of her skin when loud banging rang against the wooden wall that separated the room she was in from the rest of the basement.

"You in there, Polly?" Liam yelled.

"Yes?" she replied as calmly as possible. There really was no reason to speak loudly, the boards were thin with plenty of space between each of the boards. She could see him through the spaces.

"Have you and Henry made a decision about that fountain yet? Do I run pipe back to it or not?"

They hadn't at all. It was one of those things they avoided talking about. Polly thought it was fun and important to keep since they hoped to maintain some integrity of the original building. On the other hand, Henry thought it was ridiculous and would only create more problems. He'd reminded Polly several times of the mess it would make and since she abhorred cleaning anyway, having to clean out a fountain on a regular basis would become a huge burden. The structure was still in place. All they needed to do was decide whether to bring water to it.

For that matter, she wasn't even sure the thing worked. The pump that had been installed a hundred years ago must be useless by now.

"You need to know today?" she asked.

"Since I'm going that way for the bathroom, it would be nice to know if I need to split water off to it."

Polly knew better than that. Even if they did want the fountain, he surely wasn't going to use the same line that would take water to a shower. The thing would never have any pressure.

"You're not splitting water off," she said. "Surely you'd run a separate line."

He heaved a great sigh. "Yeah. You're right. But if I'm taking one line down, I could take two while I'm at it."

She gave her head a quick shake and made a decision. "No. We're not going to run the fountain."

"That's a good plan." He walked away a few paces and then returned. "Look, Polly. I could probably just run the Pex pipe anyway. I won't hook it up to anything, but if you ever decide differently, at least that part will be done."

She smiled to herself. "Thanks, Liam. I appreciate it."

"Yeah, yeah, yeah. I'm just a good guy." He muttered nonsense to himself as he walked away.

Polly's phone buzzed and she pulled it out of her back pocket.

"I forgot my flute for band practice. Can you bring it to school for me?" Rebecca asked via text.

That girl had better be between classes. Polly had given strict orders that her phone was to reside in her locker during the day. If she got caught using it in class and Polly found out, she was going to be without a phone and would have to use Polly's when she wanted to talk to her friends. This other behavior was driving Polly nuts, though. At least once or twice a week since school started, Rebecca forgot something important. They'd had a discussion just this morning that Polly was finished taking things to her.

Polly set her jaw. It nearly killed her, but she simply texted back. *"Nope."*

"But I need it. What am I supposed to do?"

"Borrow one or go to study hall. We talked about this. You are responsible for your things. I'm busy."

"Your not fair."

"You're," Polly texted.

"Whatever."

"Go to class. Deal with it."

Polly asked Sylvie if she had this problem with Andrew and Sylvie laughed. Of course she didn't have a problem like this. Sylvie fixed it years ago. But then, Sylvie had also never been available during the school day. The boys would have been foolish to try to pull that on her. She wouldn't have answered the phone, much less left her job.

The phone rang and Polly grinned when she saw that it was Henry.

"Hi there,"

"Hey, Meanie Woman," he replied.

"She did not," Polly spat, the grin quickly leaving her face.

Henry laughed. "Who did not do what?"

"Tell me that Rebecca didn't call or text you." Polly walked out of the room into the tunnel and locked the door. If Henry had said no to their daughter, Rebecca would keep going down the line. Fortunately, Heath was at school, but Rebecca knew full well that Hayden didn't have classes until late afternoon today.

"She called. Said you wouldn't bring her flute to her and wondered if I was in town."

"I'm going to have her head," Polly said. She ran through the tunnel to the steps leading up to Rebecca's art room, out the door, and then pulled to a stop in front of the side door.

"She sounded desperate."

"Yep. One day of desperate will stop this behavior, though. I'm willing to suffer through it."

"Okay," he said with a laugh. "You know I'll always suffer with you."

The side door blasted open and Hayden came outside. He smiled at Polly and didn't say anything since he could see she was on the phone, but she grabbed his arm.

"Where are you going?"

"Just going to run an errand," he said.

"I'll talk to you later, Henry," Polly said. "I need to deal with this."

"Love you, Bunnykins."

"Uh huh."

"What's your errand?" Polly asked Hayden.

"Well, I, uh."

"Gonna go pick up a flute and take it to your sister?" She grinned as she waited for an answer.

"Is that so bad?"

"How many times have you done this for her?" Polly asked.

"Just a couple."

She shook her head. "You're not doing it today."

"But she's expecting me to show up with it."

"I'll take care of it," Polly said. "Unless you need to go somewhere else, you march right back inside and work. You are not coddling that child any longer. Got it?"

"Really?"

"Really. Today we break her habit. She can take responsibility for her own things."

"Mom used to always have to bring things to us at school. I was forever forgetting gym shorts or homework." Hayden protested.

"And if she'd said 'no' one time, would you have been better about organizing yourself before you left for school in the morning?"

"I suppose."

"What do you do now if you forget something you need?"

"Just deal." He slunk away and went back up the steps. "I get it. Tell her to be mad at me, too."

Polly laughed. "I've got this." She opened her messaging app and typed, *"Nobody is rescuing you. And trying to go behind my back? That's an entirely different discussion we'll have tonight."* She sent the text and wandered to her truck.

"Fine. Sorry," was what she got back.

Polly got into her truck and backed out of the driveway. She was furious and needed to be far away from people. For that matter, she needed to be far away from crates of china. She knew better than to let Rebecca get to her, but just about the time things were going well, the girl pulled something like this. She came to a stop sign. Straight ahead would take her downtown. A left turn would lead to the highway and Polly could at least hit the gas in a few miles. She turned left, even though a cup of coffee sounded good. Man, that girl made her angry.

Polly drove past the hotel and the entrance to the winery. A little further and she drove past Davey's. Finally she was clear. As soon as the speed limit climbed to fifty-five, Polly hit the gas. She turned cruise control on at sixty-two. There was no reason to get a ticket because she was furious.

She chuckled. There was no real reason to be out here. Polly wondered how many times her father, or even Mary, had gotten in a car and driven away from Polly's bad behavior. Probably more than Polly even realized. She pulled into a field entrance to turn around, and headed back to Bellingwood. She was getting over her fury at Rebecca more quickly every time this happened, but the girl had to know there would be a squeaky clean bathroom in her future. She was good for at least a once a month cleaning.

When Polly's phone rang again, she was driving past the hotel and smiled at Henry's picture on her screen. She swiped it open. "Hello there."

"How mad are you?"

She laughed. "It only took two miles this time."

"Did she really contact Hayden?"

"Yes she really did. He's covered for her a few times," Polly said, frustration lacing her tone. "Henry, she's been back in school less than a month. I had to stop it."

"I get that. Don't let this eat at you. She screwed up. She'll figure it out. Rebecca is sweet and caring, kind and giving, but that doesn't mean that she gets away with manipulating her family."

"And anyone else who will let her," Polly said. "Oh, Liam is running pipe toward the fountain, but I told him not to hook anything up. You're right. I don't want that mess inside the house.

If they'd installed it on the front lawn, I would have pushed harder to restore it, but not this."

"Do you want to leave it in the foyer?"

"We don't want to rebuild that section of the floor," Polly said. "Nothing would match. Maybe you could just put a big box around it."

He chuckled. "I suppose. We'll let your creative mind process on it for a while and see what you come up with."

"Okay, I'm back at the Bell House. I'll head down into the hole and uncover great wealth."

"Go for it. I could use a new truck," he replied. "I love you, Num-num."

"That's weird. But I love you, too." Polly also loved his ridiculous attempts at endearments.

She got out of the truck and unlocked the door to Rebecca's workshop, then headed down the steps and into the tunnel. Once she was back in the old office, she flipped the light switch that Henry had installed for her and stood in front of the wall of tally boards. One by one, she took them down and carried them to the desk.

Each name had been burned into the wood at the top of the board. Polly ran her fingers across several as she stacked them into neat piles. If she remembered right, Ken Wallers had said that his grandfather was M. Langer. She leaned back in the chair and looked at that board, trying to think about what life was like a hundred years ago, making whiskey from the corn on your farm, worrying that the law might catch you. Maybe the local lawmen knew what was going on. Maybe they were part of the industry.

She turned the board over and heard something rattle. That was strange. Polly shook it and heard the rattle again. Had she shaken something loose? Tugging at the sides and edges of the board, Polly discovered a small wooden plate that slid open just behind where the name was etched. She placed the board face down on the desk, slid the panel off, and after peering at the three bits of something, shuddered when she realized she was looking at teeth. They'd been embedded in a substance that felt like candle wax and somehow had finally come loose. The wax held two more teeth as well as the impressions of the three that rattled around.

Polly slid the plate back on again and set the board aside, then took another board, turned it over and felt around for the same plate. Sure enough, she slid it off and found the same waxy substance, this time holding a gold ring. Things had just moved from interesting to creepy. Why in the world were there teeth in her basement? Polly opened each of the boards. Not only did she find teeth, but found three more rings, one with a red stone in it, a small metal cross, a metal whistle, and coins of various denominations. Unless kids had found their way down here, none of this made any sense.

Since she had time, she took pictures of everything she found, along with a picture of the front of the board, so she knew what was in each of them. Polly needed answers and she was starting with Ken Wallers. Maybe his grandfather had said something about losing his teeth. But how could he possibly explain tucking them in the back of this tally board?

When she was finished, she stacked the boards beside the desk, out of the way, then dragged the closest crate over. Polly had brought a box of large black trash bags with her, so as she unpacked the top layer of china plates, she jammed the shredded wood packing material down into one of the bags. Mice had made hash of packing material below the first layer. By the time she was finished, Polly desperately needed a bath. At the very least, a good scrub from the elbows down. That was the last crate she'd unpack without rubber gloves. She unpacked ten dinner plates and six cups and saucers. Before leaving, Polly took a picture of the front and the back of one of the plates to research at home.

It was close to noon, so Polly went out the way she'd come in, shutting lights off and locking doors behind her again. She used the pump behind the garage to wash her arms before leaving for the morning.

After cleaning up, Polly went to the side door and inside. "Hayden, are you still here?" she yelled out.

"Yeah. I'm about ready to leave." He came through the kitchen door to meet her. "Are you done downstairs?"

"For now. I found something weird down there."

"What more could you find? Tell me it wasn't another body."

It was a fair statement. Just not one Polly thought would ever be part of her makeup. So much for childhood innocence. Her life was full of construction and dead bodies. "Yeah, no. This was weird little bits and pieces of things. They were tucked into wax in a little hiding place in the tally boards. Like teeth and coins and rings."

Hayden huffed a laugh. "That *is* weird. What do you think it's all about?"

"I have absolutely no idea. I found the teeth in the board that belonged to Ken Wallers' grandfather. I'll ask him what he knows."

"That's a good idea." He patted his back pocket and then took keys out. "So how mad do you think Rebecca will be at me?"

Polly lifted her eyebrows at him. "Mad at you? Little Missy doesn't get to be mad at you. She's the one who was in the wrong. You can't give her the world just because she asks for it, you know."

"It's fun, though," he said, holding the door open as Polly crossed through and headed down the steps. "I like making her happy."

"Well stop it," Polly said. "I'm nipping this in the bud." She snapped her index finger and thumb together. "In the bud."

He laughed. "Got it. So I'd be in trouble if I called this afternoon and told you that I'd forgotten my laptop?"

"Yes you would," Polly replied. "Are you going home now?"

"Just to get my stuff. And don't worry, I packed everything I needed last night. I don't want to be in trouble."

"That's my good boy." Polly patted him on the back and then stopped to give him a quick hug. "I'm heading for the police station. I won't see you before you leave. Have a good afternoon."

"I've got the dogs, then," he said. "I might be home late for dinner. I can pick something up."

They had this discussion every week. "You know there will be food at home for you if you want it. But if you're craving fast food, I'm fine with that." Polly got into her truck and backed out of the driveway. This place would be finished someday. Just when, she had no idea.

CHAPTER TWO

Heading for the police station, Polly slowly approached Sweet Beans Coffee Shop, torn between pulling into a parking space or driving past. Ken would at lunch now anyway. He wouldn't be in the office. There, that made everything better.

She waved at Jen Dykstra who was arranging fabric and a quilt in the front window of the quilt shop. Jen beckoned for her to come in, so Polly veered and headed that way.

"What's up?" she asked.

Jen smiled. "Come on back here. I wanted you to see some of our new Christmas fabric. You're going to love it."

Polly stopped in her tracks and held her hands up, crossing her two index fingers. "Get thee behind me, woman. You know I don't have time for this."

"I know you don't," Jen said with a naughty giggle. "But you're going to love it. Think of the beautiful runner you could make for that big table you told me about. You'll be in the new house by Christmas and it would be such a pretty part of the celebration. Sonja also has patterns for Christmas tree skirts. We talked about her doing a class in October for those."

Polly turned for the front door, dramatically dragging her feet. Then she stopped again and turned back. Okay," she said with a sigh. "Are all of your customers as weak as me?"

"Every single one of them," Jen said. "If I didn't sell this stuff to you, I'd buy it myself. My poor sewing room is already bursting at the seams."

"Henry would build on for you."

"Come on. See what we've got."

The front of the shop was decked out in autumn colors - quilts, table toppers, wall hangings and pillows all done in reds, golds, greens, oranges and yellows. Cute little pumpkins were scattered in nooks and crannies, some with LED lights poking out and others with adorable faces sewn on. Sycamore House did its own decorating for fall and Halloween, making it easy for Polly to not worry about what she did upstairs in the apartment. Next year things would be different. She wanted to decorate for every season.

They stopped in front of a lap quilt done in rich reds, greens, and golds with metallic accents. "Wouldn't that be beautiful on the dark wood table?" Jen asked. She picked up a brightly wrapped collection of fabric. "Everything you need is here." She patted a crate filled with rolls of strips and small packs of five inch squares. "You could do an old-fashioned Christmas pattern for the tree skirt. It would go together in a jiffy."

"You have more confidence in my skill than I do," Polly said.

"It's all straight lines," Jen replied with a laugh. "Come on. You'll be happy you did it."

Polly took a deep breath, shook her head and grinned. "You know I'm useless. Are you really going to hold a class for the tree skirt?"

Jen nodded. "Sure. What morning is good for you?"

Polly laughed until she snorted. "I'm the only one?"

"So far, but once we set a date, more people will join us." Jen gave Polly her sweetest grin.

"I don't care," Polly said, shaking her head. "Pick one and send me an email. Plan on me being there."

"I told Sonja you'd do it."

"Don't make me buy fabric today, though," Polly said. "Henry is already questioning the piles in our bedroom. I really need to finish a couple of projects before I bring more home."

"I understand." Jen nodded. "It will wait for you here." She chuckled. "Maybe that's what we should do. Buy the building next door and rent storage space. That way, people can buy what they want and take it home when they're ready to use it."

Polly looked at her sideways. "Isn't that what your store is supposed to be for?"

"Yes," Jen said, laughing. "Of course. But what if we were out of stock when you wanted it?"

"Great," Polly muttered. "Okay, ring me up. I don't need the added pressure of worrying that I'm going to miss out on something." She picked up the stack of fat quarters and ran her fingers across the top piece of fabric. "This is so pretty."

"Which fabric do you want for the tree skirt?"

"The silver snow scene," Polly replied. "And that bright one there, too. Oh, and I love this blue set of colors. I'd better get it as well. I'm going to have Christmas trees everywhere in the house. They'll all need skirts. Right?"

Jen picked up the fabric and walked toward the front counter. "We'll talk about mantle scarves and ornaments another time."

"That's so very wrong," Polly said. "Please let me get out of here with my dignity today."

Polly tossed the bag of fabric into the front seat of her truck before heading into the coffee shop. It was strange to be thinking about Christmas decorations. It was mid-September and summer was still holding on. The few beautiful days they had soon gave way to intense heat and humidity. Between that and having everyone back in school, work on the Bell House had slowed way down. Polly wasn't sure if they'd get in there by Christmas or not.

A new set of duplexes and apartments was being built south of Sycamore House on the other side of the road. Ralph Bedford told Eliseo he didn't know whether to worry or look forward to someone trying to buy his home and land. He was holding out for a lot of money if they wanted to develop down that way. It wouldn't happen for a few more years, but new construction was popping up all around Bellingwood. Henry had more work than he could handle.

"Hello there," Skylar called out from behind the counter. "You're running late today. Really late."

"No sass, just caffeine," Polly said.

"You know my best drinks come with a side of cheeky retorts," he replied. "Have you eaten lunch yet? Rachel made an amazing ham salad today and we're serving it on Sylvie's sourdough with tomato slices and lettuce. What do you think?"

"I think you're a great salesman. That sounds wonderful." So far, Polly was zero for two up against salespeople in Bellingwood.

"Have you talked to Stephanie this morning?" he asked.

Polly shook her head. "No? What's up?"

He grinned. "I just wondered if she said anything. We went to Pufferbilly Days in Boone this weekend."

"The two of you? Like a date?" Polly couldn't believe she hadn't heard about this. Kayla and Rebecca should have been talking about it all weekend.

"It wasn't a date. We just thought we'd go Saturday morning to see what it was all about. She met me down there and then we walked around. They have a parade and then there are all of these stands around. It was a blast."

"You?" Polly stared at him. "And Stephanie?"

"Yeah. Is that okay?"

"It's great. I just can't believe Kayla didn't tell Rebecca and the two of them didn't tell me!"

He pushed her drink across the counter and leaned in to whisper. "She didn't tell Kayla. Just told her she had an appointment."

"You and Stephanie are sneaking around?"

"Well, not sneaking." He frowned at her. "I'd never sneak with her. She's great. She's a lot of fun."

"You and Stephanie," Polly said, musing to herself. "I can't believe I didn't know."

"I'm surprised she didn't tell you. We aren't trying to hide anything. Stephanie doesn't want to tell Kayla in case things don't work out. She says Kayla has had enough to deal with."

"So has Stephanie," Polly said. She watched Skylar make her sandwich.

"Yeah. I know. We've talked a lot about her history. That's crazy. How could one man be so evil and have such great daughters?"

"I don't know," Polly said, shaking her head. "But Stephanie is pretty strong."

"Yeah. She's cool. Chips?" Skylar pointed to the rack of potato chips.

Polly nodded.

"You want a pickle?"

"Sure," she said. "Are you guys doing good business with lunch?"

He shrugged. "Pretty good. We're keeping it low key. Camille and Jeff don't want to make it a big deal until we see if it's something folks around here want." Skylar grinned. "That's why I offer it to everybody. I talked you right into it, didn't I?"

Polly laughed. "So far today, I'm an easy target. Is Sylvie in the back?"

"Nah. She and Camille are over at Sycamore House. They're interviewing new people for the bakery and catering. Sylvie wants to get some permanent employees on staff." He glanced up at the clock. "They'll be back here before one, though. I have to get to class."

Polly picked up the plate and walked away, then turned back. "I'm happy for you and Stephanie," she said. "I hope things go really well."

"Me too." His face lit into a huge grin. "She's awesome."

"Young love," Polly murmured as she headed for a booth. "I was not expecting that today."

Skylar was right. The ham salad was delicious. Polly tucked back into the corner of the booth, its tall back giving her plenty of privacy. She shut her eyes and thought about the morning.

Rebecca had so much growing up to do before Polly let her loose in the world. These were the days she missed her father. It was one thing to talk to Lydia and Andy, but it would be nice to be able to relate what she was going through with Rebecca to what her dad dealt with when Polly was a girl. She grinned. He was so easy going, but when she messed up, he didn't let her get away with it.

And all of that weird stuff she found in the tally boards. Polly popped her eyes open and picked up her phone to make a call.

"Bellingwood Police," Mindy said.

"Hey Mindy, it's Polly."

"Something going on?"

Polly laughed. "No, not today. Is Ken around this afternoon? It's personal, not a crisis."

"I'm sorry. He's not. There's a training class down in Des Moines. Can I help?"

"No. That's okay." Polly frowned. This wasn't working out the way she expected. "Leave him a note to contact me when he's got time, would you?"

"I'll tell him. But I'm not sure when he'll reach out. Is that okay?"

"Yeah. No hurry. Thanks, Mindy." Polly hung up and put her phone on the table, then took a drink of her iced cold brew. She'd hoped that Ken could point her to families of some of the other names on those tally boards. Without him, she wasn't sure where to start.

The bell on the front door jangled and Sky smiled. Rather than turning to see who it was, Polly waited.

"It's all ready for you," he said, holding out a cup.

"I love the way you take care of me. It's miserable outside." Lisa Bradford put several pieces of mail on the counter in front of him and took up her cup. She popped the lid open and blew on it, then smiled. "I love the way iced coffee feels on my face."

Sky laughed. "Every day, Mrs. Bradford. One of these days you'll order hot pumpkin spice. Fall is coming. I promise."

"You keep promising me that, young man. I'll believe it when I see it." She turned and saw Polly, then waved. "Back into the furnace I go."

Polly remembered another name on the tally boards. "Lisa?" she called out.

"Yes, dear."

"Can I walk with you for a few minutes? I have a strange question."

"If you can keep up, you can walk," Lisa said with a laugh. "What am I saying? You'll have no problem today. I'm dragging something terrible. The weather is going to make us wait until the very last minute to cool off." She gritted her teeth. "Just so it doesn't turn from ninety degrees to nine degrees overnight, though. That would really frost my biscuits. What can I help you with?"

They paused at the door and Polly turned back to Skylar. "I'm coming back for that. Okay?"

He nodded.

"Your husband's grandfather might have made whiskey back in the teens and twenties," Polly said. "I found tally boards in my basement that I think recorded the number of gallons people sold to Franklin Bell. One had the name Bradford on it."

"That sounds like Paul's grandpappy," Lisa said. "He was always looking for an easy buck. There are stories about that old man. From what I hear, he even lost his wife's wedding ring in some kind of deal gone bad. She nearly divorced him over it, but never got around to it. Excuse me, just a second. I'll be right back." Lisa ducked into an office and within moments was back. "You should go over and see Paul. He'd be able to tell you more about it. Come to think of it, he should have talked to you earlier this year. I'll bet he has a couple of old Bell's Whiskey bottles tucked away. You would have liked those."

"We have a bunch," Polly said and waited while Lisa took mail into another office. She didn't realize there were so many businesses and offices on these side streets.

"You have bottles already?" Lisa asked.

"Yeah. We found a stash in those underground rooms."

Lisa stopped. "Now I feel bad that we didn't get over there during Bellingwood Days. We were just so busy with everything downtown."

"You're welcome anytime I'm there," Polly said. She crossed the street with Lisa and waited as the woman entered another door.

"Go in and see Paul," Lisa said when she came back out. "He'll talk your ear off with his stories." She stopped at another doorway. "This is going to take a while. There are a bunch of offices upstairs."

Polly smiled. "Thanks for your time. I look forward to talking to your husband."

"I'll tell him what you were asking about. Who knows. Maybe he has some pictures of that group his grandpappy was part of." Lisa opened and shut the door a couple of times, fanning Polly with cool air. "Now skedaddle back to the cool of the coffee shop. Only one of us needs to melt today."

Polly wanted to ask more questions. "What group? What did they do?" But Lisa was long gone and she was right. The afternoon heat and humidity had gotten worse and Polly was ready to melt. She was also done at Bell House. Mornings were about the only tolerable time of day to be over there when the weather was this out of control. She crossed the street and walked in through the patio door of the coffee shop.

"Hello there," she said to Camille. "That changeover was quick."

"Sky was ready to leave. He has something going on before class starts today." Camille pointed at Polly's booth. "He told me I wasn't supposed to touch it. What did you think of Rachel's ham salad?"

"It's good. I'm glad you're working with the catering business. That's pretty cool. Is Sylvie back?"

"Not yet. She had another interview with Rachel for the kitchen at Sycamore House."

"How are things going now that Elise is back in school?" Polly asked.

"I never see her," Camille replied. "She's a night person and I'm here early in the mornings. By the time she gets home from class, we say "hello, how are you" and I'm off to bed. But she seems happy enough."

The bell on the door rang again and Polly went back to her table. She didn't recognize the young couple who came in, so she scooted in and leaned against the wall before taking another long drink. What group was Paul Bradford's grandfather part of? Was Ken's granddad part of it, too? What did they do other than make whiskey? And why had no one talked about this before today? It could have been an interesting part of the sesquicentennial celebration. She huffed. People in town probably knew all about it and it was no big deal. Just part of their history that meant nothing. All Polly needed to do was ask the right questions of the right people and she'd find out that those little bits and pieces of things tucked into the tally boards were nothing more than betting chips. They probably lost poker games to Franklin Bell and he'd tucked his winnings away, not telling anyone where they were before he was killed.

"Don't try to make something out of nothing," Polly muttered to herself. "You have enough trouble with the things that *are* real."

"Hey Polly, talking to yourself?" Dylan Foster, owner of Pizzazz across the street, rapped twice on her table as he walked by.

"Yeah," she said, leaning forward. "Thinking about selling pizza over here. You know, build up the lunch crowd."

He laughed and turned back. "I'll put anchovies on your pizza next Sunday night if you aren't good."

"I'm good. I'm good," Polly said, holding her hands up.

The bell jangled again and three women came in, chattering at each other about something awful happening at one of the churches in town. Polly smiled. She didn't want to know, so she gathered up her trash and headed for the front door.

Polly got into her truck and turned it on, then backed out of the parking space, hoping for the air conditioning to kick in before she got home. Her phone buzzed with a text and as she waited for traffic to cross on the highway, she checked to see what it was.

"I'm really sorry about this morning," Rebecca texted to her. *"I know I'm in trouble. But I'm sorry."*

"I love you," Polly replied. *"We'll talk tonight."*

"Cleaning the bathroom?"

"Floor to ceiling."

"Gr8." Rebecca followed that up with a heart.

She really was a good girl. It was just going to take time for her to grow into it.

CHAPTER THREE

Early the next morning, Polly was at the desk in her home office, digging through numbers. She'd never thought of herself as a business person, but the last few years had taught her a lot. Fortunately, she wasn't alone. Her friend, Steve, in Story City took care of most of the accounting and Stephanie was becoming more and more proficient with their in-house accounting software. The girl actually enjoyed it. Polly didn't mind doing the work, it was just that she often caught herself staring out the windows, wondering what else was going on in the world.

The phone rang beside her and she swiped it open, even though she didn't recognize the number.

"This is Polly Giller."

"Ms. Giller, this is Larry Stoner in Boone. I'm the vice principal here at the high school."

"Certainly, Mr. Stoner. What can I do for you?"

He took a deep breath. "I need to ask you to come to the school. Heath has been suspended for the next three days."

"He what?" Polly yelped. "Why?"

"There was an incident with a teacher. Heath became

belligerent and aggressive, stopping just short of pushing the teacher. It's a good thing, too. That would probably have resulted in expulsion."

"He what? That doesn't sound like him at all."

"No ma'am. It doesn't. But he won't speak to anyone here. Suspension is our policy for something like this. He's lucky we didn't call in law enforcement and push for expulsion. It's his senior year. We'd rather fix it."

"I can't imagine what's going on with him. He hasn't been showing anything..." Polly let her voice drift off. They'd been so busy with the house and school re-starting, she could easily have missed something with Heath. They didn't see each other much these days. He was always quiet and she'd just accepted it for what it was.

"Ms. Giller?"

"I'll be there in less than half an hour. I'm so sorry. We'll deal with this."

"Thank you. Come directly to the office. We'll send for him from there."

"Okay." Polly closed the call and swiped another one open as she pushed back from the desk.

"Hey there, Cuddly-Wuddly, wud's up?" Henry asked.

She shook her head. "I'm going to Boone. Heath has been suspended for getting aggressive with a teacher."

"He what?"

"Huh," she said. "Exact words I used."

"Polly, were you ever suspended in your entire life?" Henry asked.

"Nope. Not ever."

"Me either. First Rebecca last year and now this. What kind of parents are we?"

She chuckled. "Parents of delinquents. That's all I've got right now. I know they're going to be great adults, but right now I want to dump them in the middle of a forest somewhere and tell them to make their own way home. They're frustrating the hell out of me."

Rebecca had come home sullen and snotty after school yesterday. She refused to speak with anyone and went straight into the bathroom, stomping and slamming things about as she cleaned. Polly went in at one point to find out what all the noise was. When she realized Rebecca only intended to escalate, left her to it, shutting the door behind her.

Kayla and Andrew hadn't come home with her, which was strange. When Polly asked, Rebecca had waved the question off, saying something about them being busy. That wasn't surprising. She was a horrible child when she was angry. Her friends loved her deeply but found other places to be when she was in a mood.

"Are you still there?" Henry asked.

Polly realized she was standing in front of the door to her truck. "Yeah. Sorry. Just thinking about how weird things were last night. I knew Rebecca was being a brat, but now I wonder what Heath was doing. Damn it, Henry. I've been so confident in him. He hasn't screwed up at all for over a year. Really responsible and working hard. What's going on?"

"I don't know, but I'll be sure to come home on time tonight. We'll sit down and talk things out. It's Tuesday. Hayden should be around, too, right?"

"Yeah. I'm going to make Heath tell him what's going on."

Henry laughed. "I'm sure that by the time Heath is back in Bellingwood, he will have discovered just how much pain you can bring. Have at it, Polly."

"I'm going to make him cry. That's my plan."

He laughed out loud. "Of course you are. I wouldn't expect anything less. How was little Miss Thing this morning?"

"She's going to cry too when I get my hands on her. I can't believe she didn't break last night. But I hugged her and told her I loved her as she walked out the door this morning."

"Did she have her flute?"

It was Polly's turn to laugh. "Yep. I asked. She patted her backpack. Okay. I need to go face this. Seriously, Henry. I never thought I'd be sitting in principals' offices waiting for them to deliver my delinquent children to me."

"Maybe it's not as bad as it sounds."

"It's bad enough."

"I love you. Thank you for dealing with this stuff."

She climbed up into the truck and then sighed dramatically. "It's my lot in life. I'll let you know when we're back." Polly was glad she'd called Henry. He always calmed her when her blood pressure threatened to pop her head off her shoulders.

Rebecca's suspension last year had been unfair, though Polly would never let the girl disrespect the principal and her decisions. The whole thing had been understandable and there was no need for any further punishment. She hoped that Heath's situation was similar; that he'd done something honorable and was misunderstood. Belligerent and aggressive behavior didn't offer much hope, though. Polly had met many of his teachers over the last couple of years at different functions and events. Sure, there were a couple she'd like to see in a different career, but you learned to deal with them and move on.

Just as she turned west to head into Boone, Polly's phone rang. She smiled when she saw that it was Lydia.

"Hello there," Polly said.

"I was just thinking about you," Lydia responded. "How are things going?"

"I don't know how you do it, but I'm heading to Boone High School to get Heath. He's been suspended for getting pushy with a teacher."

"Oh dear. What happened?"

"I don't have all of the information yet. But I will soon. Is it too late to turn in my Mom title?"

"I'm sorry. You're stuck with it for a lifetime," Lydia said. "But trust me. In a few months, this will just be another blip in the journey. Don't panic."

"I'm not panicked yet. Just mad. And Rebecca isn't having fun with life either. It's gonna be joyous at our house tonight."

Lydia laughed. "I'm not helping by laughing, but I'd love to be a fly on that wall. You are great with those kids. I'm proud of you."

"Thanks," Polly said. "I just pulled into the parking lot. I should go in and face the enemy."

"Just a second. Someone's birthday is coming up and it calls for a party."

"My birthday? You aren't supposed to do anything about that."

"It's like you don't know me at all," Lydia said. "Are you free Thursday evening? It will just be us girls at my house. Say yes. Please?"

Polly smiled. It had been a long time since the five of them had spent time together. "I don't have anything going on. That sounds great."

"Wonderful. It's a plan. Everyone else is already on board. Now be patient and find out the whole story before you explode all over poor Heath's head. Okay?"

"I'll try."

"I love you, my dear." Lydia was gone before Polly could respond.

Every year Polly hoped to get through her birthday without much fuss. Her friends would have none of it, so there was always something. Someday she'd like to just escape with Henry. Actually, these days, she'd just like to have an entire weekend with him without spending every waking hour at the Bell House. The project was so much bigger than she'd ever dreamed. It consumed all of their free time and felt like it was never going to progress to a point where they could begin finishing things.

Polly stood in front of the main doors to the building, took a deep breath and pulled one open, then went inside. Nothing about this would be pleasant. Best to just get into it and get out of it.

She made her way to the main office and asked for Mr. Stoner. One of the secretaries gave her a smile and came around the desk. "If you wouldn't mind waiting in this office, Mr. Stoner will be in to meet with you." The woman pushed open a door and Polly walked in to see Heath slouched over a table, his head in his arms.

"Heath?" she said quietly.

He didn't move or look up.

Polly crossed the room and put her hand on his back. When he flinched away from her, she pressed forward, maintaining contact. "Will you tell me what happened today?"

He refused to respond and pulled further away from her. She sat down in the chair next to him, scooting it close to him so she could touch his back again.

"We can do this all day," Polly said. "You're going to run into the wall before I run out of patience."

That elicited a shrug.

"At least I know your hearing works." She looked up as the door opened, then stood to shake Larry Stoner's hand.

"It's nice to see you again," he said. "I wish it was under better circumstances."

Polly nodded. "Is there anything more I need to know right now?"

"I'd like Heath to tell us what happened in his own words."

They both turned to look at Heath, but he kept his head down, buried in his arms, the hood of his jacket pulled over his head.

Polly set her jaw. She wasn't about to allow this type of disrespectful behavior. At least not when she was in the room.

"Sit up straight, Heath," she said, pulling the hood back.

Heath shrugged her hand off and sat up. He crossed his arms in front of his chest and leaned back in the chair, spreading his legs under the desk. Not once did he look at either of them, keeping his eyes down.

"I don't know what is going on," Polly said to him, "but you aren't getting away with acting like this. Are you going to talk to us?"

He gritted his teeth and looked down and away from them.

Polly knew she could push and create a scene, but hoped that Mr. Stoner wasn't asking that of her. All she wanted to do was get Heath out of this room and somewhere private so he could tell her what in the world was going on. The disrespectful behavior could be dealt with once he let go of whatever was hurting him so badly.

She looked at Mr. Stoner, who gave her a slight shrug. "He's been like this all morning," the vice principal said.

"May I take him home?" Polly asked. "We'll deal with this as a family and then get back to you."

He frowned at her, obviously not expecting that response.

"You've already suspended him, right?" Polly asked.

"Well, yes."

"Then he's my problem now. But trust me, we'll get to the bottom of it." Polly put her hand on Heath's upper arm. When he tried to shrug her off again, she gripped it through the jacket. "Nope. You're coming with me. Come on. Out the door. My truck's out front."

It occurred to her that his truck was probably also in the parking lot. "Give me your keys," she said.

Heath looked at her in confusion.

"Just give me your keys."

He dug down into his jacket pocket and pulled out his key ring, then handed it over.

She turned to the vice principal. "Is there any way to reach Jason Donovan? I'd like to ask him to drive Heath's truck back to Bellingwood. He comes to Sycamore House every day after school."

The man looked back and forth between the two of them. "We can find him. Ask Sharon out front. Are you sure?"

Polly took a breath. "I've got this. All of it. Don't worry." She took Heath's arm again and guided him out to the main office and stopped to speak with the same woman who had helped her before. "Could you ask Jason Donovan to come down to the office?" Polly asked.

"Are you a relative?"

"No. But he works for me," Polly said, her patience nearly exhausted. "I would like to ask him to drive our truck back to Bellingwood after school today. Is this a possibility or would you like me to contact his mother and make her call you to ask the same question?"

Sharon glanced at the vice principal who gave her a nod. She typed Jason's name into her computer and then placed a quick call. "He'll be here in a few minutes. He's in the middle of a class."

"I understand that," Polly said. "Thank you."

She led Heath out of the office and took a deep, cleansing breath. "You," she said, pushing him toward a bench. "Sit and wait for me. I don't want you to move."

Polly went back into the office and stopped at the young woman's desk again. "Now I need to ask about classwork for Heath. Since he's suspended all week, I'd like for him to not fall behind."

"All of the teachers should have their classwork posted online," Sharon said. "As long as he has his books, he can do the work. If there are any tests, he'll have to make those up."

"We'll need to go to his locker, then," Polly said. "Do I need a pass for that?"

"If the security officer goes with you, you'll be fine."

"Hey Polly," Jason said, surprised at seeing her in the office. "I didn't know why they called me down here. What's up?"

Polly pressed Heath's keys into Jason's hand and led him away from the desk. "Heath has been suspended. Can you drive his truck home tonight?"

"I heard about that," Jason said. "I couldn't believe it was him. All up in Mr. West's face. The guy's a jerk, but I never would have thought Heath would lose it like that."

"What does Mr. West teach?" she asked.

"English and literature. I don't know which class Heath has with him. How bad is it?"

"End of the week. Can you drive his truck?"

Jason shrugged and smiled. "Sure. I'll park it in the regular spot." He tossed the keys up and caught them before shoving his hands in his pocket. "See you later. I better get back to class."

Polly turned back to the secretary. "Security Officer?"

"Dave," Sharon called. A man in uniform came out from another office. "Would you escort Ms. Giller and Heath to his locker and then make sure they leave by the front door?"

Polly tilted her head. Really? She rolled her eyes as she turned to walk back out and gave her head a jerk. "Come on, Heath. We're getting your books."

He stood up and walked behind her as they negotiated the hallways to his locker.

"Everything," Polly said as she held the door open.

Heath picked his backpack up from the floor of the locker and jammed books and notebooks in, stuffing it to the brim.

"Is that it?"

Pushing the door of his locker closed, he spun on his heels and headed back for the front door of the school with Polly and Dave, the security officer, scrambling to catch up.

Dave walked them to the front door and held it for Polly after Heath pushed through and out into the sunshine. The heat and oppressive humidity did nothing to help Polly's temper.

Heath looked up and around, spotted Polly's truck and strode across the parking lot, waiting for her to arrive. She deliberately refused to open the locks until she was there. Her little rebellion made her chuckle to herself, but his attitude was so alien she wasn't sure what was coming next.

As soon as she unlocked the doors, he opened the back door, flung his backpack in, then slammed it before opening the front door and climbing in. He pulled his belt on and slouched against the door as far from Polly as he could get while still being in the same small space with her.

Polly sat behind the steering wheel and realized how hot and miserable she was, so she turned the truck on and prayed for the air conditioning to cool the cab quickly. "Are you going to tell me what happened?" she asked him.

He didn't move or speak.

"Do you understand how much trouble you're in?" she asked, backing out of the parking space. They had to get moving to force the air conditioning to come up faster. What a miserably hot day.

"You'd better figure this out soon," Polly said. "I don't know what to think right now. You're acting so out of character, it makes me worried that something hit you in the head last night and changed your personality." She glanced at him to see if he would respond and got nothing. "I haven't seen this Heath since the night you showed up in my garage. I can tell you right now that I'm not at all happy he's here again. Where in the world do you get off being such a jerk to everyone? That's not how you behave, no matter what happens."

There was still no response. His facial muscles didn't twitch, his eyes didn't change from the same flat stare he'd pasted on when she entered the office. If only he would talk to her. Say anything. Even if he told her to go to hell, that would be better than this. Maybe she'd just sit on him once they got up to the apartment. That would startle him.

Polly glanced his way again and caught him snapping his head back toward the front of the truck. He'd been looking at her. At least that was progress.

CHAPTER FOUR

The moment she pulled into the garage, Heath put his hand on the door handle. Polly reached across and grabbed his forearm. "We need to talk."

"I'm not talking. There's nothing to say. I'll just work over at the house this week."

"Oh no you won't," she replied. "You're staying here. If anything, you'll work at the barn with Eliseo."

He looked at her as if she's lost her mind. "I hate working down there. I thought you knew that."

Polly nodded and smiled. "I do know that. But it wouldn't be much punishment if you spent the week doing something you love, now would it."

He lifted his upper lip in a near snarl. "Whatever."

At his attempt to pull his arm away, she gripped it harder. "What in the world is going on? You don't get to talk to me like that. You don't get to act like this."

"You're not my mother and you can't tell me what to do."

"Like heck I can't. And just in case you weren't paying attention, I am your mother for all intents and purposes. You're my son and I love you, but this behavior is unacceptable. However, if you don't want to talk to me now, I can be patient. When Hayden and Henry get home this afternoon, we'll all sit down and have a conversation. You can explain why you've suddenly chosen to take on a piss-poor attitude. This behavior disgusts me. I'm not terribly excited about spending more time with you as it is. Go up to your room. There will be no television, no video games. In fact, I'll take your phone."

"You can't take my phone."

"I can certainly take your phone. Hand it over."

Heath put his hand on the truck door again and Polly released him.

"Go upstairs to your room. I'll be there in a moment," she said.

He got out and opened the door to the house, turned to look at her and then went inside.

Polly took three deep breaths. "You can't curse at him. You can't lose control. You can't cry. You can't put out worthless ultimatums or threats. Now go be a big girl and take his phone."

She leaned back and swiped open a call.

"Hey there," Henry said. "How are you doing?"

"Mad as hell. He won't talk to me. He's refusing to give me his phone. He said I wasn't his mother."

"You corrected him on that, didn't you?"

"I certainly did. I just gave myself a pep talk and since it didn't work, I called you."

"Do you need me to come home?"

Polly shrugged to herself. "No. I'll deal with it. I'm just going to give him a few minutes upstairs." She chuckled. "That's not true. I'm giving myself a few minutes. I wish I knew what was going on so we could have a cogent conversation."

"I have every faith that you'll figure it out. Do I need to find a way to get his truck home?"

"No. I took care of that. Jason's driving it back to town."

"You've had quite the morning."

"Can I send him to his room with only bread and water?"

"You can do whatever you want. I trust you."

"I told him that he can't work at the Bell House this week. He gets to help Eliseo in the barn."

Henry laughed out loud. "Oh, that will make Eliseo so very happy."

"I didn't think of that," Polly said, laughing with him. "I'll talk to him before I say anything to Heath. But he's good with those boys. He'll help me."

"Of course he will." Henry paused. "Okay. Are you ready for this?"

"Almost," she said.

"One, two three ..."

"Yeah, yeah, yeah. Here I go. I'm going to need a hug when you come home. You know that, right?"

"Hugs it is. I love you, Polly. You're going to be fine."

"I love you too." Polly swiped the call closed and climbed out of the truck. She went up the back steps and stopped for a moment to hug the dogs that came to greet her. Luke had jumped up on to Henry's desk, a position he had discovered got him a good rubbing whenever anyone came in the back door. "Hey there, buddy. Is the bad boy in his room?"

Luke leaned into her hand as she rubbed his head, then down his back and up his tail. Polly smiled when she spied Heath's phone at the end of the desk. She picked Luke up and cradled him in her arms as she walked through the house over to Heath and Hayden's bedroom.

Knocking twice, she softly called his name, "Heath?"

"I left the phone for you."

"Thank you. I appreciate it. Are you ready to talk?"

"Not likely," he said from behind the closed door.

"I'll have lunch ready at noon. If you want something, you can come out and eat with me. No strings. But when Hayden and Henry are here, this crap is over. Got it?"

"Why do they need to know?" he asked.

"Because they're some of the authority figures in your life and they're family. We're all in this together, no matter what's going on. And by the way, Heath. You'll feel much better when everything is out on the table and we start moving forward. Until that point, all you will think about is the garbage that is hanging over your head."

"I'm fine with that."

"Lunch is at noon," Polly said and walked away. Even with a three-and-a-half-day suspension, things just couldn't be that horrible. Nothing ever was. As long as he hadn't killed anyone, or did something to be sent to prison, everything else could be worked out. She dropped Luke on the sofa as she passed into the dining room. "Obiwan. Han. Want to go outside?"

The dogs dashed for the back stairs. Polly crossed to the charging station where the kids' phones were kept overnight. She dropped Heath's into it and jogged to the back steps, then followed the dogs down. Once they were outside, she watched them head for the tree line along Sycamore Creek. The trees were still full and green, and Eliseo had pumpkins and squash in the garden. A few tomato plants were still producing, but he'd pulled the rest of the sweet corn out several weeks ago.

Polly loved the seasons and was ready for autumn and harvest. It felt like she was more aware of the seasons now that she was back in rural Iowa. Not only were they defined by the change in weather, but by the ebb and flow of the farming seasons.

Han let out a yip and dashed along the tree line toward the pasture. Obiwan soon caught up and the two dogs wagged their tails and barked at Eliseo's dogs who were on the other side of the fence. Polly grinned, ran to their sides and opened the gate so they could go in. She wandered into the barn and found both Hansel and Gretel, the two barn cats, stretched out on the cement floor of the alley, a fan blowing air not far from them.

Hansel stood and stretched, walked over to Polly, rubbed against her legs and then dropped back down onto the floor. He rolled over onto his back and wriggled on the cool cement. She bent over and rubbed the top of his head, avoiding the belly he presented. She knew better than to fall for that trap. Gretel was a little better about tummy rubs, but not much. "Where is everyone?" she asked.

Eliseo stepped out of the donkeys' stall. "We're all here," he said. "I was sweeping up. Just about ready to take the mower out. I heard your dogs. How are you?"

"Give me a broom. I can help," Polly replied. "I should work out some of my frustration anyway."

He laughed. "Frustration on a Tuesday morning? Maybe it's not enough caffeine."

"I wish that was it. I just brought Heath home. He's been suspended for getting pushy with a teacher. I think he's lucky they didn't expel him."

"Heath? That doesn't sound like him."

"Well, actually it does. There's so much buried in him that we haven't uncovered, but I don't know what set him off. I thought things were going well. I'm frustrated."

"Have you talked to him?" As soon as the words were out of his mouth, Eliseo put his hands up to stop her from responding. "Sorry. The better question is what has he told you?"

"He's not talking yet. But he will. I don't know what it will take, though."

"A concentrated effort by you, I'm guessing." Eliseo pointed at a bench and sat down across from it. Gretel stood and stretched, arched her back, then flopped on the floor beside his feet. "Poor hairy beasts don't like this heat any more than we do," he said. "At least the cats can soak up the cool from the floor."

Polly wasn't surprised to see him wearing a light-weight, long-sleeved shirt like he did every day. He never wore anything that would expose the rest of his scars. It was probably enough that people had to see his face and hands. She wished there was some way to make it safer for him to be himself, but this was the best she could do.

"Could you use some help this week?" Polly asked.

Eliseo chuckled. "I can always find things to do. This might be a good week to whitewash the walls and doors inside. And since the horses are spending so much time in the pasture, maybe we'll do a complete wash-down of the stalls. Top to bottom. Jason would love to not have to do that work."

It made Polly so grateful that he understood what she was asking without her having to actually say the words. "That's awesome. Heath thinks he'll get to work over at the Bell House, but he enjoys doing that. I don't want there to be any question that he's been punished when this week is over."

"You always bring me the best help when I need it," Eliseo said with a laugh. "I was going to wait until it was cooler and hope that Jason and his buddies wouldn't mutiny. This is much better."

"It won't be this afternoon," Polly said. "We still have to face down whatever is going on, but tomorrow morning, he'll be here. I don't want to see him until the afternoon."

"Got it," Eliseo said. "I'll take him uptown for lunch. Ralph and I eat together on Wednesdays and Fridays at the diner."

Polly reached into her pocket. "I should give you money for that."

Eliseo gave her what could only be called a scowl. His eyes lit with fire. "No you won't. If Heath isn't carrying money of his own, I'll pay for it and he can pay me back. Let the boy take responsibility. He's making good money, he can pay for his lunch."

"You're so good for me," she said. "How are things at home?"

He nodded and his face softened. "Pretty good. The kids are doing well in school and Elva likes her job. She's working mostly lunch shifts which is nice, but I enjoy being with the kids when she gets those late night shifts. They're well-behaved. You know, like kids are."

"Do they ever ask about their dad?"

"Not really," he said, shaking his head. "It's too bad that man couldn't see what he had. It sounds like she's going to get the rest of her things shipped up here by mid-October. Some extra furniture in the house will be helpful." Eliseo grinned. "It is a little sparse, you know. I just hadn't thought about buying anything. I had what I needed. Elva thinks it isn't homey enough. Once their things arrive, I've told her we can figure out what we keep and if she wants something new, we'll get it."

"How are the two of you getting along?" Polly asked.

"We're fine. It's taken a few discussions to work things out, but we don't want the kids to hear us, so at least it isn't loud yelling. I remember Elva as being very ..." He paused. "Let's just call it passionate. She was very passionate about getting what she wanted." He slumped. "Larry drove that out of her. I'll see if I can get some of the fiery Elva back."

"By what? Fighting with her?"

"No," he said, laughing. "Somewhere, though, there has to be deep passion in her. She can't have lost it all during her marriage. When she was a little girl, she wanted to do everything. She wanted to travel and see the world. She wanted to open a sanctuary for abandoned or abused animals." A tear escaped one of his eyes. "Dad used to bring horses home that had seen some pretty awful abuse. He was good with them, but Elva was amazing. Those horses seemed to know that she wanted to love them. Even the most skittish let Elva come near them. Sometimes she was the only one who could put a lead on a horse so Dad could start working with them."

He took a breath. "The first time she was only about eight years old. Mom nearly lost her mind when Elva climbed over the fence and walked toward an angry, angry mare. Dad was in the pasture heading her way when the horse dropped her head and slowly walked beside Elva while my sister just talked. They walked around the pasture once and then a second time. Elva never touched her or did anything, just talked. Then she left the pasture and came back the next day. They did that for a week, with both Mom and Dad absolutely terrified something bad might happen.

"Then one day, Elva told us that the mare's name was Athena and she was ready to work with Dad. It was the best horse he ever trained. And by golly, she knew her name, too. I miss that Elva."

"Why don't you bring her here?" Polly asked.

"I've asked. Like I said, she just doesn't have passion about things anymore. She thinks they're beautiful horses, but they don't do anything for her. She loves my dogs, but hasn't fallen in love with them yet. Right now, she's just going through the motions. I can't wait for this part of the process to be over."

Polly frowned. "The process?"

"I went through it, too. She needs time to sort through the trauma of what's happened to her this last year. She's all dried up. No real emotions at all."

"I guess you are the best one to understand what she needs, then. I'm glad she came to Bellingwood to be with you."

He shook his head. "I don't think I'm what she needs. But we'll figure it out. At least she and the kids are safe and healthy. That's all that matters. Right?"

"Right. So. Have you asked Sylvie out on a date yet?"

Eliseo snapped his head to look at her. "What?"

"You heard me. Are you guys dating? She won't talk about it." Polly shrugged. "If I don't ask, I'll never know. You guys spent a lot of time together at Bellingwood Days in July. It's been two months. Are you doing anything about it?"

"Not that it's any of your business, but ..."

The barn phone rang and both of them jumped. Eliseo came to his feet and strode over to the telephone hanging on the wall. "Sycamore House barn, can I help you?"

He listened for a moment. "I'll be right there. Don't you worry, bud. I'll be right there." Eliseo slammed the phone back onto the wall. "Ralph cut himself. The bleeding won't stop. I need to run over there. Sorry."

"But..." Polly was never going to get anything out of him about Sylvie. "What about your dogs?"

"I'll take them with me. I'm so sorry to leave you. Send Heath down tomorrow morning and I'll put him to work." His eyes sparkled with laughter. "Thanks for the talk this afternoon. It was nice to tell someone about how terrific my sister is."

He stepped outside, gave a sharp whistle and clicked his teeth. His two dogs, Khan and Kirk, came running in, then stood on either side of him. Obiwan and Han lumbered in and wandered over to Polly.

"Come on, boys. We're heading back to the house." She turned back to Eliseo. "If you need any help with Ralph, let me know. Okay?"

"We've got it," he said. "But thanks." His back shook with laughter as he left the barn.

"He's a brat," Polly said to her dogs. "It almost makes me wonder if he had Ralph programmed to call him just about the time I was digging into his dating life."

Han yipped and stopped in front of Hansel, who had jumped up to the top of Daisy's stall door. The cat looked down, then turned and began cleaning a paw.

"You've been ignored too, young man," Polly said. "Let's take our forlorn selves up to the house where we can put up with more abuse by a certain son of mine."

She made sure the gates were tightly latched after letting the dogs out and the three of them headed for the back of the house. She waved at Rachel through the kitchen windows. The girl had a wedding coming up in a month and a half and didn't seem at all freaked out by it. She kept insisting there wasn't much to worry about. The food was settled, the location was settled, she had her dress and Billy had his suit. Instead of hiring a DJ, Doug and Billy were working on a compilation of their favorite songs which would play in the background. Rachel wanted it simple and short. The ceremony and dinner were all she wanted to face that day. Polly thought that was great. With the number of brides and their mothers that came through Sycamore House, Rachel couldn't see herself going through any of the stresses they brought with them. So she wasn't going to.

Polly opened the garage door and looked at the door leading up to the kids' apartment. Doug and Billy had lived here nearly as long as she had and now Billy was about to move out with Rachel. So many changes ahead.

She let the dogs into the main building, then opened the door leading up to her apartment. Obiwan and Han ran up the steps, then stopped and waited for her. She didn't want to do this. It would be so much easier if someone else faced the dragon. Heaving a deep sigh, she closed the door and headed up.

CHAPTER FIVE

Everything was ready for lunch. Polly looked over at the clock, smiling at the sketch of Noah and Elijah hanging beneath it. They'd received three letters from the boys since they'd left Bellingwood. The letters were written by Noah, with little drawings done by both boys. They sounded happy, and he wrote about how much they liked their new school. The couple who took them in had two small dogs that the boys had become quite attached to. Polly wasn't sure what she would have done if they hadn't been happy, but at least she had no reason to worry about them.

The bell on the clock chimed and Polly sat down. She'd told Heath lunch would be ready at noon. She could wait.

When the last chime tolled, she sat back in her chair. If he wanted a battle of wills, she was willing to take him on, even though she didn't want it to come to that. Time ticked past, second by second. At five after, she shook her head and stood up, then sat back down when Obiwan rose to his feet, looked at the living room, and wagged his tail.

"Sorry I'm late," Heath said, rubbing his eyes. "I fell asleep."

"Okay." Polly gestured to his chair and he sat down. She served herself from the large bowl of salad she'd made, then passed it to him. Except for the sound of clinking silverware on dishes, the room was silent as they filled their plates.

"Thank you for leaving your phone for me," Polly said. She nodded at the charger. "It's where it always is. Unless you have a specific reason to use it, the phone will stay there for the time being. Understood?"

Heath nodded. He stirred the salad around on his plate, then cut his sandwich into quarters.

Polly took a drink from her coffee mug before digging into her salad. She was going to miss the fresh vegetables from Eliseo's garden this winter. After she finished chewing a bite of her sandwich, she realized Heath hadn't eaten anything yet. "Aren't you hungry?"

"I don't feel good."

"That's not surprising. Your stomach is in knots and you feel like you want to throw up. Right?"

He looked up at her. "How'd you know? Is there something going around?"

"Guilt and shame. That usually does it."

Heath dropped his head again.

"Talking about it usually makes the symptoms go away," she said quietly.

The look he gave her was filled with so much pain, Polly wanted to jump up and wrap her arms around him. But it wasn't time for that yet.

"Heath," she said. "You've got to start this conversation. You have to talk to me."

"No," he replied, pushing his plate back. He stood up. "You can't make me. You aren't my mother." Heath walked out of the dining room.

Polly jumped up and followed him. Before he reached his bedroom door, she made a grab at his arm and missed, so she hurried and stepped in front of him. "That's the second time you've said that to me today. I'm still offended by it. I have never tried to replace your mother and you have no right to speak to me this way because you're upset at your own bad behavior."

"Who cares how I behave?" he spat. "I'll be out of here next year and you won't ever have to see me again."

"What?" Polly asked. "Where did you come up with that one?"

He slid past her, doing his best to avoid making contact, but brushed against her. Once he was inside his room, he tried to push the door shut. Polly braced herself in front of it and touched his arm.

"Stop it," she said. "I don't know what you're doing, but stop it right now."

He shrugged her hand off and slunk over to drop into his desk chair. "It doesn't matter."

"Heath, I want to understand what's going on. Something happened yesterday to send you over the edge. The problem that we have right now, though, is that you are working my last nerve. I go back and forth between wanting to scream at you and wanting to wrap my arms around you and hold you while we both fall apart." She put her hand on his shoulder and he looked up. "Seriously, Heath. Like minute to minute these things are happening in my head." Polly gave him a small smile. "I'm trying to control both. Now you have to help me. Which one do you want?"

He shrugged, but didn't pull away from her. "It doesn't matter," he repeated.

"What doesn't matter?"

"Nothing matters. They're right. I'm a loser."

There. That was something.

"Who's right? Who says you're a loser."

"I don't want to talk about it."

Polly pulled Hayden's chair over so she could sit beside Heath. It wasn't close enough for her, so she pulled the chair closer. When that still didn't elicit a response, she pulled the chair closer and moved so she was leaning on Heath. He scooted back and gave her a confused look.

"What are you doing?" he asked.

"Nothing matters. So I'm just going to get close to you. If nothing matters, your personal space doesn't matter anymore either. I'm invading it," she said and moved closer.

Heath scooted his chair back.

Polly moved hers again. "You know I can do this all day. Right?"

He smiled and put his hands out. "Okay, okay," he said.

"That's better. And I didn't have to scream and yell."

"I really don't want to talk," Heath said.

Polly nodded and sat back in her chair, crossing her legs. She crossed her arms in front of her. "Well, okay, then. That's your choice."

"Really?"

She lifted her shoulders and gave him an appraising look. "Yes. You can make that choice. Since I'm your guardian and I also love you, I'm going to make a few choices too."

"Like what?"

"Like I'm going to sit here with you until you do talk. The only place in this house that you're safe from me is the bathroom. However, if you decide to try to hide in the bathroom, you will have exactly five minutes before I warn you and come in. I will then sit with you in there, too. That's *my* choice."

Heath dropped his head again.

"This is going badly for you, isn't it," Polly said.

"Have you already told Henry?" he asked.

"Of course I have. He knows everything."

"I don't want Hayden to know what happened."

Polly shook her head. "If you didn't want him to know about your bad behavior, you probably shouldn't have done what you did. Sorry, honey. You made a really poor choice this morning and with choices come consequences."

"Rebecca?"

"Well, Rebecca doesn't need to know everything until you tell her. But you'll have to tell her at some point. She'll wonder why you aren't going to school in the mornings."

"I really am a loser. Why do I always screw everything up?"

Polly uncrossed her legs and arms before sitting forward. "What are you talking about?"

"I'm never going to amount to anything. I don't know why you even bother."

"What in the world?" Polly frowned, trying to understand what he was saying. "Where is this coming from?"

"Isn't it obvious?" he asked. Heath stood up and stepped around Polly, pacing to the other side of the room. He strode back and forth a couple of times before sitting on the edge of the bed. Han took a running jump and leaped up to sit beside him. When Heath ignored him, Han pushed his nose under the boy's elbow.

"He doesn't give up either," Polly said. She went over to stand at the front window, looking beyond the parking lot. Up this high she could look over the barn and see the construction of the new apartments and duplexes going in. Henry was just not that far away these days. She really wished he was here now.

"I went to see them last night," Heath said, barely a whisper.

Polly turned around. "You went to see who?"

"She called me. Told me they had some of my dad's things and I could have them if I wanted. I didn't think it would be that bad. It's been over a year. So I lied to you. I just thought I'd go out and pick up whatever they had and I'd be home. No big deal."

"You went out to see your aunt and uncle?"

He nodded.

"What did they have for you?" Polly asked tentatively.

Heath got off the bed and dug a plastic grocery bag out from under a pile of clothing, then handed it to her. "She said that since they didn't have kids we might as well have this." He dug down into his pocket and pulled out an old class ring. "And this too. It was Dad's. But I'm supposed to give it to Hayden. I don't deserve it."

"She said that?"

He nodded and dropped it on the bed.

Polly took an old black leather scrapbook out of the bag and placed it on the bed beside the ring. "Is this your father's scrapbook?"

"I guess. They went on and on about how my dad was so smart and how he played football and ran track in high school. He had some school track record that was never broken, I guess. I never knew that. She had dinner ready and told me that I should eat with them, so I did. They asked me a lot of questions about you and then she started talking about how you were worse than my mom, thinking you could do whatever you wanted. She said she knew Bill and Marie and couldn't believe they raised a son who would marry the likes of you."

Heath slid down to the floor and dropped his head onto his knees. "I couldn't say anything. All I could do was sit there and listen to her say terrible things about you and Henry and me and Mom. Hayden's like some sort of golden child, but she says you're ruining him. He was supposed to go be a doctor and once you got your hands on him, you screwed him up. Just like Mom screwed up Dad.

"Then she told me that I should have gone to Eldora. That's where they were hoping I'd end up so it would teach me a hard lesson. I'd had it too easy all my life and I was never going to be anything anyway, so I might as well have been locked away. She told me it was part of my DNA. I got it from my mother. Hayden got all the good genes. At least one of us was going to do something with our lives."

He looked at Polly, tears in his eyes. "She's right, you know. I don't know what I want to do with my life. I can't just live with you and Henry forever. I'm a total loser. She even told me that at least if I was in prison, I'd have a roof over my head and be fed every day."

Polly had been seething since his first sentence. She looked down at her hands and realized they were clenched so tightly, she had to concentrate to loosen her fists. She glanced at Heath to see if he was finished. He'd wrapped his arms around his knees and rested his head on them.

"You are never to go out to see those people by yourself again," Polly said, her voice low and angry.

"I know."

"No, Heath, I don't think you understand. What that woman did to you was beyond reproach. She used that scrapbook and ring to put you in a position where you had to listen to her unload on you. She's had no one but her husband to tear apart for the last year. She's been planning how to get you under her thumb again."

"Why?" he asked.

"Some people are so angry and bitter, they look for ways to hurt others. You're an easy target. You'd been beaten down by her for a long time and when you left, she only had her husband to take her anger out on. No one else would take that garbage from her, but you'd been trained to believe the terrible things she said about you."

"I should have stopped her from saying things about you and Mom. I couldn't, though."

Polly sat down beside him and put her arm around his shoulders. "Oh, honey. I don't need you to protect me from the likes of her. What can she do to me?"

His shoulders lifted in a shrug.

"And your mother. How did she handle your aunt and uncle?"

Heath huffed a pained laugh. "She was so sweet to them. Even when they said bad things to Dad about her." He looked at Polly, tears filling his eyes. "It didn't matter if Mom was in the room, they still said bad things."

"What did she do when that happened?"

"One time she broke a plate in the kitchen sink. Dad was afraid she had cut herself. But it was on purpose. Like she was letting off steam. I saw it. But she never let them know. They thought they were being so sly and clever and she was too stupid to realize they were saying mean things. They even told me that one night. That she was too stupid to realize how much they hated her. But Mom always knew and she was always nice in front of them. Dad told them to stop all the time and if they were at our house when it got really bad, he'd just tell them it was time to go home." Heath rolled his shoulders. "A couple of years before they died, Dad told his brother he never wanted to see him again because they couldn't be nice to his family. Mom tried to stop him. She said that family was important, no matter what. Mom and Dad had a big fight that night."

"About what?"

"About sending his brother away. Mom said that they were bitter because they had tried so hard to have children. Then we came along and that's when my aunt changed. Dad said that didn't matter. He was tired of them treating his family like second-rate citizens and his wife like a dumb whore." Heath looked down. "I didn't even know what that word meant. Hayden cried all night. But I stayed on the top step and listened. Mom never hated them. She never did, no matter what they said. She told us that we couldn't either. She had enough love to share because Dad and Hayden and me filled her bucket every day. Nobody could take that away from her with nasty words."

Heath started to sob. "I just sat there and let her say terrible things about everyone I ever loved. I didn't stop her. I didn't do anything. I never did anything. I just turned into a loser because I was too scared to stand up. I'm no different than I was when I lived there."

Polly turned him into her arms and held him while he cried. "It's not your job to stand up for us. Your mother never expected that and I certainly don't. Honey, I'm so sorry that you had to listen to that woman spew such awful garbage. It's not about you at all. It's about her own pain and the fact that she has no self-confidence. The only way she can feel powerful is to destroy someone."

She rubbed her hand up and down his back until his wracking sobs subsided and he sat back against the bed. He rubbed his sleeve across his nose and then wiped the tears on his face with the inside of his shirt. Yep, that was going right in the laundry when this was over.

"Heath," Polly said, waiting for him to pay attention to her. He looked up. "Heath, the only power that woman has over you is what you give her. Those things she says about your mother aren't true and they mean nothing. What can she actually do to you? "

"I don't know."

"She has no control over you any longer. This little supper was her attempt to regain that. But you walked away and came home to us. You aren't the person she was trying to create. You are your own person. You have a family who loves you and you have a future in front of you that is filled with potential. So what if you don't know what you're going to do with the rest of your life?" Polly chuckled. "I was going to be a librarian. Do I look like a librarian?"

"Sometimes," he said with a tiny smile.

Polly jostled him. "You're going to college and you'll experience life. You might hold down a lot of jobs until you find what you want to do with yourself. And maybe the jobs you have are only a way to pay for the dreams you want to live out. Who knows? I can promise you that as long as you do your best, possibilities will always open up. Just don't shut your eyes to what's available."

"What if I fail at everything? It's just like she says. I'm a loser."

"You're going to fail. That's how we learn some of our best lessons. But we don't focus on failure; we learn from it and move on."

"I failed big time this morning."

"Yes you did," Polly said. "We haven't even gotten to that yet."

"I don't want to," he said.

She laughed out loud. "Like that's worked so well for you today." Polly’s stomach growled. "I'm starving. Can we go back to the dining room so I can eat a sandwich?"

Heath nodded slowly.

Polly stood up and reached out her hand. He brushed it aside gently and stood up, then surprised her by hugging her. She wrapped her arms around him and held on tight.

CHAPTER SIX

As Heath worked his way through two of the sandwiches Polly put in front of him, she waited. There was more to talk about, but she didn't think it fair to cause any more stress until he was finished with lunch. They didn't speak at all.

He finally took a last, long drink from his glass of water and sat back. "You want to talk about this morning."

"You know I do," she said. "You have to tell me what happened."

He sighed and looked down at his empty plate, then pushed it away. "I feel so stupid. He was doing what he does every day, but this morning it was too much and I lost it."

"What does he do every day?"

"He picks one person to read a passage and then interrupts over and over to ask questions." Heath looked at Polly.

She shook her head. "That doesn't sound so bad. Teachers have their own way of delivering the material."

"Yeah, but he's rude and condescending. If you don't read it the way he thinks you should, he makes fun of you. He especially goes after people who are bad readers."

"There can't be very many of those in a senior literature course," Polly said.

"More than you think."

"But you're a good reader," she protested. "I've heard you. You do great."

"Yeah. That wasn't what he went after today. It was personal."

"What do you mean? Is it the book you're reading?"

Heath nodded and Polly waited for more. He didn't give it.

"What book are you reading, then?" she asked.

"*Prayer for Owen Meany.*"

It had been some time since Polly had read the book and she shut her eyes trying to remember enough about it to understand. "The boy who killed his friend's mother?" she asked.

Heath nodded again.

"Okay, so what happened?"

"I think he knew Mom when she was alive," Heath said quietly.

Polly frowned. "Why do you say that?"

"Because he said something about how I'd relate to the character and my mom was even more wonderful than Johnny's mother. Then he made me read the part about where Owen killed her. And he kept interrupting me, like after every other sentence. And when they were talking about the baseball that killed her - that it was the instrument of her death, he had the f..." Heath stopped before he said the word. "He told everybody that Mom and Dad died in a car wreck on an icy road."

"He what?"

"He asked them to consider whether it was the ice, the car, Dad's driving, or Hayden's ball game that was the instrument of her death."

Polly's voice rose in fury. "He what?"

Heath rolled his eyes and shook his head. "He does sh..." He stopped himself again. "Stuff like that all the time. Emma Leslie has a sister with Down syndrome and he makes everybody talk about mental deficiencies in front of her. One day he said that he was desensitizing us so that when we were out in the real world, we'd be able to handle it. He always says that our parents coddle us and that's why we're so entitled. He talks about trigger warnings and how stupid those are and that if any of us want to get along, we just have to face our darkest things and accept them."

"So that's when you lost it?" Polly was seething. She wanted to show this man his darkest thing and scare the life out of him.

"No," Heath shook his head again. "I knew when we started reading this book he was going to make me do it."

Suddenly, Polly knew exactly where this was going and she wanted to stop the conversation before it even happened. But she stayed silent, waiting for the pain of Heath's last summer by himself to show up. She swallowed.

"Then he asked me how it felt when Ladd Berant killed Julie and Abby. And he wouldn't stop pushing. He wanted to know about their deaths. Did they struggle? Did their eyes close when they died? He kept asking questions, even when I wouldn't talk. When he asked why I didn't save them, I wasn't really there any longer." Heath looked at her. "Polly, I swear. I didn't know what I was doing. I just had to make him stop. I told him to stop a couple of times and then he was standing in front of me. I just stood up and walked toward him, telling him to stop talking about it."

Heath had gotten involved with an awful kid - Ladd Berant - who controlled his little gang of hoods by fear and power. Ladd confronted Julie Smith at the coffee shop because she'd told him to leave when he found the front door open after hours. He'd killed her with Grey's walking stick and left her body beside the dumpster in the alley behind the shop. Abby Belran had been part of the group and the murder scared her. Ladd killed her to keep her quiet and to remind the rest of the kids that he would hurt anyone who threatened to go to the police.

"You were yelling at him," Polly said.

He slowly nodded his head. "I probably was. I don't even remember. Somebody grabbed my arm and I remember Debbie Thomas stepping in front of me. She said something about him not being worth it. I went back and sat down and Mr. West called security. They took me away and then you came."

Polly had no idea what to say next. "I'm sorry."

Heath shrugged.

"Losing control was the wrong thing to do," she said. "Life is going to hand you things that push you over the edge. I'm glad that you stopped before you got physical."

"I don't know what I would have done if Debbie hadn't stopped me," Heath admitted. "I wanted to punch him."

"It's never okay to hit someone. Especially an authority figure." Polly put her hand up as Heath prepared to protest. "Even one who is wrong. I can't tell you that you were right to get aggressive with him, even when he was being abusive. Not as my son. But I will tell you that I'm so sorry he did this to you and I understand your response. Does that make sense?"

"I guess. But was I just supposed to take it? That doesn't seem fair."

"Life isn't fair. Returning abuse for abuse will never make it better. That never fixes the problem, it only lowers you to that person's level."

"So if someone comes at me with a bat, I'm just supposed to take it?"

Polly smiled. "No, you aren't supposed to take it. You can protect yourself. I've been known to make people hurt when they hurt me. There are stories. But unless you're in immediate danger, you don't treat people badly, no matter what they're doing to you. Walk away and find an acceptable way to handle the problem."

He made a noise in the back of his throat and frowned. "That still doesn't seem fair."

"I know it doesn't, but look at what happened to you. You've been suspended from school. That policy is in place ..."

"It's not a fair policy." Heath interrupted her.

"It's absolutely fair," Polly said. "You don't ever get aggressive with a teacher."

"Well, he shouldn't have gotten aggressive with me." Heath set his jaw and glared at her.

Polly put her hands up. "Whoa. Stop right now. We were on the right track, and now your anger is taking over again."

"Maybe it should. Mr. West is a jerk. He hurts kids every day and the school just lets him get away with it."

"Have you told anyone that he's doing this?"

"No, but they have to know."

"Exactly how are they supposed to know this? Does he act like this when he's being observed by administration?"

"Well. No."

"And have you ever told me or Henry or Hayden that he's being abusive?"

"No."

"And is it your job to monitor a teacher's behavior?"

Heath snarled out a 'no.'

"Have you talked to the counselor at school or even the vice principal?" Polly kept pressing.

Heath shook his head.

"Backing him down isn't your job. You have no authority over him. But he has authority over you and you will respect that, no matter whether you respect the man. You go to someone who has authority over him and tell them what he's doing."

"They wouldn't believe me."

Polly sighed. She was getting nowhere. "I'm not arguing about this. It's not the issue. The issue is that you were out of line this morning and were suspended. You don't get to try to transfer the problem. This is your mistake. It's your problem and now you have three days ahead of you that aren't going to be fun."

He looked up at her in confusion.

"Did you think that suspension means vacation?" she asked. "Because, no, that's not what it means at all. You will log on every day after school and get your assignments. Starting tomorrow morning, you will go to the barn and help Eliseo until he's finished with you. Then you will come back here and work on your schoolwork until it's time for your afternoon job for Henry. Your evenings will be spent finishing homework or whatever projects Henry has for you. Do you understand me?"

"Whatever," he said.

"Don't you dare 'whatever' me," Polly replied. "This is on you.

Every single moment of the day you get to choose what your response is to any given situation. When you choose to respond poorly, there are consequences. No matter what Mr. West said or did to you, the issue at stake right now is your response." She stood up and looked down at him, then slowly and measuredly said, "Do. You. Understand. Me?"

"Yes, ma'am."

"Good. You can help me clean up the kitchen and then it should be time for your job with Henry."

"So I can't work at the Bell House or over at the shop?"

Polly shook her head. "Unless Henry or Hayden is working at the Bell House, you can't go. If Bill has work for you in the evenings and everything else is complete, you can do that. Remember, I said this isn't a vacation. You don't get to do the things you love doing just because you think you have extra time."

"You weren't this mad at me when I showed up in your garage last year," he said, picking up his plate.

Polly gathered more things up from the table and laughed. "I had no expectations then. Now I know who you are and what your potential is. I expect you to be an honorable young man, no matter what."

He opened the cabinet and returned half-empty potato chip bags to their shelf, then went back to the table. "That's really not fair," he grumbled.

She chuckled. "If you learn nothing else from me, I want you to always remember that fair is never part of life's equation. It's a man-made construct meant to bring everyone to the same state of mediocrity. Humanity is better than that."

Heath took the two plates they'd used from her hands and put them in the dishwasher. "Sometimes you make no sense."

That made her laugh out loud.

~~~

Heath was running end-of-day errands for Henry's crews. Polly was back at her desk, trying to finish the work she'd started
~~~

earlier in the day. Was it really the same day? It felt as if she'd been through a week's worth of trouble.

When Han and Obiwan ran through the house, stopping at the top of the stairs, Polly looked up. "Are they home?" she asked.

The downstairs door opened and three sets of feet came thundering up the steps. Andrew, Kayla, and Rebecca stopped in front of her desk.

"How was your day?" she asked them.

Andrew opened the top of his backpack and pulled out a folder, flipped it open, then slammed it down in front of her. "Bam," he said. "One hundred percent. Mom's buying breakfast this weekend."

He was pointing at a short story he'd written.

"Congratulations." Polly smiled at him. "That's awesome." She gave Rebecca a glance. "How about you?"

Rebecca shrugged. "I did okay. Not a hundred, but okay."

"Well, let's see it."

"Later. Okay?" Rebecca slung her backpack to her side and walked out of the room.

Andrew lifted a shoulder and followed.

"I got a ninety-two," Kayla said softly. "Stephanie will think that's cool."

"It *is* cool. Very good," Polly said. "There's juice in the fridge and I bought popsicles. Something to cool y'all off after a hot day."

"She bought popsicles," Kayla yelled, chasing after her friends. "I want grape!"

Polly leaned forward and put her head in her hands. What was Rebecca's problem today? Polly had read through the short story and made a few typographical and grammar corrections, but it was good. The girl couldn't have failed that badly. But at this age, anything could set Rebecca off. Polly chuckled to herself thinking back to the first few months with her brand new daughter. She'd been so excited to have someone in her life that was bright and energetic, loving and kind. Friends tried to warn Polly that it wasn't going to always be that way, and though she thought she knew what was coming ... nope!

These were the times when Polly wished her mother were alive so someone could tell her what she'd been like as a kid. Polly's dad, Everett, saw much of it, but he reacted to things like Henry did. Nothing much phased him and when Polly got too far out of line, he put his foot down and there was no more discussion.

Her phone buzzed, making Polly jump. When she saw who had sent the text, she shook her head. How did the woman always know?

"How's your day going?" Lydia had texted.

"Up and down and all over the place. Having kids is no picnic," Polly sent back.

"Is Heath still alive?"

Polly smiled. *"Alive and healthy. I'll tell you all about it sometime. I just need to get through the conversation with Hayden and Henry, then we can move forward. Rebecca is going to be the death of me, though."*

"Ahh, daughters," Lydia wrote. *"Marilyn was the bane of my existence when she was in junior high and high school. Oh, the angst. Everything was sooooo important."*

"We'll get through this?" Polly asked.

"You need to know that much of the problem between you is that you both love each other so much."

Polly laughed out loud at that. *"Like Rebecca says. Whatever."*

"It's true. You're safe for her to be her ugly self with. Trust me on that."

"Do you know how much I love you?"

"To the moon and back. Same me with you, dear. Now go surprise her and tell her how much you love her. She won't know what to do with it."

Polly blew a breath out between her lips. Lydia was right. She'd already had it out with one kid today and things weren't finished with him yet. She pushed back from the desk, heaved herself out of the chair and went to find the kids. They were all in Rebecca's room, playing with their phones.

"Phones in the chargers, guys. You know that," Polly said, pointing at the kitchen. "Kayla, take Rebecca's. I need the room."

They all sighed dramatically. Kayla waited while Rebecca finished whatever she'd been doing and then pressed the phone into her friend's hands. Polly followed them to the door and pushed it closed.

"I love you, Rebecca," Polly said.

"But?"

"But nothing. I love you. I know you have bad days and I want you to always know that I love you."

Rebecca looked at her. "That's it?"

"There's always more. But yes, pretty much, that's it." Polly sat down on the bed beside Rebecca, then slid an arm around the girl's shoulders. Before she'd finished settling in beside her daughter, Rebecca leaned in and breathed out.

"Sometimes it's just so hard," Rebecca whispered.

"What's hard?"

"Life."

"What happened?"

"Can I tell you something and not have you get mad at me?"

"I'll try."

"Sometimes I wish I was like Kayla." Rebecca was still whispering and Polly pulled her upright so she could see as well as hear what the girl was saying.

"What does that mean?"

"It sounds so mean."

"Okay?"

"You know Andrew and I are the smartest kids in the class. Right?"

Polly smiled. "I know you're both very smart."

"No, Polly. We're the smartest. When it comes to grades, we're the top two all the time. Kayla is okay, but she's not as smart as us. I help her with homework and stuff so she keeps up."

"And I'm proud of you."

"Sometimes I wish I wasn't the smartest and that I didn't have to compete with Andrew. He's supposed to be my boyfriend. It really made me mad today when he got a hundred percent on that paper. Mine was just as good, but the teacher gave me a ninety-nine percent." Rebecca dug down into her backpack and pulled out a folded-up paper. She turned to the second page and snapped her finger at it, making the sheet rattle. "She took off points because I didn't describe Eddie."

"She took off a single point. And you were told to fully describe your characters. Apparently, you didn't write enough to please her."

"I know." Rebecca flung the paper on the bed beside her. "But it was a good story and I thought it was perfect. But no, Andrew gets the perfect grade and I don't. If I were like Kayla, I'd be happy with a ninety-two. But I'm not. It's not fair."

"Oh good heavens," Polly said. "Not this again."

"What?"

"How many times do I have to talk to you about fair?"

"Yeah, yeah, yeah. There's no such thing. But I hate it when Andrew beats me."

Polly laughed. "Good for you."

"What do you mean?" Rebecca was shocked.

"You have a very healthy competitive side. Good for you. As long as you aren't mad at anybody but yourself when you don't win, I'm fine with that. It's not Andrew's fault that he did better than you and it's not your teacher's fault that she had an expectation you didn't meet. You will do better next time."

"I'll never know what she expects, though."

Polly reached across Rebecca for the paper. "Honey, she was very clear about what she wanted. You and I both see that you didn't do it. I wish I had paid better attention to her requirements."

Rebecca stood up. "I can blame you. You didn't fix it for me."

"Yeah. Okay. We'll see about that."

"It was a good try, don't you think?"

Polly walked to the door of the bedroom and opened it. "I think I'm just going to stick with my opening salvo. I love you. Now go on out to the dining room and start your homework."

"And have a popsicle. I deserve a popsicle."

"Yes you do."

CHAPTER SEVEN

Cupboards in Polly's life emptied as soon as she filled them. After everyone finally left for school or work the next morning, Polly headed for Boone and the grocery store. She'd learned to enjoy ordering her groceries on line. That happened not long after her discovery of a young woman's body in the back of her truck this summer. That parking lot was no longer to be trusted. She also needed to pick up a second desk for Heath and Hayden. They had one nice desk in their room, but that meant the other had to work at the dining room table or in the office. They'd found what they wanted and it was finally ready to be picked up.

Boone's furniture company had moved from its in-town location to an immense new space at the corner of Highways 30 and 17. It meant a little extra driving and felt like it was way out in the country, but it was a beautiful day. The sun was shining and her family was finding its way back to normal.

The conversation with Hayden, Henry and Heath last night had been tough. Hayden's shock overwhelmed the first few minutes, but once he assimilated the whole thing and understood what had actually happened, he calmed down. There were a lot of tears from Polly and Heath. Polly ached for the pain her boy was dealing with; Heath was embarrassed to admit to everything.

The only thing Henry added to Heath's punishment was that he needed to apologize to Mr. West for his behavior. Heath wanted to refuse, but when Polly thought about it, she agreed. These were the moments that would define Heath's character in the future. He would never forget this. Henry assured him that he would go with Heath to do that, but it *was* going to happen. And it was going to happen today so Heath wouldn't have to think about it any longer than necessary. Henry would make the appointment with the school and they'd just go deal with it.

Rebecca was dying of curiosity since they'd gone into the boys' room and shut the door. The poor girl spent her time in the bathroom, scrubbing down the walls. This would be the cleanest that bathroom had ever been. Tonight Rebecca would tackle the tub and shower and she would be nearly finished. Now all Polly needed was for Rebecca to really mess up just before they moved over to the Bell House.

Polly didn't want to think about what a huge pain that move was going to be. When she'd moved into Sycamore House, there had only been a few things to carry up the steps. Little by little the rooms had filled. Her father's things had been brought to the garage and slowly boxes were emptied into the apartment. With three kids now, the apartment was filled to the brim. Moving was going to be ugly.

She turned onto Highway 30. She'd chased a murderer down this highway with a young Rebecca in the seat beside her. They'd had to go see Sarah Heater, Rebecca's mother, in the hospital after that chase and Polly ended up admitting what she'd done. That was when she knew how much Sarah trusted her with her daughter. The woman hadn't worried that Polly was racing down the highway. She knew Polly would keep Rebecca safe.

Polly took the exit for Highway 17 and drove south, then turned into the parking lot for the furniture company. She wasn't sure where to go to pick up the desk, so pulled over to the side and took out the paperwork. The parking lot seemed empty and she looked at the time. Eight forty-five. The place didn't open until nine. She drove on in, pulled into a parking space and leaned back. After two minutes of tapping her fingers on the steering wheel, Polly put the truck back into gear. She'd never been here before and when the company expanded out to this location a year or so ago, it had been a big deal. She drove around the side of the building and smiled at the number of pickup trucks in the back parking lot. Iowa was made of pickups. She rounded a corner and wondered at the cost of landscaping this place.

Then her heart stopped and she swore. Lying there for all the world to see was a naked man on his back, his arms and legs stretched out. A bright red line was painted across him. As Polly took in the entire scene, she realized he was lying inside a painted red circle and the line slashed across him. He'd been stabbed several times and Polly hoped that the red was paint and not his blood. She took out her phone, snapped a picture, and sent it to Aaron Merritt's number before calling him.

"What in the hell?" he asked.

"Did you see what I sent?"

"Yes I did. Where did you find that?"

"I'm at the furniture store on Highway 17. In the back. They aren't open yet, but will be soon. Can you send someone out?"

"Like you have to ask," he said. "Do you recognize him?"

"No. I've never seen him before. But there's a big 'no' symbol spray-painted across him."

"And you're sure he's dead?"

Polly took a breath. "Okay. Let's think about it. I found him. He has red spray paint on his body. He's naked. Oh. And I found him. Do you really want me to mess with the scene and walk over to see if he's got a pulse? Because, let's remember. I found him."

"You have me there," Aaron said. "They're already on the way. Deputy Hudson will be in charge. I like the way the two of you work together."

"So I should call her instead of you?"

"Oh no. Not that," Aaron replied. "Always call me. It's our thing, you know."

Polly glanced in her rearview mirror. "Someone's coming."

"One of mine?"

"I don't think so."

"Okay. Wait for my people if you don't mind, would you?"

"Of course. I'll talk to you later."

Polly put her phone down on the console between the seats and opened the truck door, just as a bright blue pickup truck pulled in behind her.

"What the hell is this?" A man jumped down from his truck and strode over to her. "Who are you?"

She smiled and put her hand out. "I'm Polly Giller from Bellingwood. I don't know what this is, but I've already called the sheriff. They'll be here any time."

He shook her hand. "Polly Giller. I've heard that name."

Here it came. She just wished that one day she'd be able to introduce herself without people associating her name with dead bodies.

"Yeah," he said. "You're married to Henry Sturtz. You have that old school up in Bellingwood. I know Henry from high school. Vaughn Laughton. I work security here. How did you know this was back here?"

Polly was so taken aback by his reference to Henry it took her a minute to realize he'd asked a question. "I didn't know it was. I'm here to pick up a desk and since I was early, I just drove around to look at the place."

He nodded, then walked around the front of her truck. When he looked as if he would step too close, she ran after him. "I don't think we should walk near it. Mess up footprints and stuff, you know."

"I was just going to see if he was alive. Did you check?"

"He's dead," Polly said.

"Are you sure?"

"Sure enough."

Vaughn lifted up on his tip toes and looked out over the circle. "Crap. Do you know who that is?"

Polly shook her head. "No. Should I?"

"He's a teacher at the high school. English or something like that. West is his last name, I think."

She flipped her head to look at the man standing beside her. "West? Are you sure?"

"Yeah. That's him. Somebody sure was mad at him. That's a lot of hate right there."

"Oh my god," Polly said breathlessly. She backed up to her truck and leaned against its hood.

Vaughn put his hand on her shoulder. "Are you okay, ma'am? Should I call Henry?"

"No, that's okay. I'll call him." All Polly really wanted was for this man to go away and leave her alone. She didn't want to explain to him what had happened with her family and Mr. West yesterday. And now Heath would be caught up in a murder investigation. Polly wasn't worried that he had anything to do with it. He'd been home all night. But there were going to be questions.

"I got cold water in my truck. Do you want something?"

She nodded. "Thanks." Anything to make him walk away for a few moments. Polly needed to think.

She heard the sirens coming down the highway and stood back up as Vaughn returned with a bottle of water. He cracked it open and handed it to her. "They'll be here any minute. I need to get on the radio and tell my boss what's going on. He's not going to be happy about this. Specially since it's a local."

Polly nodded and took a long drink. The beautiful morning she'd been enjoying was giving way quickly to high heat and humidity again. This summer was never going to relent.

Vaughn drove his truck up beside hers and rolled the window down. "I'm gonna get outta here so my truck don't get trapped. But I'll be back to talk to the cops. Tell 'em I'll be here."

She waved and breathed a sigh of relief. This was going to be hard enough to explain without him trying to be helpful. Polly watched as Deputy Tab Hudson approached.

"We meet again," the deputy said. "Are you trying to make a believer out of me?"

"No. I promise," Polly said with a wan grin. "I swear I don't go looking for this stuff."

"I believe you. Did you approach the body?"

Polly shook her head. "I know better. If I'd seen any sign that he was alive, I would have, but there's no way. And besides, the odds of me finding a live one are pretty slim. Like ... once."

Tab smiled. "Got it. Can you wait a minute? I want to check this out and get everybody to work."

"I can wait," Polly said. "Do you mind if I call my husband?"

"No problem."

Polly opened her truck door and climbed in, sitting on the edge of the seat. She swiped open a call to Henry.

"Hey there, Love Bug," he said.

"Hey there. I did it again."

"You did what?" Henry's voice changed. "You didn't."

"Yeah. And don't bother scheduling an appointment with Heath's teacher."

"No!"

"Yeah. I met an old friend of yours. Vaughn Laughton. He told me who the guy was."

Henry laughed. "Old Vaughn, eh. Yeah. He got thumped a few too many times during football season. Good guy, though. You're picking up the desk this morning?"

"Well, I'm actually waiting for Deputy Hudson. This was a bad one, Henry. The guy was stabbed and then a big red 'no' symbol was painted around and across him. Oh. And he's naked. That's not something a girl wants to see in the morning. Dead naked guys are way worse than dead guys in clothes."

"You shouldn't have to know that either way, Polly."

"Well I do. And this was pretty weird. Then knowing who it is makes it weirder."

"Heath is going to be dragged into this, isn't he?"

"I can't imagine how he'll avoid it. I'm just going to tell Tab everything right now."

"What's everything?" Tab asked, coming from behind Polly's truck.

"I gotta go, Henry. I'll talk to you later."

"I love you."

"Love you, too." Polly ended the call and put the phone back on the console. "I know who the dead guy is," she said.

"Yeah. Mr. West from the high school. What are you going to tell me?"

"My son had an altercation with this man yesterday. Only verbal, not physical. He was suspended from school for the rest of the week because of it."

Tab nodded. "Do you think he did this?"

"Heath?" Polly was shocked. "This? Not at all. He's been with us since I picked him up from school. This morning he's working at the barn. He hasn't been alone since I took him out of school."

"Okay," Tab said. She gave Polly a big smile. "I knew he wasn't involved. If he had been, you would have handled telling me a lot differently. But I am going to need to talk to him. This is too much of a coincidence. What was the altercation about?"

"Mr. West was awful to his students, taking perverse pleasure in finding and exposing their weaknesses. He pushed Heath about his mother's death, making Heath read a passage aloud about a kid killing his friend's mother. Then he talked about killing people and pushed Heath about that summer when he was with Ladd Berant. You know, the kid that killed those girls in Bellingwood?"

Tab nodded again while taking notes in a small black notebook. "Did Heath say Mr. West did this to a lot of students?"

"It sounds like it happens all the time. I don't know how he got away with it."

"We all had teachers who found ways to get under our skin. It's a good thing we didn't have too many, but there's always one."

"I guess."

"Can I call you later to set up a time to talk with Heath?" Tab asked, tapping her notebook.

"Sure. He's stuck at the house for the week, except for a couple of hours every afternoon when he's running errands for Henry's construction crews."

The deputy pointed down the road. "You should be able to get out of here. Thanks for your help."

"Thanks." Polly pulled the truck door shut and put her seatbelt on. There was just something about driving away in front of this much law enforcement that made her want to do everything properly. She left the parking lot and pulled out onto the highway, then swore. She'd forgotten the desk. She turned onto the next gravel road, turned around and went back.

~~~

Henry's truck was in the garage when Polly got home. She texted him.

"What are you doing home?"

"Just wanted to talk to you."

"Come help me carry in the groceries, then."

She opened the truck door and hooked bags onto her arm.

Before long, Henry was beside her. "You don't have to try to take them all," he said.

"One trip. You know I'll do whatever it takes."

They got everything upstairs and into the kitchen. As she put food into the cupboards, Polly finally asked. "Are you really just here to talk to me?"

"Yeah. I had some extra time. Since I don't have to take Heath to Boone, I figured I'd check in with you. You've been taking it on the chin with the kids this week."

She hefted herself up on the counter. "Do you ever wonder what they'd be like if we'd raised them from babies? No baggage. Just us?"

"There'd be baggage. Trust me," he said. Henry opened the cabinet door and she shifted while he put boxes of cereal inside.

"Do you think so? I think the reason I'm so calm is because I don't feel guilty for their behavior. Someone else raised them and all I'm doing is trying to direct them down the path without letting them fall into the pit of alligators on either side."

"That's one way to look at it. Did it occur to you even for a minute that Heath might have been mixed up in that murder?"
~~~

Polly scowled. "Not for a minute. You?"

He bowed his head. "Yeah. But it was only a split second and then I felt guilty. Heath could have hit that guy yesterday and he didn't. Even though he was pushed as hard as he was, the boy sat down."

"Only because his friend stopped him. I get it that he's angry, but he can't let that take over. People are going to make him mad all the time."

"He's fine," Henry said. "But I'm not. What are we going to do about his aunt making him go out there just to abuse him?"

Polly grabbed Henry's arm and pulled him in front of her so she could wrap her legs around him. She kissed his lips and then put her head on his shoulder. "I'm all for getting in her face and telling her to leave him alone. We know where they live."

"Do you think that will matter?"

"Probably not. I told Heath that he needs to tell us if she ever contacts him again. I think he will."

"You know that I think the world of how you interact with those kids," Henry said.

"I couldn't do any of this without you," Polly replied.

He pushed her back and kissed the tip of her nose. "Yes you could and you'd be great."

"But I don't want to. The only reason I have the courage to take any of this on is because of you."

"You just keep thinking that."

Polly put her head on his chest, then sat straight up and looked at the clock. "Heath won't be back for at least another hour. Are you in a hurry to go to work?"

"What about all of this food here and the desk in the truck?"

"Hand me the meat and cold stuff. We can be done in two minutes."

"Then I'm not in a hurry to go back to work." Henry wrapped his arms around her and kissed her lips. Polly felt every muscle in her body relax as he held her. This was why she could get through her days, no matter what happened.

CHAPTER EIGHT

"Hello there," Skylar said when Polly walked into Sweet Beans the next morning. "Where in the world have you been the last couple of days? I swear, we wondered if the earth had stopped spinning."

"I've been busy," Polly said. "And grumpy. Girlfriend needs her fix. Why isn't it already waiting for me?"

"Sorry. Sorry." Skylar snapped a cup into his hands and turned away and then back. "I forgot. What is it you usually order?"

Polly scowled at him and he grinned.

"Oh yeah. The Grump-Fixer. Large. So, you did it again," Skylar said as he focused on making her drink.

"Did what?"

"You know. That voodoo that you do so well. Heard it was some teacher that Heath told off on Tuesday. Was he really naked and covered in red spray paint?"

"He wasn't covered in paint," Polly said quietly, looking around. The coffee shop had quite a few customers, but none seemed to be paying attention to their conversation.

Skylar put her coffee down on the counter. "How would you like to try a cinnamon muffin with Rachel's newest condiment?"

"What's that?"

"She's making pear honey. It's the good stuff."

"That sounds terrific."

"You're going to sit here for a few minutes, aren't you?"

Polly really didn't want to go home, so she nodded. Her regular booth was empty and she was not at all averse to hiding up here for a few minutes.

Skylar swirled a thick golden syrup into a tiny cup and placed it on a plate with her muffin. "So, he was really naked? Like all of his diddly bits were hanging out?" he asked, his voice low and quiet.

"You nut," Polly said with a laugh. "Yes, I guess they were. Naked would definitely imply that."

"You see the weirdest things. Death is strange, isn't it? We spend our lives covering things up and then in a flash, we're no longer in control and none of that is really important anymore."

"There's so little that's important after death," Polly said.

"Polly Giller," a voice boomed as the bell on the front door jangled. "I heard you were looking for me. You're a hard woman to find." The Chief of Police, Ken Waller, strode across the floor. He nodded to several people as he passed them and reached out to shake her hand. "Mindy told me I might find you up here this morning and when I saw your truck parked out front, I decided I needed something to drink."

"Your regular, Chief?" Skylar asked.

"Yessiree, son. And whatever Polly's having on that plate, make another one for me." Ken put his hand on Polly's arm and steered her toward the booth. "Just wave at me when it's ready."

He waited while Polly sat down and then took a seat across from her. "Mindy said you called. Sorry I've been busy, but it sounds like you've had your own messes to clean up."

She shook her head. "It's been a strange couple of days, that's for sure. What I have to talk to you about isn't any less odd. I wanted to ask more questions about your grandfather. I thought I might stop over and see Paul Bradford, too. His grandfather was involved in whatever I have going on."

"You've got something going on that involves our granddads?"

"I found something weird in those tally boards in my basement. I don't know what to make of it and was hoping that somebody might have some stories."

Ken grinned and took out his phone. "Let's get Paul over here. He has enough help this morning and I'll bet he could use a cup of coffee." He stood up, took out his phone and walked to the counter before Skylar finished putting his coffee together.

Polly laughed as she watched him try to pay. He tried every single time he was in the shop and received the same rejection. He slipped some money into the tip jar while he talked on the phone.

"He's intrigued," Ken said when he got back to the table. "Lisa told him that you'd been asking questions. He'll be here in a few minutes. How are things going over at your new place?"

"Slow. It's driving me crazy. I want it to come together as fast as Sycamore House and the hotel did. But Henry isn't quite as motivated."

Ken laughed. "He's gotten busier since then. Isn't he putting up those apartments just south of you?"

"And duplexes and houses too," Polly said. "It's nice having him in town, but he's still putting in a lot of hours."

Her phone buzzed and she looked down at it. "Do you mind if I take this? It's Deputy Hudson."

Ken nodded and Polly swiped the call open. "Hello, Deputy."

"I'm sure we got past that," Tab said.

"If this is official business, I feel like I should be a little more official. What can I do for you?"

"Will Heath be available right after lunch? I'd like to speak with him about Mr. West."

"Sure. Do you want us to come down to your office?"

"Would one o'clock work?" Tab asked.

"We'll be there." Polly put the phone back down on the table and closed her eyes for a moment to regather her thoughts. "I hope that goes well."

Ken nodded and smiled as he looked up. "Looks like we're adding one more."

"Who?" Polly craned her neck and smiled. She hadn't expected to see Simon Gardner, the owner of the antique store come in the door with Paul Bradford.

The two men came over to the booth and both she and Ken stood up. She took Simon's hand. "I didn't expect to see you today."

"Paul gave me a call. It might be your granddaddies, but my mother helped keep whiskey flowing in this town."

"She what?" Polly asked with a laugh.

"I might have a few stories for you."

"Let me get you some coffee. Would you like a muffin or something sweet?"

Simon took her arm and walked to the counter. "I'm not so old that I can't take care of myself, sweet girl. Let's see what delicacies your friend, Mrs. Donovan, has made today." He glanced up at Skylar. "Good morning, young man. I'd like a cup of your Darjeeling." As he leaned on Polly's arm, he said, "Thanks to your wonderful shop here, I get to experience all of my favorite teas without having to keep a large stock of my own. I can have something different each day of the week. And a slice of that lemon berry pound cake. Maybe you could sprinkle a little extra powdered sugar on it?" He grinned. "I'm being bad today."

Skylar grinned back. "You're bad every day."

"Shhh, young man. Don't be telling my secrets to the pretty girls, now. A gentleman must maintain some decorum."

"I'll bring it over to your table," Skylar said.

Polly and Simon walked back to the table and she slid in first, moving her coffee and muffin with her. He sat down beside her and took a long, leather wallet out of a pocket in his jacket.

"The boy is a treasure. He knows how to make his customers happy," Simon said. "I hope you pay him well or I might have to steal him."

Paul Bradford slid in across from Simon with a cup of black coffee. He looked at the muffins in front of Ken and Polly and groaned. "I promised Lisa that I wouldn't do this, but it's not fair. I'll be right back."

"No willpower," Ken said with a laugh. "But I'm afraid that's not what this shop is all about."

"No sir, it isn't," Simon said. He smiled at Skylar as he set the plate and mug on the table. "Here you are, son. The change is yours. Thank you for your service."

"Thank you, Mr. Gardner," Skylar said. He looked at Polly and Ken. "Wave at me if you need anything."

"Thanks, Skylar," Polly replied.

In a moment, Paul Bradford was back with a chocolate muffin. "What Lisa doesn't know won't hurt me." He waggled his finger at the three of them. "And don't any of you tell on me." He took a bite and elbowed Chief Wallers. "Did you hear about that big walleye ole Jeff Denton pulled out of the Des Moines River last weekend? Nearly fifteen pounds from what I hear."

"All I've been able to catch is channel cat in there," Ken replied. "Caught some good walleye down at Rathbun, though. You heading up to Fort Dodge for trout fishing in a couple months?"

"Yeah, buddy," Paul replied, winking at Polly. "You want to go fishing with us sometime, Ms. Giller? Lisa has a good time."

Polly laughed. "No, thank you. I have enough going on without getting dumped in a river with the likes of you."

"What do you hear about those trees coming down out by the winery?" Simon asked.

Ken shook his head. "Somebody's probably stocking up for winter heat. We haven't figured out who it is, yet. As long as they don't hurt anything else, I'm not too worried."

"Archie Westerfield says they've been having trouble with kids shoplifting," Paul said. "You on that, Chief?"

"Bert ran 'em down the other day. Just a couple of kids daring each other," Ken said. "But I'd have to guess Polly has better things to do than sit here and listen to you two hens chatter about town gossip. What did you want to ask us, Polly?"

She took her phone out and scrolled through her photos to those she had taken of the items found in the back of the tally boards from her basement. "These things. I'm curious as to what their significance was and why they might have been hidden away. Did your relatives ever talk about any of this?" Polly stopped on the picture of the teeth. "These were found in the back of your grandfather's board, Ken. Why would he have put teeth in there?"

Ken laughed. "Granddad was famous for his false teeth. He had a couple of different sets, which was a big deal because they were so expensive." He tipped his head back and looked at the ceiling. "One of them was missing a bunch of teeth. I wonder if these belonged to that set. Do they look false to you, Simon?" He pushed the phone toward the older man beside Polly.

Simon Gardner made the photo larger and moved it back and forth in front of his eyes. "I'd have to see them in person to know for certain, but they probably are. How'd you find all this, Polly?"

"I was working in the room in my basement and when I took the board off the wall, it rattled. I wanted to know what was rattling."

He set the phone back down and smiled. "My mother used to tell stories of a group of men that met in secret in the basement of the Bell House. I guess that once I knew they were cooking whiskey for young Mr. Bell, I assumed that was the purpose of their meetings."

"What did she do at the Bell House?" Polly asked. "And why did you never tell me that she worked there?"

Simon shrugged. "I didn't think about it. She worked in the hotel's dining room. Mother was a lovely young lady and I think she had a small crush on Mr. Bell. But then Father moved to Bellingwood, swept her off her feet and she never looked back. She wasn't there very long. Less than a year."

Paul Bradford had picked up the phone and was scrolling through the pictures as Polly and Simon Gardner spoke. "I asked my grandfather why he didn't wear a wedding ring. He said he lost it. I wonder if one of these rings was his," Paul said. "Dad told me not to bother Grandpa with questions like that. I didn't think much about it at the time, but now I wonder if they weren't hiding something. He wasn't too happy with me that day."

"Sounds like we have a mystery," Ken Wallers said.

Polly scowled. "I'm curious, but I don't want to make any more of it than it is. These things were put in there eighty or ninety years ago. Nobody is alive who would have known what was going on."

"You really need to talk to Greg Parker," Ken said. "You know, Lucy, from the diner? Her husband."

"He doesn't speak," Paul said.

"Lucy can talk to him. They communicate pretty well. Greg remembers everything. If he heard or saw something, that man's mind trapped the information. It's just a matter of pointing him in the right direction and then giving him enough time to write it out."

"He can write?" Simon asked.

"A little bit."

"He needs one of those fancy computers. You know, like that scientist has. The one who is in a wheelchair and can't talk." Paul waved his hand at Polly. "You know who I mean."

"Steven Hawking?"

"Yeah. Him. If he can communicate using a computer, Greg should be able to do it." Paul turned to Ken. "Why haven't we figured that out for him?"

"Because he's a stubborn old man who won't accept help."

"But what if we need *his* help? Polly needs his help. Maybe she can talk him into letting us get him a computer."

"Me?" Polly gasped. "Why me?"

Paul Bradford laughed and pointed at her phone. "Because you're asking questions about things that happened decades ago. And now you have us curious."

"Aaron's a good friend of Greg's," Ken said. "You should talk to him first, Polly."

"Wait. How did this become my deal?" Polly asked.

"Paul already answered that, my dear," Simon said, putting his hand on her arm. "And besides, you're the youngest one here. Surely you know all about that assistive communication technology."

Polly laughed until she snorted. "I think you're trying to

buffalo me. You even know what it's called. Don't give me that 'I'm too old' crap. You're smarter than most people."

"I might have read a thing or two about it."

"On the internet, am I right?" she asked. "And you used a fancy tablet to do it. While seeing you in your old-fashioned store with an old-fashioned cash register and your antiques might be good for business, you'd have me believe that you don't have the latest technology under the counter? Let's see your cell phone." She beckoned to him with her hand. "Come on, bring it out, Mister."

Simon grinned and took out a shiny, flat phone. "It's not the latest, but it does the job."

"Wow, old man," Paul said. "That's newer than mine. I suppose you have an e-reader and a tablet, too?"

"I built my own computer," Simon said with a grin, leaning forward. "Don't you dare tell anyone. It would ruin my reputation. But that baby blazes right along."

"Do you play video games too?" Polly asked, shaking her head.

"Every now and again. I had to stop with that, though. It was cutting into my reading time in the evenings."

"So what do you know about this assistive communications technology?" Ken asked Simon.

"It's not that expensive. I could get some information for you. Maybe you talk to Lucy about it and see what she has to say. She'd know whether Greg would go for it. And while I'm at it, I'll look back at some of my mother's journals. She kept a diary. Maybe she wrote something about those secret meetings. I know it felt odd to her, but it was a part of her life that she left behind when she got married. After Mr. Franklin left town ..." Simon shook his head. "... died, I guess. She always talked about him leaving town on a whim. It never made sense to her. But after he was gone and the hotel shut down, she really did just quit thinking about it. If we drove by the old hotel, she talked about it as if it were a far-off place. For a while they had that tuberculosis asylum in there. That didn't last too long. And then the Springers bought the place. Mother was happy to see them bring it back to life. She would be glad to see you restoring it, Polly."

"I'm thankful for your help," Polly said.

Paul Bradford put his hand on the table. "So we have a plan. Mr. Gardner is going to research the technology. Ken, you'll talk to Lucy since you're in the diner all the time. And Polly, you're going to ask Sheriff Merritt to talk to Greg about using the technology to communicate. Are we set?"

"This is why you've been in business so long, isn't it," Ken said. "You just delegate tasks and then sit back and do nothing."

"I'm the boss. I do that very well," Paul replied with a laugh. "I've got some old photographs and things of my grandfather's. I'll go through those and try to figure out who the rest of the people are in Polly's basement. Would you send me those pictures of all the tally boards? I'll try to identify the other names. Maybe there are more people in town who might know something. It's Thursday. How about we see what we can come up with over the weekend and have coffee again here next Monday. Will that work?"

"You really are the boss," Polly said with a smile. "But that works for me."

"I'll put it on my calendar," Ken replied.

Simon nodded. "I look forward to it."

Paul stood up. "I'd best get back to the shop. They get nervous if I'm gone too long. But being here gives me a good excuse to take some of Mrs. Donovan's muffins back with me. And maybe a loaf of her sourdough bread for home."

"I should make my way back to the shop," Simon said. "I'm never terribly busy in the mornings, but you never know when a stray customer might show up." He reached over and squeezed Polly's arm. "You be sure to stop in any time. Your smile lights up a room."

CHAPTER NINE

"Eat something," Polly said when Heath came in from the barn. "It will be a long afternoon."

"No time. Too nervous. Need a shower."

Heath ran through to his room and then back to the bathroom. He was right. Whatever Eliseo had him doing was dirty, smelly work and the fact that the temperature was still in the upper eighties hadn't helped.

She really hadn't expected him to be hungry. Heath skipped meals when he was stressed. Polly usually went straight for the ice cream sandwiches. So far, she'd been in good shape this week. Even after finding Mr. West's body yesterday, she'd been okay. Maybe she should be more nervous than she was about taking Heath down to meet with Tab Hudson, but many of the deputies were friends and she was learning to trust Tab as much as she did Aaron Merritt. And besides, any member of her family who might have had a problem with the teacher had been safely ensconced in the house last night. No matter how hard they tried, no one could connect this murder to Heath.

The ears on both dogs perked up as sirens screamed through

town. Polly wondered if she would ever get used to that sound. When she lived in Boston, sirens were part of background noise, but Bellingwood was a quiet community. A siren meant there was every possibility something had happened to someone you knew. She took a deep breath, praying that whoever was involved would be okay.

"I'm ready," Heath said, coming into the dining room. "Do I look okay?"

He'd changed into a clean pair of blue jeans and a dark blue, button-down shirt.

"You look great. But maybe some shoes and socks." Polly pointed to his feet.

Heath moaned and ran back through to his bedroom, emerging a few minutes later with his shoes on. "I'm really nervous."

"I understand, but you don't need to be. This isn't about you, it's about Mr. West and people that might have been angry enough to kill him."

"I'm really glad I was here with everybody."

She reached out and squeezed his hand. "Me too. Now remember to think before you speak. Don't offer information that isn't pertinent and make sure you are completely truthful. Don't make something up just because you think that's what she wants to hear. Okay?"

"Yeah. That makes me more nervous. What if I screw up?"

"You can't screw up. If you get too nervous, just look at me. Take your time, slow down, breathe deeply and look at me. Can you do that?"

He gave a little chuckle. "I don't know. But I'll try. Why do I keep getting involved in this stuff?"

Polly shook her head. "I have no idea. When I ask myself those kinds of questions I realize that I'd rather it be me than anyone else. I know that I can handle it. You've got this. You can handle it. You've been through much worse."

"I'm ready," he said. "Thanks for coming with me."

Polly rubbed her hand up and down his back. "I promised you I'd always be there for you, no matter what." She slipped her arm through his as they walked through the media room. "Except when you forget to tell me that you're going to spend time with your aunt and uncle."

Heath slumped.

"Oh come on," she said. "Not ready for me to tease you about that yet?"

"That was so dumb of me. She just said she had stuff that I'd want. I didn't know she wanted to mess with my head."

"How could you have known?" Polly asked. "Put it down to a lesson learned." She let him go down the steps first and waved goodbye to the dogs as she slipped out the downstairs door.

The ride from Bellingwood to Boone was quiet. Heath closed his eyes, in essence shutting Polly out. When she pulled into the parking lot at the sheriff's office, she reached over and took his hand, startling him to alertness. Polly was surprised at how clammy he felt.

"It's going to be okay," she said.

He just nodded.

They went inside and he hung back while she asked for Deputy Hudson. Tab came right out and invited them back to a conference room. Pleasantries were exchanged and both Tab and Polly noticed that Heath's face had lost much of its color.

"Heath," Tab said quietly.

His head jerked up and he looked straight at her. "Yes, ma'am?"

"I'd like to ask you a few questions about your encounter with Mr. West on Tuesday."

Heath nodded.

"Was that the first time that you had gotten aggressive with him?"

Heath sat back, confusion written across his face. "Yes. Of course."

She nodded. "I understand that he had been pushing you pretty hard that morning. Was that a regular occurrence in the classroom?"

"Not just with me. But yeah. Everybody put up with it. Except for some of the popular girls. He was always nice to them."

"The popular girls. Can you give me some names?"

"I don't know. Maybe he just hadn't gotten to them yet."

"That's okay. How many girls do you think it was?"

"Two or three."

"And you said that he pushed kids pretty hard. Had everyone else in the class been through something similar to your experience except those two or three girls?"

Heath looked at Polly and she nodded.

"Yes, ma'am."

"Did Mr. West call on more than one student in a class period?"

"Sometimes." Heath nodded. "Yeah. Usually."

"Was Tuesday the first time you'd experienced this occurrence?"

"No, ma'am. He made me read out loud the first week of class and asked personal questions that time, too."

"Did it feel like abuse the first time he put you on the spot?"

Heath glanced at Polly again and then looked at the floor. "It was embarrassing, but no big deal."

"Can I ask what he pressed you about that first time?"

"What it felt like to be alone in the world without any family that loved me."

Polly huffed. "Pretty hard to make a case for abuse when it sounds like he's just asking them to be introspective, doesn't it."

"Yes it does," Tab agreed.

"That's why nobody ever talked about it," Heath interrupted. "We knew what it sounded like. He always made it sound like he was teaching us how to be deep thinkers, but the questions were always pointed at something that had hurt us or was wrong in our lives. Things that should have been private. One girl hadn't told anybody except the school counselor about what he talked about in class."

"What was that?" Tab asked.

"I shouldn't talk about it. It's her story. I know it sounds weird, but it's like we all knew that if our secrets were going to be revealed in that room by him, the rest of us were going to protect each other."

"You've only been with that class for a few weeks," Polly said. "Amazing how you closed ranks so quickly."

"He asked that girl the question on the second day. She cried and asked him how he knew because she'd never told anyone."

Polly took a breath. "There's a problem with the counselor if private information is getting to teachers who abuse it."

"I'll ask that question," Tab said before turning back to Heath. "Do you think this girl who was questioned on the second day of class would have wanted to hurt him?"

"I don't know why," Heath said. "It was already out and none of us talked about it after class. She'd seen him say other bad stuff to the rest of the class."

"So you believe he had access to private information?"

Heath pursed his lips in thought. "I didn't think about it that way. He said he knew my parents and the rest of the things he talked about were public knowledge. Everybody knew it. Just nobody taunted me anymore. I thought it had finally blown over."

Tab put a sheet of paper in front of him. "This is a class list. Would you please tell me the names of the girls who had not yet been singled out by Mr. West?"

"Kaylee Butler," Heath said, pointing to a name. He breathed loudly through his nose. "I don't want to do this. They were the lucky ones."

"Just tell her," Polly said.

He set his jaw. "Jen Johnston and Emmy Dill."

Polly's phone buzzed. She took it out of her pocket, saw that it was Henry, swiped to ignore the call and put it back. She'd call him when they were done. The man felt horrible when he couldn't be there for the tough things the kids had to go through. Polly could hardly believe that she finally had a life that allowed her the freedom to be part of these kids' lives during the day.

"Looking at this class list," Tab said. "Are there any kids who were pushed so far that you think they might have retaliated?"

Heath frowned in shock and shook his head violently. "No. Nobody. I was the only one who got so mad. That was only because I had such a bad night the night before."

Tab looked at Polly and then asked. "The night before?"

"He had to spend time with his aunt and uncle who are pretty abusive themselves," Polly said. "Mr. West picked a terrible time to pile onto Heath's emotional baggage."

"I see." Tab put her hand back on the class list. "You can't think of anyone on this list, or maybe friends or family of someone on this list who might have retaliated for what Mr. West did to a student?"

Heath shook his head, more slowly this time. "I really can't." He ran a finger down the names on the list.

"No boyfriends or brothers?"

"If they'd taken his class before, they'd gone through it. It's one of those things everybody knows and nobody talks about. If I'd known before I got in there, I would never have taken that class."

"That's so crazy," Polly said. "In this day and age, everybody talks about everything ... everywhere."

"Not this," Heath said.

"I can't believe there wasn't any video or audio," Polly went on.

"We had to drop our phones in a box by the door," Heath said. "If he found out that someone had a phone with them, he took it away completely and sent it down to the office. You couldn't get it until school was over."

"I have a question that is completely off the record, Heath," Tab said. "Can you think of any reason, other than him singling out students in class, why someone might have killed Mr. West?"

Heath looked down at the table and tucked his lips between his teeth. He looked back and forth between Polly and the deputy, then slowly shook his head. "No, ma'am."

"Are you sure? Nothing at all?"

When Polly put her hand on his arm, he flinched away. "What aren't you telling us, Heath?"

"Nothing. There's nothing."

"There's something."

"It's probably not even true. You know how kids are always making sh.." He stopped, had the decency to blush, and shook his head. "It's just rumor."

"What's the rumor, Heath?" Tab asked.

"I don't want to be a snitch. This is just wrong." He put his head in his hands.

"It's off the record."

"Yeah, but as soon as you hear it from me, you'll investigate and then everything will be on the record," Heath protested. He put his hands on the table in front of him, bracing himself and then said. "If you're the right kind of girl and you are pretty enough and flirt with him and maybe, even, you know ..." he let the sentence drift off.

"Have sex?" Polly asked.

"No, not really sex. But you know." He whispered. "A BJ."

"I understand," Tab said. "Go on."

"Well, some of the girls got on his good side by doing that. At least that's the rumor." He put a hand up. "But I don't know if it's really true. It could just be some of the other girls saying bad stuff because those three didn't get picked on. And, you know, they always kind of had a rep with the boys, even though they're really popular."

Tab smiled at Polly. "High school really never changes, does it?"

Polly laughed. "I guess not."

"You guys know about this stuff?" Heath asked.

"These kinds of rumors have been floating around about girls since before time began. Sometimes they're true; most of the time, they're not. Would there be any other possible reason those three girls wouldn't have been chosen to be in the hot seat?"

"I don't know," Heath said. "I just assumed it was probably true. They're always flirting with the male teachers and it feels like they never have to do as much as anyone else to get by."

"Just these three in the senior class?" Polly asked.

"No," he said. "There's a bunch of 'em. They all hang around together. It's just that these three are in his class together." He stopped talking and looked straight at Deputy Hudson. "Do you really believe that he was killed because of the way he treats us in class?"

"We're just beginning the investigation, Heath. I'm trying to develop an idea of what the man did during the day in the classroom. We are also looking into his life. This is only a small part of the picture."

"I never saw him other than at school. I don't think he was ever at a game. Somebody said he was a class sponsor one year, but that was a long time ago. They said he was pretty creepy about it."

"Creepy about it, how?"

"Never talking to people; just sitting and staring at the kids during meetings. Kind of like he did during class. And then he'd ask weird questions. Never about what they were working on."

"Did you ever see him spend time with other teachers or staff?"

"Honestly, I didn't pay too much attention. Sometimes the teachers walked around in the halls, but they're always going somewhere, not talking to anybody." He shrugged. "Well, the coaches are always in the hall, shooting the sh ... Sorry. But no, I never saw him with ..." Heath paused. "Wait a minute. I guess I did see him talking to one of the teachers in the parking lot before school one morning. I couldn't hear what they were saying, but she was pissed at something. I don't know if she was mad at him, but she was waving her arms around and pointing at something in her briefcase."

"When was that? Do you know who it was?" Tab asked.

"It was last week. Maybe Wednesday morning. Yeah. It was Wednesday because I remember I had toast crumbs on my shirt. I was late and Polly let me take toast with me. I don't know the lady's name. She teaches math. She's new."

Tab wrote down a few more notes in her ever present notebook and then closed it. "I think that's all for now." She stood up and put her hand out to Heath.

He stood and shook it. "That's it? That wasn't so bad."

"Thank you for talking to me," Tab said. "Let me show you two out. I'll be in touch if I need anything more. Polly, I still need to get up to Bellingwood and take you to lunch."

"I need to take you to lunch. You and Anita," Polly said. "I haven't seen you two in forever."

"Anita?" Tab said, her eyebrows creasing. "You haven't seen her?"

"No. Why?"

Tab looked bemused. "No reason. I just assumed you'd see her."

"Why?"

"You'll have to ask Anita." Tab gave Polly a wicked grin walked with them back to the main door. "I really appreciate your time today. I'm sorry you had to deal with this, Heath."

"I hope you find who killed him. It's kind of freaky that it happened after I yelled at him. People are going to think I had something to do with it."

"Yes, they probably will, but we don't. Have a good day, you two."

Tab went back into the building.

"I wonder what's going on with Anita?" Polly asked out loud.

"You mean, other than her going out with Doug?"

Polly grabbed his arm. "Shut up. How do you know this?"

"She's at his place all the time these days. I can't believe you haven't seen her."

"What?" Polly had stopped in the middle of the parking lot, her mouth wide open. "Why didn't you tell me?"

Heath laughed and pushed his hand through his hair. "I figured you knew. You know everything. Can we get something to eat? I'm starving now."

"I'll bet you are." Polly turned back toward the building. "I should go in there and talk to her. Those brats. Going behind my back."

"I don't think they went behind your back. Everybody knows," he said. "Lunch? I'll even buy."

She hooked her arm in his. "No. I've got this one today. Where do you want to go?"

"That barbecue place downtown. I want a rack of ribs."

"Of course you do." Polly unlocked the truck and then climbed up into her seat. "Let me call Henry to tell him that we're done and you lived."

"It wasn't that bad. I can't believe it wasn't that bad. She's like a normal person and everything."

"Most of them are. You know, they were born and had real live parents."

"Yeah and then somewhere along the line they forgot all about it."

"Now, Heath," Polly scolded. "You know a lot of peace officers. They're all pretty good people, right?"

"Yeah. Now that I know them."

She chuckled as she swiped her phone open. "Huh. He left a voice mail. Just a second." Polly called her voice mail back, input her code and waited.

"Polly. Call me as soon as you get this," Henry said. "Dad had a heart attack and they're rushing him to Ames. I'm on my way. Just call me. Polly, oh god, my dad had a heart attack. He's not supposed to have more heart problems. What am I going to do? I have to call Lonnie and ... Polly, call me."

Tears fell from her eyes onto her cheeks.

"What's wrong, Polly?" Heath asked.

"It's Bill. He's had a heart attack and the ambulance is taking him to Ames. Henry's falling apart. I have to call him."

"Do you want me to drive? You can talk to Henry."

Polly looked around the truck, trying to force her brain to focus. "I can drive."

"No you can't. Let me." Heath jumped out of the truck and ran around the front to her door. He opened it and put out his hand. She took it and jumped to the ground, then stopped as she looked at him.

"Go get in the passenger side, Polly," Heath said. "I'll drive us to Ames. You call Henry."

"Okay. Thanks. Sorry about this."

"No problem. I'm fine now."

"But you're hungry."

"Please, Polly. That can wait. Go on, get in the truck and call Henry."

CHAPTER TEN

Racing through the halls of the hospital as fast as they could without upsetting any of the staff, Polly and Heath finally found Henry with his mother, Marie. They were in a waiting room by themselves. Marie's face was drawn and Henry didn't look much better.

He stood when he saw Polly and waited until she drew close, then pulled her into a hug, holding her tightly.

"I'm so sorry," she whispered. "I wish I could make this okay for you."

"Mom's really scared."

"Of course she is. Have you heard anything?"

Henry released Polly and put his hand on Heath's shoulder.

"What can I do for you, Henry?" Heath asked.

"I don't even know," Henry replied. "I haven't been able to think straight yet."

"Did you talk to Lonnie?" Polly asked them.

Marie nodded. "She's speaking with her boss. Hopefully she'll be here by the weekend unless something terrible happens and she has to come earlier."

"Nothing like that is going to happen, Mom," Henry said. "He's in good hands here."

"What about Betty and Dick?" Polly asked quietly, referring to Henry's aunt and uncle.

Marie looked up at them, her eyes opening wide. "I didn't even think ..." She broke down into tears and Henry rushed to sit beside her.

"Don't do this, Mom. We'll make the call."

"Don't make me sit here alone," Marie said, grabbing his hand.

"I'll call Betty," Polly said. "Heath, could you come with me?"

They walked away and Polly touched his hand. "I need you to do what you normally do for Henry after school. Go run the errands for the guys and ask if they need anything from Henry. Take good notes, pay attention and if you see anything he needs to know about, write it down somewhere. Let the guys know that Henry won't be talking to them today. If I know him, he'll try to be there tomorrow."

"Sure," Heath said. "Thanks. I need to do something. Do you want me to call Hayden or talk to Rebecca and the kids?"

"I'll call Stephanie and Jeff to let them know. Yeah. When you're done, stop by the house and make sure the kids take care of the animals and that they're doing okay. I'll let you know what's happening here."

"What about Hay?"

"Of course you can call him," Polly said. "But I will too. He and Marie have a close relationship. He might be good for her."

Heath smiled and started to walk away, but Polly stopped him and gave him a quick hug. "Get yourself something to eat before you leave town. I was proud of you today. You did really good with Deputy Hudson."

"Thanks. I'll call you later."

She watched him walk down the hall and took her phone out, then scrolled through her list of contacts until she landed on Betty Mercer's phone number and swiped to make the call.

"Hello, hello," Betty sang out. "My phone tells me it's Polly. Is that you, sweetheart?"

Polly smiled in spite of all that was going on. "It is me, Betty. But I'm calling with bad news. Bill had a heart attack and he's here in Ames at the hospital."

"He did what?" She must have put her hand over the phone because Polly heard muffled sounds before she returned. "I just told Dick to change his clothes. We'll be there as fast as we can. Tell Marie that whatever decisions she makes, I'll support her. Kiss Henry's head for me. Should we bring anything?"

"Just yourselves, I think," Polly said.

"Do you know anything yet?"

"I'm sorry. I just got here myself and offered to call you."

"Then don't you worry. I'll find out what I need to know when I get there."

With that, she was gone and Polly smiled again. Her arrival would certainly lift everyone's spirits.

Alerts on Polly's phone showed that she had several text messages. Lydia and Andy had both messaged her asking questions about Bill and Marie. There was a message from Jessie. The poor girl had to be worried sick, but Polly decided to wait until she knew something before making any more calls.

She sent Hayden a quick text and hoped he would see it before leaving Ames.

She went back into the waiting room and sat down beside Marie. "Betty and Dick are on their way." Polly leaned forward. "Heath is going to head to the work sites just like normal. I told him to pay attention and make sure they didn't have any big questions for you, Henry."

Henry nodded. "The doctor says Dad is stabilized, but they're taking him into surgery to do an angioplasty. This is going to be a long night."

"I'm so sorry," Polly said, taking Marie's hand. "I know this is stressful, but they're moving forward."

"I know. I just want this to be over and have him home again."

"What happened?"

Marie looked past Polly long enough that Polly turned to see if someone was there.

"If Len hadn't been there, I don't know what would have happened. Bill could have been lying on the floor of the shop for hours before we found him."

"Then I'm very thankful for Len," Polly said. "Did he have to do CPR?"

"No," Marie said. "I don't think Bill's heart stopped until he was in the ambulance. Len and he were talking and Bill complained about his arm. He tried to say it was from running the table saw, but Len knew exactly what it was and he didn't hesitate. He just called for the ambulance. He didn't even come get me until they were already there. He just called and told them to hurry." She gave a slight chuckle. "Bill said he was crazy. But Len refused to listen and made him sit back and then gave him an aspirin. Who carries aspirin?" Marie started crying again and slumped against Henry. "I'm never leaving the house without a bottle of aspirin in my purse, that's for sure."

Polly's phone buzzed with a text and she opened it.

"I'm just getting out of class," Hayden wrote. *"I'll be there in a few minutes. Is everything okay?"*

"In surgery. Angioplasty. Marie will be glad to see you. Thanks."

"Can I bring anything?"

Polly turned to Henry. "Hayden's coming up. He's done with class. Do you want him to bring anything?"

Henry shook his head. "Mom? How about you?"

"No. I can't eat anything. It would just go to waste."

Polly texted back to Hayden that they didn't need anything, though she knew that soon her stomach would be growling.

"I'm going to call Jessie," Polly said. "She's pretty worried."

Marie looked up. "Poor Molly was scared. She didn't know what was happening." She fumbled in her pocket for her phone. "I should call Lonnie again. Tell her what's going on." The phone slipped from her hands into her lap as she stared off into space.

"Mom?" Henry asked.

"I'm sorry. I was just thinking about Bill on that table. He's so strong and he takes care of everyone. How could this happen? What will I do without him?"

"You aren't going to have to do without him," Henry said. He rested his hand on the back of the chair and gently rubbed his mother's back. "Do you want me to call Lonnie?"

Marie handed him her telephone. "Call her. I want to talk to her, though."

Polly nodded at the two of them and slipped out of the room and placed a call to Jessie.

"Polly? Is he okay?" Jessie asked.

"He's going into surgery to have an angioplasty."

"Oh that's good," Jessie said. "I've been reading all about this stuff on the internet and this is better than anything else."

Polly chuckled. "Of course you have. How is your little girl doing?"

"She's making get well cards. We talked about how the EMTs and doctors are helping Bill and aren't scary people. I just want that to be true for her. Is there anything I should bring for Marie?"

"Let's wait until she knows more about what's going on," Polly said.

"But we can come over after work, can't we?"

Polly glanced back at the small room. Marie hadn't rejected the idea of having people around. Jessie and Molly were as much a part of her family as anyone else. "Of course you can come over. You're family," Polly said.

The sigh of relief on the other end of the call told Polly how important that had been to Jessie. "I know where her travel bag is. I'll toss a few things in and bring it with me in case she needs to spend the night. She shouldn't have to do without her things."

"Thank you, Jessie."

As soon as Polly hung up, she knew she needed to call Lydia. The woman would be worried. She dialed the call and waited while it rang.

"Hello Polly," Lydia said. "Are you in Ames at the hospital?"

"I am. He's gone into surgery."

"How bad?"

"Angioplasty. I don't know how bad."

"Andy called me. I'm so sorry. This is a terrible stress."

"Yes it is," Polly said. "But Marie said that Len knew what was happening right away and called the ambulance before Bill even realized what was going on. He also made Bill take an aspirin. What was that about?"

"Len had a heart attack six years ago," Lydia said. "He says that he thought his life was over. He's pretty sensitive to that nowadays."

"Well, Marie thinks he's a hero. So do I, but she's pretty grateful."

"Aaron said that you and Heath were down at his office today and didn't stop in to say hello."

Polly gasped audibly. "I didn't. Should I have?"

Lydia laughed. "No. You're fine. How did it go with Heath and Deputy Hudson?"

"She had a lot of questions for him about his classmates and their experience with that teacher. What kind of weird, freakin' man was in that classroom anyway, Lydia?"

"It will be interesting to find out how he managed to dodge questions about his tactics," Lydia replied. "But for every ten or fifteen excellent teachers, there will always be one who slips through the cracks. Just like with any business."

"I suppose. And I know that my kids can't avoid the terrible things that life has to offer them, but I'm pretty sure Heath has had his fill. The universe could be finished messing with him at any moment and I'd certainly be glad of it."

"What doesn't kill you makes you stronger, yes?"

Polly wasn't quite sure how to respond. Lydia rarely spoke in platitudes. "Yeah," she finally said. "He'll be plenty strong, I guess."

"I'm sorry, Polly. I got distracted. Beryl just walked in. She's waving at me to hand over the phone."

"I should ..."

"You should what, Miss Thing?" Beryl interrupted. "I know you don't have time to talk to me. I just wondered if you needed me to take Rebecca tonight. I'd get her to school on time and everything tomorrow morning. I promise."

Polly chuckled. "You're awesome. I'll be coming home one way or the other tonight, so she should be fine. But thank you."

"Well don't forget that. I have plenty of room and she's a sweet girl."

"Thank you. If something comes up and I need a place for her, I'll let you know."

"I love you, missy. Take care of your people, okay?"

"Got it."

Polly walked back into the waiting room. Henry was still sitting with his arm around his mother and the two of them were silent.

"Did you talk to Lonnie?" she asked.

Henry nodded.

"When's she coming into town?"

"She wanted to start for home tonight, but it's nearly a nine-hour drive," Marie said. "I told her to wait until tomorrow morning. I don't want to worry about one more person tonight."

"Lonnie will be fine, Mom," Henry said. "She's a smart girl."

Marie nodded. It nearly killed Polly to see her mother-in-law this way. Not only was Bill strong and vital, but Marie didn't let much of anything get to her. She handled most things with equanimity. Bill was the one who let his emotions get the better of him.

Henry's head had to be all over the place. He continually opened his phone and looked at it, then he'd shake his head and put it back down. There were so many things going on right now. For the first time in months, he was coming home at a decent hour in the evenings. He'd hired a couple of new foremen whom he trusted, and rather than taking on more new projects, he was looking forward to slowing down a bit when winter arrived. In fact, his father had been talking about heading south again for a few months. Polly didn't know whether this heart attack would keep them in town, or force them back to Arizona for good.

His last heart attack had occurred in Arizona after a car crashed into their house. That was only a few years ago. Henry had to be considering the fact that his father needed to slow down, or even stop doing all that he was doing. That would kill Bill Sturtz, though. Retirement hadn't been good for the man. As much as he and Marie enjoyed their lives in Arizona, they were both thrilled to be busy in Bellingwood again. Marie's relationship with Jessie and Molly was a huge joy for her. They couldn't run away again. There were too many young people in their lives now who would miss them desperately.

She looked up at the sound of a slight cough and jumped out of her seat to greet Hayden.

He sat down beside Marie and took the woman's hand. "I'm so sorry, Marie."

She touched his cheek and smiled. "I'm glad you're here. Your brother was here earlier, but he's gone to take care of things for Henry. We're all so lucky that you're in our lives."

"We're the lucky ones," Hayden said.

"Did you have a good day in class today?" she asked him.

Hayden nodded. "It was okay." He looked up at Polly. "How'd things go with Heath?"

"He did great," Polly said.

"I never took that guy's class," Hayden said, still holding Marie's hand. "I heard he was creepy, but this stuff was over the top."

"Do you think he was high?" Marie asked.

Everyone turned to stare at her.

"Well, I had a professor that came to class every day, higher than a kite. Like we all didn't know it. He thought he was so clever and could hide it, but we all knew. Of course, that was in the early seventies. It wasn't all that odd. Half the class was high, too."

"You?" Henry asked.

She swatted at him and chuckled. "Of course not me. I was there to get an education."

"Uh huh," Henry said.

"I might have gone to a few parties, but I stayed away from the hard stuff. I just knew that as soon as I did something, I'd get caught."

A young woman in a white coat came into the room and Marie tried to stand up.

"I just want to let you know that it's taking a little longer than expected," the nurse said. She put her hand up. "But it's fine. He's doing really well and as soon as he heads for recovery we'll let you know."

"Did something happen?" Marie asked. "Are there complications?"

"No. Nothing like that. The doctor is just being extra careful. Now I need to get back in."

Marie nodded and sat back. "Do you think she was lying to us?"

"No, Mom," Henry said. "She wouldn't do that."

"There you are," Betty Mercer said, striding into the room, her husband right behind her. She crossed over to Marie and Henry, knelt in front of them and reached up to hug Marie. "I've been worried about you. Nobody should have to go through this twice."

"It's Bill that's going through it," Marie said.

"No honey, it's you, too. You're scared out of your mind, aren't you?"

Marie nodded, then melted into Betty, sobs wrenching out of her.

Both Henry and Hayden pulled back in surprise. Dick Mercer chuckled a little and walked over to put his hand on Henry's shoulder. "Sometimes they just need a woman to cry on."

"She's been crying a little all day," Henry said, "but nothing like this."

Dick nodded. "Trust me. When this passes, she'll be a whole lot better. You boys come with me. We should maybe get something from the cafeteria to fill you up. Have either of you eaten anything since breakfast?"

Henry shook his head and looked over at Hayden, who just shrugged.

"Mother there, told me to take you away so she could spend some time with Marie. I'm taking you away. You too, Polly. Let those two hug on each other for a time and we'll come back before the doctor is finished with old Bill. You don't need to worry, they can't take him too far in this place without us finding him."

Henry gave a little shake of his head, started to say something to his mother and got a look from Betty. He chuckled and stood up. "Okay, Uncle Dick. I guess you're the boss."

"No, son. She's the boss. Always has been. Always will be. I learned a long time ago that all I had to do was pay attention to her and I'd live a very happy life. So far it's been pretty good. Come with me if you want to live."

Polly laughed out loud. "Really? Terminator?"

Dick winked, then said out loud, "Hasta la vista, baby."

CHAPTER ELEVEN

Polly stood at the door to the hospital room while Henry went in to say hello to his father. Marie and Betty both insisted that he go home and he was exhausted enough to let them push him out. Betty intended to stay as long as Marie would let her, grinning when she told everyone that she'd made Dick bring his own truck. She wasn't about to leave her brother until it was absolutely necessary.

Jessie and Molly had come up to see Marie for just a few minutes. The peace that happy little girl gave Marie was palpable. When Jessie handed Marie the bag she packed, the older woman had fallen into tears again.

It was strange for Polly to watch the strong bond Marie had with that little family. Polly loved her mother-in-law and her kids loved spending time with Bill and Marie, but something special had happened between Marie, Jessie, and Molly. Something Polly would never have. She realized that, instead, that was the relationship she had with Lydia. It had never occurred to Polly to be jealous of Jessie and she hoped Lydia's daughters never felt threatened by her relationship with their mother.

Then she shook her head. What strange things to be thinking about today.

Hayden had gone back to Bellingwood. He promised to make sure that the kids were all where they should be, supper was fed to them, and things were okay before he and Heath went over to the Bell House. They were working in the immense front foyer, ripping out the lath and plaster on the walls. Henry had brought scaffolding over for the boys since some of the walls were two stories high. They hadn't yet made a decision about tearing out the ceiling, but Henry did intend to bring the chandelier down and check all of the wiring. Polly couldn't wait to see that chandelier at eye level. It was in desperate need of a cleaning. The pulley system that brought it down had long since rotted away, but Hayden thought that with enough scaffolding in place, he had the courage to climb up there and rig something up. Henry had agreed with Hayden's plans. Polly just didn't want to have to watch.

When she and Henry got to his truck, he tossed her the keys. "Do you mind?" he asked.

"Not at all." Both of them chuckled when the keys hit the ground and Polly had to bend over to pick them up.

"Sorry," Henry said.

"Whatever." Polly opened the truck door. Since it was a bigger truck than hers, she used the panic bar to pull herself up and into his seat. She waited for him to open the passenger door and was startled when her door opened again.

Henry stood there, his eyes filling with tears. "I can't lose my dad," he said.

"Oh honey." Polly turned in the seat and slid down to stand on the running board. Henry put his arms around her and buried his head in her shoulder. She held him while he cried, stroking his back. "He's going to be okay. The worst is over."

They stood like that for a few minutes as the sun went down and parking lot lights came on. She felt his crying subside and his breathing become more normal.

"It isn't going to be okay. Yeah, he'll be alive, but he can't keep working like he has," Henry said. "Mom is going to have a fit if he tries to keep up that pace. And I don't blame her. Polly, this was my fault."

"How was it your fault?" Polly asked.

"I needed him so bad, so I could just quit thinking about work at the shop. He and Len have been handling it and Dad is forever telling me how much fun he's having. How he never thought he'd be able to do this after he retired." Henry shook his head. "I've been taking him for granted. And Len too. What would I do if I had to call Andy and tell her that her husband died from a heart attack?"

Polly kissed Henry's forehead. "Honey. I know you're stressed, but if I started talking like this about the people who work for me and around me, would you let me get away with it?"

"What do you mean?"

"Did you stick an electrical charge in his heart? Did you build up all that plaque in there?"

"No. But I shouldn't have let him work like he does."

Polly chuckled. "He's your dad. How in the world are you supposed to tell him what to do? Have you ever succeeded at that in the past?"

"No, but ..."

"No. What would your father say to you if you were discussing someone else in the same situation?"

"That it wasn't my fault and I should quit blaming myself and decide what to do going forward."

"Oh, look how wise he is."

Henry stepped back so Polly could turn around, then helped her get back into the driver's seat. "You get awful practical on me sometimes."

"Do I now? I guess I've learned from the best. Now get in this truck. I'm still starving. That cafeteria food did not hit the spot and we're stopping for sandwiches before I head home."

He pushed her door closed and walked around the truck, climbed up and pulled his belt on, then laughed. "It's messy over here."

"Whaddya know," she said with a laugh. "You've had a busy week and no one else has been in your truck."

"I hope he makes it through the night."

"Henry, I love you, but you have to have a little faith. Absolutely no one is talking about him dying tonight. The doctor was positive and upbeat about the procedure and says your Dad will be home by the weekend."

"But anything can happen."

Polly stopped the truck to wait for a light to turn green and turned to glare at him. "I did not just hear you say that."

"What?"

"Some pessimistic baloney about the worst possible outcome."

"No feeling sorry for myself tonight, is there?" he said.

"You can feel sorry for yourself as long as it isn't crazy talk coming out of your mouth. You don't let me get away with it, I'm certainly not letting you do it either."

"Can I stress out about what I'm going to do at the shop?"

Polly nodded. "Absolutely. Those are decisions that you have to make. You can talk your way all through those until you've come up with a plan. Tell me what's bothering you the most."

"These homes that we're in the middle of. Cabinets and facings. Everything."

"Your dad and Len weren't building all of those things, were they? How?"

He shook his head. "No. Most of it's just stock stuff, but they were working on specialty trim for a few of the customers. And Dad was coordinating all of the product coming in."

"Can I help?"

"No. Maybe I can pull Ben off the jobsite and bring him over to the shop."

"There are other cabinet shops around. Would any of those guys help you out?" Polly asked.

"Competition is pretty stiff. I don't want to ask for their help unless I absolutely need it."

Polly let him work through the problem while she headed into a drive-through for sandwiches. He didn't even look up when she asked what he wanted, so she ordered what they usually got. She put the ice tea beside him and absentmindedly, he picked it up and took a drink, then dropped it back in place and went back to work on his tablet.

"These are great notes that Heath took today. Thanks for having him do that," Henry said. "I need to make some calls tomorrow morning, but with him checking job sites this afternoon, that really helped."

"I'm glad." Polly unwrapped his sandwich and put it on the console beside him, then popped open a bag of chips. He continued to work and eat as she drove home.

She pulled into the garage and Henry looked up. "I'm sorry," he said. "I didn't mean to ignore you."

"It's all right," Polly assured him. "You've had a long day and a lot on your mind."

"Are the boys here?" He craned his neck, looking for their vehicles.

"I don't think so."

"Okay. I just needed to talk to Heath about a couple of things. I can do that when he gets home."

"Come on. Let's head upstairs and you can settle down in the bedroom and work to your heart's content."

"What did I ever do to deserve you?" he asked, reaching across the console for her hand.

"It was all that good livin'," Polly quipped.

He gave her hand a squeeze, slid his tablet into a briefcase and got out of the truck, waiting at the door for her. "Do we need to let the dogs out?"

"I'll take care of it. You don't need to worry about anything."

He nodded distractedly and they headed up the steps.

"Is anyone here?" Polly called out.

"I am!" Rebecca yelled from another room. "Are you both here?"

Polly and Henry walked into the dining room and met Rebecca, who had come running across the living room floor. Rebecca threw herself at Henry and he pulled her into a hug. "I was so worried. Everybody I saw asked me about Bill and I didn't know what to say."

"Everybody you saw?" Polly asked.

"Yeah. Beryl came and got me and took me to Davey's for dinner. She said I shouldn't be home by myself while everybody else was at the hospital. I called Heath and told him not to worry and I was home by the time Hayden got here. He said he was going to make supper, but I gave him my leftovers instead. Heath and him are at the other house. They said they'd be back by nine. They should be here any minute. I took the dogs outside so you don't have to." She dipped her head. "I didn't do any more in the bathroom tonight. Are you mad at me?"

Polly shook her head. "That's fine for tonight. We'll finish it another time. That was pretty wonderful of Beryl to take you to dinner. Did you tell her thank you?"

"Of course I did." Rebecca scowled at Polly. "A bunch of times. If Bill is still in the hospital tomorrow, will you take me over to see him?"

"Let's wait and see," Polly said.

Henry had slipped away while Rebecca was talking. Han and Obiwan followed him into the bedroom and moments later, Obiwan left with the door shutting behind him.

"He's really upset, isn't he," Rebecca said.

"Yes he is."

"It's not easy to see your parent lying in a hospital bed," Rebecca calmly observed. "I wish I could say the right thing to him."

"What was the right thing that people said to you?" Polly asked.

"I love you and I'm sorry."

"You can say those things to him any time. He'd really appreciate it. Did you finish all your homework?"

Rebecca nodded. "Yes. And I told Heath that he had to finish his when he got home tonight even if he isn't going to school again tomorrow. He can't get behind or he'll never catch up." She looked at Polly with a small smile. "Do you think he still has to read all of those books for his literature class? Maybe they'll just give everybody a grade and call it good."

"They have substitute teachers. But he likes reading, doesn't he?"

"Maybe he will now."

Obiwan ran to the back stairs and in moments, Heath and Hayden had crested the top step and were coming into the dining room.

"How did it go?" Polly asked.

"That foyer is going to take forever," Hayden said. "I'm glad we got the other rooms done first."

"Hay figured out the pulley. We got the chandelier down," Heath said, clapping his brother on the back. "It wasn't that bad, the chain just got stuck. Somebody wrapped it around a gear and it was all messed up."

"Probably the ghost," Rebecca said. "You guys are a mess. Shouldn't you, like, shake like dogs before you come into the house?" She bent over and shook herself. "It's not that hard."

"Yes, ma'am," Hayden said. "I think I'll take a shower."

"Heath, I think Henry wants to talk to you. He's in the bedroom. You did a good job for him today."

"Yeah?"

She nodded. "He appreciated it."

"There were a lot of things that I had questions about, but I figured he just wanted to know them all."

"You did exactly right. He's in there working."

Heath had come back to life, his face brightening and his stride a little longer as he left the dining room and headed for Henry.

Rebecca dropped into a chair at the dining room table, reaching out to rub Obiwan's head as he settled beside her. "I feel like I'm not doing anything to help. But I don't know what to do."

"You could have finished cleaning the bathroom," Polly said, turning away so Rebecca couldn't see her smile.

"That's not helping. That's punishment."

"The boys might have appreciated it being clean when they used it tonight."

Rebecca rolled her eyes heavenward. "They're going to make it worse. I should have finished tonight so I don't have to clean up after them." She smacked her forehead with the butt of her hand. "I'm so dumb."

"Come on. Let's make cookies and brownies. We need to tell a few people thank you tomorrow."

Jumping up from the table, Rebecca opened the pantry door and pulled out ingredients. "Like who?"

"Like Len Specek."

"What'd he do?"

"He saved Bill's life. He realized Bill was having a heart attack and called for the ambulance before anything bad happened."

"Wow," Rebecca said. "That's a big deal. What if he hadn't been there?"

"But he was."

"But I mean, what if he wasn't?"

Polly turned and put her hands on her hips. "What is up with you people letting your imagination create scenarios that don't exist? He was there. If he hadn't been there, we wouldn't have thought about him being there. So why are we thinking about him not being there when he was."

"What?" Rebecca asked, creasing her forehead. "What did you just say?"

"I said ..." Polly opened the refrigerator and took out a one pound box of butter. "It's ridiculous to try to make a bad situation worse by imagining a different outcome. We have what we have. This time it worked out wonderfully. If I were to say to you, 'What if Kayla's dad had never escaped from prison,' what's your response?"

"He wouldn't have kidnapped me and he'd still be alive."

"But he did and he's not. Your life is what it is today because those things happened. You can't change it by wondering about a different outcome. What if Joey Delancey hadn't ever met me?"

"You wouldn't have come to Bellingwood and you wouldn't have known Andrew and then I would never have met you and I would have been all by myself when Mom died."

"But he did meet me. I did come to Bellingwood and look where we are. All of those other paths ..." Polly twisted her hands around to represent a winding path. "Those paths don't exist. So trying to come up with much worse scenarios in order to create some kind of fearful drama is just ridiculous. Yes?"

"I was just wondering."

Polly chuckled. "Len was there and it worked out the way it worked out. And we're all very thankful."

"Was Marie upset?"

"She cried a lot. It's going to take some time before she is confident he won't just die on her at any minute."

"Will she ever get there?" Rebecca asked. "I don't know if I would."

"I'm not sure. This is Bill's second heart attack. The confidence that Marie had rebuilt is eroded again. It won't easily come back."

"Yeah. That makes sense," Rebecca said. "I'd never let him out of my sight."

"He'd drive you crazy. Imagine never letting Andrew out of your sight."

Rebecca stopped in her tracks. "Yeah. I'd lose my mind. You won't believe what he did today."

"What's that?"

"He asked Joel Spotter to take Kayla to the dance next week. And Joel said yes!"

"Is Joel a nice boy?"

"Come on," Rebecca said. "He's one of Andrew's friends. He'd never set her up with a bad guy."

Polly shrugged. "I was just asking. Have you told Stephanie?"

"Me? No. Kayla was going to tell her about it tonight. I hope she doesn't have a cow. It's just a stupid eighth grade dance."

"I guess you'll know tomorrow." Polly poured the chocolate chips into the mixer, and after letting it mix for a minute, turned the thing off.

"My timing is impeccable," Hayden said, walking in. His hair was still wet and he'd changed into a t-shirt and shorts. "Are we doing some baking therapy?"

"Polly says we're making thank you gifts. Did you know that Len saved Bill's life?" Rebecca asked.

Hayden nodded. "I heard about that. It was a really amazing catch. Most people would never see it that early. And then they'd try to ignore it or act like it was no big deal. It sounds like he didn't let Bill protest at all. Just made the call. That man is so quiet, I never would have thought he'd be that bold." He took a spoon out of the drawer and scooped up a chunk of cookie dough. Before Rebecca or Polly could protest, he licked it clean and dropped the spoon in the sink.

"What if we don't have enough cookies because you did that?" Rebecca asked, swatting at his hand.

He opened the drawer again, took out another spoon, filled it and handed it to her. "You were just jealous. You know I'm right."

Rebecca looked at Polly, who grinned at them and then back at Hayden. She hesitated long enough that he snatched the spoon out of her hand, licked it clean and dropped it into the sink beside its mate.

"Hey. No fair. I was going to eat that," she complained.

"You snooze. You lose."

CHAPTER TWELVE

Rolling over, Polly was surprised to find that she was alone in the bed. No Henry. No dogs. It was still dark, so Henry hadn't gone to work. She checked the time - only three fifteen. They'd stayed up late talking. Henry was pragmatic about many things, but this had him rattled. Polly wasn't sure whether it was the terror over losing his father or worry about how to run the business without him. Bill and Henry had become much better friends these last couple of years. Bill was Henry's anchor when he took on too much stress over the business side of the construction company.

She opened the bedroom door and saw light coming from the media room, so she walked through. When she didn't see Henry on the sofa, Polly tapped lightly on the door to his office. In moments, he pulled the door open.

"What are you doing up?" he asked.

"I was lonely. I'm used to having the bed filled up with men and dogs."

"Men?"

"Okay, one man. But still, you three fill up the bed. Now it's too much for one measly little girl."

He chuckled and kissed her nose. "You're a nut."

"A nut who was lonely. What are you doing?"

"I had too many things going on and thought I'd just start dealing with them since I couldn't sleep."

"Did things really fall apart that much after you left yesterday?"

He walked back over to the chair behind the desk and pointed at another chair sitting against the wall. "No. But since I was upset and thinking, every bit of information I've needed to deal with in the last month took up residence in my frontal cortex."

"Dad used to tell me to keep a notepad and pencil by my bed so I could take notes when this happened. That way I'd be able to go back to sleep."

"He was a smart man. I could use your father right about now." Henry tipped the chair back and put the pencil he'd been using behind his ear. "I'm so worried about Dad. I don't know what I'm going to do. He'll try to come back to work early if I need him. I can't let that happen." He took a shuddering breath before looking up at her. "What if I'm killing my father?"

"Henry!" Polly snapped. "Don't even say that out loud. You're doing no such thing. This is his body and his life. You, your mother, and your father all talk about how he's having more fun than ever before. Don't make his life less than it is by taking this onto yourself."

"But this might not have happened if he hadn't ..."

Polly interrupted him. "Hadn't what? Come back to Bellingwood? He had a heart attack when he lived in Arizona. Hadn't gone to work for you? What was he supposed to do, sit around and twiddle his thumbs? Would you prefer visiting him in a nursing home because he gave up and didn't want to live any longer? You stop beating yourself up right this minute."

"Can't," he said, not looking up.

"Can't what?"

"Can't stop beating myself up. I feel guilty."

"Well, you're making that stuff up all on your own," she said. "Did your mother say anything at all to you today that was meant to elicit guilt?"

"No." Henry stuck his lower lip out in a pout.

"Have your parents ever talked about how he shouldn't be working any longer? Did his doctor ever tell him to quit working for you?"

"No. And no," he said. "But I can't help myself."

Polly shook her head. "I love you more than life itself, but you drive me absolutely batty sometimes. You can't take this on. The heart attack is for your parents and his doctor to deal with. Your business? That's yours. You can worry about your business and the ramifications of Bill stepping back a bit. But I'll tell you another thing. You'd better not start treating him like some pitiful old man. You don't get to act like he's unable to make good decisions for himself."

Henry looked up at her in confusion.

"You know what I'm talking about. People who think their parents are too feak and weeble to make any decisions without the kids' input. I've never seen such disrespect. Their parents lived amazing lives, helping people, making big decisions, some even running their own companies. And then because someone fell and broke a hip or got cancer or needs a little assistance, they're no longer able to think like an adult. It infuriates me."

"Whoa," Henry said. "I'm not doing that. And did you just say feak and weeble?"

She nodded. "Well, actually, you're starting to. You're trying to replace Bill without waiting to talk to him and your mother. Your Dad is going to be scared enough as it is trying to come back from this heart attack. He doesn't need to think that you believe he's unable to take care of your mom or their house or his job. You have to let him know that he's important to your business and that you'll wait as long as he needs you to wait for him to regain his strength and stamina."

He blew air out of his nose. "You're not fair."

"What do you mean?"

"You're right. But it's not fair. I'm supposed to be able to be an idiot around you and not get yelled at."

Polly laughed. "You can always be an idiot around me, but I

don't remember making that kind of a silly promise. If you're an idiot, I'll still love you, but I will call you on it."

"What am I supposed to do about the shop, then?"

"You said you were moving Ben over. Do that."

"But I can't do that forever. I need something more solid and permanent."

"Maybe it's time for you to add another employee."

"Dad will see right through that."

Polly put her hands out in exasperation. "Then be honest with him. Tell him that you need someone and that you know it's going to take time for him to come back to full strength. Get an apprentice in there. Henry, you and I know that your Dad won't be around forever, but forever doesn't have to start tomorrow."

Henry shuddered. "It almost began today."

"It didn't though. And tomorrow he'll be a little better and then every day after that, he's going to come back a little more and a little more. And he needs to have a place to get back to."

Henry gave a small shake of his head. "I hadn't talked to you about it, but I was kind of hoping that he had another five or six years in him. I want Heath to get through college, but then I was hoping he'd want to come back to Bellingwood and help me run the business."

Polly smiled. "I love you so much. I think Heath would love that. He really likes working with you. But he can't be Bill's apprentice right now. He's still in school. It needs to be someone else."

"Then who?" Henry asked jamming his fist on the desk. "That's my biggest issue. I have no idea how to get someone in who gets along with Dad and Len well and yet knows what they're doing with those machines."

"I'm going to tell you that you need to talk to your parents before you make any decisions. Once you've had that conversation, we can think about where to find an apprentice. And then maybe you can get some sleep." Polly yawned, covering her mouth as she did so. In just a split second, Henry did the same.

"You're coercing me," he said. "You want me to go back to bed."

"A little bit." Polly leaned forward and looked at the little clock on his desk. "It's nearly four o'clock. Can you at least try for a couple of hours of sleep?"

~~~

Polly waited until Henry had taken his shower and was outside with the dogs before she got out of bed. She usually savored the extra hour before she needed to get moving with the kids, but this morning it felt like Henry needed more support.

They'd finally drifted off to sleep around four thirty and even though it had only been an hour and a half, Henry popped out of bed like he did every morning. He planned to go to the hospital early before checking on his construction sites. He needed to rearrange where people would be working for the next few days to allow Ben Bowen freedom to work at the shop.

Polly wanted to head down and talk to Eliseo this morning, too. If he didn't need Heath, she was hoping he could ease some of Henry's work load today. At least tomorrow was Saturday and the weekend would give them time to regroup.

The sound of the dog's feet dashing across the floor caused Polly to turn around from the coffee pot.

"What are you doing up?" Henry asked.

"Making you coffee."

"I can get something on the way."

Polly held out a thermal mug. "It's all ready to go." The microwave dinged and she took out a sausage breakfast sandwich wrapped in a napkin. "And so is this. Now go see your dad and call me when you leave him, okay?"

"I still don't know what I did to deserve you."

"I keep telling you, you must have been a saint when you were younger." Polly grinned and leaned forward to kiss him. "It's all going to be okay. Got it?"

He took a deep breath. "Just keep telling me that. As worried as I am about the business details, none of it will make any
~~~

difference if Dad isn't healthy. He took the sandwich from her, then leaned against the counter. "I hate to admit how worried I am that Mom blames me for this."

"What?" Polly asked.

"She was really strange with me yesterday. I know she loves me and I know she was worried about Dad, but something was off. I finally landed on why I was feeling so weird with her when I stood in the shower this morning."

"I didn't sense any of that," Polly said.

"No matter what has happened, Mom has always had an easy way with us kids. She's affectionate and easy to talk to. When Dad was in the hospital in Arizona, she was still that way. But yesterday, she never reached out to comfort me or ask how I was doing. She didn't push me away, but it was just a strange feeling."

"I think you're reading too much into it. Your mom was just worried about Bill. From the heart attack into surgery, things moved pretty quickly. And there were more people around her yesterday. Your aunt and uncle were there, Jessie and Molly, and Hayden. She had a lot of people to pay attention to."

He nodded, his lips quivering. When his eyes filled with tears, Polly took the cup and sandwich out of his hands and pulled him into her arms. "She doesn't blame you, Henry. Your mom doesn't think that way."

"I blame me. How could she not?"

Polly pulled back enough to look into his eyes. "Nobody blames you. You have to stop this. We need to be thankful that he's on this side of the experience. Your dad is alive."

"I'd miss him so much if he was gone, Polly. How do you not talk to your dad every day? I don't know how you do it." Henry broke into tears again and Polly pulled him close.

Sometimes she didn't know how she did it. She missed her dad every single day, but some days were worse than others. By now, most of the time she just let it sit on her heart as a dull ache, but when she thought about what he was missing with all the fun she was having in her life, it was really difficult. She let out a small chuckle.

"What?" he asked.

"I was just thinking that Dad would have loved to help you right now. He'd be at the shop in a heartbeat, doing whatever you needed him to do."

Henry smiled and kissed her lips. "I love you. I know, I know. I'm being dramatic about this and need to get over myself. I will. Right now, I just need to see Dad and be assured that he's still alive and then talk to Mom and hear her tell me that it's okay."

"Call me when you leave the hospital, will you?" Polly asked.

"I love you so much." He kissed her again, then gathered up his coffee and breakfast and headed for the back door.

Han tried to follow, but Polly lured him back to the kitchen with the rattle of food hitting their dishes.

"Was that Henry leaving?"

Polly stood back up and saw Hayden in the doorway. "Yeah. He's heading down to the hospital."

"It's Friday. I'm done at eleven. Can I help him today when I get back to town?"

"Text him and let him know what your schedule is. If he can use you, he'll say so. He'd better say so."

"I was going to head over to the Bell House this afternoon anyway, but if he needs me..."

Polly nodded. "Thanks. Is Heath up?"

"He was just stirring. Do you want me to wake him?"

"Not yet. I'm going to bail him out of barn house jail today. He can work at the shop with Ben and Len." She chuckled. "Hey, that rhymes and there's no getting around it."

Hayden shook his head and laughed. "You're weird. I won't wake him up, then."

"If I'm not back here by seven, would you wake little Miss in there? She won't like it, but she has to get up for school."

"On it."

Polly went back into her bedroom, pulled on a pair of boots and headed out the front door and down the steps. The building was still quiet. Jeff and Stephanie wouldn't be in until late since it was Friday. Kristen opened the office at nine and Rachel usually got to the kitchen by ten unless she had an early meeting to prepare for. Friday mornings were generally quiet, but gave way to the bustle of activity by early afternoon. Then everyone held on to their hats until late Saturday night. Polly loved the excitement of the place on the weekends, even if she wasn't involved. The energy level rose and everyone was at the top of their game.

She slipped out the side door and headed for the barn. The horses were already out and standing around the big hay pile munching away. That meant Eliseo was here. Not that she didn't expect that. He was usually in by six. The man worked incredible hours, but insisted he'd rather be here with his friends and his horses than anywhere else. It had gotten worse since his sister and her children had moved into his house. As much as he loved them all, Polly was sure that the added noise of four children was a little much for a man who was as solitary as Eliseo.

Elva had settled in at the Alehouse. She worked mostly during the day when the kids were in school, so they'd worked out that childcare issue. The tips were better in the evenings, but she took the early shifts that the younger staff didn't want. So far the children had done well with their new school. Rebecca didn't see much of them since they were in the other end of the building, but every once in a while the kids found her. She told Polly that they seemed to be fitting in okay.

Polly opened the main door and went inside. "Eliseo?" she called out.

He stepped out of the feed room. "Good morning, Polly. You're down here early." He glanced up at the clock. "Really early. Is everything okay?"

"Yeah. You did know that Bill Sturtz had a heart attack yesterday, didn't you?"

Eliseo nodded. "I'm so sorry about that. Yeah. Jeff told me. Is there anything I can do?"

"Well, I'm wondering if you've worked Heath hard enough these last two days. I didn't say anything to Henry, but I think he could really use him over at the shop."

"Of course," Eliseo said. His eyes twinkled as he chuckled.

"This place is cleaner than it has been in months. I was making up work for him by the time he left yesterday. We cleaned and oiled tack and things have been sorted and organized. I don't think I've ever gotten this much done in such a short period of time."

Polly sighed. "I'm glad he helped you. I was a little worried that I'd forced you into taking care of one of my problems." She grimaced. "I guess I did. But I'm glad he was helpful."

"We had a good time. It was good for him to be down here doing something other than slopping stalls. He spent time with the animals, got a little more familiar with the things we do here and he and I got to know each other better. Heath is a good kid. I'm glad he found you."

"I love him," Polly said. "Even after every crazy thing this week, I can't imagine life without him and Hayden."

"Tell Henry that if he needs anything, I can help. In fact, I'd be glad to bring Ralph and Sam Gardner along to do any kind of work he needs from us. Those guys are always ready to dig in."

"They're older than Bill," Polly said with a laugh.

Eliseo nodded. "But they like feeling necessary. Sam's wife, Jean, told me that as happy as her husband was to retire from the university, he was just as happy to work with me on the gardens. She was worried about him."

"What do you mean?"

"He'd always had something to do every day and once he retired, she said his days no longer had a purpose, so he watched television or puttered around the house. He slept a lot and tried telling her what to do. She wasn't sure which of those was going to bring about his early demise."

Polly laughed. Sam and Jean Gardner lived just down the street from Sycamore House. The two of them were wonderful people. She couldn't imagine Jean putting up with much from her husband.

"Even if he's over here for a few hours every couple of days, it's enough for him," Eliseo said. "He just needed to know that someone else needed him. And I'm glad to have him here."

"Are we paying him?" Polly asked.

Eliseo nodded. "Jeff and I talked about it. Sam didn't want anything. He just liked coming over and helping, but both he and Ralph are on the payroll. It was the right thing to do."

"I'm so glad. Looks like we're going to have a big Sycamore House Christmas party this year. Our employee list is growing like crazy."

"It sure is. You've got a good thing going here, Polly."

"It's got little to do with me anymore," she replied. "Everyone else is doing the work. It's the most amazing thing." Polly stood up. "So you're really okay with Heath not showing up?"

"Actually, I'm relieved," Eliseo said, standing as well. "I wasn't sure what we were going to do this morning. I was a little afraid we'd have to resort to re-painting the wagon or something."

"Does it need it?"

"Not in the least."

They walked toward the main door. Polly stopped and took his arm. "Thank you for being here, Eliseo. I don't say it enough. You have no idea sometimes how comforting it is to know that I can count on you, even if it is just to listen to me blather on while I work things out." She looked up at him and felt tears glisten in her eyes. "Where would I have been without you?"

"I'm glad we don't have to answer that question," he said.

In a surprising move, Eliseo gathered her in for a hug, then just as quickly released her. "Make sure to let Henry know we'll be there for him if he needs us."

"Thank you."

CHAPTER THIRTEEN

"I love it." Polly walked into the kitchen as Hayden put a large plate of pancakes on the dining room table. "But you spoil them."

"There's enough for you, too. Rebecca is up and dressed and Heath's doing something with his hair in the bathroom." Hayden shook his head. "I was never like that."

"Like what?" Rebecca asked. She smiled at Polly. "Can I take the day off? It feels like it should be a family day."

"Nice try," Polly replied. "You'll be out soon enough and then we can have a whole family weekend."

She dropped her shoulders and slopped her feet across the floor to the table. "You're no fun."

"I'm a grinch. No party at all in this girl." Polly choked off her words and gasped. "Oh no. I totally forgot."

"Forgot what?"

"I'll be right back." Polly ran into her bedroom and took out her phone to call Lydia.

"Good morning, Polly. Is everything okay?"

"I'm so sorry! I completely forgot. Can you ever forgive me?" Polly asked.

"Honey, we canceled your birthday party as soon as I heard Bill was in the hospital. We have plenty of time. Your birthday isn't until next Tuesday. I just wanted to do something before the rest of your family took up all your time."

"I am so, so sorry, Lydia. I feel just awful. The least I could have done was talk to you about it."

"Honey, if the worst thing you ever do is forget about a party, you're in good shape. You've had a wild week and you're allowed to misplace a few events."

Polly sat down on the edge of the bed. "Thank you. The world feels like it's closing in on me. Henry's taking everything on and I don't know how to help him."

"He just needs to know that you're a safe haven, dear."

Polly chuckled. "I guess he's been that enough times for me."

"Exactly. You two will work it all out and if you need help, please call. I can always find some way to motivate people."

"Yes you can. Okay, I'll let you start your day. I just realized what I'd done and had to call. Thank you for being so understanding."

"I love you, dear. And if you need anything, don't hesitate to call me."

"One more thing. Has Aaron said anything about the murder of that teacher?"

"Just that they haven't gotten much information about it yet. The final coroner's report won't be back until next week. Though he did say that the site where you found him wasn't where he was murdered."

"What?"

Lydia chuckled. "Aaron just walked in and gave me the evil eye. I wasn't supposed to tell you that. Keep it under your hat, will you?"

"Are you in trouble?"

"Not in the least. He knows I'm talking to you and trust me, if Aaron tells me anything, the only reason he does so is to ensure that you find out about it unofficially. Now he's rolling his eyes."

Han came into the bedroom and pushed his nose into Polly's

hand. She absentmindedly rubbed his head. "He tells you things he wants me to know?"

"Aaron won't admit it, but that's exactly why I find things out. Otherwise, he's as tight-lipped as a ... what's a good metaphor for tight-lipped, Honey?" Lydia chuckled. "He doesn't know one either. Anyway, if he wants to talk about one of his cases, he always, and I mean always, makes sure to preface it with a reminder not to talk. If he doesn't include that caveat, I take it as license to tell you what's going on. And I make sure to let him know that's what I'm doing, too. It keeps us all out of trouble."

"You two are weird."

"That's what keeps it interesting. Give my love to your husband. What?" Lydia paused and listened. "Aaron just said to tell you that if Henry needs any help at the shop, he's got a couple of deputies who are pretty good craftsmen and they'd be glad to make some extra money working for him."

"Really?" Polly asked.

"You might be surprised who comes out of the woodwork." Lydia giggled. "Aaron caught that one. I didn't even hear myself. Okay. I need to finish feeding him so he can go to work. I have things to do today and one of them isn't managing my husband. I love you, dear."

Polly was smiling by the time she got off the phone. Han wagged and followed her out to the kitchen where the three kids were already eating.

"We didn't want to be late," Hayden said.

"That's cool. I just needed to apologize to Lydia for missing a birthday party last night."

Rebecca frowned. "You had a birthday party? I was with Beryl. Wouldn't she have been there?"

"Lydia canceled it when Bill went into the hospital." Polly sat down beside Heath. "Did your brother tell you that you were off barn duty this morning?"

"Yeah. Thanks," Heath said. "But it hasn't been too bad. I like Eliseo."

"He likes you too, and said you did a lot of good work. Thank you for being honorable to that." She turned to Rebecca. "Speaking of being honorable. You need to finish your project tonight. There has been a lot of craziness around here, but it shouldn't take a reminder."

"Yes ma'am," Rebecca said. "Sorry." She looked at her plate, then just as fast, looked up and grinned at Polly. "So, Kayla and I were wondering if we could do a girl's sleepover at the Bell House some time. It would be like camping but with four walls."

"Girls?" Polly asked.

"Yeah. You and Stephanie and maybe Jessie and even Molly if Jessie wants to bring her. We were thinking we'd invite Kristen and Rachel and I don't care if you want to invite all of your girlfriends. There are a couple of girls from school that would be fun, too. It could be a huge thing. We could take sleeping bags and maybe a bunch of games and have candles for light. Can we do it sometime?"

"That actually sounds like fun," Polly said.

Rebecca's eyes grew wide in surprise. "Really? I thought you'd hate it."

"I don't like the idea of not having a bathroom, but I don't hate it."

"If you wait a couple of weeks, Liam can probably have the toilet off the kitchen finished. Especially if he knows that you want it," Hayden said.

Rebecca jumped up and ran over to Hayden. "Would you ask him? Please? Tell him we can't have the party until he's done that because Polly won't go."

"You're darned right Polly won't go," Polly said. "Polly refuses to go in the back yard, that's for sure."

"That's not what I meant," Rebecca said, scolding her. "But it's funny."

"Tell you what," Polly said. "Hayden, you ask Liam how close he is and get a pretty firm date. Once he sets it, tell Rebecca and let her loose with her plans. I think it sounds like fun. Whether we have two people or twenty, we can break in that new house."

"Do you think Beryl would come?" Rebecca asked.

Polly nodded. "If I get enough air beds over there, she's always game for something a little wild."

"Can I tell her about it tomorrow at my art lesson?"

"You certainly can. But don't be disappointed if she turns you down, okay?"

"You just said she's always game."

"But you never know. Make the invitation, but have no expectations. Got it?"

"Do you care how many of my friends I invite?"

"Let's limit it to ten."

"Including Kayla?"

"Including Kayla. Then if Stephanie and some of her age group want to come, that's great and I'll talk to some of my friends."

"The maids, the mothers and the crones," Hayden muttered.

Polly snorted laughter. "Where do I fit in?"

"That was out loud?" he asked, laughing. "I thought I only said it in my head."

"Well the good news is," Polly said, "at least they're all goddesses. And I'm for that."

Hayden stood up, and took his empty plate into the kitchen, then came back and bowed in front of Polly. "May I take your plate, my goddess?"

"I'm having another pancake," she replied. "But don't you soon forget that part about goddesses."

"Never." He took Rebecca's plate. "Hurry up, little maiden goddess. I'll drive you to school." He glanced at Polly and then back to Rebecca. "Don't you forget your flute."

"Should I head over to the shop?" Heath asked Polly after the other two were gone.

She pursed her lips. "I'm not sure yet. I wanted to wait until Henry called after seeing his dad. I don't know where he needs you today."

Heath opened the door of the dishwasher and filled it as Polly handed him their breakfast dishes. "I could go do some of my homework, I guess." He sounded as if he was about to be sent to the stockade.

Polly laughed. "It shouldn't be too long before Henry calls. I'd hate for you to start and have to walk out in the middle of it."

"That sounds really good," Heath said, nodding. "I'm caught up on the reading for that lit class at least. It's easier to just read when Hayden's in there studying."

"We haven't had much time to talk about things after that interview with Deputy Hudson. Have you given it anymore thought?"

Heath yawned and stretched. "I've done nothing but think about it this week. Yeah. He was weird around the pretty girls." He put air quotes around the word 'pretty.' "But I don't think he did anything to them. I would definitely have heard about that."

"And that argument with the math teacher?"

"I don't know." He looked at Polly and shrugged. "Wouldn't it be weird if you just had a normal every day argument with someone and then you were a suspect if they died?"

"Yeah. Sometimes things mean nothing, but then again, sometimes insignificant events are important," Polly said. "Nobody else was strange around him?"

"Everybody was strange around him, Polly. But other than that, I don't know. Trust me. I didn't want to have anything to do with him outside of class. I mostly ignore the teachers anyway."

Polly looked at him and grinned.

"No. I promise," he said. "I pay attention in class. I just meant out of class."

"I know," she replied.

Her phone rang and she smiled again. "It's Henry, I'll find out what's happening today." Swiping the call open, she said, "Hey there, how are things?"

"It's not great, Polly."

"What do you mean?"

"Dad isn't doing very good. This is going to take a long time. I don't think he's going to be able to come back to work. Even he said so this morning."

"Oh Henry, I'm sorry."

"It was the hardest thing to see him in that hospital bed.

Monitors everywhere; he's all pale. Mom's eyes are red from crying and not sleeping. It was only two days ago that he was just normal Dad. Everything was fine. And now I'm terrified that he's going to die."

"What are you doing now?"

"I can't just sit here and watch him drop in and out of sleep. I have to go to work but my head isn't in it."

"Do they need you on-site?"

"I don't know. Probably."

"Where are you right now?"

"I'm just walking out to the truck. I called you as soon as I left his room."

"Are you going to be okay to drive home?"

"What? Of course I am."

"Okay. Sorry. Do you want to just come home?"

"I need to at least get down to the apartments."

"Heath is here. Why don't you let him run for you this morning? He can check with your foremen and if there's anything you need to do, he'll contact you. Is Ben over at the shop?"

"Yeah. I've already talked to him and Len. They'll be fine today. Next week is going to be rough."

"Can I send Heath out for you?"

"No, that's okay. I'll go. Maybe I just needed to hear your voice and settle myself down."

Polly chuckled. "Yeah. That's not something I usually hear from you. It's nearly always the other way around. But seriously, Heath is here with nothing to do. Hayden will be home just after lunch and I talked to Aaron. He said he has a couple of guys that might be able to help out at the shop, too."

"You've been busy, haven't you?"

"I'm just asking questions."

"Let me talk to Heath."

Polly held her phone out to Heath and nodded.

He took it and said, "Henry?"

She went into the living room and sat down on the sofa and dropped her head into her hands. Bill was too young to give up and much too young to die. Not that that really made any sense. Death came no matter the age. It didn't matter whether Henry was ready for his father to go or not. If it was over, it was over, but this hurt so much right now. And she didn't know what to do to help.

"Polly?" Heath was standing in front of her, holding out the phone. "I'm taking off. I'll talk to you later."

She smiled and mouthed the word, "thanks" before returning to the call. "Are you going to let Heath help you out today?"

"Yeah. It will be good."

"How's your mom doing other than being a wreck? Can I go sit with your dad while she comes home and cleans up? I could meet Hayden there and he'd drive her back and forth."

"I doubt that she'll leave him. And Lonnie is coming in late this afternoon."

"Do you think she'd sleep if I was there to sit with him?"

"I don't know," Henry said. "Maybe. You'd do that?"

Tears filled Polly's eyes. "Of course I would. Let me call Jessie and see if she can put some fresh clothes together for Marie and I'll take them over. And let's figure out where Lonnie is staying while she's in town."

"Why wouldn't she stay at the house?"

"Because it's big and she'd be lonely. She can sleep on our couch or in Rebecca's room. Rebecca could maybe spend the weekend with Kayla. We can work this out. But the two of you are worried about your dad and she shouldn't be alone. Unless your mom would come home."

"Not until the hospital forces her out. She won't come home until Dad does." He paused. "Or doesn't, I guess."

"Honey, you have to stop thinking like that. It's destroying you."

"If you don't feel the same way after you see him today, I'll be surprised," Henry said. "Polly, it scared me. It feels like he's given up."

"Did he say that?"

"Not in so many words, but that's what it felt like."

Polly stood up from the couch and gave Heath a quick hug as

he headed for the back door. "Heath's leaving. You get in the truck and come back to town. Focus on your driving and think about the things you need to take care of. I'm calling Jessie and then heading to Ames myself. Henry, I have to believe this is going to be okay. That means you do, too."

"I love you, Polly. I don't know what I'd do without you."

"Same goes. We're a pair, aren't we?"

As soon as he was gone, Polly called Jessie.

"Sturtz Family Construction, how can I help you?"

"Hey Jessie, it's Polly."

"Hi there. Have you heard anything about Bill yet?"

"Henry was just there and he's scared."

"Oh no," Jessie moaned. "I've been afraid to bother Marie, but I'm so worried. And Molly keeps asking where Marie is. What can I do?"

"Could you pull some more clothes together for Marie? She's not coming home until Bill does, so I'll take things over to her and maybe sit with him so she can rest. I guess Lonnie will be here this afternoon."

"I like her," Jessie said. "She'll be good for them. I should probably make sure there are clean sheets on her bed upstairs. Tell Marie not to worry about it, okay?"

Polly wasn't going to say anything. If that's what Jessie wanted to do, it was the right thing. And besides, maybe everyone would be home tomorrow. "Thanks, Jessie. You're amazing. I'll be there after I let the dogs out one more time."

"Come on, guys," Polly said. "Let's go outside."

The dogs ran for the back steps and waited for her to catch up. She opened the overhead garage door and they ran for the line of trees at the creek - their normal spot. Polly leaned against the wall and watched them. It sounded as if Bill's recuperation was going to take a lot more work than anyone had realized. Marie could do it, but not alone. And this was killing Polly. They just didn't have enough information yet for her to help make decisions. Everything was still up in the air.

She turned around when she heard the door leading up to

Doug and Billy's apartment open and then laughed out loud. "Anita Banks. What are you doing here?"

Anita's face flushed red. "Hi Polly. Um. I-uh. Well, uh."

Polly started laughing until she realized she couldn't stop. Tears flowed down her face and she hugged Anita. "I'm so glad to see you," she said.

Anita hugged her back and then looked at her with confusion written across her face. "Why?"

"Because I needed to think about something else and you are the perfect diversion for my thoughts. So really?" Polly pointed up the steps.

"It's not what you think."

"You aren't dating Doug?"

"Well, okay. If that's all you think, then yes. But we got in late last night and nothing happened. I swear."

Polly frowned. "If you think that I care what's going on up there, you're crazy." She shrugged. "Okay, so I care because I love those boys, but I'm not about to make any judgment. You're all adults. But really? You're finally dating Doug?"

"We have been for a few months. I don't know how serious it is yet. And I swear, we're not doing anything."

"I don't care," Polly said again. "That's your business. Not mine."

The door opened again and two dogs ran out the garage door. Doug stepped into the garage and his eyes grew immense when he saw Polly and Anita standing together.

"Uh, hi, Polly. Uh. It's not what you think," he said.

"I hear that," Polly said. "Apparently it is what I think, though. Anita has been telling me everything. And I mean everything. Doug Randall, you should be ashamed of yourself. I'm absolutely disgusted with you."

"I didn't do anything wrong," he protested. "Tell her, Anita. I haven't done anything to be ashamed of."

Anita smiled. "I think you might have."

"What?" he asked. "I'm sorry if I did anything."

Polly chuckled and took his arm. "You didn't tell me you two were dating. That's what you did wrong. I can't believe you managed to pull this off under my nose."

Doug's entire body collapsed with relief. "I didn't want to jinx it. I never thought I'd end up with someone like Anita."

Anita stepped toward him and kissed his lips. "I need to hurry and get to work. See you tonight?"

"Uh huh," he said, standing in place, stunned.

They watched her walk around the side of the house and Polly patted his shoulder. "So. Are you going to tell me about your first date?"

CHAPTER FOURTEEN

Easing it open a bit, Polly hesitated before tapping lightly on the door to Bill Sturtz's hospital room. She waited a moment and before she could put her hand on the door handle, Marie pulled it open.

"Hi Polly. Henry called to tell me you were coming over. You didn't have to," Marie said.

Polly wanted to hold this strong woman, but Marie already looked as if she was ready to fade away, from both exhaustion and worry. Instead, Polly held out an overnight bag. "Jessie packed up a few more clothes for you so you could have something fresh to wear. I'm glad to take anything back with me and we'll get it washed."

Marie took the bag. "Come on in. Bill's sleeping, but he'll be glad to see you when he wakes up."

Polly took a deep breath and followed Marie into the room. There were several bouquets of flowers and a balloon tied to one of the vases. She hadn't even thought about bringing flowers up. What a bad daughter-in-law. Polly finally pulled her eyes to the one thing in the room she didn't want to look at and breathed a sigh of relief. It wasn't as bad as she expected. Bill looked like the man she knew and loved, though it was strange to see him in a hospital gown rather than street clothes. His glasses were on the table in front of him and that made him look a little odd, but she didn't see the pallor that Henry described.

"How's he doing?" Polly asked.

"He's alive," Marie responded. "That's all I can ask for. I think he's doing better now than he was this morning, though." She smiled. "He's always been a night owl. Mornings are his worst time. If Bill ever got sick, his fever spiked in the morning and then as the day wore on, he got better. I tried to tell Henry that, but he was worried when he left."

"He's concerned about both of you," Polly said. "I didn't know what to expect."

"There's a room down the hall where I can take a shower." Marie smiled and patted the bag Polly had brought in. "It will be good to clean up."

"You can certainly do that now if you'd like," Polly said. "I'm glad to sit here."

"That would be lovely, dear. The call button is right here." Marie picked it up from the bed where it had been lying. "They'll be here in a minute if you need something. But I'll hurry."

"Marie. Take a long, hot shower. I'll be fine."

Marie wrapped her arms around Polly and the two women held each other for a moment. "Thank you. I won't be gone long, but I will take the time I need. Maybe I'll take a walk down to the cafeteria. Can I bring you anything?"

"Coffee," Polly breathed. "A large coffee."

Polly sat down beside Bill's bed after Marie left and hoped that the fact the woman was taking some time for herself meant that things weren't so dire. She leaned her head back in the chair and closed her eyes after placing her hand on the bed beside Henry's father's hand. Just in case.

It wasn't a but few minutes later when she felt Bill brush her hand. Polly opened her eyes to look at him.

"Every time I wake up, there's another pretty girl in my room,"

Bill said. "It certainly makes a man want to keep opening his eyes. What did you say to finally get Marie to leave?"

"She's taking a shower and getting something from the cafeteria. How are you?"

"Better than I deserve." He put his hand on top of hers and squeezed. "Did my boy scare you this morning?"

Polly chuckled. "He sure did. I think he's certain you're planning to die today."

"Don't do that," Bill said, trying to stop himself from laughing. "It's not fair. I'm supposed to be a very sick man."

"You've scared us all."

He pressed the button to lift the head of his bed and moved it just a few inches. "There. That's better. Polly, my dear, I scared myself. All I could think about was Redd Foxx. 'It's the big one. I'm coming, Elizabeth!' But I don't know any Elizabeth and I'm not ready to go anywhere."

"You're kidding me," Polly said with a laugh. "Redd Foxx?"

He lifted a shoulder in a shrug. "I can't help it."

"We're not ready for you to go anywhere either. Here, make a face." Polly took out her phone and opened the camera app.

Bill screwed up his face and stuck his tongue out and she snapped a quick picture.

"Why did I just make a fool of myself?" he asked.

"I'm sending this to your son so that he can see what a difference a few hours makes."

"You're a good woman, Polly Giller." He glared at her. "Even if you aren't a Sturtz. Polly Sturtz. That would have sounded just fine."

"I like it," she said.

"So you'll change your name for me?"

Polly looked at him, trying to decide what he was asking.

Bill chuckled. "I've got to get better at this. If I'm going to milk the whole asking for favors thing because I might be dying, I have to really mean it."

"You really are feeling better."

"It might have something to do with all of the strange things they've put in my body. Maybe it's the extra blood flow through my heart. Yes, that's it. Extra blood makes me say things I shouldn't." He grinned at her. "Imagine how fast alcohol would flow through these veins right now. It wouldn't take much for me to be drunk on my ass."

Polly laughed out loud. "What are you doing?" she asked.

He sighed. "I'm still being careful with Marie. She's worried sick. Henry doesn't have a sense of humor about this yet either. So far, you're the only person who won't be offended if I'm a little off the wall. And I feel like I need to be off the wall. I just beat death a second time. At least I hope I've beaten it. That's a big deal for me. I don't know whether to be terrified or ecstatic."

"I'm leaning toward ecstatic," Polly said.

"Except for the fact that I'm never going to be allowed to eat another hamburger in my life," he muttered. "I'm about to have the most boring menu on the face of this earth. And I can count on the fact that no one will go up against Marie in order to sneak me in some ice cream."

"Not me."

"If I can't get you to help me buck the system, I'm sunk. That wife of mine..."

"That wife of yours what?" Marie asked, coming into the room.

"Is the most amazing woman I've ever known. She is a gem in the crown of humanity."

Marie handed a hot cup of coffee to Polly. "How's he doing?"

"A lot better, it seems," Polly said. "At least his sense of humor is returning."

"Did he make a comment about all of the pretty girls?"

Polly glanced at Bill. "Well, yes."

"And tell you that he was Fred Sanford, worried his heart attack was going to take him home to his Elizabeth?"

Polly frowned. "Uh yes."

"And complain about never eating steak again?"

"This is old shtick, isn't it?" Polly asked Bill.

"I'm still woozy," he replied.

She attempted to stand up so Marie could take the seat, but

Marie waved her back down. "I'll putter around the room. That shower rejuvenated me."

"I was kind of hoping you might be able to take a nap while I was here," Polly said.

"Don't worry about me. Once I realized the old man was going to live through the day, I started feeling better." Marie rearranged flowers in a vase, turning it so the roses faced Bill's bed.

"My boy thinks I'm dying today," Bill said.

Marie spun to face him. "He what?"

"Evidently I scared him this morning."

She nodded. "You were pretty scary."

"Polly took a scary picture of me and sent it to him." Bill turned back to Polly. "Has he responded?"

Polly was in the middle of taking a drink of coffee. It was blazing hot, but she quickly swallowed and took out her phone. "He asks what I did to you."

"Come here, Marie," Bill said. "Kiss my lips and let her take a picture of that. Just because I'm an old man who's had a couple of heart attacks, doesn't mean I can't love my wife."

Polly shook her head. "Nah, nah, nah. I don't want to hear it." But she took a quick picture of Marie standing beside Bill, leaning in to kiss his lips and sent it off to Henry.

Her phone rang and she smiled as she answered it.

"Is he really that much better?" Henry asked.

"I think so. He's got color in his face and he's talking about the pretty girls who keep showing up in his room."

"Tell him you're mine."

Polly looked at Bill. "Henry says to tell you that I'm his."

"That's fine," Bill said. "I think he's the only one that can handle you."

"Did you hear that?" she asked Henry.

"He *is* doing better. How's Mom?"

"She's had a shower and been to the cafeteria. She brought coffee to me so I'm doing better too."

Henry laughed. "I'm glad it doesn't take that much for you. Thanks for being there for me."

"I love you." Polly winked at Bill. "Even if I haven't taken your last name."

"Did he give you trouble about that?"

"A little bit."

"I did not," Bill said. "I was just teasing."

"Bill Sturtz, you leave those kids alone," Marie scolded.

"I didn't do anything," he protested.

"Now they're fighting about it," Polly said. "I'd better let you go before I start something else."

"Call me later. I love you," Henry said.

"I love you too."

Polly put her phone back in her pocket as someone rapped lightly on the door.

"Come in," Marie called out.

Andy Specek and Lydia Merritt came into the room, both bearing gift bags. Andy gave Marie a quick hug, before releasing her to Lydia's embrace.

"More pretty women," Bill said. "Won't any of you hug me?"

Marie shook her head. "Ignore him. He's just glad to be alive and getting all of this attention." She reached out for Andy's hand. "I don't know how we'll ever be able to express our appreciation for what Len did yesterday. If it weren't for his quick thinking and insistence on calling for help, this could have been a very different outcome. How is he?"

"He was pretty shook up," Andy said. "But he had a lot of work to do and I think that helped take his mind off it. We're both glad that he was there." She slipped in beside Polly, who had backed her chair up to give them room. Andy took Bill's hand. "You are one of Len's best friends. He's not ready to have you go anywhere yet."

He smiled up at her. "He's a fine friend. The kind every man needs in his life. He gave me quite a gift yesterday. I can never repay him for that."

"Len certainly wouldn't want you to think that you should. We're just grateful that you're still here." Andy put her gift bag beside Bill on the bed. "He stayed last night and turned these for you. His mind wouldn't shut down, so I took supper over to him and sat while he worked on the lathe." She reached into the bag and drew out two gorgeous candlesticks, turned with ridges and rills.

"Those are beautiful," Polly said.

"Marie," Bill choked out.

His wife stepped over and took up the two candlesticks and stroked the polished wood. "He does beautiful work." She put her hand on Bill's shoulder, her finger reaching up to caress his cheek. "Thank you."

Andy stepped away, smiling. "Lydia and I didn't want to bring flowers."

"So you left Beryl at home?" Polly quipped.

Lydia laughed. "That's a good one. I'll tell her you said that." She held out the bag she was carrying to Marie. "I assume you'll be staying here and I wanted to bring something that would make your time more comfortable. It's a little silly, but I've spent a few nights in hospitals and this strange neck pillow really helped me sleep in those awful chairs."

Marie accepted the gift. "Thank you. I don't plan to go home until Bill does."

"We'll make that happen tomorrow," Bill said.

"You'll stay until they kick you out," Marie retorted. "This will be terrific, though. I don't really care how much or how little sleep I get, as long as I know he's coming home."

"There are some chocolate chip bars at the bottom of the bag," Lydia said in a stage whisper. "But none for the man in the hospital bed, right?"

"That's not fair at all," Bill said, yawning. He leaned his head back on the pillow and closed his eyes.

"We should go," Andy said in a quiet voice.

Marie shook her head. "It's really okay. He's been awake this time longer than any time before. He slips in and out of sleep. He'll be fine."

"We didn't want to stay long anyway," Lydia said. "We just wanted you to know that we were thinking about you and praying for you all. If there's anything you need, be sure to ask. And if you don't ask, I'll find a way to figure it out."

"Thank you." Marie followed them to the door and then she stopped Andy. "Please tell your husband how much his actions yesterday meant to all of us. When I see him, I'll tell him, but words don't seem to be enough."

"I'll let him know. He's so thankful that he was there," Andy replied.

"So am I."

After they left, Marie sat down on the edge of Bill's bed. "They're such good women. You're lucky they found their way into your life."

"I really am," Polly said. "My start in Bellingwood would have been so much different if they hadn't shown up. Have you heard from Lonnie?"

Marie shook her head. "Not yet. I know she's on her way, though."

"Jessie is making up her bed at your house, but I've talked to Henry about inviting her to stay with us until you and Bill are at home. There's no reason for her to stay in that house by herself."

"Thank you," Marie said, breathing an audible sigh of relief. "She could have stayed with Betty and Dick, but I think she'd have more fun with you, Henry, and the kids."

Another rap at the door and an older woman carrying a bouquet of flowers walked in without waiting for an invitation. "Oh Marie," the woman said. "I've been so fretful since I heard about Bill." She gave an imploring look at the bed. "Is he going to be okay? How are you? This is just such an awful thing to have happen. I told Trudy that Bill needed to slow down. He's not a young man anymore."

The woman noticed Polly. "I'm sorry. I didn't realize you had company. Maybe I should have phoned first, but you just never know and I didn't want to bother you if you were in the middle of something. I feel as if I should know you."

Marie stepped up to the woman. "Louise Fender, this is Henry's wife, Polly. You know who she is. She bought the old schoolhouse in town and now she and Henry are renovating the old Springer House."

"Yes, that's why I know you."

Louise Fender's voice was grating on Polly's nerves. All sweetness and concern, just a little too high pitched to be genuine. But Polly stood and put her hand out. "It's nice to meet you, Mrs. Fender."

"It's *Miss* Fender," the woman corrected her. "I've never been married. I'm just too much woman for a man, I guess." She turned away from Polly and pushed past Marie to put her vase on the table beside Bill, moving Marie's book and Bill's glasses to make room. "There, that should lighten up the room. Has he been sleeping long? Will you be going home soon or are you going to have to stay in this tiny little room all weekend?"

"We don't have a good answer for that yet," Marie said.

"Surely you're going to make him slow down now," Louise said. "This is his second heart attack, right? It would be a shame if he died because he felt it necessary to work so hard. Your son shouldn't expect that of him. He should know better." She patted Bill's arm. "It's hard to accept that we're getting older, but sometimes we just have to face facts. People get to a certain age and their body just starts giving out."

Miss Fender had turned her back to Polly, who gave Marie a surprised look. Marie barely shrugged as she smiled and nodded at the woman.

"I was just telling my friend, Trudy, the other day, that she should consider getting someone to help her clean that big old house. None of her children are around. They all moved away, leaving her here by herself. Now how is she supposed to manage that house alone? What were they thinking? They're too far away to help, but she's expected to do everything. All of the cleaning and the yard work. She's not a youngster anymore. But will she even consider asking them? Oh no. She doesn't want to be a burden. Well, what kind of a burden is it, anyway? She took care of them and supported them until they finally had their own lives and now that they're all grown up, they don't give her a second thought. At least your son keeps an eye on you. But he shouldn't be working his father so hard. And where is your daughter? Why isn't she here? You'd think that she could at least come home when her father has a heart attack. What if he died before she got here?"

"It is so good to see you, Louise," Marie said. She touched the leaf of one of the flowers in the bouquet. "This was such a sweet gesture. I'll be sure to tell Bill that you were here to check on him. He'll be sorry that he missed you. The doctors don't want visitors to spend too much time here, though. It exhausts Bill and we're trying to help him rebuild his strength."

"Oh," the woman said, clearly flabbergasted at being dismissed. "I would have thought you'd be glad of company. But I suppose that if the doctors say Bill needs his rest, then he should have it." She turned to Polly. "If you would like, I could walk down to the parking garage with you."

Polly looked at the woman and then back to Marie. "Ummm."

"Well, come on now, young lady. If Bill needs his rest, we should be going."

"Uhhhh." Polly looked helplessly at Marie, who was just as helpless. "Okay. You're right. I need to get back to town anyway." She walked over to hug Marie. "I'm sorry," she whispered.

"We'll talk later," Marie whispered back. "Thank you for everything."

Polly walked out with Louise Fender, still at a loss as to what had just happened. They stood in front of the elevator doors and the woman began talking again.

"I've never been fond of hospitals, but it seems that I spend a lot of time in them. Whenever any of my friends is in one, I feel it is my duty to go see them." She nodded her head. "And funeral homes. Now that I'm getting older, more people I know are dying all the time. You'd be surprised at the number of funerals that don't happen in a church. Why wouldn't you have your funeral in a church? We have many good churches in Bellingwood. But instead, they'd rather have it in a funeral home. I never understood that. When I die, I want them to cremate my body.

I've already paid for it, you know. You can do that. I don't want anyone looking at my dead body. Bill didn't look like he was dying. I was afraid that he'd look terrible and I wouldn't have known what to say if I'd had to look at that."

The elevator door opened to the lobby and Polly stepped out.

"Which way is your car?" Louise asked. "I'm just out this way."

Polly was too, but she pointed at the other end of the hall. "I came in a different door. It was very nice to meet you, Miss Fender."

The woman walked off and Polly stared at her, still in shock. She considered going back upstairs, but hoped instead that Marie might be able to get some rest while Bill slept. Both of them looked better than what Henry had described earlier today and if Bill continued to move forward, he'd soon be recuperating at home.

CHAPTER FIFTEEN

Driving past Sycamore House, Polly headed straight for the coffee shop. She'd probably had enough coffee, but spending a few minutes there every day or so gave her sanity. And she never knew who she might run into. After these last few days, Polly wanted to spend time with people other than her immediate family. If nothing else, a chocolate chip muffin and another cup of coffee couldn't hurt.

She glanced at the quilt shop next door and shook her head. She'd just get sucked into another project she didn't have time for so she veered and headed inside Sweet Beans.

Camille looked up from waiting on a young couple and gave her a small smile. Polly looked around the room and nearly collapsed with joy when she saw Sal and Joss sitting in a corner with their three little ones.

"I'm so glad to see you," Polly said.

Cooper and Sophia were looking through a pile of books that Joss had put on the floor beside them. She'd tossed out a beautiful quilt for them to play on and so far, they looked like they had stayed fairly well contained.

"Polly," Sophia cried out and ran to get a hug. Her feet hit the edge of the quilt and she stopped, then looked at her mother.

"May I?" Polly asked.

Joss smiled. "Absolutely. If they stay on the quilt while we're here and play nicely, we'll stop at the grocery store and get them each an apple or an orange for an afternoon treat."

Polly reached down and scooped Sophia into her arms. The little girl's dark brown eyes sparkled with joy. "We got a puppy," she said.

"You did?" Polly sat down and hitched Sophia around on her lap. "When did this happen?" She looked at Joss. "Why didn't you tell me?"

"I haven't seen you," Joss said. "Jasmine came home with Nate on Monday. She's a lab mix and we're having a lot of fun. Aren't we, Coop?"

He looked up before crawling to the edge and holding his arms out to his mother. Joss picked him up and placed him so he could touch both Polly and his sister.

"Jass," he said.

"Or Jazz," Joss echoed. "Whatever is easiest for them. She'll be a great dog. I wanted to bring a puppy into the house before we brought any more children in."

"More?" Polly asked. "Are you making plans?"

Joss nodded. "I was just telling Sal. We have an appointment with the adoption counselor next week."

"When are *you* going to start again?" Polly asked Sal with a wicked grin.

Sal looked heavenward. "I really don't want to have more than one in diapers. Joss was telling me about having twins in the house. I'm not ready for that much fun. She stroked her sleeping son's head. "But I don't know how much say I'll have in the matter. At least two years between them. I never want to turn into that dumpy woman who hasn't a brain in her head because she has fifteen babies tugging at her over-sized muumuu."

"Sexy Sal," Polly said. "Wouldn't your mother love that." She frowned. "Speaking of your mother, I can't believe she hasn't come out to Iowa yet to see her little prince. Are you heading to Boston with Alexander soon?"

"We'll fly out mid-October," Sal replied. "I want to wait until after Rosh Hashanah. We might not be terribly religious, but Mother still insists on celebrating the high holidays. Introducing an infant to that isn't what I want to do this year. Especially since it would also be the first time Mark experienced it. We'll wait until Alex is a little older for those events."

"Mark's going too?"

Sal nodded. "He offered and I jumped at it. It will be a fast trip. Just over a long weekend." She peered at Polly. "Speaking of that. Do you think Kayla and Rebecca would take care of the dogs again?"

"I'm sure they will." Polly took out her phone. "Tell me the dates again."

They discussed the travel dates and Polly made sure to get things written down so she would remember to ask.

"How's Bill?" Sal asked.

Polly smiled. "He's good. They were pretty scared for a while, but I just saw him and he looks and sounds good. Marie is less stressed about it now, too, so that tells me he's better."

"It is scary," Joss said. "I can't imagine worrying about my husband. How's Henry with it?"

"He's been worried sick. Blaming himself and then worrying about how he's going to get everything done without his dad to help."

Sal creased her forehead. "Bill won't go back to work with him?"

"Of course he will," Polly said. "But it's going to take some time."

Sophia poked Polly's collar bone and said, "Horses."

"Yes, I have horses," Polly said.

"Big horses. Me."

"Do you want to ride on the big horse?"

Cooper grabbed Polly's sleeve and when she turned to look at him, his eyes were bright and huge. "Horses!"

"We see your horses when Eliseo, Jason and some of the others are out riding," Joss said. "I make sure to tell them that they're your horses so they make the connection. One day Eliseo and Jason came over to the house so the kids could pet the horses, didn't they?" She bounced Cooper on her knee.

"Did you get up on the horse?" Polly asked.

Sophia shook her head and in a split second, Cooper was mimicking her. "Horses are big. We might fall off."

"Big," Cooper echoed.

"Eliseo said they were too big?" Polly asked.

"The kids were nervous," Joss said. "He mentioned needing helmets for them, too. We'll get those one of these days and then when Eliseo brings the big horses over, you can sit up on them. How does that sound?"

Sophie shook her head again. "Too big."

"I want the kids to learn to ride," Joss said. "When they're older and the house finally feels like we've laid claim to every inch, I want to build a barn and get a couple of normal-sized horses. It was always something I wanted. With Eliseo so close, I'm finally going to do it." She looked at Polly with her brows furrowed. "We'd pay him to help us, of course."

Polly laughed. "I didn't even go there. You can work that out when it happens. I know that I couldn't do it without him. Maybe by then, even Jason would be good help. He could teach the kids too. He loves showing those horses off."

"Mark says we're going to have horses. He wants to move out to an acreage," Sal said quietly. "Is he kidding me?" She gave a dry laugh. "I'm living about as rural as I dare and he wants to drag me out to the country." She tapped her fingers on the table. "I had to buy a coffee shop in town so that I didn't go stir crazy. What's he doing to me?"

"He likes the quiet?"

"But I don't. Not that much quiet. And think about the kids. I don't want their closest neighbors to be three miles from the house. Who will they play with?"

"Each other?" Polly asked.

Sal scowled at her. "I'm a city girl. It's in my blood." She smiled down at her son. "It's in his blood, too."

"That's a fight I don't want to know about until it's finished," Joss said.

Polly's phone buzzed. She ignored it the first time and when it buzzed again, she reached into her pocket and pulled it back out. The text from Heath asked if it would be possible to have a bunch of kids up at the apartment this evening.

"Apparently, his friends missed him," Polly said.

"Who's that?" Joss asked.

"Heath. He's been on suspension this week. He wants to have some of them up to the apartment tonight. I just don't know if that's a good idea. Henry will be exhausted. He's still worried about his dad. Rebecca's fine and so is Hayden, but we're also having Henry's sister stay with us. She'll be wiped out from driving down from Ann Arbor and then spending time with her parents."

Polly sighed and drooped her shoulders. She kissed Sophia's cheek. "It's so much easier when they're young like you. You'll never get in trouble at school, will you? You won't make your mother crazy trying to figure out how to give you a good life while there are so many strange things happening in it, right?"

Sophia giggled and snuggled into Polly's arms, then squirmed to be put back down on the floor. Polly put her on the quilt and Joss put Cooper down beside his sister. "Remember, kids. Stay on the blanket. Got it?"

Cooper nodded and Sophia smiled at her mother.

"I'm not sure what to think about that smile," Joss said. "She's usually pretty good about doing the right thing, but one of these days she's just going to let loose and I'm going to be in trouble."

"I'm trouble," Sophia said with a smile. She turned back to one of the books on the floor, then picked it up and handed it to Cooper. "Your turn. You read."

"She's got that right," Polly said. "I need to call Henry before I say anything to Heath." She shook her head. "This week is exhausting me."

"How are things at the other house?" Sal asked.

Polly groaned. "I don't even know. I'm just so frustrated. Every time another big job comes up for people, they take off and don't come back to me until they have time. The electricity isn't finished yet. Liam Hoffman is almost done plumbing the main floor, but there are just a few more things that he needs to get before he's done. And then, a few more things after that because something else broke or exploded on him. It's not that he isn't doing a great job. It's just that place is overwhelming." She grimaced. "I don't even want to think about how long it will take to get into the second level. I don't know why I want to live there so badly. We have a perfectly wonderful home, but ..."

"It's starting to feel a little cramped?"

"Can you believe it?" Polly asked. "First I was cramped because I only had the one bedroom and couldn't have guests stay with me." She turned to Sal. "Remember when you stayed in one of the guest bedrooms that first time you were in town?"

Sal nodded.

"And now I can't let Heath have friends over because we don't have room for Henry to escape or his sister to stay with us. It won't be that much better at the Bell House until we move into the second floor, but at least it will be bigger and we'll have room to spread out." Polly threw her hands up. "Don't mind me. I'm being a whiner. I have a great life and a great home. I think I'm just tired."

Polly leaned down and kissed first Sophia and then Cooper on their heads. "You two are the sweetest things ever." She touched Alexander's arm, making him stir in his sleep. "And you're an adorable baby, no matter what they say about you."

"Hey," Sal said.

"Just kidding. Everyone knows that child is going to be killer gorgeous. He can't help it. If you guys are still here when I'm done talking to Henry, I'll be back. Otherwise, I love you." Polly slipped back out the front door of the coffee shop, not at all surprised that she still hadn't had her chocolate muffin. She was getting it to go the next time she walked in the door.

"Hello, Chippy," Henry said. He sounded better than when she'd talked to him this morning.

"You sound chippier. Things going well?" she asked.

"Things are going great. Everyone's doing their job and Hoffman called me. He said that we're going to have running water in the house before the weekend."

Polly was so grateful, her body sagged with relief. "Real water?"

"No hot water until they hook the electricity up, but you'll be able to flush a toilet and turn on a sink."

"I might cry," she said. "Real tears of joy. I was just whining about that."

"Whine no more. We're getting there."

"Have you talked to Heath?" Polly asked.

"Yeah. A couple of times. What's up?"

"He texted me asking if he could have some friends over tonight. I haven't said anything because I wanted to hear from you whether it was a good idea. I know you're exhausted and Lonnie is going to be there. What do you think?"

Henry took so long to answer, Polly thought she'd lost the connection. "Did I lose you?"

"No. I'm still thinking. He's had a pretty rough week, too. Lonnie probably won't show up until late in the evening, so don't worry about her. She and Mom will spend a lot of time talking..."

"Speaking of talking, remind me to ask you about someone I met this morning."

"Okay," he said. "I can hide in our bedroom. What are you thinking?"

"Well," she breathed out. "Okay, how about this? How about I call Stephanie and see if Rebecca can spend the night over there. Her room isn't horrible. I'll get her and Kayla to change her sheets and Lonnie can sleep in there tonight. We can do it again tomorrow night if your dad isn't home yet. That gives her some privacy. Heath and his friends can have the media room and dining room. That will give them access to the kitchen and bathroom out there. Would that work?"

"You're always thinking," Henry said. "That's fine with me. I'm going over to the hospital when I'm done here for the day. I'll say hello to Lonnie and see Mom and Dad for a while, then I'll come home."

"You don't need me to go with you?"

"I can do it by myself," he replied. "Can you handle the mess at the house preparing for the party?"

"Heath can help when he gets there, but I'll make Rebecca, Kayla and Andrew help me out after school. They'll love that."

"So we're good?"

"We're good. We really get water at the house this weekend?"

"I think so."

"Now I'm going to go have a chocolate chip muffin. I need to celebrate."

"I love you."

"I love you, too. Things are starting to look up, aren't they?"

"When Dad goes home, I'll agree with you. For now, though, I'm just going to be happy for water."

"Me too." Polly hung up her phone, did a little dance step and went back into the coffee shop. She danced over to Joss and Sal. "Henry says we're going to have water at the house this weekend. No electricity yet, but water. I can go to the bathroom." She stopped and chuckled. "Of course there is no door on the bathroom. They took it off. But that's okay. I can scream at anyone who comes close to me. I get water!"

"It's the little things," Joss said, smiling at Sal. "I should gather my children and head out. Mrs. Hart will be at the house to watch the kiddos while I work at the library. They love their Mrs. Hart, don't you, Cooper and Sophia."

"Mrs. Hart!" Sophia sang out. "She sings to us."

"She's always singing," Joss said, gathering things into her bag. She picked up the books and put them back on the shelves, sorting them into some order that Polly didn't pay attention to. Then she took two books out of her bag and put one in each of the kids' hands. You hold onto those until we're in the car. You have to decide whether you want an apple or an orange when we get to the grocery store. Now, walk over and stand beside Polly while I fold up the blanket."

Polly put both hands down and smiled as the two little ones each grabbed a few fingers. "I can walk out to the car with you," she said, then turned to Sal. "Save my seat. I'll be right back. Do you want anything?"

Sal smiled. "I'm still building up my caffeine for the day. A refill, please."

"Got it." Joss grabbed up Sal's cup and herded Polly and the children to the side door and out to her car. "Sal has been lonely," she said quietly. "She called me this morning to see if I had time for coffee. Of course I did, but she misses you. You're too busy."

Polly lifted Sophia into the car, then bent down and picked Cooper up to heft him in the open door as well. "She what? I had no idea. She never says anything."

"She wouldn't. She knows how much you have going on."

"I feel terrible. I have plenty of time for my friends."

Joss smiled. "We haven't seen each other in weeks other than Sunday nights. And those have been haphazard since school started."

Polly put her hand on her forehead. "I don't know what to say."

"I know you're busy and have kids that need you and a job and now Bill's heart attack. And you've got that house and everything else. I'm not mad at you. But you need to know you're missed."

"I was supposed to have a birthday party with Lydia and those guys last night. I totally forgot about it after spending the day at the hospital."

"Whose birthday?"

Polly looked at the ground. "Mine. It's next Tuesday. Thank goodness Lydia just takes care of things. She called it off, knowing that I wouldn't have time, but that's not the way my life is supposed to be. I make time for my friends. I am so sorry."

"I didn't say anything to make you feel guilty," Joss said. "And I can't believe I didn't know it was your birthday." She giggled. "I would have thought Rebecca would have done something, at the very least."

"She's overwhelmed with school this year and having a boyfriend and everything that is going on in her body." Polly stopped. "I can't let her become like me at my worst." She made sure that Sophia was safely buckled inside the car, then shut the door and ran around to Joss and gave her a hug. "I love you. Don't let me get away with this. Last week Henry was talking about wanting to work on the Woodies, but now with Bill out of the picture at the shop for a while, I don't know what is going to happen. I'll be better. I promise."

"Still not trying to work the guilt on you, Polly," Joss said. "I love you, too. That's the thing with friends. When you're at your craziest, we're still friends. It will all work out." She picked Sal's cup up from the front seat and pushed Cooper's door shut. "Sit with Sal for a few minutes. It will all be fine."

Polly gave her friend another quick hug and ran inside with the cup. She waved at Sal, then approached the counter.

"How are you today?" Camille asked.

"I'm okay. Just a little frazzled."

"So more coffee?"

"Yes please." Polly put Sal's cup on the counter. "And a refill for Sal. And two of the chocolate chip muffins."

"How's Henry's father?" Camille filled Sal's cup and put it back on the counter, then took down a fresh cup and filled it for Polly.

"He's doing better. I saw him earlier this morning."

"That's good." Camille put the muffins on plates and came around the counter. "I'll walk over with you."

"What's this?" Sal asked.

"I'm celebrating," Polly said and turned to Camille. "Henry just told me we're getting water at the house this weekend."

"Congratulations," Camille said, patting Polly's back. "I'll let you two talk. It's good to see you, Polly."

Polly sat down, brought the coffee up to her nose and drew in a long breath. "I'm sorry I've been such a lousy friend," she said quietly.

"What?"

"Joss told me how long it's been since we've done anything

together and I realized it was probably even longer with you. I'm sorry. Being busy doesn't excuse any of it."

Sal bit her lip, then said, "I just figured you didn't want to be around the baby. It's okay. I get it."

"That's not it at all. I love Alexander and I love you. I've just let my life take over and I can't do that to you. You're my friend and I'm so proud of you and happy for you and then I turn into a lousy friend. I'm sorry."

"It's okay." Sal touched Polly's hand. "It's really okay. I have plenty to keep me busy."

"So tell me about your trip to Boston," Polly said.

"I think the more entertaining time to ask that is when I get back," Sal replied. "Mom is making plans for a big dinner party on Saturday and a brunch for all of my friends on Sunday. She thinks it's important for their husbands to meet Mark. You know, so we can feel that we're part of the old gang." Sal shrugged. "Like there was a gang. We were a bunch of girls thrown at each other by our mothers. They'll want to talk about their jobs and their fancy houses and how many servants they have. Where their kids are going to grammar school and if they have nurses and nannies and ..." Sal let her voice drift off. "I can't tell you how glad I am to not be living that life. I don't want Alexander to have a nanny or a nurse or governess taking care of him. That's what I want to do."

"And you do it really well," Polly said.

"So are you having a party at your house tonight?"

"Ohhhh," Polly moaned. "I forgot. Do you mind? I need to call Heath."

Sal laughed. "Go ahead. I'm going to eat some chocolate. Thank you."

CHAPTER SIXTEEN

If this place was going to be ready for guests Polly needed to keep moving. Rebecca would be home from school soon, but Polly could get started. She wasn't sure where to begin, though. She went into the kids' bathroom and picked up the spray cleaner. She could finish this for Rebecca. And for Lonnie.

She sprayed down the tub and yanked dirty towels, tossing them into the hallway. The toilet was usually the last thing that Rebecca cleaned, hoping that someone else would either get punished and have to do the work instead or Polly would forget or better yet, take pity on her. Today was a pity day. Polly went after the walls and floor around the toilet with a vengeance. This wasn't her favorite job in the world, but when she was finished, at least she felt as if she'd accomplished something. She flung more towels and cloths to the hall and wiped down the mirror and counter tops before heading back to the tub.

"Polly?" Rebecca yelled. "We're home. Where are you?"

"In your bathroom," Polly yelled back.

Rebecca walked in. "I really was going to do this tonight. I promise. I'm sorry I didn't finish it last night."

"It's okay. Lonnie is staying here tonight. What do you think about spending the night with Kayla? I've already talked to Stephanie."

Kayla was right behind Rebecca and jumped up and down. "Cool!"

"Really?" Rebecca asked.

"Yeah. Maybe you and Kayla could clean up your room and change your sheets so Lonnie can sleep in there."

"Awesome," Rebecca said. "But you can't have a party here without me. That's not fair."

Polly sat down on the edge of the tub. "We are having a party, but that's just Heath."

"Tonight? Here?" Rebecca asked.

"Uh huh. So get moving on your room. You need to help me clean the rest of this place."

"Why am I cleaning it for Heath's party?" Rebecca whined. "He should be cleaning."

Polly scowled. "Heath is helping Henry this afternoon. Do you want to whine about that? We can do this."

"Whatever."

Polly stood up, grinned and took a breath. "You know what? I'll change your bed. I cleaned the toilet, but you get to finish the tub. Make sure you get it scrubbed down well. I'll be back to check in a bit."

"I'm sorry," Rebecca said quickly. "I didn't mean to whine."

"Too late. No takebacks." Polly bent over and picked up the towels she'd tossed to the floor. "Oh. And put out a nice set of towels for Lonnie, would you? Thanks."

Before Rebecca could say anything more, Polly headed for the washer and dryer, chuckling evilly to herself. Someday Rebecca would learn, but until that day, she was going to suffer for her bad mouth. She started a load of laundry, then glanced around the bathroom and replaced the towels. She wasn't sure how long they'd been there, but it wouldn't hurt to have fresh. She tossed the old ones on top of the washing machine, made sure there was plenty of toilet paper in the holder and walked out.

"Where's Andrew?" she asked Kayla, who was walking into the kitchen with a stack of glasses and several small plates.

"He'll be up in a minute. He had to go ask Eliseo something about horses for a story."

"Is that from Rebecca's room?"

Kayla nodded and opened the dishwasher.

"The dishwasher is dirty. Go ahead," Polly said. "I'll meet you back in her room." The kitchen could wait until last thing. That way Polly could bake while she cleaned. The living room was in good shape. A quick dusting would take care of it. She stood in Rebecca's doorway and took a breath. That girl could turn clean into chaos in no time at all. Polly opened the closet door and found it to be pretty much empty. She took the two empty laundry baskets out and put them up on Rebecca's bed.

"What are we going to do with her?" she asked Kayla when the young girl walked back in.

"I don't mind cleaning."

Polly laughed. "You're a good friend. Okay. How do we know what's clean and what's dirty?"

Kayla pointed to the opposite side of the bed. "That's usually her clean clothes. She drops her dirty clothes on this side."

"Yeah. Wouldn't want to get them into the basket." Polly filled the first basket, then walked around the bed and filled the second with what she assumed were clean clothes. At least that pretty much cleared the floor. While she was doing that, Kayla picked up books and put them back on shelves. She emptied Rebecca's night stand of wadded up pieces of paper, tissues, broken pencils and other trash, then moved things around, rearranging Rebecca's stuff back into her desk and in drawers. It took them about a half hour, but by the time Polly pulled the light blanket back off the bed, the room looked less like a disaster area.

She pulled the sheets off, only to discover that it was going to be a nearly impossible task with the two cats that had come in to find out what she was doing.

"I thought maybe I'd get away with it," Polly said with a laugh. "But they always know."

"They're funny," Kayla said. "I like playing with them when we put new sheets on."

"I'll be right back with those. I'm going to take this all to the laundry room."

Kayla sat down on the bare bed and rubbed Leia's back until the cat rolled over. Kayla touched the soft belly and snapped her hand back, as if she knew instinctively that she was inviting a scratching. Polly smiled and left the room with the laundry basket.

"Hi Polly," Andrew said, walking in the front door. "What are you doing in Rebecca's room?"

"We're cleaning. Are you ready to help?"

He slumped where he stood. "It's Friday. We've had a long week at school. Where is everybody?"

"Rebecca's cleaning the bathroom and Kayla's waiting to help me make her bed. Which would you like to help with?"

His eyes grew big and he shook his head. "I don't know. That all sounds terrible."

"Then why don't you take the dogs outside. Make it a nice long run. They haven't had much time out today."

"I'll do it!" Andrew ran to the back door. "Come on, dogs. We gotta get out of here right now."

Polly laughed as she crossed the room. It was much more fun cleaning with people helping, even if they were teenagers and whined about it. She transferred the towels into the dryer and started another load, then went back to the closet on the far side of the living room where they kept extra towels and sheets. It would be weird to live in a house where there was a real linen closet - maybe even more than one. The Bell House had a lot of storage that she didn't even realize she was missing here. Henry had done a wonderful job of creating extra storage, but it wasn't the same as those old houses. She could hardly wait.

"I put Rebecca's clothes in the dresser and hung things up in the closet," Kayla said. "She won't know where to look for them, but at least things are where they should be."

"You're a gem," Polly said. She dropped the pile of sheets and pillowcases on the desk and drew off the fitted sheet, then shook it out over the bed.

Luke pounced under the sheet, trying to grab at the billowing fabric. Polly tucked in one top corner, while Kayla tucked in the other, then the two of them tried to chase him off the end of the bed. He continued to prance around underneath the sheet until Polly finally pulled it back, scooped him up and put him on the floor. "Hurry," she said, grabbing the end and pulling it down.

Kayla giggled and laughed while they put the top sheet and a blanket on top and tucked them in. Both cats wrestled, but got pushed to the head of the bed while Kayla and Polly smoothed things out. The comforter had been draped over a chair, on top of pillows with shams covering them.

"There," Polly said. "This almost looks like a guest room."

"What did you do to the place?" Rebecca stood in her doorway with her hands on her hips.

"We cleaned," Kayla announced.

"Where's all my stuff?"

"Where it belongs," Polly said. "I have your clothes in the washing machine. When they come out of the dryer, you're going to put them away neatly and then pack a bag to take to Kayla's. I don't want any of it lying around. Got it?"

"This is weird," Rebecca said. "It's all sterile and cold."

Polly looked around and laughed. The room was anything but that. Rebecca accumulated knickknacks and stuffed animals, toys, posters, photographs and sketches. Easels sat in two corners of the room, one with scarves and hats draped over it, the other with a work in progress. "You'll have to suffer with sterile and cold," Polly said. "It's your sacrifice for family, okay?"

"I guess. I'm done with the bathroom."

"Did you get towels for Lonnie?"

Rebecca frowned. "I forgot those. I'll go get them."

"Bring them in here and put them on the bed. Then at least she'll know what's hers and the boys won't use them. Get the pretty green set for her."

Rebecca nodded. "What next?"

"Would you girls dust the furniture in the living room?" Polly asked. "I'll start in the kitchen."

"We're dusting for a party for Heath?" Rebecca asked.

"No, silly girl," Polly said. "Because Lonnie will be here. But it's nice to clean up for guests."

"Did I hear Andrew?"

"Yes. He ran away with the dogs. I think cleaning scares him."

"His mom is worse than you," Rebecca said. "She makes him clean his room every morning before he goes to school."

"Maybe I should do that."

Rebecca slapped her forehead. "Why did I say that out loud?"

"Grab the towels and then dust the living room. I'm going to make brownies and cookies for tonight while I clean the kitchen."

~~~

Polly stood in front of the kitchen sink and looked out the window. For a few minutes, the place was completely quiet. The dogs were lying down somewhere. Andrew had run them pretty hard this afternoon. The kids were all gone. Stephanie took them with her after she was finished with work. There was no wedding reception tonight, but two tomorrow, so she and Jeff would be on site all day.

Hayden was somewhere between the shop and the Bell House. He'd gone straight to the shop after class and then was heading over to check on things after Liam Hoffman finished for the day. Polly was still waiting to hear whether she really had water over there.

Heath would be home in fifteen minutes or so. They'd talked several times and she'd ordered three pizzas to arrive about seven o'clock. As soon as he finished with tasks for Henry, he was picking up snacks and drinks at the grocery store.

Plates, cups, napkins. Everything was out on the peninsula. Polly was glad that they'd been able to pull this off. He told her there would be ten or twelve people here. Even Jason was coming up. He and Heath had become better friends this year and that
~~~

filled Polly's heart. She loved both of those boys so much. Henry had told her to let them be, that they'd figure it out or not. And if they didn't, it would be okay. But Polly liked it when everyone got along.

She hoped that Jason's friend, Mel, would be here tonight. Polly really liked the girl. She was bright and self-assured. He was still trying to figure out whether she was girlfriend material.

The football game must be out of town, Polly realized. These kids would generally be at the football field on a Friday evening. While many of Heath's friends were girls, there were a few boys mixed in. She noticed some of them paired off, but usually they all just wanted to spend time together. They watched movies or played games, ate, laughed, talked and were pretty good kids.

Both Polly and Henry were glad that Heath felt comfortable enough here that he asked to have friends over. It had never occurred to Polly that he wouldn't, but one night it hit her that it was a pretty big deal for Heath. He'd come a long way since the day he moved in. She was thankful that Hayden was also living with them. He gave his younger brother a lot of support and strength. He was the one person in Heath's life who knew his entire history - not just the time after their parents died, but what a great kid Heath had been up until that day. He saw Heath through their parents' eyes, the hopes and dreams that they had for their kids.

Polly's phone rang, startling her out of her reverie. She smiled when she saw Henry's photo on her screen and opened the call. "Hey, Loverboy," she said.

"You beat me to it. Are you ready for the onslaught?"

"All ready. Rebecca is gone, the dogs are settled in, the house is clean, and pizza is ordered."

"Lonnie's following me back. She got into town about two o'clock and I think she's done in. What do you think about dinner for us?"

"Does she want to go out?"

"I doubt it."

"Probably not pizza either."

Henry laughed. "I've had enough this week. Do you want to call Davey's? I can pick it up."

"Do you know what she wants?"

"Oh. Rats. No."

"Why don't you two both come home. I can go out and pick it up while you two settle in. We'll eat in our room. We can turn the television on and you both can relax."

"Really?"

"Really. It's perfectly clean in there. We have plenty of room."

"I know it's clean, but you're good with taking care of us?"

Polly smiled. "I'm really good with it. You both must be exhausted. Just come home."

"I love you. Have you heard from Hayden yet?"

"Not yet. Oh ... we should feed him, too."

"I'll be home soon. I love you."

"I love you, too." Polly closed the call just as she heard footsteps coming up the back stairway. The dogs bounded out of wherever they had hidden themselves, wagging their tails as they chased each other through to meet the new arrival.

"It's me, Polly," Hayden said.

"Hi there. So?"

He looked at her, confused. "So?"

"Do I have water over there?"

"There is water and it is flowing," he said with a laugh. "But no, not flowing on its own. Just when you tell it to."

Polly jumped up and clapped her hands together. "I have water! Thank you, thank you!"

"I didn't do much, just helped Liam finish. He's coming back on Monday to make sure it's all still good, but until we get to the upstairs, he's done."

Polly hugged him. "I'm so excited. You have no idea."

"I have a little bit of an idea." He looked around. "What's going on here?"

"Heath's having friends over. Henry's sister, Lonnie is staying with us tonight. She'll be in Rebecca's room. Rebecca is at Stephanie and Kayla's."

"Wow," he said. "A guy goes to class in the morning and comes home to complete craziness. How's Bill?"

"He's doing better. I saw him earlier today." Polly stepped back. "That was really just this morning, wasn't it. Anyway, he was teasing and cracking jokes. Henry and I just talked. He sounds more normal too. He was really worried earlier today, but it's amazing what a few hours can do to turn something around."

"I'm glad. I was going to stop by after class, but I didn't want to intrude. I figured friends and family would show up today. And if things were bad, I knew you'd let me know."

Polly nodded. She wasn't sure that was true, but he didn't need to know that. She was trying not to feel as if she'd lost complete control of things around her, but so far, the people in her life were taking the brunt of her distractions. She didn't like it at all.

"Once Henry and Lonnie get here, we'll decide on supper. Unless you want to eat pizza with Heath and his friends."

"Oh no," Hayden said, putting his hands up as a defense. "None of that." He grinned. "I had an invitation to go over to Iowa Falls for the football game tonight. I said no because I thought you'd all be here and we should do family stuff, but if I'm just a third wheel, I'm going out instead."

"A date?" Polly asked.

He shrugged. "Just some friends. We'll be out late, though."

"Would you mind texting my phone when you get in?" she asked. Rather than worrying about whether he was home or not, they'd taken to just having him send a text to her phone when he got home. That way, when she woke up in the middle of the night, she could check it and fall back to sleep. Having adult kids living under her roof played havoc with her sense of responsibility and their sense of independence, but they'd finally come to a good place about it. Hayden wanted to honor her concerns, and Polly couldn't imagine not knowing that he was safe. It all worked out.

"Of course I will. You don't have to ask. I'll always let you know," he said. "I'll take a quick shower and then be out of here."

"Rebecca cleaned the bathroom," Polly called after him as he headed for the bedroom. "Take care of it when you leave, okay?"

She saw his back shaking as he laughed. When he got to the bedroom door, he turned around. "I will. I promise. If she ever figures out how to be an obedient child, you're going to need to hire someone to clean bathrooms."

"I hope she never does," Polly said. "Not just because of the bathrooms. As annoyed as she makes me, it's just that behavior that will serve her well when she's older."

He nodded and went into his room, shutting the door behind him.

"One more down," she said to Obiwan. "And by the way? We're all sleeping in tomorrow. Got it? Good."

CHAPTER SEVENTEEN

"Namaste, Ms. Giller," one of the boys said from the dining room table, with his hands together and a slight bow.

She smiled and nodded. Kids were awesome. They all turned to wave at her or say hello as she wandered into the kitchen. Heath was trying to shake the last of a bottle of ranch dressing into a dish.

"We have more," she whispered and went back to the pantry. Polly opened the bottle and handed it to him. "How are things going?"

"Not everyone is here yet. It's okay if more come later?"

"Fine with me. Lonnie and Henry are watching some old John Wayne movie."

Heath looked at her and laughed. "John Wayne?"

"I don't know," she replied, shaking her head. "Something they grew up with. Evidently, Marie loves them."

"Any of you watch John Wayne movies?" he asked the group.

"No, but Dad made me go down to his birthplace once," Mel piped up. She shrugged a shoulder. "It was okay. It's kind of cool that he was born in Iowa."

"The Superman guy was from Iowa," another girl said. "What's his name? He's been in a couple of shows. Brandon something."

The conversation bled off into celebrities born in Iowa and then to celebrities the kids had met.

Polly's ears perked up when someone mentioned Beryl's name. Jason blushed when they asked if anyone knew her. Was she really a crazy old lady who painted in the nude whether it was summer or winter? In the split second it took for Polly to decide whether or not to interrupt, Jason lifted his head.

"I know Beryl," he said. "She's one of my mom's best friends and she's not crazy. And she doesn't paint in the nude."

Good for him.

The kids didn't care; they moved on to someone else and while she was still standing there, the topic turned to Heath and his suspension.

"I heard he likes to look at girls'..." The girl stopped speaking and looked at Polly.

"Sorry. I'll go," Polly said, putting the last dish in the dishwasher.

"It's okay," Heath said. "You guys know she's the one who found Mr. West's body, don't you?"

"Was he really naked?" another girl asked. Polly thought her name might be Emmy. But this wasn't the Emmy Dill that was in Heath's literature class with Mr. West. This was a different girl. The other girl at the table was Cate with a 'C'. Yeah. She remembered that.

Polly nodded.

"And you saw everything?" Cate asked.

Polly chuckled. "It's a little different when the person is dead. You don't pay attention to anything but the fact that you need to call for help."

"This happens a lot to you, doesn't it?" a boy asked.

Polly wasn't sure who he was.

She nodded. "It does."

"Last summer I heard there was a guy killing people just to see if you'd find them," Cate interjected.

Polly decided she didn't really like that girl. And then she felt guilty. She barely knew these kids.

"You're right. He was a little off his rocker," Polly said.

"But you found them all. He knew something was up." The girl was persistent.

"Let it go," Heath said.

"You'd rather we talk about what Mr. West said to push your buttons? Rumor is you were going to punch him until Debbie got all up in your face," Cate said in a rather snotty tone.

Polly felt less guilty for not liking the girl.

"I wasn't going to punch him," Heath said. "Debbie just was there."

"So who killed him?" Mel asked, changing the subject. "Nobody liked him, but we all know Heath didn't do it."

"Maybe his big brother did it for him," Cate said.

"Like the police didn't check all of that out first thing," Jason retorted. "How dumb are you?"

Polly lifted her eyebrows. It seemed as if the rest of the kids didn't have much time for Cate either. So why was she even here?

"I heard he was cooking meth," the boy Polly didn't know said quietly. "You know, like on that TV show?"

"But he's not a science teacher," Cate said. "How would he know how to do that?"

Jason leaned forward and scowled down the table at her. "You can find everything you want to know on the Internet. Don't you know how to use Google?"

"The police wouldn't let that be out there for just anybody," she protested.

"Because the police control the Internet," Jason muttered. He sat back, turned to Polly and rolled his eyes. She shook her head and smiled at him, hoping to stop him from ruining the evening.

Even if it was Cate who was doing the worst bad-mouthing, Jason knew better. It didn't seem as if the girl had a single clue about what people thought of her. She just kept talking.

"Okay," Cate said. "But wouldn't we have heard something if the police found stuff at his house?"

Polly nodded. That was a good question.

"What idiot would cook meth in their own house?" Jason asked.

"What kind of idiot would do what he did to kids in school?" Mel asked. " From what I've heard, he didn't used to be as bad as he was this year. It's like he got way worse over the summer. He used to make kids read out loud and then ask them if they could relate to the passage and maybe ask some difficult questions, but it sounds like he was going for the kill every time he got someone in the hot seat. Maybe he was doing his own drugs."

"If he wasn't cooking, maybe he was just taking drugs," Jason said. He reached forward and took a piece of pizza out of the box and then gestured to Mel, asking if she wanted one. She put her plate out and he slid another piece on for her, then reached across to grab a bag of chips.

Polly leaned on the counter, tucking herself into a corner to try to stay as unobtrusive as possible. This was better than asking questions of Aaron or even Anita. The kids might not have all the right information, but they certainly had heard opinions. She wagered that somewhere in the middle of everything they heard was bits and pieces of the truth.

Mel got up and then bent over to whisper in Jason's ear. He nodded and she slipped around behind him and came into the kitchen. "Need some more pop," she said to Polly.

Polly opened the refrigerator door. Mel grabbed two cans and went back into the dining room.

"Miss Vincent was having a fight with Mr. West before school last week," Emmy said. "Heath and I saw it when we were going into the building. She was really yelling at him about something. Do you think she's involved?"

Heath shook his head. "I already told the police that people have fights. It was probably no big deal."

"But what if it was?" Emmy asked. "Teachers don't just have fights with each other at school. It's not like they know each other so well that they are mad before school even starts for the day. Unless they were dating."

"Ewww," Cate said. "He was creepy. And he had those weird relationships with girls. Why would any self-respecting adult want to date him?"

"She isn't married. Maybe they *were* dating," Jason said. "I have her for math. She's kind of weird. Really intense."

"Mom said she has a kind of autism. What's that other kind?" Emmy asked.

"Asp..." Jason turned to look at Polly.

"Asperger's."

"Yeah. That."

Emmy nodded. "Mom said that's why she's so good with math. She's like really focused. I can't believe that she teaches, though."

Jason shrugged. "She knows what she's talking about. But she's hard. Have any of you had Mr. Bills for computers?"

As the conversation moved away from Mr. West, Polly decided she didn't need to hear any more. The meth cooking was new information. She wondered if Aaron or Tab Hudson knew about that. She glanced at the clock. It was after eight o'clock. She wouldn't bother him tonight. Tomorrow would be soon enough. Polly slipped out of the dining room and stopped when she heard a tap at the front door.

"I've got it," she said and crossed to answer it. Three more high schoolers were standing there. Two girls and another boy. If these boys didn't figure out that they had a wealth of talent in front of them, they were dopes.

"Is Heath here?" one of the girls asked.

Heath spoke up. "Hey, Allie. You came, Bails." He'd come up to stand beside Polly and lifted his hand. "Yo, Jose." The two boys clapped up a high five. "We're in here. There's still a lot of pizza."

Polly pushed the door shut as they wandered away, chattering about what they'd heard regarding the score of the game. It sounded like Boone was ahead. She smiled as the decibel level in the dining room increased and went back to her bedroom.

"Are they having fun?" Henry asked.

"It sounds like it. I was just listening to them talk about that Mr. West."

"The guy you found this week?" Lonnie was sitting in Henry's place on their bed, propped up against the headboard.

"Yeah. Him. There's a rumor that he was cooking meth. The kids have linked him and a math teacher together. It feels like I should let someone know about these rumors. If even a little bit of their information is correct, Aaron should know."

Henry frowned. "You aren't calling him tonight, are you?"

"I can talk to him tomorrow. What were you talking about while I was gone?" Polly asked.

"Henry was telling me about that new subdivision," Lonnie said. "I can't believe little old Bellingwood is growing like that. He says that a lot of the apartments are already taken. He just has to get them built. And all of those new homes? That's just crazy."

"I gotta pay for the renovations at the Bell House," Henry said. He winked at Polly. "Gotta keep my girl happy."

"We have water," Polly said with a happy sigh. She sat down in the chair under the window and waited for Luke to climb up into her lap. "I can go to the bathroom when I'm working over there and wash my hands in a real sink. I don't even care if there's no hot water yet. I'm just thankful for this little bit of forward motion. It's the best thing ever."

Henry turned to Lonnie. "I give her happiness a little bit at a time. Don't want her getting too excited on me or she'll find more for me to do."

"Hah, like you're doing all of the work," Polly said.

"I really like Heath," Lonnie said. "He's such a sweet boy. If I were ten years younger, I would have made a move."

Polly laughed. "You should see what he's got going on out there. Four boys, including him and Jason, and eight girls. And the worst part? Those boys have no clue that the girls are only there because they are interested in them. It's adorable."

"When are you going to hook yourself a husband?" Henry asked nonchalantly.

Lonnie grabbed one of Polly's pillows and swatted him over the head.

"Hey," he complained.

"Hey nothing," she responded. "How old were you when you finally talked Polly into marrying you?"

"Yeah, yeah, yeah."

"Well, just because I haven't found a man that's worth my time and energy doesn't mean that I'm a loser. Got it?"

"You're not a loser," Henry said in protest. "I never said that. I just thought maybe you'd want to get married someday."

"What if I don't? Does that make me less of a person?" she asked. "What if I like my life? I have my friends and I have my job and I have a great house and when you don't annoy me, I like coming home and seeing my family."

Polly just pursed her lips and watched the entertainment.

"Sorry," Henry said. "You really like being alone?"

"Didn't you hear me?" Lonnie swatted him in the head with a pillow again.

Henry grabbed the pillow and tossed it across the room at Polly, who missed it completely. "Stop that. I heard you."

"Being alone and being lonely are two different things," Lonnie said. "And I'm neither. There's always someone around and I love my friends. And when I took Duchess back with me, I had someone who would sleep in the bed with me. That's a whole lot easier to manage than some guy. At least she doesn't snore." She looked at Polly and grinned. "Much. But it's so cute when she does, I never complain."

"Your roommates like her?" Polly asked. Lonnie had taken her Uncle Loren's dog back to Michigan with her after he'd been killed.

"Like her? They love her. Nance would steal her every night if she could. I might have trouble getting Duchess back into my bedroom if I'm gone too long. She's such a good dog. We're talking about getting a puppy now. It seems crazy when we're all so busy, but maybe after the holidays."

"Cats?" Polly stroked Luke's head and down his back, then put her hand on his chest to feel his purr.

"Dar's allergic to them."

"And not to dogs?" Henry asked.

"I don't get it, but there it is." Lonnie yawned. "I should really go to bed. This is really nice of you to let me stay here."

"Hopefully the kids won't bother you," Polly said.

Lonnie looked around. "I can't even hear them.

"Good insulation," Henry said. "If you keep your door closed, you shouldn't hear too much."

Polly laughed. "And the dogs won't try to sleep with you."

"That would be okay." Lonnie rubbed Han's head as it rested on her thigh. "Okay, pretty boy. I need to get up. It's time for me to go to sleep." She swung her legs over the side of the bed and giggled when one of them kicked Henry. "Oops. Sorry."

"No you're not."

"What time are you going down to see Dad tomorrow morning?"

"I don't care," he said. "Whenever. Do you want to go with me?"

"I'd like that. I don't want to stay all day. Maybe you guys can show me what's going on at the new house. I haven't seen it in forever."

"What time do you want to go?" he asked.

She shook her head and turned to roll her eyes at Polly. "If I go to sleep now, I'll get up early. Is eight too early?"

Polly sighed. "You morning people."

"I wouldn't be if I didn't have to be," Lonnie said. "But my body is programmed for it. And besides, it's an hour later where I'm from. Eight o'clock tomorrow will be late morning for me."

Henry laughed. "We can go earlier. I'll be up. Do you want to leave about seven? Let's run up to the coffee shop. Maybe we can pick something up for Mom."

"Sounds great." Lonnie stood and mussed his hair. "You're pretty cool, Henry. No matter what they say about you." She skittered out of the way before he could respond, stopped at the door and turned back. "Thanks, you two."

Their door pulled shut and Polly bent over to retrieve her pillow, then tossed it up on the bed. She stood and deposited Luke on the cat tree, then jumped on her bed and positioned herself so she was lying on her stomach, looking at Henry. "It's been a long day."

"It's been a really long day. We're not staying up until Heath's friends leave, are we?"

Polly shook her head. "We don't have to. He knows to come get us if there's a problem. Hayden will be out late. He'll text me when he gets in and if the kids are still here, he'll deal with them."

"Who are the kids that are here?"

She laughed. "You're kidding, right? I've tried to remember their names, but they come and go so fast. Jason and Mel are there. Some girl named Emmy that I've met before. At least she's hanging around. Then, Cate something." Polly set her jaw. "That's Cate with a "C", mind you. And three more showed up. An Allie, Bails - probably Bailey, and Jose. I have no idea who the other boy is or the other girls that were at the table. Would you believe the kids even thought that Hayden might have killed that teacher?"

"They're just testing out their thoughts," Henry said. "I wouldn't worry too much about what they say."

"But what do you think about the whole meth cooking thing?"

"It wouldn't surprise me. It sounds like Iowa is a hotbed for that stuff."

Polly shook her head. "I can't get over that. I'll never understand why people have to screw things up so badly."

"Money and power," he said. "It always comes down to money and power."

"Well, that's ugly." She sat up and then got off the bed. "I'm going to tell Heath that we're turning in."

"I'll take the dogs out the front door," Henry said.

They headed out of the bedroom and Polly gave Lonnie a little wave as Henry's sister ran back to her bedroom from the bathroom. The kids were no longer at the dining room table and she was surprised to find them gathered around the television watching a movie.

"Heath?" she called out.

He jumped up from the floor and ran back to her. "Yeah? Are we too loud?"

"No, not at all. I was just going to tell you that we're turning in. Don't hesitate to come get me if you need anything, though. Hayden will be back later, too."

"Oh. Okay. Thanks for letting me have them over. We'll be quiet."

"You'll be fine. No worries. But do me a favor and text me when everyone is gone and you're heading for bed. That way I know what's going on if I wake up."

He nodded. Heath looked like he wanted to hug her, so Polly just took things into her own hands and pulled him in. "I love you, Heath. I'm glad your friends showed up tonight. Monday is going to be okay. Right?"

"I was a little worried," he said. "This is cool, though. And we'll clean up."

"I know you will. Have fun."

She watched him make his way back to the cluster of kids in the media room, then turned and headed back for her bedroom. This had been a long, crazy week and she was glad it was over.

CHAPTER EIGHTEEN

Those grey skies would most certainly bring a thunderstorm or two today. It was a perfect day to stay under the blankets. At least for a few more minutes.

The house was blessedly quiet. Henry and Lonnie were long gone and the boys were still asleep in their room. She'd come awake at three o'clock and checked messages on her phone. Heath had sent his text about twelve thirty, telling her that everyone had gone home and the kitchen was clean. If he'd missed anything, he would take care of it this morning. Hayden's text came in about one o'clock, telling her he was home and safe. She was sure the dogs had probably tried to tell her that the boys were home, but she'd slept through it all.

Luke and Leia jumped down from where they were perched on the cat tree and before Polly knew it, both dogs jumped off the bed and headed out of the room.

"What's going on?" she asked out loud. She didn't expect Henry and Lonnie to return for another few hours.

"It's just me, Polly," Rebecca called back. Polly sat up in bed. She hadn't been expecting this.

Rebecca tapped on her door.

"Come on in."

"Stephanie had to come over early because of the wedding receptions, so we came with her."

"Did you have a good night?" Polly asked.

"It was okay. We had to go to bed early, but Kayla and I stayed up for a while talking. We brought you a coffee from Sweet Beans. And Stephanie bought sweet rolls." Rebecca sat down on the bed and leaned toward Polly. "I think she likes that guy who works there. Skylar? Kayla says they go there before school sometimes, but it isn't every day." She smiled. "I told her it's probably only the days he's working."

"Everybody's finding someone," Polly said. Her memory flashed and she laughed. "Did you know Doug was dating Anita?"

"No way," Rebecca replied. "Doug next door and that girl from the sheriff's office? No way."

Polly sighed contentedly. "I'm glad I'm not the only one who didn't know. I forgot to say something to Henry last night."

"Are they at the hospital this morning? I kinda hoped I'd get to go over and see Bill."

"They left early." Polly shook her head. "I hate morning people."

"You're more of a morning person than me," Rebecca said.

"Only because I have to." Polly pushed the blanket off and scooted to the edge of the bed. "Where are the sweet rolls you're talking about?"

"On the counter with your coffee."

Polly wrapped a robe around herself and then hugged Rebecca before they left the bedroom. "Thanks for doing that. I probably would have found a good reason to go up there this morning, but now I can stay here and be a slug. What's Kayla doing?"

"She's downstairs with Stephanie. Something about decorating tables for the first reception. Stephanie needed help."

"And you came up here?"

Rebecca scowled. "They didn't need me. I think they like doing things together. I was just in the way."

Polly's eyes were immediately drawn to the beautiful Sweet Beans cup on her counter. It was as if everything else was a blur around it. She brought it up to smell the essence of bean and took in a deep breath. "Ahhhh."

"You're weird," Rebecca said, lifting the lid on the sweet rolls. "Will I ever like coffee?"

"When you're twenty-five years old, you can start drinking this blessed liquid. Until then, you're too young."

"When did you start drinking coffee?"

Polly thought back. She couldn't remember a time when she didn't drink coffee. It started with Sal. Polly had been up late one night writing a paper, desperately trying to stay awake to finish the thing. Finally, Sal put a cup of coffee in front of her with some creamer beside it just in case Polly didn't like it black. She hadn't. At all. But it had kept her going that night. Not long after, she realized that she might have an addiction to the stuff.

"I don't remember," Polly said.

"You looked like you were remembering. Tell me it wasn't high school."

"Oh no," Polly said. She reached to the end of the peninsula and grabbed the container of napkins, bringing it forward. "It was at least college."

"Then I'll try to wait until college."

"You do that. Or the age of twenty-five. I'd be fine with that."

"What's all this noise out here?" Hayden asked. "I thought we were sleeping in."

Rebecca put a sweet roll on a napkin and held it out to him. "What? Did you have a hot date last night?"

When he reached for her offering, she snatched it back and took a bite. "Fooled ya."

"She's mean, Polly," he whined. "Make her stop being mean to me." Hayden glanced at the empty coffee pot. "Why is there no coffee?"

Polly put her hand with the Sweet Beans cup behind her back. "I haven't gotten there yet."

"What's that?"

"What's what?"

Hayden stuck his lower lip out in a pout. "She loves you more than she loves me." He flipped the coffee pot switch and leaned against the counter. "Everybody was talking about that murder at the game last night. Sounds like Mr. West was a lot worse this year than ever before. There are so many rumors, it's hard to figure out what might be real."

"Did you hear about a meth lab?" Polly asked.

Hayden nodded. "Can you believe it? Why would he do that? He's supposed to be helping kids get smarter, not make them dumber. It makes no sense to me."

"So you think that's real?"

"It probably is. That was the main story going around. But the police didn't find anything at his house."

"Why would he do something like that at his house?" Rebecca asked. "People can smell it from the outside."

Polly turned slowly to look at her daughter. "How do you know about that?"

"People talk. And hello, I watch television and read books."

"About cooking meth?"

"Yeah. Duh."

The girl was such a teenager.

"Heath and I are going over to the Bell House to finish tearing off the plaster on the ceiling in the foyer," Hayden said. "Someday we're going to stop making dust over there."

"I can hardly wait," Polly said. "But at least there's water."

Hayden nodded. "He put a toilet in. There's no door, but there's a toilet and a sink. That's going to be so much better."

"I might have done a little happy dance last night." Polly lifted up on her toes and pranced around the kitchen. "I'm still doing it." She brought her cup to her mouth, drank deeply and grinned. "And I have yummy caffeine."

Heath came into the kitchen, rubbing his eyes. His hair was sticking up all over the place. "What is going on around here?" He swatted his brother's arm. "You left the door open and the dogs wouldn't go away."

"Oh sorry," Hayden said and smirked at Polly. "Did I do that?"

"What time is it anyway?"

Everyone looked at the clock in the dining room.

"Eight thirty?" Heath complained. "That's only like seven hours of sleep. On a Saturday. After a Friday night party. I'm going back to bed."

"We have sweet rolls," Rebecca said, holding the box out.

He peered down at her, squinting at the box. "Where did you come from? I thought you were gone for the weekend?"

"I'm back." Rebecca laughed. "Come on. Stay awake. We never get to see each other anymore."

He shook his head. "What are you talking about? I see you all the time."

"Not to just talk. How are you?" Rebecca put the box down on the dining room table and took Heath's arm, leading him over to sit at the table with her. "Come on, you guys. Join us. We're a family, aren't we?"

Hayden and Polly looked at each other and Polly shrugged. "I guess we're having family time."

"Just let me get my coffee," Hayden said.

"So do you two know that Polly's birthday is on Tuesday?" Rebecca asked. "Do you have plans?"

Polly laughed. "I don't think we need to worry about making plans for my birthday. The more I ignore these, the faster they go away."

"Nonsense. We're going to have a really nice dinner." Rebecca tapped the table. "Hayden, you're cooking. We'll plan a menu."

He nodded, a little bemused by her direction.

"Heath, what about you?" She waited only a split second and said, "Nah. We'll talk about you later when you're more awake." Rebecca pushed the box of sweet rolls at him. "Eat. Do you want juice or milk?"

"Milk."

"Polly?" Rebecca looked expectantly at Polly, who was still standing in the kitchen.

"I'm good," Polly said. "Got my coffee right here." She knew what Rebecca had asked, but wondered what the girl would do when Polly ignored her request.

"Fine," Rebecca said. "I'll get it. I want some, too."

The dogs ran to the back steps and Polly looked up. "That was a fast trip. I hope Bill's okay."

Rebecca poured out two glasses of milk and came back to the table, putting one in front of Heath. "He would have called if something was wrong, right?"

Polly nodded. "I'm sure of it."

They all stopped talking as they waited for Henry to come up the steps. When he and Lonnie walked through the door to his office, he laughed. "That's a welcoming committee. I can't believe you're all up and moving."

"Some of us are moving better than others," Polly said. "Rebecca brought sweet rolls from Sweet Beans."

"She did," he said, appraisingly. "That's interesting."

Lonnie moved out from behind him with two fast food bags. "We bought breakfast biscuits and burritos. There's a little bit of everything in here. Sausage, chicken, bacon. Henry said you'd have coffee."

Hayden jumped up and went into the kitchen to bring plates back to the table. "How's Bill?" he asked.

"Funny," Henry replied. "That's why we're home early. Lonnie and I are heading over to the house to get things ready. Dad's coming home this afternoon. I'll go back over with their car to bring him home."

"Can I help you?" Polly asked Lonnie.

"I guess. We're bringing my bed downstairs so Dad can sleep there until he's recuperated."

"Do you have one of those Japanese screens?" Polly asked. "Your parents are going to have lots of visitors and I'm guessing Marie wouldn't be happy with everyone seeing Bill's bedroom. If you're putting the bed at the other end of the living room, you can at least give him some privacy."

Lonnie shook her head. "I could go back to Ames and buy a couple, I guess."

"Let me make some phone calls. I might find some." Polly knew she'd seen a couple somewhere, she just needed to remember whose house they were at.

"Heath and I can help you bring the bed down," Hayden said. "Then we'll head over to the other house to work."

"That's great." Henry couldn't stop smiling. He walked around the dining room table and sat down beside Polly. "It's the best news I've had in a while. Dad's okay and he's coming home. And Mom's not mad at me."

"Why would she be mad at you?" Lonnie asked.

"He was worried she was upset because Bill was working so much in the shop."

"Like you could slow Dad down. He does what he wants. He probably won't even wait until he's fully healed up before he's out there again. That's his life. Mom knows that." Lonnie glared at Henry. "Why don't you?"

"Because Dad's been working really hard. He's too old to work that hard."

Lonnie laughed. "Think about it for a minute. When you're his age, do you want someone telling you that you work too hard? Especially your son? What if Heath said that to you?"

"I'd be annoyed."

Lonnie smiled at Heath. "Never say that to him. He'll be annoyed." She pushed a chicken biscuit to her brother. "Don't treat Dad like a child. Ever."

"Yes ma'am." Henry winked at Polly. "You women. One of you gets an idea in your head and it passes from brain to brain. The rest of us are just clueless."

"We're just so smart that we know what's right and what's wrong," Polly said. "When you're right, it's always obvious."

~~~

Polly drove slowly as she approached Sweet Beans. They'd gotten the bed downstairs and set up, moving furniture around in the far end of the living room to make it comfortable for Bill and
~~~

Marie. She still couldn't remember where she'd seen the Japanese screens, but it would come to her. Hopefully, visitors would give him time to settle in at the house before arriving for long chats. Lonnie was heading to the grocery store to re-stock the refrigerator while Henry spent time in the shop, making sure that things were ready for Monday morning.

She was on her way to the Bell House. She could hardly wait to turn on a faucet and feel water running over her fingers. This was one of those steps in the process that gave her confidence she might actually be able to move in someday.

Heath and Hayden were already there. They'd helped Henry bring the bed downstairs at Bill and Marie's and then left so they could get to work. She still couldn't believe how fortunate she was to have these boys in her life. They worked hard and usually without complaint.

Just as Polly was ready to pass the coffee shop, she realized that Lydia's Jeep was parked there. Taking a chance her friend would be inside, Polly swung her truck into a parking space.

When she got inside, she was thrilled to see Lydia there with Andy and Beryl.

"Polly!" Beryl said, jumping up. "What are you doing out and about this morning?"

"Just heading over to the other house," Polly said. "What are you doing here? Aren't you supposed to be giving my daughter a lesson?"

Beryl smiled. "I'm picking her up. We're going up to the park."

"It's going to rain," Polly said.

"I know that. We'll sit under the shelter and draw rain drops bouncing off leaves. It's the perfect day for this."

"Okay," Polly said. "You're the teacher."

Beryl nudged her. "And I'm a good one. Get your coffee and join us."

"I've had enough this morning. I saw Lydia's Jeep and wanted to say hello."

"Then it's good to see you, dear," Lydia said. "Have you heard anything from Marie and Bill?"

"They're coming home this afternoon. Henry's so much better now that his dad is doing better."

Andy took her phone out and typed in a text. "Sorry. I just wanted Len to know. We were thinking about going up to see them today, but if he's coming home, we'll call tomorrow."

She glanced back at her phone. "I'm training him." She showed them Len's response which was a heart emoji. "He's taking to all of this new technology pretty well. He likes being able to talk to Ellen any time without worrying about what it costs. They talk more now than ever before. Sometimes he even wakes up in the middle of the night so he can say good morning to her before she goes to work. It's pretty sweet."

"When are you going back to Spain?" Polly asked. Len's daughter lived in Barcelona.

"Maybe in January. It will be our Christmas present to each other." Andy shrugged. "We'll see what happens with Bill, though. If Len needs to be here, he won't go."

"Isn't he retired?" Polly asked.

Andy shook her head. "I think real retirement would kill him. He's been so happy since he started working with Bill and Henry. And I'm at the library several days a week. We weren't ready to stop, I guess. Someday."

"You!" Polly said, pointing at Beryl.

"What about me?" Beryl asked. "What did I do this time? I swear I'm innocent."

"You have Japanese screens."

Beryl nodded. "I have two of them. Why?"

"Are they imperative to your decorating scheme?"

"No, not at all."

"I told Henry they'd be great at Marie's house. They moved a bed downstairs for Bill. This way they could close off the space." Polly grimaced. "You know they're going to have people show up. And if Bill needed to take a nap, at least Marie wouldn't worry about him being bothered."

"That's a great idea. They can certainly use mine," Beryl said. "But they won't fit in my car."

Polly smiled. "I'll come get them. Maybe this afternoon. Thank you."

"How's your boy doing?" Lydia asked.

"Heath?"

Lydia nodded.

"He's doing okay. He had friends over last night. They stayed up late, watched television, and ate pizza. It was good for him to see some of them before he goes back to school on Monday. That will be hard enough as it is." Polly stopped. "Can I ask a weird question, Lydia?"

"Of course."

"Has your husband said anything about that Mr. West cooking meth? The kids are talking about it. If he knows, I won't call him."

"He does," Lydia said. "They've heard all the rumors, but have yet to discover where the man might have been working on it. They don't know if that's why he was killed or if it was something else."

"Okay. It was such a shock to hear them talking about it last night, I wondered if Aaron and Tab Hudson knew. I hadn't heard it yet. Heath acted like he didn't know about it either."

Lydia shook her head. "Aaron sees this pretty regularly. It's sad, but true. I think we'd be very surprised to find out who in town is making drugs."

"I know it's not the same," Polly said. "But do you think that people talked about the moonshiners during prohibition like we're talking about meth cookers?" She huffed a laugh. "They called it the same thing. Cooking whiskey, cooking meth. We want to wax poetic about those people who had stills going in their barns, but it was against the law and some of that stuff was really dangerous to drink. Maybe it wasn't as romantic as a hidden room in my basement might make it. One man died over there and even though it was a hundred years ago, he had friends and family that cared about him." Polly looked up. "Did that Mr. West have any family?"

"Not around here. He has an ex-wife who lives in Omaha. No kids, though."

Polly looked at her watch. "I should get over to the Bell House. The boys were expecting me a half hour ago." She put her hand on Beryl's. "Can I call you later this afternoon and show up?"

"Rebecca and I will put the screens just inside the front door," Beryl said. "Stop by and take them. Don't worry about trying to find me. It's a perfect day to hunker in the studio and work."

"I love you guys," Polly said, standing up. "Talk to you later."

She took one last longing look at the counter, then walked out. She'd had plenty of caffeine. It was time to work some of it out of her system.

CHAPTER NINETEEN

"Okay, this feels good," Polly said. After this last week, it felt good to do something physical. While Heath and Hayden ripped plaster away from the ceiling in the grand foyer, Polly filled her trusty wheelbarrow with the debris they'd dropped to the floor over the last week. All she had to do was haul it to the driveway. Henry or one of the boys would use the bobcat to lift it into the dumpster. She wasn't sure why Henry refused to show her how to use the bobcat.

Then she chuckled. Maybe it had something to do with her aiming skills. At this point in her life, Polly was no longer embarrassed by the whole thing. It had turned into such a joke, that she figured if she ever truly caught something on purpose, no one would believe it anyway.

She'd worked to clear one corner of the massive foyer and looked out over the room. When they planned for heating this place, she and Henry agreed that radiant flooring would work in here. She couldn't believe they were going to have to install two furnaces in order to heat the rest of house. What kind of insanity had she walked into? If they had simply torn this building down, she would have gladly built a more reasonably sized home and been glad of an immense lot to mow. She still had a big lawn, but there was also this massive building to deal with.

Polly jumped when a large chunk of plaster hit the floor across the room.

"Sorry," Hayden called out. "Bigger than I thought."

Polly walked up the stairs in front of her. It had been a while since she'd spent any time on the second floor. Her plan was to move her family into the main level and then start working upstairs. Rebecca had already identified which room she wanted.

"What is all of this?" she asked Hayden, pointing at the ceiling joists.

"I don't know yet," he said. "It looks like some kind of symbol. Do you suppose the Freemasons worked here and painted their symbol on the ceiling before it was plastered?"

She shook her head and smiled. "That's not the Freemason symbol. You'd see the compass and square with all that you've pulled away. This is a star with other symbols. Would you two hurry up and finish so I can see what it is?"

"Henry told us not to hurry. We're supposed to do the job right and be safe."

"Okay, okay." Polly stopped on the landing and looked out over the ceiling. The star had definitely been painted there before the ceiling was plastered on. What a strange thing to uncover. She sat on the floor and then laid down, trying to take it all in.

Hayden stopped and turned to her. "What are you doing?"

"I'm trying to decipher what this is."

"Patience, Polly. Patience. We'll have this all off soon. Then you can see the whole thing."

She peered at the star a little longer and then jumped up. "I'll be back after a while. If you need me, I'm in the basement." Polly steered the wheelbarrow out to the driveway, looked up at the grey sky and said, "Don't you dare." She dumped the plaster and headed for Rebecca's studio.

Cursing when she tried to turn the locked door handle, she ran back to the garage and went inside, digging around in an old coffee can filled with nails. When they threatened to puncture her skin, Polly poured the nails out on a shelf, retrieved the key, and ran back to the studio. Within minutes she was standing in front of the doorway to the basement room, fumbling to get the key in the lock.

"Slow down," she breathed to herself. "It will still be there, no matter how long it takes you."

Polly lit the lamp on the old desk and picked up the top tally board. She didn't even bother to check the name on the front, but flipped it over and slid the cover off the hiding place. There it was. Etched into the wood was a five-pointed star with a sword on one side and a crude image of a plow on the other.

"Swords into plowshares," she breathed and picked up another tally board. Just like the first, the symbol was etched into the wood inside the small hiding space. Each of the tally boards had the same thing in the same place. "What is this? What were they doing?"

Polly took pictures of the image, then turned out the flame in the lamp and headed back the way she'd come. She took a moment to put the nails and key back into the can and shoved it to the rear of the shelf where she'd found it before heading back into the house.

"It's a plow," she said, walking into the foyer.

Hayden craned his neck. "Yeah. I guess it probably is. How did you know?"

"And when you uncover the other side, you'll find a sword."

He furrowed his brow. "Okay. That's officially weird. How do you know that?"

"Because it's on those tally boards downstairs. Did you guys see anything else like this in any of the other rooms?"

Heath shook his head. "We weren't really looking. You know, mass mess?"

"Check in the library," Hayden said, pointing at the back corner. "I might have seen something on the door frame."

Polly pushed the double set of doors open and stepped into the hallway, turned left and walked to the corner room. This would end up being her sanctuary. In her mind's eye, she saw walls filled with floor to ceiling bookshelves, a dark red Persian rug lying across the hard wood floors, and a deep ebony desk with a black leather chair in the center of the room, facing the fireplace. But until that finally happened ... she figured in ten years or so … it would first be the room she and Henry claimed as their bedroom.

She looked up and down the door frame, but didn't see anything, so she scoured the studs in the room, looking for anything that might be another representation of the sword and ploughshares symbol. And she finally found it on a window frame. Polly snapped a picture and went through into the living room where she discovered another small image on the door frame. There were more rooms on this main level, so she walked down the hall, back past the library and turned into the next room.

This would be their office. A door along the back wall led outside. It was boarded up right now, but when the back porch was finally attached, it would open up to their beautiful back yard. She searched for the symbol and found it on a window frame along the back wall. The next room had been the formal parlor for the Springers. Polly wasn't yet sure what it would become. There were a lot of doors in this room. The double doors leading into the hallway didn't have the symbol, so she checked the double doors into the dining room. No symbol there. This room also had a door that was boarded up on the back wall. Instead of bothering with that, she went to the window that matched the one in the office and found the symbol. It was everywhere in this house and she had no idea what it meant.

The dining room was a gorgeous room. Polly wasn't quite sure how she wanted to end up decorating it but with that massive table in the center of the room, she wanted rich, dark colors on the walls. Maybe a deep green with wainscoting from the chair rail down. The big pieces from this room - the buffet and hutch - were in the garage, covered with tarps until she could deal with them. She checked the door frames first, one leading from the parlor and another leading out to the hallway. A small door opened onto the back porch, but nothing was there. Polly looked around the large fireplace and then found the symbol underneath the window seat that filled the back wall.

The last room on this floor was the kitchen. With the floor mostly ripped out, Polly made her way across on the planks that had been put down. She checked the patio door and then the doorways leading to the mudroom and pantry. Nothing there. The windows were bare of the symbol and she grew frustrated. It was everywhere else, why not here? She finally went through to the bathroom and then into the back storage area that also contained a stairway leading upstairs. This had been the servant's stairway that led to their rooms on the second floor. She looked everywhere, on every piece of wood available and found nothing.

Polly finally went out the back door and stopped, then went back inside. There on the exposed face of the door frame was the symbol once more. She took another picture and sat down on the steps. Was that simply the sign of the construction company? But why wasn't it in the kitchen or storage rooms?

Taking a deep breath, she opened her phone and made a call.

"Miss Polly Giller," Ken Wallers said. "To what do I owe the pleasure of a conversation with you?"

"Have you guys talked any more about those things I found in the tally boards?" she asked.

"Not yet. Has something else come up?"

"I don't know what to think. I just discovered that there is a symbol all over this house and it's also in the backs of those tally boards. I thought it was just a maker's mark, but it's painted on the ceiling in the foyer and I also found it in every single room on the main level of the house."

She heard him breathing on the other end of the phone.

"Ken?" she asked.

"That's weird."

"Tell me about it."

"What's the symbol?"

"It's a five-pointed star. On one end of it is a sword and on the other end is a plow."

"Swords into plowshares," he said.

"You know what this is?"

"It's a Bible verse about peace after war. But I don't know what it means in your context. You're sure it's a five-pointed star and not like the Star of David or something else."

"No. Five points. I counted. I can send you a picture. It's not great, but you should be able to see it."

"Yes. Send the picture to me. I'll forward it to Paul and Simon. Maybe one of them knows more about this."

"Have you talked to Greg Parker yet?"

"He chuckled. "No. Sorry. I mentioned something to Lucy and she wasn't excited about any of us getting involved in Greg's disability, so I left it alone, hoping maybe we could decipher this mystery without him."

"That makes sense." Polly sighed. "Maybe I'm making a big deal out of nothing. It's not like it matters any longer."

"Crap," Ken said.

"What?"

"I'm an idiot. I need to talk to Margie Deacon. If we have a historical society in Bellingwood, she's it. She's collected more history on this town than anyone else."

"How have I never met her?" Polly asked. "No one ever mentioned that name to me."

"She's old and most people have forgotten about her. She doesn't get out very often. In fact, I didn't even see her at the Sesquicentennial this year. Maybe she doesn't have her collection any longer. It's been years since we've talked."

"Do you want me to go with you to see her?"

"No. Not this first time. She's a crusty old gal, but she likes me. She was always a little paranoid. Used to talk about people who didn't want the true history of Bellingwood to be made known. I chalk it up to too many years of living by herself."

"That sounds ominous."

"They used to call it hardening of the arteries. Now it's just called dementia. Who knows, the old lady might not have any faculties left, but I can certainly give it a shot. I probably won't do anything with it until next week. Maude and I are taking the girls to Omaha for the weekend. Naomi has been talking about going to the zoo. Hopefully the forecast is correct and tomorrow will be bright and sunny."

Polly smiled. She and Rebecca had been talking about a girls' weekend to one of the larger cities. Chicago, Minneapolis, Kansas City, Omaha. It really wasn't that far to drive to any of them.

"Have a great weekend and we'll talk again on Monday," she said.

"We'll figure it out," he replied. "I hope this isn't worrying you too much."

"Not really. It's like an itch that needs to be scratched. I hate it when I don't know what's going on."

He laughed. "I get that. You should go into law enforcement."

"Don't say that too loudly. Aaron wouldn't like it."

"That's right. You're too close for him as it is. I hope you have a good weekend. We'll talk on Monday."

She slid her phone back into her pocket and grabbed the empty wheelbarrow to go back inside. That was all she needed - one more mystery to solve.

Polly pushed the wheelbarrow over the planks in the kitchen, then stopped and turned around. She wanted this room to be everyone's favorite place to be. The long side wall facing the garage would probably be where the appliances and counters ended up. She was working on a design for an island in the center, and there was a large space along the back wall for a table. The windows there were small and useless, but she hoped to turn it into a sun room, with nothing but windows. Looking to the east, the sunrises would be glorious. Even if it did look out over the cemetery. She wanted a patio put down just outside the back door with a grill and picnic table.

Poor Henry. He really was never going to be finished with the construction projects she had planned for this place.

Polly heard another crash of plaster in the foyer. At least she had those two boys helping. She wondered how much she could get done this next year before Heath went off to college. Hayden would be around for several more years. As long as she could make it easy for him to live here and still maintain his independence. Who else in the world adopted one son and got two in the bargain?

"Are you two okay in here?" she asked, walking through the double doors into the foyer.

"We're fine. Sorry. Every once in a while a big chunk pulls off and it makes noise," Hayden said. "Where did you go?"

"I found those symbols in every room on this main level except for the kitchen. Ken says the sword and plow is from a Bible verse. I guess I knew that. Beating swords into plowshares. But I really wonder what it means around here?"

"Maybe it was a secret society," Heath said. "You know. Stopping war?"

Polly lifted her eyebrows. "This place was built in 1916. Right in the middle of World War One. Seems odd that there would have been a bunch of peace radicals in the middle of Iowa. Those wars weren't like the wars we fight now. Once the President and Congress declared war, most everyone in the country supported them." She shook her head. "No. That doesn't make sense."

"Why not?"

"It just doesn't sound right. This is a normal little town in Iowa, for heaven's sake. Okay, so we had some moonshining going on, but that other stuff is for movies and spy novels."

"Can't you just see it now?" Hayden asked. "The Bell House was the home for a secret society that supplied spies who traveled throughout Europe during the war. Rather than the hammer and sickle or the Nazi symbol, they used the sword and plowshare to identify themselves to each other. One guy would draw the sword in the sand with the toe of his boot and the other would draw the plow. Then, they'd both bend over to wipe it out while drawing the star."

"You should write a novel," Polly said with a laugh. "That's ridiculous."

He shrugged. "Do you have a better story? I'm sticking with mine until you come up with something more interesting."

"How much longer are you two going to work here today?" she asked.

Heath looked up at his brother on the scaffold and Hayden shrugged. "I don't know. Maybe midafternoon."

"I'm heading out. I need to run to Beryl's to pick up her privacy screens for Bill and Marie. Then I'm going home to take a shower before going over to make sure Lonnie has everything she needs."

"Tell Bill hey," Hayden said. "I don't want to bother him tonight, but sometime this week I'll stop by to see them. Maybe I'll make my famous Chicken Parmesan and take it over."

"You haven't made that in years," Heath said. "Wasn't that Mom's recipe?"

Hayden nodded. "Yep. I make it better, though. A little brown sugar and no one can stop eating it."

"Maybe you need to try it out on us first," Polly said. "I can't believe you haven't."

"If everyone's home tonight, I'll do it."

She smiled. "Send me a list of the ingredients. I'll make sure they're in the house. See you guys later!" Polly went back outside, got in her truck and sighed a contented sigh. One of these days they'd live here, but for now, she was glad to have a wonderful home waiting for her. First the screens, then a shower.

CHAPTER TWENTY

Henry followed Polly out to the kitchen.

She gave him a quick peck on the cheek and headed for the back steps. "I'm just going to walk up to Pizzazz. No need to take my truck. If I don't feel like walking home, one of the girls will bring me."

He nodded distractedly while thumbing a message into his phone. She thought it was odd that he was texting someone on a Sunday evening. Even *he* didn't bother his crew during their last hours of the weekend.

"Polly," Rebecca said, running up to catch her.

"What's up?"

"Can I do another load of laundry tonight?" Rebecca turned to look at Henry. "I want to wear my jeans that are dirty."

"Sure." Polly frowned at her daughter. "You can do laundry any time. I don't care."

"Okay. Thanks."

Polly's phone rang and she pulled it out of her pocket as she walked through the office. Sometimes her family was just odd. "Hey Sal," she said after picking up the call.

"I need a huge favor. Have you left yet?" Sal asked.

"No. I was just getting ready to head out. What do you need?"

"Can you come get me? My car won't start and Mark won't let me take his truck. Something about a mare about to give birth. He doesn't want to be without a vehicle if they need him."

Polly turned and went back into the living room to get her keys. "Sure. I'll be there in a few minutes."

"What are you doing back in here?" Henry asked. "Forget something?"

"I'm picking Sal up. I don't know when I'll be home. Is that okay?" Polly was a little worried about leaving her family. What a bunch of oddballs they were being tonight.

"If you're out after midnight, let me know," he said with a grin. He came forward and kissed her, then gave her a gentle shove on her way. "I love you."

"I love you, too."

Polly made it down the back steps and out to the garage without any more trouble. She and the boys had spent the afternoon at the Bell House while Henry and Rebecca went over to see his parents. Bill was happy to be home. Lonnie planned to take a few more days off to help her mother. Polly enjoyed having Henry's sister around. She was like him in so many ways and yet, she was her own person. It was fun to watch someone enjoy life as much as Lonnie did. She and her friends had gone to Florida for two weeks a year ago, intent on spending every minute they could at the Disney and Universal parks. This year, Lonnie would miss Christmas because they were heading to Greece and Rome over the holiday break. If everything worked out, she'd meet her grandparents there. Polly had never cared to travel, but she certainly enjoyed it vicariously. Especially with someone as excited as Lonnie was for these big trips.

Sal was waiting outside her front door when Polly pulled up. "I'm so sorry. Thank you for doing this," Sal said, breathless, as she buckled her seatbelt. "I would have died if I had to miss it tonight. We were so haphazard over the summer and now that we're getting back to normal, I didn't want to mess it up."

"You're a nut. Of course I'll come get you. Any time."

"Have you heard anything more about that dead guy?" Sal asked.

Polly shook her head. "Aaron never tells me anything. I have to either fall into the clues that are out there or pin him down until he talks."

"I can't believe you had to look at an old naked guy while you waited for them to show up."

"Everyone thinks it's so weird that he was naked. But I was more focused on the fact that he was dead."

Sal nodded. "I suppose. You get yourself into the oddest stuff."

Polly huffed a laugh. "I do that. I found a weird mystery at the Bell House and I don't know what to do with it. We discovered a strange symbol painted and etched all over the house."

"What?" Sal snapped her head to look at Polly.

"I know. Totally weird. It's painted on the ceiling in that big foyer. We'd never have found it if the boys weren't stripping the plaster. And then I found it on door frames and window frames in the other rooms on the main level." She put her hand on the console beside her. "But not in the kitchen."

"Because that's where the servants were," Sal observed. "That whole end of the house was for the servants. Right?"

"Yeah. Even the bedrooms upstairs. That's gotta be the reason, but I don't know what the symbol means." Polly drove down the block past Pizzazz. "The place is really busy tonight. I hope they saved our table."

Sal laughed. "Of course they did. It's not like we don't call them when we won't be there. We're predictable and responsible." She shook her hair out after combing her fingers through it. "It's hell getting old. All of that responsibility just isn't right."

Polly parked and jumped out of the truck. She met Sal on the sidewalk and as they walked, Sal hooked her arm through Polly's. "Do you ever think about how different our lives are now? It's only been a couple of years, but we're both married and living in Iowa. I have a baby, you've adopted two kids. We have dogs and houses. What happened to us?"

"I don't know," Polly said. She smiled at Sal. "I'm a lot happier now than I was in Boston. And I was perfectly happy out there. Who knew that I could actually step it up so many notches?"

"That's exactly how it feels. Some nights I wake up to take care of Alexander and I know I should be mad because I'm not getting enough sleep, but then he smiles at me and I wonder how lucky a girl has to be to have all of this joy in her life."

"Pretty lucky." Polly put her hand on the handle to the pizza shop, and Sal put her hand on the door above Polly's head to let Polly go in first.

"Surprise!" The room erupted with 'Happy Birthdays' and more 'Surprises.' Polly looked around in astonishment. Pizzazz was filled with her friends. Henry, Hayden, Heath, and Rebecca stood close to the door with immense grins on their faces.

"How did?" Polly stammered. "What did? How? When? Is that what the weird texting was?"

Henry nodded. "I was telling Sal to call you. We wanted it to happen at the last minute so you wouldn't come up with some other strange plan and not give us time to get up here."

"And your laundry?" Polly asked Rebecca.

"I had to divert your attention from Henry. As soon as it was out of my mouth, I realized how stupid it sounded." Rebecca giggled. "When do I ever volunteer to do laundry?"

"I know!" Polly said with a laugh. She stepped on into the room and shook her head at the number of people that had gathered. Even Jean and Sam Gardner were there with his brother, Simon, from the antique store. Eliseo stood at the back with Sylvie and Ralph Bedford. His sister, Elva, and her four children were at the table near him; the youngest, Matty, standing close to Mr. Bedford, trying to get his attention. The older man bent over and lifted the child up so he could stand on a chair and see the action. Matty kept his hand in Mr. Bedford's. Just the sweetest thing ever.

"Come on in, dear," Lydia said. "You have all night to make your rounds of the room. If we missed anyone, I'm terribly sorry. We tried to think of everybody that you might like to have here tonight."

"Who did this?" Polly asked. "You?"

"Henry and I have been talking about something all month, but Sylvie said that you never miss a Sunday night and no matter what, you'd be here. Even if you found another body."

"No more bodies," Aaron said, standing beside his wife. "One is more than enough. After this summer's spate, Polly can slow down for a while."

"I agree," Polly said.

"Your attention! Everyone! Attention, please!" Beryl wasn't getting the room to quiet down, so she stepped up onto a chair next to Aaron, put her hand on his shoulder for stability and yelled. "Hey! Shut up!"

In a split second, the room quieted and Beryl looked down at Polly. "Did you want to say something? I have their attention."

Polly laughed. "No. I didn't know I was supposed to talk."

"You aren't. I was just checking." Beryl grinned, then turned back to the group in front of her. "So that you can leave when you want, we're going to embarrass Polly by singing to her now and giving her the cake. Dylan will cut it and you can have cake before you eat supper, instead of supper, or in spite of supper. There's plenty. Our Sylvie made sure of that. So, Master Jeff, will you lead us in song? Are you ready? Uh-one. Uh-two. Uh-three."

Jeff Lyndsay gave Beryl a strange look, laughed and then began singing, "Happy Birthday to you. Happy Birthday to you. Happy Birthday, dear Polly. Happy Birthday to you."

A much smaller voice rang out with "And many more." Polly looked for its source and laughed at Andrew, who made a sweeping bow to her.

"We told them no presents," Lydia said. "I hope that's okay."

"Thank you," Polly replied. "I'm so glad."

Beryl clambered back to the floor, leaning on Aaron the entire time. "But that doesn't mean us. We're doing lunch this week to celebrate."

Polly nodded.

"No arguments either," Beryl said. "Or there'll be trouble. Big trouble."

"Got it."

Jessie and Molly made their way to Polly. "We can't stay, but I wanted to tell you Happy Birthday."

"Did you stop over to see Bill and Marie?" Polly asked.

"No. I'm a little worried about tomorrow with Molly, but Marie insisted that it would be okay. She says Lonnie will be there, too. Molly loves Lonnie."

Polly nodded and gave Jessie a hug. "Marie would tell you if it was too much trouble. Trust her to know what she can handle."

"Okay. Thanks." Jessie knelt down beside her daughter. "Tell Polly Happy Birthday, Molly."

"Happy Birthday," the little girl said, clear as a bell. She looked back toward the kitchen. "Cake, Mommy?"

"We have treats at home. No cake for the little girl tonight." Jessie smiled at Polly. "Happy Birthday again."

Polly watched them walk out. She hadn't had a chance to see the cake yet, though she was certain Rebecca had taken a photograph of it. If she missed seeing it before it was cut into pieces, that would do.

Mark Ogden brought Alexander out to his wife, who took the little boy into her arms and smiled.

"Thought you were working tonight," Polly said.

He shrugged. "A man's gotta do what the woman tells him to do sometimes. Ain't that right, Henry?"

Henry laughed. "You just wait until you have more than one woman in the house. Between Polly and Rebecca, I'm just a shadow of my former self. I've learned how to say 'yes ma'am' before they're even finished with their commands."

Rebecca opened her mouth to speak, but Polly took her arm and guided her away. "Sometimes they attempt humor and fail. It's not nice of us to point it out to them."

"Can I go sit with Andrew now?" Rebecca asked.

"Of course."

Rebecca leaned in. "This isn't our family birthday party for you. Remember that," she whispered.

"I will."

Polly was quickly gathered up in conversations around the room. It felt like everyone from Bellingwood was there.

"I'm only here for a few minutes." Elva gave Polly a quick hug. "The kids wanted to say hello and Eliseo said he'd take them home. I'm on a break from work."

"Thank you for coming over," Polly said. "It's good to see you."

Elva smiled and made her way around the milling people to the front door.

Polly nearly didn't recognize Tab Hudson out of uniform and with her hair down and loose, soft around her face.

"You're quite the celebrity," Tab said, looking around the room.

"They're just my friends," Polly replied. "I'm glad to see you actually take time off."

"The boss is pretty strict about that," Tab replied. "We take it when we can get it. Otherwise, he starts kicking us out of the office right when we're in the middle of something."

Polly shook her head. "He works all the time."

"I know. But Sheriff Merritt always says that we're better able to handle emergencies if we go home when we're supposed to. Unless," she grinned, "we're in the middle of an emergency."

"No emergencies tonight, then."

"Not yet. How's your son doing?"

"Heath?" Polly asked.

Tab nodded. "Wasn't he out of school all this week?"

"Yes. I think he's ready to go back. He's nervous, but life will go back to normal after a day or so. Have you come up with anything on the murder?"

Tab's lips thinned into a flat line. "No. And it's frustrating. We've talked to quite a few students, both past and present. There's something hinky about the way that teacher treated the pretty girls." She lifted her upper lip and rolled her eyes. "Isn't that always the way?" Then she let loose with a tight laugh. "Either you're not pretty and you're jealous that they're getting the attention, or you're one of the pretty girls who can never seem to get the right kind of attention."

"Which were you in high school?" Polly asked.

"Well, I wasn't one of the pretty ones, that's for sure. But I can't say I was all that jealous. I was too busy with my own stuff to worry about that. You were probably one of the pretty girls."

Polly shook her head. "Not really. I was just normal. Never part of the pretty-girl clique. I didn't have to worry about weird attention from boys or teachers. I suppose I was a little jealous of the girls who were always getting what they wanted, but honestly, I did my own thing. I had good friends and plenty to do, so I didn't waste much time on it."

She put her hand on Tab's arm. "You're gorgeous. You know that, don't you?"

Tab looked at her in surprise. "That's a weird thing to say."

Polly grinned. Tab Hudson really wasn't comfortable having normal conversations with people. She'd noticed the deputy's abruptness this last summer, but felt like she'd made some inroads by the time they discovered who had been murdering people to get Polly's attention. "It's not so weird," Polly said, stepping right into it. "You said that you weren't one of the pretty girls and you said it like you didn't think you would ever be one of them. But you are. You're absolutely beautiful."

"No one has ever called me beautiful," Tab replied. "Now her?" She nodded toward Sal. "She's a bombshell."

"And she knows it," Polly said. "She's my best friend from college and is completely confident in who she is. She loves turning men's heads, but the thing she adores most right now is her family. It's settled her and given new depths to that beauty."

"Her husband is that gorgeous hunk?"

"That's the one," Polly said with a laugh. "Mark Ogden. He's a veterinarian."

"Man, that's not fair."

"What? That two beautiful people found each other?"

Tab raised her eyebrows. "Exactly. Leave some for the rest of us."

Sal walked past Polly, carrying Alexander on her way to the counter. Polly grabbed her arm. "Sal, I'd like you to meet Tab Hudson. She's the deputy working on that murder case."

"It's nice to meet you," Sal said. She fumbled with her hands, while trying to balance her son. "I'm sorry. I feel like a klutz."

"That's okay," Tab said. "It's nice to meet you, too. What's his name?"

"This one?"

Tab looked around, trying to figure out who else Sal might have meant. "Yes."

"This is Alexander." Sal glanced at Polly. "Do I sound as dense as I feel?"

"Maybe a little. Tab and I were just commenting on how it wasn't fair that gorgeous you married gorgeous Mark."

"Well, if I stand here and talk to you any longer, you'll probably decide that what everyone else got in brains went into my looks." Sal narrowed her eyes. "That sounded completely egotistical. See? I can't even hold a decent conversation tonight." She held Alexander out to Polly, who hesitated for just a moment.

"Can I hold him?" Tab asked.

"I'd hate for him to mess up your blouse," Sal replied.

"But it's okay for him to mess up *my* shirt?" Polly asked. "Tonight is supposed to be my party."

Sal laughed out loud and handed Alexander to Tab. "I'm going to get some cheese bread and a coke. Maybe carbs and soda will help my brain return to normal."

She walked away and Tab nestled the little boy into her arms. "He's going to be a heart stopper. Look at those eyelashes."

"It's not fair, is it," Polly said.

"She seems like a nice lady."

"I love her."

"All of these people are your friends?" Tab looked around the room again, careful to move slowly so Alexander could see what was happening around him.

"They really are." It was hard to believe how many people Polly had become close to in just a few short years. She smiled at Tab. "You're awfully comfortable with him."

"My mother had me when she was still in high school. I was eight when she got married and eleven when she started having babies. Built in baby-sitter. That's about all I was. She had five kids after me, so I learned how to be around babies."

"I'll bet she was glad to have your help."

"I guess."

"Are you from around here?"

"My parents live up near Sioux City in a little town. I left as soon as I could and don't go back much."

That conversation was going to take longer than they had, so Polly simply nodded, reached out to touch Alexander's head and let her hand fall to touch Tab's before backing up to grin at Sal.

"Nobody has put any food or drink in your hands tonight," Sal said. "Here's an iced tea and a slice of your favorite pizza. Hurry up and jam it down before someone else comes up to talk to you. You need to keep your strength up." She looked at Alexander, who was falling asleep in Tab's arms. "Wow. You're good at that."

Tab nodded. "He's sweet. So innocent and trusting. I wish they could stay like that forever."

"Do you have children?" Sal asked.

"Just brothers and a sister," Tab replied. "They're all younger than me. I haven't held a baby in a long time, though. This is ..." She stopped to consider the word she wanted to use. "Comforting." Tab gave them a sad smile. "With all of the ugliness I see, sometimes it's nice to look at something as beautiful as a baby's face."

"Any time you want to look at this baby's face, you let me know," Sal said. She reached out to take Tab's elbow. "I'm not just saying that, either. My little prince and I spend a lot of time at the coffee shop across the street. You could get a baby fix along with your caffeine. It's a good deal."

"You don't even know me."

Sal shrugged. "I'm still getting to know people here in town. I don't have nearly the number of friends Polly has. In fact, the only reason I have any is because of her. We should be friends. Stay right here. Don't move." Sal darted off to where Mark was standing with several other people and grabbed her extra-expensive diaper bag. She came back, opened it, removed a business card holder and opened it to slide out a card. "Where can I put this?" she asked, giggling.

Tab took it from her and slid it into a pocket. "Thanks."

"I'm serious. The next time you're in Bellingwood and need a cup of coffee, call me. I'm always up for a fix."

"I might just do that," Tab said. She handed Alexander back to his mother. "Thanks for that. I should probably get going. Tomorrow morning is coming early." Without another word, she ducked through the crowd and out the front door, leaving Polly and Sal gaping after her.

"Thank you," Polly said.

"What? I just want to make friends, too."

"You know what. Thank you. That was awesome."

"And look, you didn't even have to hold the baby."

CHAPTER TWENTY-ONE

"Epic fun," Rebecca said as she and Polly walked home.

Henry and the boys needed to do something at the Bell House, so rather than making them go back home to get Henry's truck, Polly just sent them with hers. Sal had left with Mark earlier in the evening. By the time Pizzazz was ready to close, Polly, Henry, and the kids had been there with Joss and Nate Mikkels, Lydia and Beryl, and Sandy and Benji Davis.

Aaron left fairly early. The man needed his sleep. Jeff scooted out around ten o'clock. He didn't plan to be in the office tomorrow, but his weekend had already been long enough. Eliseo took off with Elva's kids around eight. Polly wanted to wring his sister's neck. Maybe she didn't know that he and Sylvie needed opportunities to be together. Whenever they were in the same room, they drifted together, but as of yet, there had been no dating. Not long after he left, Sylvie had taken off, too. That made sense. She would be up hideously early in the morning to work at the bakery. She'd left strict orders for Jason and Andrew to be home by nine thirty, which is when most of the people really started vacating the restaurant.

The cakes Sylvie baked were nearly gone, but Dylan pulled a small box out. Sylvie had decorated one in miniature for Polly, a beautiful sycamore tree with its branches reaching out over a gazebo on one side and four little horses on the other. That pretty well described the passions in Polly's life right now. Except for her kids.

"It *was* fun," Polly said to Rebecca, yawning. As they stood at the corner waiting to cross the highway into the Sycamore House parking lot, several cars filled with high schoolers roared down the highway, kids hanging out of windows and yelling. "What was that about?" Polly asked.

"I don't know. I'm not in high school."

Polly grinned at Rebecca as they hurried across to the park on the corner. "Yeah, but you know everything that's going on around here."

"It was probably just them being idiots. There's nothing going on tonight," Rebecca said.

Polly looked up at her building. They always left a light on in the living room while they were away. A warm glow filled the windows. "It is going to feel strange not to live here."

"Somebody should live upstairs," Rebecca said. "You shouldn't turn it into offices."

"Why do you say that?"

"Have you given any thought to the fact that a handicapped person can't get up there if they want to have a meeting?"

"We'd have all of the meetings down in the conference room," Polly replied.

"But what if you wanted to hire someone who used a wheel chair or had trouble walking or maybe they were blind. You wouldn't expect them to go up steps, would you?"

Polly shook her head. "You're right. I just hadn't thought of it. But why are you thinking about this?"

"There's a new girl in my class. Her name is Janna. She's in a wheelchair. She can do a lot of things, but she can't do stairs. Janna is really smart and shouldn't be stopped from getting a great job because she can't negotiate stairs."

They'd arrived at the back door beside the garage. Polly swiped her phone over the lock so it unlocked and they went in. They walked on into the storage room in silence.

As Rebecca put her hand on the door to go upstairs, Polly stopped her. "I feel guilty for not thinking about this myself, but you're right."

Rebecca put her hand out and rubbed her fingers with her thumb. "I should be paid for all of my good ideas. Don't you think?"

"Go on upstairs and send the dogs down," Polly said with a laugh. "By the way, who do you think should live in the apartment after we leave?"

"I haven't figured that out yet." Rebecca slipped past Obiwan and Han, who barreled down the stairs. "But I'm working on it."

Polly shook her head and let the dogs out into the back yard. She leaned against the door frame as they ran across the yard, yipping and chasing each other in their excitement at being outside. Life was so simple for those animals. They loved their people, they loved their food and playtime, and they loved to sleep. Everything else was just icing on their cake.

Sirens sounded and Polly stepped out onto her driveway to see what was happening. Two sheriff's vehicles drove past and just as she was turning to head back to the safety of her doorway, the ambulance and another emergency vehicle followed.

"I hope it wasn't those kids," Polly said, but she didn't hold out much hope. They'd been going far too fast. The road was a straight run over to Highway 17, but anything could happen.

Obiwan barked twice and Polly turned to see what he was doing. This was different than his usual yipping and yapping conversational noises. "What's up?" she called out.

He barked again, a sharp sound that had her moving toward him and Han. "Please no body, please no body," she whispered as she picked up the pace into a trot.

The dogs were on the north edge of the lot, near the highway. When Polly arrived, Obiwan whined and looked up at her. Han was pacing back and forth.

"What did you find, boys?" she asked and moved so she wasn't creating a shadow from the street light. Down in the creek bed she saw something move. "It's not a body," she muttered. "Now please don't let it be a skunk or a raccoon or something I don't want to deal with tonight." She put her hand on Obiwan's head. "You wouldn't bring me over here for a raccoon or possum, would you?"

He whined again and scrambled down the embankment to stand over whatever it was he'd found. "Okay," Polly said. "I'm coming." She didn't usually like to go down into the creek bed from this position, the bank was shorter to the south, but Obiwan didn't want to wait, so she grabbed a young tree, apologized for making its life miserable and slid down to Obiwan, making a muddy mess of her pants. "What did you find?"

Polly bent over and discovered a worn-out mama cat with four newborn kittens tucked in around her. She looked up toward the highway and saw a cardboard box that had been tossed into the creek bed, tipped on its side, the flaps pushed open from the inside.

The cat didn't have the energy to hiss or bat at Polly. "I'm so sorry, mama," Polly said. "You shouldn't have to be out here alone like this." Something glinted in the light and she realized that the cat wore a collar. "Are you freakin' kidding me?" Polly asked. "Someone dumped you because you were pregnant? It was their fault you hadn't been spayed. Damn it. Well, you managed to land in just the right place, but I have to go get something to carry you back to the house, okay?"

She took a look at the bank and cringed. She could climb up, but it would play havoc with the knees of her pants. "Obiwan, stay here with her. I'm going to get a crate and some blankets. I'll be right back."

The dog sat down beside the little family and gave a little yap.

"Yes," Polly said. "You know I'll be back. Tell her that she's safe now." She didn't want to make the climb, so she ran to the shallow bank and climbed up and ran over to the garage. There had to be a box in here. Then she had a thought and ran upstairs.

"What happened to you?" Rebecca asked when Polly walked into the media room.

"Obiwan found a cat and her new baby kittens down in the creek bed. I'm going to get some towels and a laundry basket to put them in."

"Are you bringing them up here?"

Polly looked at her. "What do you think?"

"I get to have kittens in my room."

"You want them? You'll have to clean out the mama's litter box and make sure she's got food and water."

"I can do that. I promise. Isn't there another litter box down in the garage?"

Polly nodded.

"I'm coming with you," Rebecca said. "And I'm keeping one of the kittens. Deal?"

"We'll talk about it later. For now, I just want them to be safe."

The two went back outside and Rebecca followed Polly down into the creek bed. As they walked over to where Obiwan sat waiting, Rebecca took Polly's hand. "I have the strangest life with you," she said. "There's always something going on."

"Yes there is," Polly said, chuckling. "Let's see what we can do about this something tonight." She put the basket on the ground beside the mother cat and arranged the towels in it, making sure to bring them up and over the sides to cover the holes. "Which first?" she asked. "The mama or the kittens?"

"Will she let you pick her up?" Rebecca asked.

"That's what I have this towel for." Polly decided to try the 'mom' pinch on the cat's neck and it worked like a charm. The cat went limp and allowed Polly to put her into the basket, but immediately attempted to climb back out until Rebecca put the first kitten in beside her. They carefully picked up the others and before long, all five cats were in the basket, the mama nestling her babies close to her.

"They're so little," Rebecca whispered.

Polly nodded. "She can't have been here very long. Obiwan would have told us."

"She's wearing a collar." Rebecca glared at Polly. "She was someone's pet."

"I know. But we're not worrying about that tonight. We need to get her upstairs and make sure she has plenty of food and water. She'll take care of the rest." Polly picked up the basket and felt tears rise. She was so thankful to have been around tonight to find this little girl.

"An extra treat for you two," Polly said, patting Obiwan's head again as they walked back to where it was easiest to climb up the bank.

Rebecca went up first and took the basket from Polly. The dogs scrambled to follow them back to the garage. Headlights turned into the driveway and Polly pressed the button to open the garage door for Henry.

"I think the litter box is back here," Rebecca said, searching on a set of shelves Henry had built for storage.

Henry drove into the garage and turned the truck off. "What are you two doing?" he asked, after stepping down to the floor. Heath and Hayden both climbed out.

"Rescuing kittens," Rebecca said. "Have you seen an extra litter box around here?"

"You're what?" Henry strode over to see what Polly had in her arms. "She's not kidding."

"Nope. Obiwan found them down in the creek." Polly touched the collar on the mama cat. "Someone abandoned her when she needed them the most."

He snarled. "Why would you even want to have a pet if you refuse to take care of them for life? That's ridiculous. So now we have ..." he peered in and using his index finger, counted heads. "We have five more cats in our house?"

"For a while," Polly said. "We'll find them homes."

"I want one of the kittens," Rebecca piped up. "Is no one going to help me find that litter box?"

Hayden crossed to where she was looking around. He turned back to Polly and Henry and with a laugh, picked up the litter box sitting right in front of Rebecca. "This litter box?"

She grabbed it out of his hands. "Shut up."

"Can I help it if you're blind?"

"I'm not blind. I was just distracted."

"Use whatever words you need to make you feel better about standing right in front of it," he replied.

"What did you guys do over at the Bell House?" Polly asked.

"Jerry caught me tonight and told me that he's going to be in there tomorrow morning. I had some extra cord and boxes from another job, so I wanted to put them inside for him." He took the basket from Polly's arms. "He's wiring for the furnaces this week, too. We might make it into the main level by Christmas if this keeps up."

She held the door while everyone tromped up the steps, then ran back to bring the garage door down and make sure everything was locked up and lights were off. By the time Polly got up to the apartment, her family was all sitting on the floor in the kitchen as Rebecca put a dish of water into the basket beside the mama cat.

"The cat is going to need a name," Polly said.

Heath looked up. "So do the kittens."

Polly chuckled. "We're going to want to wait a while for that. You'll never be able to tell what their sex is right now."

"Wonder Woman," Rebecca said, tentatively reaching in. She let the cat sniff her hand and then the water. When the cat didn't drink right away, Rebecca looked up, concerned.

"It's okay," Polly said. "She's had a lot happen to her today. Give her time. Why Wonder Woman?"

"Look what she did," Rebecca said. "And the little orange cat we should name Flash. The grey one could be Arrow and those two could be Batman and Robin."

"You've been watching too much television," Heath said.

"If you give them powerful names, they'll live powerful lives," Rebecca retorted. She put her hand back into the basket and when the mama cat didn't flinch, stroked the cat's head and down its back. "She let me pet her and I think she's purring."

Polly backed up, nearly tripping over Luke, who was in his loaf-cat form. This was the shape he took when he wanted to be alert, but unobtrusive. He knew something was going on, but wasn't quite sure how it was going to impact his life. She looked around for Leia and realized that the cat was on the peninsula looking down at the tableau on the floor.

"Our other cats are quite interested in what's happening here," Polly said. She reached over to pet Leia, but got a hiss instead. "Why don't you take the new cats into Rebecca's room? I'll bring in supplies for tonight."

Hayden picked up the basket after Rebecca removed the water dish and then followed the girl into her room. Luke refused to move, so everyone just stepped around him.

"What are you going to do with them during the day?" Henry asked.

Polly shook her head. "They'll be fine in Rebecca's room with the door closed. She hasn't had enough time to completely return it to chaos, so hopefully the cat won't get lost in all of her clutter." She pulled the bag of litter out and handed it to Henry. "Do you mind carrying that in for me? I'm going to give Luke and Leia some treats and see if I can make them happy again."

Heath was staring at his phone, shaking his head.

"What's going on, Heath?" Henry asked.

"There was a wreck out on the highway. Five kids are going to the hospital. Nobody died, though." He looked up at Polly. "It was a good thing you were finding baby kittens, I guess."

"Stop that," she said. "I wonder if it had anything to do with those two cars of kids that went tearing through town when Rebecca and I were coming home from the party tonight. Anyone you know well?"

"Jose," he replied, not looking up from his phone. "You know, the one who came with Bailey and Allie? He's in the worst shape. I'm surprised they weren't with him. He's dating Allie."

Polly walked over and put her arm around him. "I'm sorry."

"Can I take my phone to my room with me for a while?"

"You bet. Let me know what's going on."

He glanced at her in surprise. "You want to know?"

"Of course I do. They're your friends. Why don't you call

Allie?" Then Polly looked at the clock on the wall and realized that it was after nine thirty. "No. Don't do that. But text her. Make sure she's doing okay."

"Thanks." He walked out and headed for his bedroom.

"Oh, I'm just ill," Polly said quietly to Henry. "What if Heath had been with those kids?"

"He wasn't. He's home and safe." Henry grinned. "Remember how you tell all of us to not let those kinds of thoughts overwhelm what really happened? Huh? Huh?"

Polly swatted at him. "Leave me alone. Okay. I'll be good." She opened the cupboard door and took out the bag of cat treats, opened it and gave a few to both of her cats. Neither acted as if they cared, but ate them up in a hurry. She scooped some cat food into a dish, then took two cans of wet cat food off the top shelf. Rebecca would enjoy pampering Wonder, if that was the name the girl decided to keep for the cat. Henry had been in enough of a shock that this horrible thing had happened to the cat, he really hadn't made much noise about them all coming into the house. Polly wondered how long that would last. He also hadn't reacted when Rebecca said she wanted to keep one of the kittens. Polly chuckled. That poor man just held on for dear life some days in this household. Maybe Bill Sturtz would like a kitten around to keep him company. They'd be just about ready to wean when he was getting back to his regular life.

Henry hadn't said much about the afternoon's visit to see Bill and Marie. And nobody was talking about the future yet. Polly couldn't imagine that Bill would want to quit working. He had too much fun and the man would go out of his mind if he had to sit still. For that matter, Marie would lose *her* mind if her husband was hanging around the house all day with nothing to do.

She reached back in and took a couple of dog treats out and dropped them to the floor. "I forgot, didn't I? You two are always in the present. Not worried about what tomorrow will bring and never fretting over yesterday. Sometimes I wish I was more like you."

CHAPTER TWENTY-TWO

Although she was in a new home, Wonder had done well in Rebecca's room overnight. She seemed grateful for a safe place to care for her babies. Rebecca had been very excited to discover that Wonder used the litter box and ate the kibble they'd left for her.

Polly sent in another can of wet food to feed the mama cat and Rebecca cleaned out the litter box on her own. No one expected that to last very long, but for now, Rebecca had certainly taken charge of the new family in the house.

Wonder didn't look to be very old herself. Polly would make a call to Marnie at Doc Ogden's office later today to ask about what they needed to do to ensure this litter stayed healthy. They'd spend the day shut in Rebecca's room, away from the other animals. Rebecca made sure they had everything they might need.

After breakfast and one last check of Wonder and the kittens, Polly followed Hayden and Rebecca down the back steps. The girl loved having Hayden drop her off at school. It made her feel important. Even though Polly was leaving the house at the same time, Rebecca made her preference known. Handsome older brother would win every single time.

No matter. That just gave Polly a few extra minutes to spend at Sweet Beans before Ken Wallers arrived with his posse. She pulled into a parking space and headed inside, to be greeted by Camille.

"Iced or hot?" Camille asked.

"Make it iced. This heat is never going to release us."

"It sure is hanging on," Camille agreed. She smiled at a woman who came out from the bakery in the back, carrying a tray of sweet treats for the display.

The woman glanced up at Polly. "How are you?" she asked.

"I'm good." Polly walked over to see what she'd brought out. "What's that one?" she asked, pointing at a muffin.

"Banana walnut. It's pretty wonderful."

"I'll have one of those, too," Polly said to Camille. When the woman had emptied the tray, Polly put her hand out. "I don't think I've met you. I'm Polly Giller."

"I know who you are," the woman said, shaking Polly's hand, a huge smile on her face. "I'm Marta Reynolds. I've been following your career since you moved to town. I've been to quite a few of the events over at Sycamore House. You put on some terrific affairs. My friends and I still talk about the barn raising and hoedown and then those gorgeous horses you rescued. You certainly have made Bellingwood a fun place to be."

Polly looked up at Sylvie who had come out with another tray.

"Good," Sylvie said. "You've met Marta. She's been training with me for the last week, and today she started working here full-time. She's a god-send."

"It's a good thing there's a coffee shop here," Marta said. "These early hours require a lot of caffeine for me to be a god-send."

Sylvie chuckled. "If you'd go to bed at a reasonable hour, you'd be in better shape." She looked at Polly. "Marta keeps telling me that her cats keep her up. I think it's all of that partying she does."

The woman shook her head and smiled, then pushed her glasses a little higher on her nose. "I need someone around to keep me off the streets, you know." She nodded at Polly. "It's nice to meet you, though. I feel as if I've known you forever, but it's good to shake your hand."

Sylvie put her hand on Marta's back as the two women walked around the corner to the kitchen.

"I didn't know Sylvie finally hired someone," Polly said to Camille.

"It was out of the blue. She'd been bringing in young people from the community college in Boone, but they were all temporary. One day a couple of weeks ago, Marta applied for a job. Jeff interviewed her and brought her right up to meet Sylvie. It could have gone either way between here or Sycamore House. She fits in really well." Camille grinned. "And she's a worse caffeine addict than nearly anyone..." She pushed Polly's coffee across the counter at her. "...except maybe you. I hope she'll give Sylvie a little more freedom. She's as steady as they come and that's what Sylvie needs. Marta says she wants to learn the front counter, too. Like Sylvie will let her have time for that, but we'll see. The woman's a bundle of energy."

"I'm really glad." Polly picked up her coffee and muffin, and headed for a table near the front door. She looked up and smiled at a group of women coming in the front door, then sat down and pulled a long drink of coffee through the straw. No matter what coffee she made at home, it was never as good as what she could get at Sweet Beans. That made no sense to her, but after another long drink, she decided she didn't care.

The door opened again and Simon Gardner walked in. He caught Polly's eye and sat down at the table with her.

"My old knees are aching something fierce today," he said. "The weather must be about to make a big transition."

Polly looked up. "Fall? Are we finally going to see cooler days?"

"I don't know about that. It's probably just another storm." He rubbed his right knee. "I left early, thinking it was going to take me a long time to limp my way up here. It wasn't as bad as I thought."

"Let me get something for you to drink," Polly said, standing up. "I'm having a banana walnut muffin. Will you join me? They're just fresh."

"No, no, no," he protested. "I can get my own tea."

Polly scowled at him and he leaned back away from her.

"Okay, okay. You're frightening when you look that way, young lady."

"Good. What would you like to drink?"

"They have an Irish breakfast tea back there. Ask the young lady for that. She knows just what I like."

Polly nodded and walked back to the counter, waiting behind the women who were oohing and aahing over the goodies in the glass front case.

"Did you forget something?" Camille asked, stepping away from the case. The women were in no hurry to make a decision.

"Mr. Gardner says you have an Irish breakfast tea that he likes. And another of those banana walnut muffins." Polly looked back at her table. "Why don't I get three more of those."

"Can you wait for me to bring it over to you?"

"We're in no hurry," Polly replied. "Can I help you?"

Camille glanced at the women who were chattering and pointing. "No. I'm fine."

"What is this one?" a woman asked, pointing at a plate.

"Go. I'm good," Polly said as Camille turned away. She went back to the table and sat down. "Camille said she'd bring your tea out."

"She's a gem, that one," he said. "Word is you've found some more interesting tidbits at the old house. What made you look around for that symbol?"

Polly opened her phone and flipped through the pictures until she came to the photo of the symbol painted on the ceiling of the foyer. "This. Why would someone paint it in such a strange place?"

He shook his head. "But how did you discover the others?"

"Hayden said he thought he'd seen something like it in one of the rooms, so I went through each of them. Of course I don't know what might be upstairs. We haven't torn into any of those walls."

"Now, what makes you think it is something other than the mark of the craftsman who built the home?"

"It could be," Polly said with a shrug. "But it doesn't feel like that."

He chuckled. "What does it feel like?"

"A mystery."

"You're known for those. Let's hope that you find no dead bodies along the way. I'd hate to think that my father was part of something nefarious." He furrowed his brow. "But if he had been, it wouldn't surprise me."

"Why do you say that?" she asked.

"There was always something about my father that was a secret. He and Mother never spoke of it, but conversations would stop and start whenever we walked into the room. I put it down to adult issues that children shouldn't be part of. But Mother was never happy when they spoke of those things."

"And you've never discovered anything about those things?"

"Secrets," he said with a sad smile. "Everyone has them. So many secrets die with each generation. In many ways that's as it should be, but when our curiosity is piqued, it can be frustrating."

"I can't imagine how much you see of that in your business."

"Old photographs make my heart ache the most. Families around the world might better know their histories if they had those photos in their hands. Lost stories and tales. A smiling woman and her boy. Did the father take the photograph or was it taken by a professional to send to her husband who was fighting in a war? Wedding photographs. You know that they are more than likely ancestors of people who would love to see the similarities, but they never will. I consider those old photos to be the biggest tragedy in my shop. I will never find their homes and no one wants them, so they languish."

Camille stopped in front of him, holding a tray. "Your tea, Mr. Gardner."

"Will you ever call me Simon?"

"I will continue to try, but I may not succeed." She put the tea down on the table and a plate of muffins in front of Polly. Taking a stack of napkins from her apron, she placed those beside the muffins. "Let me know if I can get anything else for you."

"Thank you, sweet girl," he said.

She smiled and walked away.

"You're a flirt," Polly said.

"Unrepentant."

"Good morning, Mr. Gardner," Ken Wallers said as he placed his hand on Simon's back. "I would have picked you up."

"It's good for me to be out and about," Simon said. "Even when my knees complain. He gave Ken a wicked grin. "Would you have put me in the back seat and run your siren?"

Ken laughed. "If you wanted me to."

Simon looked at Polly. "Wouldn't that be a sight? Me in the back seat of the police chief's car with my face pressed to the glass, pleading with someone to rescue me."

"Your brother would be mortified," Polly said.

"Then we should do it as soon as possible," he replied. He nodded at the plate of muffins. "Polly bought treats for us. All you need is coffee."

"I'm about to get that," Ken said. "Can I buy anyone a refill?"

Polly shook her head and Simon chuckled as he lifted his still-full mug to his lips.

The doorbell rang again and Paul Bradford walked into the shop. "Hey old man," he said, stopping beside Simon. "You aren't supposed to wander off without me."

Simon rolled his eyes. "They worry about me too much."

"You bet I do. My wife would be destroyed if something happened to you. Some days I think she likes you better than she does me."

"Some days I'm nicer to her than you are," Simon retorted. "Just like this here. I'm a grown man and can take care of myself. I lived a long time before you were even a twinkle in your mother's eye, Paul Bradford. I can walk to the coffee shop by myself."

"Grown man," Paul muttered. "You're going to give me palpitations." He walked away and up to the front counter.

"I'm probably a little hard on him," Simon said. "But that man and his wife think they need to take care of me. Do you know how many times last month I had dinner at their house?"

Polly laughed. "The horrors."

"You're not being very sympathetic, little missy," Simon said, wagging his finger at her. He leaned forward and spoke in low tones. "Sometimes it's frustrating when young people think that because I don't get around so well, I'm incapable of caring for myself. I'm fairly certain that Lisa Bradford believes I exist on TV dinners and out of date cereal. She probably worries that I'll forget I turned the stovetop on and fall asleep in my overstuffed chair with a blanket falling off my lap and drool running out of my mouth."

Polly laughed out loud at the image he described. "That's not true?" she asked.

"The overstuffed chair, the nap and the blanket are real, but I don't drool. At least not often. And I enjoy cooking. Very much. One of these days I should write a cookbook for older single men. Delicious dinners for one are not that easy to create. There were many years that I lamented every garbage day because I knew I had to throw away food I'd spent good money on. It was just too much. Why they don't sell fresh vegetables in smaller quantities so one person can eat a healthy meal, I'll never understand." He huffed a laugh. "Oh, I understand. They make more money when I throw food away, but it's so wasteful."

Ken and Paul sat down across the table and Polly pushed the plate of muffins toward them. "Have you discovered anything more about the items I found in the tally boards at the Bell House?" she asked.

Paul dipped his head. "I'm ashamed to admit that I forgot about it until Ken called this morning. We had a busy weekend."

"You know I was out of town this weekend," Ken said. "I was going to call Margie Deacon this afternoon or tomorrow morning."

Polly felt her frustration rising. This reminded her of staff meetings back at the library in Boston. A whole lot of meeting without much substance. If these men just wanted to get together and have coffee, that was fine, but she'd hoped for more than that this morning. Then she scolded herself internally. It wasn't like she had that much to do, but still.

"Margie Deacon is dead," Simon said flatly. "A year ago."

Ken frowned. "Dead? I didn't know that."

Simon shrugged. "I received a few of her things. A few kids and grandkids came to pick over her belongings, but most of it went up on auction."

"What about all of the Bellingwood history she collected?" Ken sounded panicked.

"Now, now, don't worry," Simon said, patting the younger man's back. "It ended up at the library. In fact, boxes and boxes of documents from her house ended up over there. I'm afraid that I had totally forgotten about them and I suspect that young Joss hasn't given them much thought. Margie had her own sense of organization and it didn't much agree with the rest of the world."

"Where at the library?" Polly asked.

"You could ask your friend, Joss, to be sure, but as I recall, it ended up down in the catacombs." He winked at them. "That's what I call them. There are shelves and shelves of things hidden down there. No one has taken the time to put any organization to the mess as far as I know."

"She died," Ken muttered. "How did I miss that?"

Polly closed her eyes and sighed. Someone was going to have to dig through boxes in the library's basement and she did not want that to be her. She wouldn't even begin to know where to look.

"Do you have any way of telling me how to find Margie Deacon's records?" Polly asked. "How many boxes were there?"

Simon shook his head. "I wasn't involved. One of her children packed everything up that looked like it was historical and unloaded it on the library. I know they found whatever they could for the celebration this summer, but I don't think the committee worked very hard on digging any deeper than just re-using information from the centennial fifty years ago." He glared around the table. "It was a great celebration, but they worked harder on the parties than they did the history as far as I'm concerned."

Ken laughed. "Old news, old man. Those protests of yours didn't accomplish much last spring and now it's too late."

Simon looked sideways at Polly. "Do you see the lack of respect I get around here?"

"Not getting in the middle of this one," she said, then turned to Paul Bradford. "You're awfully quiet."

"What?" He looked up, startled. "Oh, I wasn't paying any attention." Paul pointed at the picture of the symbol he had on his phone. "I've seen this before, but I don't know where. It's been a long time ago, though." He turned the phone so Simon could look at it. "Are you sure you haven't seen it anywhere?"

"No," Simon replied, shaking his head. "It isn't familiar to me, but that doesn't mean much. I'm old and senile, you know."

Paul laughed. "Stop it. You know we care about you. You're the last person I would consider senile."

"But you consider me to be old?"

Polly watched Simon's eyes and caught the twinkle in them as he pushed Paul Bradford's buttons like a skilled master.

"You're my dad's age if he was alive. Yeah. You're old. Not as old as dirt, but maybe as its younger, more interesting cousin."

"I see, so I'm young dirt."

Paul had still been concentrating on the image in front of him. He looked up and frowned. "What? That's not what I meant."

"Maybe you should pay attention to conversations occurring around you," Simon said. "Especially when you're involved."

"What did I do to deserve this?" Paul asked with a laugh, looking for help from Polly and Ken.

"You scolded me for not being at the store when you arrived," Simon said. "I'm not used to being scolded by young upstarts."

Paul lifted his eyebrows in mock shame. "I'll be better, sir. I promise. Will you forgive me?"

"Only if you and your lovely wife accept my offer of dinner in my home," Simon said. "It is time I return the gesture and I'd enjoy cooking for more than just myself."

"That would be fine," Paul said. He turned the phone toward Ken. "You've never seen this in any of your grandfather's things?"

Ken shook his head. "Nope. You're going to have to find it down deep in your own memory, I'm afraid."

"So," Polly said, waiting until she had their attention. "I don't want to be the one who has to dig through boxes of dusty papers in the basement of the library."

"But it's your house. Your mystery," Paul said.

"These people are your ancestors," she protested. "It's your mystery too."

Ken put his hands up. "Talk to your friend, Joss, and see what she knows about Margie Deacon's inventory. We'll find people to help you go through it." He reached for a muffin. "Now enough of this talk. Who's going to win the football game Friday night? I think we have a real chance at going to state this year."

Polly tuned him out. This was what it sounded like at her house. She was already contemplating the trek down into the warrens beneath the library. How bad could it be?

CHAPTER TWENTY-THREE

The new cat and her kittens were in Rebecca's room with the three kids. Polly had purchased a scale so the kids could weigh them and keep track of their growth. Rebecca was ecstatic at having something productive to do. She'd cleaned and replaced the bedding in the basket and in her frenzy of activity had even put many of her own things away.

The conversation with Marnie had gone as expected. There hadn't been any calls about a missing cat, but when Wonder was stronger and the kittens a little older, they'd check for a chip just to make sure. Marnie told Polly to keep an eye on things for the first couple of weeks. As long as the kittens were growing every day, that meant they were getting nourishment from their mother. Wonder would take care of everything else. Cats had been doing this since the dawn of time.

That made Polly smile. Birth and death were such natural processes and yet people spent so much time preparing for and then dealing with the aftermath of each. Joy and grief, life and death - all so inevitable.

She was thankful that Bill Sturtz was home and doing well.

Marie wasn't letting him out of the house yet. He kept trying to come up with excuses to go over to the shop, but she wasn't ready to let him leave her sight.

Lonnie was staying in town for the week. They'd come too close again to losing Bill and she wasn't ready to leave. Henry hovered as much as he dared. He'd gone over for lunch and stayed until Marie told him to go back to work. Even Hayden had gone by to check before leaving for class this morning. He'd called Polly to say that he was going to take supper in to them before heading to the Bell House to work.

Polly patted at the piles of paper and envelopes on her desk when she heard the phone ringing. Luke jumped up from his perch in the middle of everything. He and Leia knew something was happening in Rebecca's room. They prowled around her doorway, then skittered away whenever it was opened. The dogs wanted to be involved and it was quite a heroic feat for anyone who tried to enter that room to do so without falling over a canine interloper.

Once Luke was gone, Polly's phone became visible and she saw that it was a call from Heath. "What's up?"

"I need some help. Something's wrong with the truck and Henry asked if I could call you. I've called for a tow, but I need to get this tile to Leroy before tomorrow morning."

"Sure," she said. "I'll leave right now. Where am I going?"

He gave her quick directions to a road west of Boone and Polly slipped her feet back into the shoes she'd parked under the desk. She went over to Rebecca's room and knocked on the door.

"Hey guys," she said. "I need to go get Heath. His truck broke down. I don't know how long I'll be gone. You okay in there?"

Rebecca opened the door and peeked at Polly, then slid out, pushing Han's nose away from the door. "We're doing our homework in here so we can watch the cats. That's okay, right?"

Polly shrugged. "As long as you get the work done. You are getting the work done, aren't you?"

"Of course we are. Wonder is sleeping right now anyway. I started a chart for each of the kittens. We're going to write in it every day and we're going to take their picture every day, too." Rebecca held up her phone and swiped through a picture of each kitten. "So we can see how they grow. Isn't that awesome?"

"It's great," Polly said. "Too bad you can't turn this into a project for one of your classes."

Rebecca looked at her in awe. "That's a great idea. I'm going to tell Andrew and Kayla about it. We should totally do that. Maybe even extra credit if we do a good job."

"Go for it," Polly said with a laugh.

"You'd better hurry. You don't want Heath to think you got lost." She gave Polly a gentle nudge.

"Pushing me out?" Polly asked, walking through the media room. "You're not planning on getting into trouble around here, are you?"

"You're gone nearly every other day," Rebecca said. She followed Polly through the house and stopped at the top of the steps, her hand on Obiwan's head. "I think we've got this."

"I love you, too." Polly opened the door and ran out to her truck.

By the time she found Heath, the towing company was already there.

"Pretty sure it's the alternator," Heath said. "Going, going ... and it was gone."

Polly shook her head. "What do we need to haul?"

"Can you wait just a second?" Heath called out to the tow truck driver, who was just starting to attach chains to the truck.

"Sure," the guy said.

"Polly, can you back up to the bed of my truck?" Heath asked. "These boxes are really heavy."

She drove around and managed to back up so that he wouldn't have too far to carry things. The next thing she knew, the young tow truck driver was helping Heath as they moved what he was carrying into her truck.

Once they were finished and Heath's vehicle was up on the flat bed, she stopped the driver and gave him forty dollars.

"You don't have to, ma'am," he said, holding it in his hand.

Polly desperately wanted to take it back and tell him to never call her ma'am again, but she smiled instead and said, "We appreciate your help today. Thank you."

He tipped his hat and climbed up into the cab and drove away.

"That was pretty cool of him," Heath said. "I wouldn't have thought to tip him."

"It's just one of those things Dad taught me. It never hurts to give people a little something extra to say thank you. Why wouldn't you put a smile on their face if you can?"

He nodded and walked toward the passenger side of the truck.

"You should drive," Polly said. "You know where we're going. I don't."

"Really?"

"I let you drive into Ames when I barely knew you." Polly started to toss the keys to him and he stopped her.

"I got it," he said, jogging to meet her. He put his hand out for her to drop the keys into it. "This is easier than chasing them into the ditch."

"Do we have time for an ice cream cone at Dairy Queen?" Polly asked, ignoring the dig. "Or are you going to be late?"

"We have plenty of time. I just need to unload these so they can start tomorrow morning. No big deal. I can even take you home and then go deliver them."

"I'm in no hurry. But I want ice cream."

He pressed the button to turn the truck on and then looked at Polly, biting his lower lip. "You're not in a hurry?"

She shook her head. "No. I'm good."

"Do you mind if I go look at something first?"

"Okay. What are we going to look at?"

Heath grasped the steering wheel with both hands and continued to chew on his lower lip. "I asked some of the right people a few questions today."

"What questions?"

"I think I know where Mr. West was cooking meth."

Polly clenched her hands into fists. "No, Heath. We're not doing that. We'll call Aaron and tell him."

"But it's right out here. I want to check before I say anything. Please? We don't have to go in. We can just drive by."

"If we just drive by, how will you know?"

"Please?"

"I should say absolutely not," Polly said. She breathed out loudly through her nose. "How far away is it?"

"A few miles. I pulled it up on my phone."

She closed her eyes, reached her left hand out and waved her pointer finger. "Just go."

"Thanks. It's no big deal. I promise."

"Uh huh. You're buying the ice cream."

Heath took one last look at his phone and drove back out onto the highway, turning south a half mile later.

"How was it going back to school today?" Polly asked.

He glanced at her. "Kinda rough. A few people asked me if I killed Mr. West. But things got better as the day went on. My friends hung out with me."

"Do they have a new teacher in that lit class?"

"Yeah. Some substitute. She doesn't know what she's doing, so class was pretty much out of control. We were just supposed to read." He shrugged. "So I read. It was weird, though."

"I'll bet," Polly said. "You know, sometimes it's hard for me to let you wade back into situations like that. Everything inside me wanted to go with you and step in front of you all day, just to make sure nobody could say something that could hurt you."

He looked over at her and smiled. "That's kinda weird, but I get it. Thanks. Nothing anybody could say today was worse than what I went through in the past. At least this time I knew I hadn't done anything wrong."

Heath laughed as he slowed for a stop sign. "Everybody wanted to talk about you finding his body, though. Now that was really weird."

"What do you mean?" Polly gripped the door handle as he skidded on loose gravel.

"Sorry." Heath brought his speed down. "Too fast. People talked about you like you're some kind of celebrity. Like you aren't my ..." He bit his lower lip again. "I don't know what to call you, so sometimes I call you my mom."

Polly felt tears well up in her eyes. Did the boy have any idea how much that touched her heart? "I'm glad you do. But I'm sorry that they think I'm a celebrity." She brushed aside the tears and laughed. "You're right. That *is* weird."

Heath turned another corner. Polly hoped he knew where he was going. She wasn't much for getting lost out in the country and always counted on her digital compass in the truck, but he kept winding and turning and turning some more until she wasn't sure where they were going to end up.

"It's back here somewhere," Heath said.

"How did you find out about this place and why couldn't the police?"

He stopped at a corner again and looked both ways, then turned to her. "Because the kids that know about it won't talk to the police. I overheard somebody talking and asked."

"So for all those people who think I'm a celebrity, don't they know that I'm always working with the sheriff? Why would they tell you anything?"

"Because I still have a reputation from hanging out with Ladd." He dipped his head in shame. "Some of the younger kids are still scared of me. I don't do anything to make them be scared. They just are." Heath put his hands on the steering wheel. "I can't wait to get out of high school and forget about that whole thing." He put the truck into park and sat back. "I don't mean that. I never want to forget what it was like, but I want to be with people who don't know me that way. They just let me be what I'm going to be and don't expect me to be who I was."

Polly put her hand on his arm. "That will be fantastic for you. But you know Henry and I don't look at you like that."

"Yes you do," he said.

"What?" Polly creased her brow in concern. "What do you mean?"

"I know you wondered what I did this time when you had to come down to the school to get me. And I get it. You were mad at me and it wasn't because I'd just done this one thing. You wondered if I was going back to who I was before. Even if it was just for a minute."

Polly nodded. "I suppose you're right. But I didn't want to believe the worst about you because I know how much you've changed. That's how I look at you now. You've changed. You still have that history, but you are building up new history with us."

"And I have a lot more to prove. I get it. But someday I will walk into a room and the people who are there won't even know that I have a past unless I tell them. And then it will just be a story they hear, not something they experienced." He turned in his seat. "I don't blame you for that. You've stood by me when nobody else would. That's important."

"Henry and I will always stand beside you." She chuckled. "Well, maybe not if you choose to go out and see that crazy aunt and uncle of yours." Then Polly smiled. "That's not true. I think Henry would like to do terrible things to them. I'd just like to find a way to arrest them and throw them in a deep dark hole for what they did to you."

"I don't get it," he said. "What did I ever do to them?"

"Sometimes people are just so broken," Polly replied. "If your mother was right and your aunt's bitterness was caused by not being able to have children, that explains a lot. She couldn't stand a family that had two happy boys."

"But wouldn't you think she'd be happy to take me in, then? I mean, I would have been their son."

"By that point, it was probably too late for her to come back from her anger and grief. And with that much pain in her heart, there was no way she was going to be capable of helping you through the grief you faced at losing your parents. You still loved them and missed them. She could have easily been jealous of how much love you had for two people who were dead."

"I wasn't easy," he said. "I didn't cry. I just sat in my room if I wasn't working for them. Sitting in their stupid living room watching television with them at night wasn't any fun. They never asked if there was something I wanted to watch." He laughed.

"When we were little, Mom couldn't wait to watch Rudolph and Frosty every year. When those shows came on, we all got in our pajamas and she brought out extra pillows and blankets. One year she even turned the heat down so the house was cold enough to pile blankets on top of us. She made hot chocolate and Dad made popcorn. Then we watched the movies and Mom sang along to all the songs. She even bought the CD. We played it all the time. Rudolph was her favorite."

"I loved it too," Polly said. "I wish you would have said something. We'd watch it together. Who hates Rudolph?"

"I didn't even think about it until after Christmas," Heath replied.

"Would you like to watch it as a family this year or would that be too difficult?"

He shrugged. "I think it would be fun. But it has to be really cold outside and we have to have lots of blankets."

"I have the blankets," Polly said. "I can't guarantee the cold, but we'll see what we can do. Are you a fan of *It's a Wonderful Life*?"

"Mom liked it. Dad didn't. He said it was sappy."

"It is," Polly said with a laugh. "All of those Christmas shows are sappy. That's what's so terrific about them. But we'll start with Rudolph and Frosty and go from there."

"Cool." Heath pointed to the left. "The house should be a mile down that way. There isn't any traffic, so we'll be the only car that goes by. I just want to find out if there's anything there."

Polly pointed. "Onward. As long as you don't pull in and don't run into the ditch or drop me off somewhere ..."

"So you can find a dead body?"

"No dead bodies. Okay?"

He chuckled.

"I mean it," Polly said. "I'll never go anywhere like this with you again if you do that to me."

"Like I can do anything about it?"

"We're taking a risk just coming out here into the boondocks," she said. "Rebecca would warn both of us that this is prime territory for something to happen."

"Just a drive-by. I'll go slow enough and you look really hard."

"Anything I should be looking for?"

"Just tell me what cars you see."

Polly put her hand on his arm. "I'm terrible at identifying cars. Really, really bad."

"Okay then." Heath pointed at her lap. "Take out your phone and video the drive-by. If there's anything there, I can look at it later."

She sat back and grinned. "You're kind of good at this investigating thing."

"Not really. Just used to using my phone."

CHAPTER TWENTY-FOUR

"Heath, I should be driving and let you take the video," Polly said as she leaned across the seat trying to get a good angle through the window. "I can't believe we're doing this." She swatted his upper arm. "I can't believe you're doing this and I'm with you. What kind of a mom am I, anyway?"

"You're Polly. You're the best," he replied, slowing the truck as he approached the farmstead.

There wasn't any activity, but Polly had her video going, just like she was told.

"That's her car," Heath whispered. Polly tried not to laugh. The windows were up and the air conditioner was running. Nobody could hear them.

"Whose car?"

"Miss Vincent's. That's the car I saw her standing beside when she was yelling at Mr. West. If this is where the kids all say the meth house is, that means she's involved too, right?"

"Don't rush to judgment," Polly said. "Maybe she's out here for some other reason. Maybe you have the wrong house."

"I don't think so. Look at the windows."

Polly looked through her phone's camera as she videotaped the property. "What am I looking at?"

"The windows are all covered. You can't see in."

She sat back in her seat. "Heath, you need to go *now*. Get out of here. I'll call Aaron and we'll tell him what's going on here."

Just past the house was a small grove of trees. Heath pulled into a field entrance on the other side of the trees. "I'm going to turn around and we'll make one more pass. Then you can call the sheriff," he said.

"No. They'll see us."

He gave her a sideways glance. "There's black plastic across the windows so no one can see in. That means no one can see out either. It's okay."

Polly shook her head, but didn't say anything more as Heath backed out onto the road and headed back the way they'd come. She brought her phone up as surreptitiously as possible and began recording once more, then slammed her foot to the floor of the cab. "Stop," she said.

"What? Why?"

"Turn in."

"But Polly, you said ..."

"I know what I said. Just turn in."

Heath took a deep breath, slowed to a stop and pulled into the driveway.

"Over there, just past the shed." Polly pointed to where she wanted him to go and he followed her finger, then stopped the car.

"I can't believe you did that," he said. "How did you even see it?"

"This is bad," Polly said. "Really bad."

She swiped her phone app open, placed the call, and waited for the inevitable ...

"Hello Polly. Just tell me where to send my people," Aaron said with resignation.

"I don't even know," Polly replied. "I'm with Heath. He got me here."

"What did you find?"

"That other teacher. That Miss Vincent that Heath said was arguing with Mr. West. It's the same thing."

"She's naked?"

"Yes, and with a big red circle painted around her with the hash cutting across her body."

"You're sure she's dead?"

Polly watched the body for a few moments, almost willing the woman to twitch. "I think so. She's not moving. Do you want me to go look?"

"You're at a meth house. Are there a lot of cars there?"

"Just hers."

"I'm not comfortable with you being there. These people are paranoid and dangerous."

"Heath is with me."

"Are you telling me that to make me more worried or because you think he'll protect you."

"I don't know," Polly said, her voice rising as her concern grew. "What do you want me to do?"

"Let me talk to Heath. Can he tell me how you got there?"

"I don't know. Just a second." Polly handed her phone to a very worried boy in the driver's seat of her truck. "Aaron wants to talk to you."

"I'm in trouble, aren't I?" Heath asked. "I shouldn't have brought you with me. I'm sorry."

"No," Polly interrupted. "He just wants directions. I wasn't paying enough attention to be able to retrace my steps."

"Oh." Heath took the phone from her and said, "Hello, Sheriff Merritt. How can I help you?"

He listened for a moment and then said, "Yes sir. I can do that."

As Heath began to describe the circuitous route he'd taken to get to this house, Polly put her hand on the door handle and opened it, then jumped out. There, she was still safe, even though she knew better. She made her way over to the body and crossed the painted circle, feeling silly for being afraid of it. She'd read enough paranormal books to hold her breath just in case something magical was going to hold her back. When she stepped inside the circle and nothing happened, Polly giggled. She was being ridiculous. She really did want to know whether the woman was still alive. Heath hadn't mentioned that the woman had missed school today, so that meant that in just a few short hours, she'd gotten to this location and then been killed, stripped of her clothing, laid out and had a circle painted around her. Yeah. This was a really stupid idea.

But now that she was here, Polly bent over the woman and picked up her wrist, feeling for any possibility of a pulse. The woman's skin was clammy and there was no pulse. She was definitely dead.

The sound of scuffling caused Polly to jump up and spin around. Two people with black ski masks pulled down over their faces were holding shotguns as they stood in front of the house. They didn't say anything, just slowly walked toward Polly as she backed out of the circle.

"Did you do this?" she asked, pointing at the dead woman.

"Polly!" Heath yelled from the truck.

The two with the shotguns stopped in their tracks, then leaned close to each other and whispered something. They seemed to be having a fairly heated conversation. Polly wished she could hear what they were saying.

Heath had gotten out of the truck and rushed to her side. He grabbed her arm and pulled her back. "Come on, Polly. Get in the truck." He yelled out to the two holding the guns. "We're leaving. We don't know who you are, so we can't tell anyone. Just let us go. You don't want to kill us."

That they refused to speak really freaked Polly out. They were dressed so she couldn't tell if they were male or female. Rubber gloves covered their hands and each wore a loose-fitting coverall and rubber boots. They stopped at the outer edge of the circle on the other side from where Polly had entered it. Both looked down and then at each other. Even from this distance, Polly could tell that they were shaken by what they saw.

"You didn't do this, did you?" she asked.

"Polly!" Heath hissed. "We have to get out of here before they hurt us."

"No. They won't hurt us," she said and pointed back to the body. "This scared them." She looked up and put her hand out. "You know who killed this woman and who killed Mr. West, don't you?"

"Go," one of the masked figures barked.

That one spoken word wasn't enough to give Polly a clue as to the gender of the person, but she was prepared to say that it was a female.

"Polly, get in the truck. Aaron is going to kill you." Heath grabbed her arm and pulled her backwards toward him.

"We aren't leaving," she said. "I won't leave them with that body."

"Yes you will. He's on his way."

Polly yanked her arm out of his grip. "No. I won't leave and they won't shoot me." She yelled out. "Will you? You're not going to shoot us. You aren't killers."

She started back toward the circle and one of the figures brought the shotgun up and before Polly knew it, the gun had gone off and dirt and dust sprayed up from the ground beside the truck.

"Okay," Polly said. "You know how to aim and shoot. At least I hope that you were aiming for that spot and not for me and just missed."

The other figure turned and ran, stopping at the car Heath identified as Miss Vincent's. They opened the driver's side door and got in. Within seconds, the car started up and the second figure ran for the passenger side and ran up against a mass of old, rusty barbed wire fencing. The coveralls ripped and tore as the downed figure struggled against the barbs. Panicked thrashing made things much worse. Blood seeped into the fabric of the coveralls as the person struggled to regain footing. The driver of the car jumped out, picked up the shotgun, and after tossing it into the back seat, ran back to help their friend.

"You need help," Polly called out. "Let me help you."

The driver glanced at Polly, flipped a middle finger at her, then helped the wounded friend into the back seat as well. Without another word or even a glance, the driver jumped into the front seat, backed the car up, sped around the truck, out onto the road, and took off.

Polly turned around and stared at Heath, dumbfounded. "What just happened?"

"They didn't shoot you." Heath bent over, then leaned on the front bumper of Polly's truck, breathing heavily. "I saw him bring that gun up and thought we were both dead," Heath said. He looked at Polly with complete panic in his eyes. "This is why Henry is always so worried about you. What in the hell were you thinking?"

"That they weren't going to kill me. Seeing that body really shook them up. Someone else killed your Miss Vincent; not those two. I'm guessing they were just kids. Probably working here to make extra cash."

He grimaced. "To buy more meth."

"Maybe. Or maybe not," Polly said. "I'd guess that if you want a good product, you'd hire clean kids to do the work. At least that's what I'd do."

Heath looked at her in shock.

"Oh come on ... you know, if I were a terrible human bent on stripping young people of their money and their brains." She put her hands out. "Which I'm not."

"I don't know how you can make jokes at a time like this. Somebody just shot at you." He stood back up, shaking his head.

"No they didn't," Polly said. "They shot at the ground, thinking they'd scare me."

"Well, it scared *me*. Aaron told me that I was supposed to get you out of here. When I told him you'd gotten out of the truck, he was so mad he yelled at me."

Polly smiled. "Then you can just sit back and enjoy him yelling at me when he finds out what I did."

"Are you going to tell Henry?"

She started laughing and realized it might be a little

hysterically out of control, so gulped twice to stop herself. "I tell him everything. You know that."

"He's never going to trust me with you again."

Polly reached out and this time took his arm. "Heath, stop worrying. These men know they can't stop me from doing what I'm going to do. They won't blame you."

"But I blame me. I should never have listened when you told me to turn in here. I shoulda just drove on by and let you call Sheriff Merritt when we were far away."

"Oh honey," Polly said. "You really have to learn when and where you have control of my actions."

He looked at her, confused.

"Exactly," she said. "You never do." Polly took a deep breath and gave him a warm smile. "Look, I saw the eyes of those two. They were kids. They weren't killers. They were scared to death of what had happened here. All they wanted was for this to go away. If we weren't going to leave, they had to run."

"But ..." He just shook his head. "I'm never going down another country road with you by myself again."

Polly chuckled. "That's probably a good idea. Rebecca doesn't like it when I take off for remote locations either."

The sound of vehicles on the gravel road caused them to turn and look toward the road.

"Sounds like you gave them good directions," Polly said.

"I guess." Heath glanced at the dead body again and turned back to watch sheriff's vehicles flow into the yard. Several emergency vehicles stayed on the road.

Tab Hudson jumped out of her truck and rushed over to Polly while waving other deputies toward the house. "Check everything," she called out. "Tell me when it's clear."

"I think it's clear," Polly said. "Two people just left in this woman's car. They wore coveralls and masks and had shotguns."

"What?" Tab looked furious. "What in the hell are you still doing here?" She turned on Heath. "I thought you said things were safe."

"I ..." He looked at Polly.

"My fault," Polly said. "Don't involve him. I went over to check the body, just to make sure she was really dead." Polly smiled. "She really was, by the way."

"And?" Tab asked.

"And two people came out of the house dressed in full length coveralls, wore rubber boots and had ski masks over their heads. Both were carrying a shotgun. One of them shot at us."

"What?" Tab bellowed.

"Okay, it wasn't really at us." Polly walked over to where the person had aimed. "Right there. That's where they shot. They were trying to scare us away, but I think they were kids and were more scared than I was."

"Why didn't you run?"

"Because they weren't going to hurt me. Those two didn't kill this woman. When they saw her body, they panicked."

"How do you know that?"

"Because I could see it in their eyes. They're scared, Tab. And when they realized that we weren't running away, they did."

Polly pulled out her phone and swiped to a photograph. "That's the car. Heath said it belongs to Miss Vincent."

"Why did you pull in here in the first place?"

"Because I saw her body and the red paint." Polly touched Tab's hand. "You know I couldn't leave her, right?"

"I don't know any such thing." She shook her head slowly. "Aaron is going to be furious."

"Why?"

"I don't know. I just know he's going to kill me dead." Tab turned as one of the deputies approached her.

"The house is clear. We're not staying in there. It's a full-blown meth lab. There's product everywhere."

"Go," she said. "Check the other buildings." Tab turned to another deputy and gestured to the body. "Bring the rest of the team in to deal with this."

Tab led Polly back to Heath. "Tell me why you're even out here in the first place." She looked around. "And please don't say that it's because the body led you here."

Polly chuckled, then put her hand on Heath's arm. "It's kind of a long story."

"I've got time."

"Well, it all started about four and a half years ago when I ran away from Boston," Polly said with a grin.

"Uh huh. Not that much time. Anyway." Tab gave Polly the come-along gesture with her hand.

"Heath called and needed a ride because his truck broke down. I met him, we transferred tiles from his truck to mine ..." Polly glanced at Tab who was telling her to speed it up yet again and raised her eyebrows. "Apparently not much time at all. Anyway, Heath had heard at school about the possibility of the meth house being out here. He said that the kids you talked to wouldn't know where it was and so he asked a couple of questions and because they still see him as being part of the bad crowd, they talked to him."

"And why didn't you call us right away?"

Heath leaned into the conversation. "If they were just yanking my chain, I didn't want to look like an idiot. All we were going to do was drive by and if we saw anything, we were going to call you."

"Anything except a body, I guess," Tab said with a slight eye roll.

"We called right away," Polly protested.

"If you had any idea how much trouble I'm going to be in because you got shot at," Tab said, "you wouldn't be feeling very good right now."

Polly pursed her lips. "I'll deal with Aaron. He knows better than anyone that he can't control me. Why he'd think that *you* can is crazy stuff. Do you want us to stick around?"

Tab shook her head. "I guess not." She pointed her pencil at Heath's chest. "But I am going to want to talk to you about what kids told you this place was out here."

" I don't want to get them in trouble," he asked. "They haven't done anything wrong."

"We just want to talk to them." Tab pointed back toward the

body. "If they know this place is here, they might know something more about why she was killed."

"Okay," he replied, his shoulders slumping. He handed the truck keys to Polly. "Here, you drive. I'll get you back to town."

Polly smiled. "Ice cream first, though. Right?"

He wrinkled his forehead. "Are you kidding?"

"You'll feel better by then. I promise." She reached out to shake Tab's hand. "Thanks for coming. We'll be around tonight and I'll be available tomorrow if you want to have coffee."

"Thanks," Tab said wearily. "I'll call if I'm in town."

Polly negotiated her way out of the yard and back onto the gravel road, then followed Heath's directions as he guided her back to the highway. They drove into Boone on Story Street and when Polly passed the Dairy Queen, he pointed at it. "No ice cream?"

"Not yet. We aren't quite finished with this excursion." She continued north and then turned on Mamie Eisenhower to go west.

"Where are we going now?"

"You'll see." Polly made a right turn.

Heath took a deep breath. "Why are we here?"

"It occurred to me that if Miss Vincent took those kids out to the house, they left their cars somewhere. So I thought that maybe they'd come back for their cars and leave hers. No one would think it was odd that a teacher's car was parked in the school lot late into the evening. Am I right?"

"I suppose."

"We're just going to see if they brought her car back and maybe see if there are some interesting items in the back seat."

"I'd put them in the trunk so no one could see them," Heath said.

"Now you're talking," Polly replied with a laugh. "But first, we need to see if I'm right about the car." She drove into the entrance and followed as Heath pointed.

"It should be in this lot," he said.

The parking lots were still relatively full.

"Something going on at school?" Polly asked.

Heath shrugged. "I don't know."

She nodded. "Of course you don't."

"It's not here," he said after they had gone around the lot twice.

"We'll try the other one." She crossed the street and headed down the first aisle, then up the second.

"Over there. You were right."

"I always am." Polly pulled in behind the car and stopped. She took her phone out and breathed. "Who do I call?" she asked. "Aaron or Tab?"

CHAPTER TWENTY-FIVE

"Stop looking for trouble, Polly Giller. You're really stretching me thin tonight," Aaron said. He was standing beside Miss Vincent's car with her. "Wasn't it enough to find another body? Now you have me out chasing down cars?"

Polly looked back at the truck. Heath was leaning against the head rest, desperately trying to ignore what was happening. "Sorry. Are you going to open the trunk? I want to know what's in there."

"Just a second. I'm not even sure this is the teacher's car," Aaron said. He walked around her and conferred with another deputy, then came back. "Okay. It is her car." He nodded to his deputy who made a call. "We'll take this back to the office and open it there. If your two masked men were in the car, they might have left fingerprints or other identifying information."

"Oh come on," she said. "Just one quick look?"

Aaron shook his head. "I'm not breaking into that trunk just to satisfy your curiosity. What do you expect me to find?"

Polly looked at the ground. "You have to promise not to be mad. And you can't be mad at Tab either."

"Why would I be mad at Deputy Hudson?" Aaron asked. He planted his feet and put his hands on his hips, looming over Polly.

She giggled, backed up a step, then matched his stance. "You can't intimidate me, Mr. Sugar-Muffin, so don't even try."

He let out with a belly laugh, but didn't relax. "Why would I be mad?" Aaron repeated.

"You might find a couple of shotguns in there."

Aaron darted a look at the trunk. "Shotguns?"

"And maybe their masks, boots, and coveralls."

"Shotguns?" He leaned forward, re-entering Polly's personal space.

"You heard me. I didn't stammer," she said. "Shotguns. One of them will have been recently shot, too."

"Polly Giller. You tell me the whole story right this minute."

"It will all be in Deputy Hudson's report, I'm sure," Polly said. "But one of them tried to scare me off the property by shooting their gun."

"At you?"

She twisted her lips back and forth. "Not really. Unless they had terrible aim."

Aaron's face got red and his eyes looked as if they were on fire.

"Stop it, Aaron," she said. "I know those two were scared. They were trying to figure out how to get out of a terrible situation. They were absolutely terrified when they saw Miss Vincent's body."

"How do you know that?" he spat out.

"Because I saw it in their eyes. They didn't know anything about the murder. They were trying to scare us away and when we didn't leave, they got in the car and took off."

"Why am I going to be mad at Deputy Hudson?" he asked again.

"Everyone is afraid that because I didn't run away, you'll blame them."

"If they only knew."

"That's what I said. It's no one's problem but mine."

"I'm more afraid of your husband and my wife than anyone is

of me," Aaron said. "If I can't keep you safe, those two will roast me over an open fire."

"Will you let me know if you find anything in the trunk?" Polly asked.

"We'll see." Aaron shook his head at her. "I might as well, though. If I didn't, I'm afraid you'd find your way into the lot and search it for yourself." He grimaced. "And probably find something we'd missed."

"It isn't like I plan to find these clues. I just stumble on them," Polly said. "I count on you to make sure everything is neatly wrapped up."

"You go straight home now," Aaron said. "I don't want to hear from you again tonight. Got it?"

"I'll do my best," Polly said. "I promised Heath we'd get ice cream. Can we do that?"

"Just stay away from any crime scenes."

Polly climbed back into the truck.

"Is he mad?" Heath asked.

"At you or at me?"

"Whoever."

"He's not mad at all. It wouldn't do him any good. Aaron worries about me and sometimes that's more than he can take."

"I've never been really involved when you're doing this. No wonder Henry worries about you all the time."

"Oh no. Henry."

"I just thought you were waiting until later to tell him."

"You'd think that," Polly said. "But if I don't tell him right away, he gets even more upset." She gave her head a quick shake. "Nope. Not going to worry about that right now. We'll go to Dairy Queen and then drop off your tiles."

Heath leaned forward and put his head in his hands. "I don't know how I'm going to get to school tomorrow."

"Surely one of your friends can give you a ride," Polly said. "I can always give you a ride."

"But I have to work after school. How's that all going to happen?"

"Don't worry about it," she said. "Everything will be okay. I promise. My goodness. After all that's happened this afternoon, that's the last thing you need to be concerned with." Polly turned right on Story Street and headed back south. She wasn't actually sure that she wanted ice cream, but she'd talked about it for so long that it seemed wrong not to stop.

"It's getting really late," Heath said. "I don't know how long they'll be there with the site unlocked."

"So no ice cream?"

"Please?"

Polly smiled at his pleading face. "No problem. We still have plenty in the freezer at home. Back to Bellingwood it is."

His body relaxed. "Thanks. I should never have taken you down there. This whole afternoon just turned upside down. It's all that stupid truck's fault."

Heath was driving the truck that Polly couldn't bear to have around. She'd finally accepted that it existed in her space, but she still couldn't look at it and not see the faces of the girls that Joey Delancy and his serial killer cohort had murdered. They'd put Polly's clothes on the girls and posed them in her truck just to taunt Polly and draw her out. That had been such a horrible experience.

"It *is* a stupid truck," she said. "I wish Henry would trade it in and get another one."

"He could sell it when I can afford my own car."

"No honey, when you're driving for Henry, you won't be expected to put miles on your own vehicle. We'll keep the stupid truck for a while longer. Maybe one day it will just quit working and I can call someone to haul it away and crush it into a million pieces."

Polly followed Heath's directions onto the work site south of Bellingwood. They parked in front of an apartment building.

"There's a two-wheel cart inside," Heath said. "I'll be right back. You can't help me with these anyway."

She nodded. She'd seen him and the tow truck driver transferring them into the bed of her truck and they were heavy.

Polly watched Heath go in the front door and return with a red cart. She took her phone out and made a call that she should probably have made much earlier.

"Well, hello there, Wifey," Henry said.

"That's a terrible thing to call me."

"Someday," he said. "I promise I'll find the right term of endearment for you. I promise. Did you get Heath taken care of?"

"Yeah. We're dropping off the tile now."

"Now?" Henry asked. "Where have you been all this time?"

"Well ..."

"No."

"No what?"

"No, you didn't find another body."

"Well ..."

"Oh Polly. With Heath? Was it connected to the other body you found?"

"Yes. And we found the house where they were cooking the meth."

"How did you find that?"

"You can't be mad at him. The whole thing is my fault. Heath just wanted to drive by it and make sure that the kids were right."

"What kids? What fault? Why would I be mad?"

"It's kind of a long story," she said. Those words hadn't worked with Tab Hudson, but she knew Henry was probably busier than Tab and she'd see him later.

"How long?"

"Long like I should tell you when we're sitting in the same room."

"Everybody is okay?"

"We're just fine. I promise. What do you want to do for supper? Hayden is spending the evening at your parent's house. It will just be four of us."

"Is it safe for us to go to Davey's or will I explode?"

Polly laughed out loud. "That's completely up to you. I would hope that you have better control than to explode in a public place."

"Polly," he said warningly.

"I don't know. There are parts of the story that might upset you, but I'd really like to not cook a meal tonight."

"I love you."

"I know," she returned.

~~~

Rebecca and Henry were playing tic-tac-toe on a piece of paper when the waitress finally arrived at their table.

"I'm so sorry," she said. "We're short tonight and we're busy too. It's crazy in here. What can I get for you to drink?"

Polly smiled. "We can give you our whole order so you don't have to make multiple trips. Right guys?"

Henry grabbed his menu, then shoved Rebecca's in front of her. "You start, Polly. I'll be ready in a second."

"But ..." Rebecca protested. She stopped talking when Henry tapped her menu. "I know what I want," she grumbled.

In moments, they'd placed their order and the girl was off to greet another table filled with a young family and an elderly woman.

"That's going to be you kids and your children with me and Henry someday," Polly said.

"She has to be the grandmother, not the mother," Henry replied. "We'll still be very young when Rebecca and Heath have their families."

Polly laughed. "Nope. No way. They don’t get to start families until they're in their late twenties or early thirties."

"And we'll be in our early fifties," Henry said.

"I will." Polly grinned at him and took his hand. "You're a lot older than me."

"It's really not that far away," Rebecca mused. "Just think. In twelve years, I'll be twenty-five. I'm almost halfway there right now and Heath is only eight years away. What if he has a kid when he's twenty-five? Are you ready for that?"

Polly shuddered. "I'm not ready to even be talking about it."
~~~

She waggled her finger at Heath. "No babies until I'm ready. Got it?"

He snickered, then laughed out loud. "Got it. I'll just tell my wife that she has to wait for the Polly Giller seal of approval."

"Exactly," Polly said. "I'm glad we have that settled. You two are not allowed to grow up for a very long time. I've just gotten started with you."

"Maybe you two should have your own babies," Rebecca said with a grin.

Henry and Polly snapped their heads to look at each other. Polly was grateful to see as much shock in his eyes as she was feeling. "No," they said together.

"Why not?" Rebecca wasn't going to give it up.

"We just aren't," Polly said. "There are too many other people who need us in their lives right now. Henry and I have spent a lot of time talking about this. It's not happening."

"But why not?"

"You're kidding me, right?" Polly asked.

"Well, I suppose. Some of my friends talk about you."

Polly frowned at her. "Your friends talk about me not having babies?"

"Yeah. I guess."

"First of all, tell them it's none of their business. Why do they care whether I have a baby or not?" Polly practically growled out. "It's not like my decision affects their lives." She felt her ire growing and took a deep breath. "Damn, that makes me mad. People in town are really talking about my procreation?"

"Polly." Henry put his hand on her leg.

"I know. But seriously. Our decisions about child-bearing are no one's business but ours." She pointed her thumb back and forth between her and Henry. "And by ours, I mean me and Henry, by the way," Polly said, looking pointedly at Rebecca.

"I was just asking."

"Women should be allowed to decide not to have children if that's what they want," Polly said, fully aware that the pace of her speech was picking up. "Nobody else gets to be part of that decision, nor do they get to be judgmental about what someone's choices are. Does that make sense to you all?"

Rebecca scooted backwards. "Sorry."

"I'm sorry for getting so riled up, but knowing that people are actually worried about whether or not I have a child is just disgusting to me," Polly said. "It is none of their business." She took a deep breath, closed her eyes and then took another long, slow breath in before letting it out. "I'm okay," she said, looking up. "I'll let it go."

"I really didn't mean to push," Rebecca said. "Sometimes I don't think."

"It's fine," Henry said. He put his hand on Rebecca's back. "These things will become more important to you as you grow up. Knowing that you have the freedom to make choices in your own life without the world coming unglued on you is really important to us. It wasn't always that way for women and sometimes it feels like it still isn't." He took Polly's hand. "But I will always fight for you two. Always."

Polly felt tears fill her eyes as she looked at the man sitting beside her. He was always strong for her when she needed him. He would always support her, no matter what. That was an incredible feeling.

She blinked away her tears as another family passed their table. The girl, who looked to be the same age as Heath, did a double take at Polly and Heath, but continued to follow her parents.

"Who was that?" Polly asked. "She acted like she knew you."

Heath leaned closer to her. "That's one of the girls I was telling you and Deputy Hudson about. "Jen Johnston. Must be her parents. I knew they lived in Bellingwood, but I don't see them around very much."

"That's Lowell Johnston," Henry interrupted. "He's a broker for farm equipment. You've seen his auction signs out on the highway by their place. This year has been tough on him. Lots of farmers wanting to unload stuff."

"Is he an auctioneer?"

Henry shook his head. "No, his partner does that. Vernon Dill."

"That's Emmy's dad," Heath said.

Even as he spoke, another family came in, following the hostess. Polly glanced at the girl with them who was limping beside her mother. "Is that Emmy?" Polly asked Heath.

He looked at her kind of strangely. "How did you know?"

"Just a hunch. Did you see her limping?"

"Yeah."

"Was she limping in school this morning?"

Heath looked off into space and then back at Polly. "I don't think so." He stopped to think again. "No. Before the teacher came into the room, she and Brandon Leden were playing keep-away with some kid's book. They were throwing it over the girl's head and Em was jumping up and down."

"What do you think about that?" Polly asked.

Heath leaned back in his chair to look at the table where the Dills and Johnstons had been seated. Polly pushed his front seat legs back onto the floor when the waitress approached with their drinks. She put a basket of fries into the middle of the table. "Davey says anyone that has to wait tonight gets free fries. They're really good. Your dinners will be out in a minute."

Rebecca grabbed the basket as Heath reached for it.

"Hey," he said, laughing.

"Did you want some of these? You'd better say please."

"Please?" he pleaded.

Rebecca shook her head. "Nope. You'd better make that pretty please. I'm not feeling particularly generous."

Polly reached across the table, took the basket from her daughter's hand, and put it in front of Heath. "For just a few minutes I think that you two are adults and then you crush my dreams. Will it always be like this?"

Henry reached over and pulled the basket back. "Oh, it will always be like this. So what's up with the limping girl?"

"I'd totally forgotten that one of the people who shot at me fell down on old barbed wire," Polly said.

Henry dropped the basket onto the table. He looked at Polly, then at Heath before swallowing. "You were shot at?"

"I told you that you weren't going to like it," Polly said. "And you promised that you wouldn't freak out while we were at dinner. Remember?"

"But I didn't know gunplay was involved."

"It wasn't that bad. Tell him, Heath."

Heath shook his head. "I'm not telling him anything. You said you were going to tell the whole story. I'm staying out of trouble."

"That's the way to play it," Rebecca said. She looked at Polly. "Somebody shot at you?"

Polly sighed. "Yeah, so, I found another body at a meth house and there were two people there in coveralls, rubber boots and ski masks. I couldn't tell whether they were men or women, girls or boys. But they hadn't killed Miss Vincent."

"The math teacher?" Rebecca asked.

"Yes. The new math teacher," Polly replied. "They were completely freaked out when they saw her sprawled on the ground with that red circle and slash painted over her."

Rebecca was agog. "Was she naked too?"

Polly nodded at her and gave a weak smile before looking at Henry. He'd crossed his arms and pushed away from the table. "No freaking out, Henry. Look. We're all here and we're safe. It's going to be okay. I promise."

"You went to a meth house. You were shot at by strangers in masks. Anything else?"

"We went to the high school to find the car that they'd driven away from the meth house. I had to call Aaron to come get it."

He nodded slowly. "And you chased down the getaway car." Looking pointedly at Heath, Henry said slowly and deliberately. "You. Didn't. Stop. Her."

Before Heath could respond, Polly put her hand out to stop him. "Oh no you don't. Not for a minute you don't."

"What?" Henry asked.

"You don't blame him for this. The poor kid was about to have a conniption. Take a deep breath and consider just how successful he would have been in trying to stop or redirect me." She lifted her eyebrows and waited for Henry to respond.

"Did you really try to stop her?" Henry asked Heath.

"Yes sir. Over and over. But she made me talk to Sheriff Merritt and then she jumped out of the truck while I was on the phone. I didn't know what to do."

"And the shooting?"

"She wouldn't come back to the truck. I tried to beg her."

Henry smiled and gave a small chuckle. "There's nothing you can do when she gets like that. You did your best, I suppose. But Polly, why would you put yourself in danger?"

"Because there was no danger. Those two weren't the killers. They didn't want to be there." She frowned. "No. I suppose they did want to be there, but not once they saw the body. They just wanted to get out and thought I was going to stop them. The person who shot at me made the shot go really wide. Probably trying to scare me."

"That was the wrong thing to do. You get stubborn when someone tries to scare you."

"I didn't have time to do anything else. The other one ran for the car, then the one who shot the gun tried to run, but tripped and stumbled across some old barbed wire fencing. There was a lot of blood until that one was rescued by the one who drove. They took off and a few minutes later, Tab Hudson and her crews showed up. Then I thought that maybe if they were high schoolers, Miss Vincent had brought them out in her car to cook meth. If that was true, maybe they took her car back to the school parking lot so they could get in their own cars and go home. There. That's all of it." She took a breath.

"What if they'd still been in the car?"

"Well, that would be crazy, wouldn't it?" Polly asked. "That would be just like asking to be caught."

"You think that girl who was limping was the one who shot at you?" Rebecca whispered across the table.

The waitress chose that moment to arrive with their plates. "Would you like ranch dressing for your French fries?"

Polly nodded. "That would be great. Thank you."

CHAPTER TWENTY-SIX

Polly's mind wouldn't stop racing while she ate. If those two girls were the ones who had been at that meth house, then Tab should know about it. They might even have a good idea as to who could have been the murderer.

"You've gotten awfully quiet, Polly," Henry said.

She finished chewing. "Just thinking."

"About how sorry you are that you make my heart race?"

"I like making your heart race. I thought you did too."

"Stop it," Rebecca muttered.

"Right," Henry said. "You know what I mean."

Polly smiled. "Honey, you know that I'm never going to stop being who I am. You married me because of that, right?"

"In spite of it. So what are you thinking about?"

"Those two girls. Wondering if they were the ones at the house."

"That's all you're going to do tonight. Wonder. Right?"

Polly grinned at Rebecca. "I think he's talking about your cat."

"Speaking of cats," Henry said. "Please tell me the two of you aren't planning to keep all five."

"Stephanie told Kayla she could have one," Rebecca said. "But Polly told me I could keep one of the kittens. I think we should keep Wonder, too. She's old and would be harder to find a home for."

He laughed. "No, Rebecca. No harder than a kitten. You just have to find the right people."

"Please, Henry?" Rebecca batted her eyelashes at him. "Please?"

"We can't make any decisions about this for several weeks anyway," Polly interrupted. "We'll have plenty of time to discuss finding homes ..." she looked at Rebecca. "...or not for Wonder and her babies."

"They'd be really good at keeping mice out of the Bell House. You know, it's so drafty there are probably lots of places for rodents to come in," Rebecca said, batting her eyes at Henry again.

"Begone, child," he said, putting his hand up between their faces. "Polly says we don't have to talk about it tonight."

"Give me one of your business cards," Polly said, putting her hand out.

Henry immediately responded by pulling out his wallet. Before he put it on the table, he stopped himself. "Why?"

"Because I need it." She waggled her fingers. "Just one. That's all I need."

"Not until you tell me why you need it."

"Trust me?"

"Not on your life."

"I'm going to go over and talk to Mr. Johnston and Mr. Dill. Between you and me, we have enough for an auction. Right? All of that stuff at the Bell House. My dad's stuff. Some of your excess equipment?"

"What are you doing?" Heath asked.

"Just a little reconnaissance." Polly waggled her fingers again. "Come on, Henry. All it will cost you is a business card. Surely a big, fancy contractor like yourself can afford to sacrifice one little business card." She mimicked Rebecca and batted her eyes at him. "Please?"

He drew a card out of his billfold and held it out, then pulled his hand back. "Are you going to be good? It really is only reconnaissance?"

"Of course. Would I lie to you?"

Henry looked at Rebecca and Heath. "None of us would ever really call it lying, but ..."

Polly snatched the card from him, then took her phone out of her pocket. She loved the wallet case that wrapped around her phone. It carried her driver's license, a credit card, her insurance card and some cash as well as a few business cards. Taking one of her own cards from the inside pocket, she slipped the two into her hand. "I'll be right back."

"Oh Polly," Henry said with a sigh. He took his phone out and set it on the table beside him. "Just in case."

Polly got up and went over to the table where the two families had just received their meals. "I'm sorry to interrupt," she said. "But when my husband told me who you were, I had to stop by."

The man Henry had identified as Vernon Dill looked up at her. "You're Polly Giller, right?"

She nodded. "I'm married to Henry Sturtz. You know him, right?" Polly turned back to her table and waved, causing everyone at the table to turn and look at Henry, Rebecca and Heath. "Those are my kids, Rebecca and Heath." She'd come up to stand between Emmy and Jen. "You know Heath, don't you? He said you're in that literature class with him. You know ..." she looked around the table. "The one that Mr. West taught. It's such a tragedy, him being killed like he was. And then today, that Miss Vincent was killed too."

The two girls looked down at the table and Polly caught Vernon Dill glance across the table at his partner. If she didn't know better, she'd have identified the look as accusatory. Lowell Johnston gave a barely perceptible shake of his head and nodded at Polly.

"How can we help you?"

Polly held out the two business cards, leaned across the table and as she did, gently brushed her foot across Emmy's leg. The girl cried out in pain and Polly jumped back. "I'm so sorry. Did I hurt you?" She knelt down and touched the leg where Polly knew it had been hurt by the barbed wire. "What did you do to yourself?" Polly asked.

"It's nothing. Just a scrape."

"It sounded like it hurt more than just a scrape." Polly looked at the girl's mother. "Have you looked at this?"

The woman shook her head, concern in her eyes. "You said you twisted your ankle but that it was no big deal, Emmy. What's going on?"

"It's nothing, Mom," Emmy spat. "Let it go."

Polly touched the leg again and realized that there was a spot of blood on the girl's jeans. "That's blood. Honey, are you bleeding?"

Emmy yanked her leg away from Polly. "Leave me alone."

"You should probably take her to see someone about that," Polly said. "Especially if she scraped it on something old and rusty. Your daughter probably needs a tetanus shot." She looked down at Emmy and caught her eyes. "You wouldn't want to get tetanus because you didn't tell your parents what happened. That's a horrible thing to have to deal with. Headaches and then muscle spasms. They used to call it lockjaw. I'm sure you know what that means. If you don't take care of it, you will get really sick. Seizures and trouble swallowing. That would be such a shame. Especially if dealing with it was as easy as getting a shot." Polly turned to the girl's friend. "You both look really familiar. I'm trying to think where I might have seen you lately." She shook her head. "I just can't place it. But I have a pretty good eye for detail. I'll remember it. Probably about the time I'm relaxing when I try to go to sleep tonight."

Polly put her hand out with the business cards again and scooted them across the table to Lowell Johnston. "I have a lot of items in the Bell House that we may not be using and I have some things from my father's house. If I wanted to put together an auction, you two men would be the ones to help me, wouldn't you?"

"We would," Lowell Johnston said.

"Well, I'm sorry I bothered you." Polly patted Emmy's back. "You should probably go to the ER in Boone tonight. You wouldn't want to wait very long."

With that, she turned around, barely able to control her grin. As Polly walked back to her table, she quietly muttered, "You're a horrible person, Polly Giller."

"What did you say over there?" Henry asked.

"I just asked if they'd be able to help us out with an auction should I want to do that," Polly said. She picked up her fork and swirled it in the pasta in front of her, took a bite and smiled. "And I might have scared a young woman into running to the emergency room tonight."

"What?"

"Well, if she hurt herself on that barbed wire, which she did, she needs to be sure that she's had a tetanus shot. Otherwise, you know, lockjaw." Polly chuckled. "I'm sure that those two girls were the ones in the house cooking meth. They were both pretty scared of me. Especially when I told them that they looked familiar."

She looked up as their waitress rushed past them with takeout containers. "Hmmm," Polly said. "Looks like someone is in a hurry to get out of here this evening."

The rest of her table was staring at the Johnstons and Dills. Polly waved her fork at her family. "Quit staring. Eat your supper. They're going to be gone in just a few minutes and then I can call Tab."

"You're calling Deputy Hudson tonight?" Heath asked.

"Of course I am. Those girls were in the house where Miss Vincent was killed. And by the way, if you ever do something stupid like they have, I'll be able to tell immediately. I could smell it in their hair."

"Seriously, Polly," Rebecca said. "How do you know this?"

"When you're my age, you'll know all sorts of things, too."

"I'm not kidding. How did you know?"

"I went online and investigated cooking meth." Polly looked around the table. "Don't be messing with my search history. It's all in the name of the investigation. Anyway, I can't believe their parents can't smell it, but maybe they've gotten used to it. Ammonia, sulfur, lighter fluid. Smells like that. And it's in those girls' hair."

"Not the pretty girl smell like you. What is your scent?" Henry asked.

"Fruity stuff," Polly quipped. "Lots of fruity stuff."

The two families scooted out of the restaurant as quickly as they could, none of them stopping to look at Polly and her family. As soon as they cleared the front door, she took out her phone and wandered out to the lobby.

"Tab Hudson here," Tab said.

"Tab, it's Polly."

"I knew it was a Bellingwood number," Tab replied. "I just couldn't figure out who. I lost my contacts about a month ago."

"Well, this is me. I know who shot at me today."

There was silence on the other end of the call.

"Tab?"

"Yes, Polly. Tell me what you did."

"I took my family to dinner at Davey's. That's all. I promise."

"There's more. Spit it out."

Polly laughed. "Okay, fine. Two of Heath's classmates came in with their parents. Do you remember those girls he talked about that hadn't been picked on by Mr. West?"

"Yes. I have their names here somewhere."

"Two of those girls. Emmy Dill and Jen Johnston. Emmy was limping."

"Limping?"

"Yeah. I completely forgot about it. She stumbled over that pile of barbed wire and cut her leg up pretty good. I'm sorry I forgot to tell you that."

"That's okay. So just because she was limping you think she's the one?"

"Well, I might have gone over to their table."

"Oh Polly."

"Funny. That's what Henry just said."

"I'll bet that's not all he said. Anyway?"

"Anyway, I brushed against her leg and made it bleed again. She'd told her mother that she'd twisted her ankle. I might have scared her a little about tetanus. And when I told them that Miss Vincent had been killed ..." Polly lowered her voice so no one could hear her. "I could have sworn that Vernon Dill looked at his partner like he knew something. I think the dads know what's going on. I wouldn't be at all surprised if one of them wasn't responsible for those deaths."

"Polly." Tab's voice took on a note of warning.

"I'm not going to do anything about it. I was just in the right place at the right time," Polly said.

"For heaven's sake, you really always are," Tab said. "I swear. You're going to make a believer out of me yet."

Polly chuckled. "That's probably going too far. You don't want to jump on the Polly Giller bandwagon quite yet, do you?"

"Anita still thinks I'm crazy for not believing."

"Speaking of Anita," Polly said. "What else has she told you about the new man in her life?"

"Only that I'm not supposed to talk about it with you."

"Come on. You're kidding me."

It was Tab's turn to laugh. "Not really. She says you set them up in the first place."

"I caught her coming out of his apartment the other morning. Does she really like Doug?"

"Doug's his name?" Tab asked, still laughing.

"Whoops. You didn't know?"

"She's keeping it pretty hush-hush. Anita's worried that the guys will harass this Doug person. She's kind of like a sister to everyone in the office."

"Doug's a really good guy," Polly said. "I love him."

"He'd better be. Does the sheriff know him?"

"He sure does."

"That's probably another reason Anita isn't saying much. She really doesn't want Sheriff Merritt to know about it until it gets serious."

Polly smiled. "She thinks it's going to get serious?"

"Wait. No. That's not what I meant. She just doesn't want people talking about it right now. If they ever do get serious then she'll probably say something. You can't tell her I said anything and you really can't tell Sheriff Merritt that you know she's dating this Doug guy. "

"Aaron really likes him. Doug took a beating for me one night. That gave him a lot of points in Aaron's book. But I'll be good. Aaron will never hear it from me."

"Now back to these people at the restaurant. You can't go back and bother them."

"I won't," Polly said. "Besides they're gone. They left halfway through their meal. Well, right after I went over to the table."

"And you aren't going to try to follow them. Right?"

"I don't need to. I'm calling you. I'd bet that the Dill family is headed to the emergency room in Boone for a tetanus shot. I scared that girl pretty badly, telling her about how awful the symptoms could be."

"She's young. She's probably had tetanus boosters as she's grown up."

"Then you better send someone to their houses. And Tab, I could smell the stuff in the girls' hair."

"You what?"

"I read, you know. A little research and some common sense and I know what to look for. When I bent over her, I could smell it. Like ammonia and sulfur."

"Okay."

"The girls are pretty scared. I'm almost positive they had nothing to do with the murders, but they're beginning to wonder if the deaths are connected to them. I suspect that with a little pressure, they'll tell you whatever you want to know about that particular meth cookery."

"We have such a problem with it in the county. It's nice to shut at least one down," Tab said. "But more will just pop up."

"So I should drive around in the country more often?" Polly asked.

"Don't you dare."

"Just kidding. Okay, I'm going back to dinner with my family."

"And I'm going to round up a couple of deputies and knock on some doors tonight. With Heath's information about how the girls were treated differently by Mr. West, I can at least begin to ask questions. This should be interesting."

"Are you going to let me know what you find?"

Again, there was silence on the other end of the call.

"You're just like Aaron," Polly said. "It's a good thing I'm not so stingy with the information that I get."

"You're right," Tab replied. "How about coffee tomorrow morning. Ten o'clock?"

"At Sweet Beans?"

"Where else?"

"I'll be there." Polly put her phone back into her pocket and smiled. She should really just set up an office in one of the booths at Sweet Beans. What a glorious place that would be for her to work. Well, except for not being able to have her animals there with her. That would make it perfect. She'd gotten used to working in the office of their apartment with Obiwan and Han sleeping on the floor at her feet and the cats sprawled across papers on the desk.

When she got back to the table, her plate had been replaced by a takeout box. "What's this?"

"We were done and wanted to order dessert," Rebecca said. "You can eat out of the box if you want."

"Or," Henry said as their waitress returned with four pieces of pie, each with ice cream and a lit birthday candle, "you can have birthday pie with us."

"This is awesome." Polly watched as the pieces of pie were placed in front of everyone. "Do I have to blow out all of your candles too?"

Henry nodded as he handed his phone up to the waitress. She took pictures as Polly leaned over the table to blow out first Rebecca's, then Heath's. She blew Henry's out and kissed him on the lips before returning to her own plate.

"Thanks," Henry said, as he took the phone back. "We'll celebrate more tomorrow night, but I think it's a good idea to declare this week Polly Giller Week. It will be a birthday party every day."

"Last night was really enough," Polly said.

Rebecca frowned. "But you didn't get any presents. You have to have presents on your birthday. Right, Henry?"

He nodded.

"Right, Heath?"

Heath just shrugged. "I don't know what you're talking about. I didn't think we did presents in this family."

Polly leaned over and hugged him. "That's exactly right. We don't do presents. Who needs 'em." She turned to Henry. "So what'd you get me?"

"You have to wait until tomorrow," he replied.

"Tomorrow morning when we wake up?"

"That's an entirely different present."

"Lalalalala," Rebecca said, putting her hands over her ears. "You two are sick."

Polly glanced at Heath, who had dropped his head while he laughed to himself. "It's better to have us this way than fighting all the time, right?"

"I wouldn't know," Rebecca responded. "I don't know what it's like the other way. All I know is that when we get to the Bell House, you two are going to have to live upstairs all by yourselves. We don't want to see any more of that mushy stuff. Tell them, Heath."

"I'm not here," he said, putting another bite of pie in his mouth.

CHAPTER TWENTY-SEVEN

Again with the empty bed. It was always surprising to Polly when she woke up without a single warm body snuggled against her. The cats weren't in the room, the dogs were gone, Henry was gone. At seven o'clock, there should be activity and noise, but the house was silent. She was a little sad that Henry hadn't even kissed her and wished her Happy Birthday before he'd gone.

Maybe they were planning some sort of surprise, but they'd already done that on Mother's Day this year, leaving the house before she got up and making her visit people all over town before arriving at the Bell House. They wouldn't repeat the same thing, especially on a school day.

Polly pulled a sweatshirt over her head and opened the bedroom door, expecting to be greeted by something … anything. She stepped out into the living room and looked around. The boys' door was open. Rebecca's was closed, but with Wonder and her kittens living in there right now, that was to be expected.

Polly tiptoed across the living room floor, hoping maybe she'd get away with surprising her family, but when she peered in, the dining room and kitchen were empty.

"What in the world?" she asked out loud.

Luke startled her by jumping from the top of the refrigerator to the countertop and then to the floor. He bolted for her bedroom. He wasn't a fan of being locked out of his favorite room.

"Weird," Polly said, looking around for anything out of place. Leia shot out of the bathroom beside the office Polly shared with Henry and ran to catch up with her brother on the cat tree.

"Well, that's one way to wish a girl a happy birthday," Polly said, loudly enough for people to hear if they were hiding. She waited a few more moments to see if anything would happen and when it didn't, walked over to the coffee pot and turned it on. Henry hadn't even made coffee for her this morning. She stuck her lower lip out in a pout.

While that brewed, she might as well take a shower. Tab Hudson would be at the coffee shop this morning. Polly thought about calling Sal to see if she wanted to do something today, too. Joss had been pretty pointed about the fact that Polly needed to pay more attention to her friends. She'd been so caught up in the work over at the Bell House, that she'd not made much of an effort for the last couple of months. That was on her. It wasn't like either Sal or Joss could spend time there while she was working. Not with their kids and all of the construction chaos she had going on.

Polly moped around her room as she tried to decide what to wear. It was still quite warm. Today's forecast called for a high in the eighties. It was late September. What in the world was that about? Polly was ready to wear sweaters and thick, heavy socks inside her favorite boots, or curl up under a pile of quilts with a good book and something hot to drink. So far, she was still relying on the air conditioner to keep her cool enough to sleep at night and while she had pretty much quit wearing shorts - it was nearly fall for heaven's sake - she flipped through her closet to find a light-weight blouse. She had no intention of working at Bell House today.

When she finished dressing, Polly set her jaw and figured she could find something for breakfast before texting Henry to find out what in the world was happening.

She opened the door to her bedroom again and stared at the dining room. "What's going on?" she asked, while striding across the living room. Obiwan stood up from where he'd been lying beside Hayden and wagged his tail.

"What do you mean?" Henry asked.

"I mean, where have you all been?" She looked at the dining room table. It was fully set with buttered toast, a breakfast casserole, and pitchers of juice. A pretty bouquet of flowers with a Happy Birthday balloon lifting toward the ceiling sat in the middle of the table.

The four of them looked back and forth at each other.

"We've been worried about you. Thought you'd never get up," Hayden said.

She gave kind of a panicked laugh. "I was just out here. I started the coffee and everything." She glanced at the coffee pot and saw that it was cleaned and prepared to be started. "No," Polly said, shaking her head. "That's not right. I was just here. I swear. I came out of the room, saw that the house was completely empty and turned the coffee on."

"Hayden made a breakfast casserole," Rebecca said, pointing at the table. "Maybe you just need food."

Heath got up and walked into the kitchen, flipped the switch on the coffee maker and took a mug out from the cupboard and put it beside the pot. "Happy Birthday, Polly," he said, giving her a quick hug. "I'm glad you're here. I don't want to be late for school."

"We're doing presents tonight at dinner. Is that okay?" Rebecca asked. She gave Polly a side-hug when Polly sat down beside her, still stunned.

"Sure, that's great. Whenever. You guys have to be messing with me." Polly looked around at the four innocent faces at her table. "Tell me you're messing with me."

"What do you mean?" Henry asked.

"You went away."

"The dirty dishes from making breakfast are all in the sink," he said, pointing over to the kitchen.

Polly turned around. When she'd been here earlier, the sink was empty and now it was filled with mixing bowls, the pan they'd used for cooking sausage, and various utensils.

Henry took Polly's plate and handed it to Hayden, who put a square of casserole on it. "Toast, Polly?" Hayden asked.

She turned back to the table and shook her head. "I'm losing my mind. I have to be losing my mind."

"What do you mean?" Henry asked.

"You know what I mean. You weren't here. I swear you weren't here." She turned and looked into the kitchen. "But where did my pot of coffee go? Where did all of those dishes come from?"

Henry put her plate back in front of her and moved a jar of elderberry jelly closer to her. "You're going to be okay. Maybe you just had strange dreams this morning. It happens, you know."

Polly glared at him. "I don't trust you."

"What do you mean?" He laughed at her. "I'm very trustworthy."

Hayden finished the food on his plate and headed for the kitchen. "I only have a short day at school today, so don't worry about cleaning up the kitchen. I'll take care of that when I get home." After depositing his dishes in the sink, he came back and gave her a quick hug. "Happy Birthday. Are you going up to the coffee shop today?"

"Of course I am," Polly said.

"I figured. Have a good day." He picked up his backpack and headed for the back door, the dogs following. Everyone listened as he said good bye to the animals and headed down the steps.

Heath took his plate out to the kitchen. "Jason's taking me to school. He has his mom's car. I said I'd meet him out front. I'd better go." With that, he was gone.

Polly looked at Rebecca on her right and Henry on her left. "Okay, you two. Spill it. Why are you messing with me?"

"We wouldn't mess with you," Rebecca said. "It's your birthday. That hardly seems fair." She pushed back from the table. "I'm meeting Kayla at school early. We're practicing with the band teacher." She darted out of the room.

"I guess that leaves you," Polly said to Henry. "Are you coming clean?"

"I'm innocent," he said. He stood and leaned over to kiss the tip of her nose. "And I'm late. But I wanted to be here for your birthday breakfast. Are you going to have any more casserole?"

Polly shook her head. She'd barely eaten what was on her plate.

"I'll leave it here for you. After you put it in the refrigerator, though, don't you dare clean this up. Hayden's got it, okay?" He carried his plate out into the kitchen.

"Okay," she said with a nod.

When he walked back past her, she caught his sleeve. "Am I really losing my mind?"

Henry shrugged. "I hope not. None of us want to visit you in the looney bin."

Rebecca ran into the dining room, clutching her backpack. "I have my flute, too," she said, patting the pack. She glanced at Henry. "Are you leaving now?"

"Yes."

"Would you want to give your sweetest daughter ever a ride to school?"

He sighed and put his hand on her back. "I could probably be talked into it." They headed for the back door and he turned his head. "I'll talk to you later. I love you, birthday girl."

"I love you too." Polly picked up the pan of breakfast casserole and went into the kitchen. She took out aluminum foil, ripped off a piece, and covered the dish. The coffee was finished brewing, so she filled a cup, then blew on it as she leaned against the countertop. Where had that other pot gone?

Shaking her head at the insanity of it all, Polly picked up the casserole dish, opened the refrigerator door and laughed out loud.

"Did you know about this?" she asked Obiwan. He'd startled when she laughed and came over to stand beside her, looking into the refrigerator. He looked up at her and wagged his tail.

There was her pot of coffee and a small box from Sweet Beans with her name and the words "open me" on it. Polly took the box back to the table with her and sank down into her chair, breathing a sigh of relief. She opened the box and found one of her favorite chocolate-chocolate chip muffins and a birthday card.

"Dear Polly,

Sometimes we can hardly contain ourselves. You're so much fun to mess with. You can blame Hayden. The whole thing was his idea. If you could have seen the glee everyone had on their faces as they created this diabolical plan to make you feel like you'd lost your mind, you would have enjoyed every moment of it. We are a crazy, wonderful family. Because of you, I have the very best family a man could hope for. Happy Birthday, my love.

Henry"

She took a breath and began to weep. Maybe some of it was relief at not having lost her mind, but they were a family and those three kids had so much fun doing things together. Their own mothers had given them an incredibly strong start to life. All Polly and Henry had to do was make sure they got to adulthood in one piece.

Polly glanced up at the drawing of Elijah and Noah on the wall under her clock. She was going to ask Rebecca to do a few more of those sketches. One of Hayden and Heath together and another of Rebecca by herself. Polly wanted one of Jason and Andrew and one of Kayla. So many kids were part of Polly's extended family and she wanted to be able to remember them all as they were during these wonderful days. They would all grow up much too soon and boys would become men, girls would grow into women. They'd all have their own families, but in twenty years, Polly wanted to be able to look at a wall filled with drawings of her favorite people as they grew up.

She smiled. That was how she would decorate that parlor room. Polly wasn't sure what else was going to end up in that room, but she wanted the walls to be covered with Rebecca's sketches. She tucked the lid back down on the muffin's box. It could wait.

"You all are pretty rotten," she texted to Henry. *"I love you so much, but that was a mean trick."*

"Not my fault," he replied.

"Does Hayden know that it's not safe to sleep around me for a few days?"

"Big talk, girlie. You're a softie. You laughed, didn't you?"

"I might have cried at your note. Thank you. I love you, too."

"I'm going to Dad's for lunch. Will you join us?"

"Are you sure it won't be too much for him?"

"Mom asked if you'd have time."

"Then I'll be there. I love you."

"I love you."

Polly finished her breakfast and cleared the rest of the things from the table to the kitchen counters, making sure there was no food left out where animals could get to it. She was supposed to meet Tab at Sweet Beans this morning, but before she headed out, she wanted to run downstairs and say hello.

When she walked into the main office, Kristen waved at her as she spoke to someone on the phone.

"Happy Birthday," Stephanie called out from behind the desk that Polly had grown used to calling her own. She came out to give Polly a hug. "I hear you had an exciting day yesterday."

Polly chuckled. "You heard already?"

"Everybody is talking about it in town. How you fingered those two girls at Davey's last night."

"What?" Polly asked.

"They were arrested. Didn't you know that?"

Polly shook her head. "How did you find out?"

"People talking about it up at Sweet Beans this morning." Stephanie blushed. "I went up before I came to work."

"They're already talking about it?"

Stephanie nodded and turned to include Kristen in the conversation when the girl was off the phone. "And one of the dads confessed to killing those two teachers."

Polly stepped back. "He what?"

"Everybody says you were the one who figured it out."

"Everybody?" Polly was in shock. How had this gotten around town so quickly?

"Yeah. What was his name, Kristen?"

"It's Lowell Johnston from the auction house."

Stephanie looked down at the receptionist. "You know him?"

"They've lived here forever. He has another daughter who's my age. Susie. She was kinda stuck up. She got married and lives up in Fort Dodge," Kristen said.

"Rumor is, Mr. Johnston was mad because he thought that man teacher was having sex with his daughter," Stephanie said. "Everybody says the whole thing tipped him over the edge. They found blood in his barn where they hose machinery down to clean it for auction. He didn't clean up very good, I guess."

Polly stood there, her mouth wide open.

"When he found out that they weren't having sex, but that his daughter was cooking meth, he totally flipped out. They arrested his partner ..." Stephanie looked at Kristen again.

"Vernon Dill."

"Mr. Johnston told his partner what he'd done and they both found out their daughters were working with that teacher and the female math teacher," Stephanie said. "People are talking about how they canceled a couple of auctions last weekend because they were driving around, asking questions, looking for the meth house. Their daughters are really dumb if they didn't know their dads were checking up on them. Who does that?"

"You got all of this at the coffee shop?" Polly asked.

"Yeah. It's all over town by now," Stephanie replied. "That Dill guy, the partner. He didn't kill anybody, but since he knew about it and I guess he helped cover it up, he's like an accessory or something."

"And that female teacher?" Polly was stymied by how much information had gotten out there so quickly. All she'd done last night was sleep.

Stephanie nodded. "They were mad because she was corrupting their daughters."

"Like those girls needed any help," Kristen said. "They think they're smarter than anyone else and can get away with whatever they want."

"That must be why the red circle and slash were painted on them." Polly said. "Mr. Johnston was trying to warn others away from his daughter."

"Somebody said he was trying to make it look like some kind of cult murder," Stephanie said. "They're still looking for the clothes." She grimaced. "Why would you want to carry somebody's naked body around?"

Polly gave her a weak grin. "There are a lot of things I'll never understand about murder. But yeah. This was a weird one. So what's happening with the girls?"

"They were arrested on drug charges," Stephanie said.

"Yeah, that will kill old Susie," Kristen muttered. "She was such a nasty hag. Always thinking she was better than everybody else. Looks like her family is just the same as the rest of us. Everybody has their problems. Bet we don't see her face in Bellingwood any time soon."

Polly chuckled. "You should be nice. This has to be hard on her and her mother."

"She can take it," Kristen said. "She dished it out every time someone got in the least bit of trouble. I remember her standing in the hallway laughing at this girl who wore braces on her legs and needed those canes that wrap around her arms to walk. Susie and her friends would laugh and laugh and call her a Weeble. You know Weebles wobble but they don't fall down? Yeah, she thought that was the funniest thing ever. And when Missy Horn got pregnant our senior year, Susie started calling her a whore and a slut. Even in class, Susie would call her names. The thing is, Missy ended up marrying the guy she was with. They'd been together for a year before that and as far as I know, they're still together and have a couple more kids."

Kristen looked up at Stephanie and Polly after her diatribe. "I might have hated Susie Johnston."

"It sounds like it," Stephanie said. "You're going to want to deal with that."

"I didn't know I was still so mad. I could never do anything. Missy was kind of a friend and I didn't have the courage to stand up to Susie and her friends. It made me feel horrible. I tried to just be nicer to Missy and to Maria, the girl with braces. But that didn't stop those other girls." Kristen frowned. "I wish I would have known what to do, but I was scared they'd find something to say about me, so I drifted into the background whenever I could."

"Bullies count on that," Polly said. "You don't need to feel ashamed. We should teach better ways to help people who are on the outside of bullying know what to do or say to stop it. Whatever happened to Maria?"

Kristen shook her head. "I don't know. I should ask around. Her family is from Boone, but somebody should know." She nodded fervently. "Yeah. I'm going to look for her. No reason to completely lose track. That's a good idea."

Polly turned back to Stephanie. "What else happened at the coffee shop this morning?"

Stephanie blushed. "Nothing much. I just had a coffee and doughnut and then came to work."

"That was a heck of a doughnut. Is Skylar working this morning?"

"Of course he is," Kristen said. "When he's not, she just comes straight to work."

"Oh yeah. That's how it works." Polly grinned at the two of them. "No Jeff this morning?"

Stephanie nodded toward his office. "He's coming in late. Getting a delivery at his apartment. New dining room furniture."

"Really. That's cool. Okay, well, tell him I said hello. If I'm around, I'll stop in later."

"Happy Birthday," Kristen called as Polly left the office.

CHAPTER TWENTY-EIGHT

"I hear it's your birthday," Ken Wallers said as he approached the table where Polly was sitting with Tab Hudson.

Last night had been long for Tab and her team and she'd spent the last half hour telling Polly whatever she could about the night. The girls were home with their mothers, but Lowell Johnston and Vernon Dill were making their home behind bars. The girls had an inkling that one of their fathers was involved in the murders, especially after Miss Vincent had been killed. That had shaken them up quite a bit and last night's dinner at Davey's was a thin attempt at smoothing waters and unifying their front. It failed.

"Shhh. We're keeping it a secret," Polly replied to Ken.

Tab laughed. "Big secret. They sang to her when we came in this morning. And oh wait, there was a party Sunday night. Yeah. No secret."

Polly shrugged and then gestured to a seat at the table. "Join us. Have you and your buddies found out anything more about that symbol in my house?"

Ken looked at the chair and then at the counter. He made a quick gesture to Skylar, who nodded at him. "It's scary that they know exactly what I want in here these days. It's your fault, you know, Polly."

"I can live with that. So anything?"

He shook his head. "I'm afraid it's going to have to remain a mystery for now. Simon is going to chat with Joss Mikkels about uncovering those boxes from Margie Deacon's estate."

"I wish I was in the Bell House," Polly said. "We could probably dedicate a whole room to that stuff and work from there."

Ken shook his head. "You're making more of it than it is, I'm sure."

"Probably. But it bothers me to not know."

"When you get plaster on the ceiling and drywall on the walls, you'll forget all about it." He gave a little wave to Sky, who had lifted a cup. "I can't stay today. Crimes to solve out there in the big, ugly world." Ken headed for the counter and then turned back. "Unless, of course, you'd like to come work for me, Polly. I hear you solved the latest murder."

"Deputy Hudson did all the work. I was just in the right place at the right time."

"And drawing the correct conclusions," Tab said. "We'd have to fight you for her, Chief."

He chuckled and reached out to shake Tab's hand, then Polly's. "You two have a good day. I'm off to keep our fair town safe."

"He's a good man," Polly said.

"Sheriff Merritt likes him. Says he's good to work with."

"I can't tell you the number of times that I think about how strange it is I'm close to so many different peace officers," Polly said. "They were just nameless people in my town when I was a kid. Now you're my friends."

"We're better at our jobs when we have friends in the community," Tab said. "Keeps us from seeing the whole world as a minefield. Sheriff Merritt is lucky to have a lifetime of friends and family in Bellingwood. He's really normal." She chuckled. "Except when you scare him by walking into something that you shouldn't."

"I don't try to do it," Polly protested. "It just happens."

Tab smiled and nodded. "You keep saying that." She looked around the room. "I suppose I should get going. All of the paperwork from last night is still on my desk. I haven't been to the office yet this morning."

"Thanks for meeting me, then," Polly said. "This was great."

"We'll do it more often. The sheriff thinks that I make a good liaison for Polly Giller."

"He's trying to shuffle me off, eh?" Polly laughed. "I'm kidding. I know he's busy."

"Never too busy to take your calls. You keep calling him and one or the other of us will show up when you need us. Happy Birthday, Polly."

Polly stood with Tab and gave the young deputy a quick hug. "Have a good day and thank you for listening to me last night and taking care of things."

Tab met Chief Wallers at the front door. He held it open for her, balancing a box of sweet treats from the bakery with his coffee.

Not sure what to do next, Polly sat back down and took the last drink from her coffee cup. She pulled out her phone and sent a text to Sal asking if she had time to do something.

"I'm kind of stuck here," Sal replied. *"Alexander isn't feeling great and I didn't get any sleep. I look and feel like hell."*

"Want some coffee and company?"

"You'd better not. I'm not sure what we have going on. I'd hate to infect you."

"What about a quick hit and run coffee? I'll bring it, ring the doorbell and tell you that I love you."

A few moments passed before Sal replied. *"You have no idea how much I need that. Thank you."*

Polly sat up a little straighter. She could do this for her friend.

"One of Sal's favorites," Polly said to Sky when she got to the counter. "She's home with a sick kid and I'm going to take her something to help perk her up."

"On it," he replied.

"How are things going with you and Stephanie?" Polly asked.

He spun to face her. "What do you know?"

"Nothing more than what you two tell me. Are you going to get up the courage to ask her out?"

"I'm a terrible chicken. What if she says no?"

Polly shook her head and sighed. "You two went to Pufferbilly Days together. She's in here every morning that you work. She'll say yes."

"What?" He frowned. "What do you mean?"

"What I mean is that Stephanie only comes in on the mornings you're here."

"Maybe I'll get up the courage on Thursday."

"No," Polly said, causing him to turn and look at her again. "You will not make it casual and random with that girl. You will step up and ask her out on a date. You will call and talk to her. Make her feel special. And you won't ask her what she wants to do. You'll have a plan and ask her if it is something she'd be interested in doing with you. Expend the energy."

"You're scary," Sky said, putting the cup on the counter in front of her. "Do I really have to do that?"

"I'll have your head otherwise." Polly pointed at the display of sweets. "I think Sal might like a couple of Sylvie's French rolls and two of those cheesecake brownies. And put a cinnamon roll in there for good measure. The girl needs comfort food today."

Sky opened a Sweet Beans box and filled it with Polly's order. "Not only are you scary, but you're the nicest person around, which makes it even worse."

"When are you calling Stephanie?" Polly asked.

"I don't know?"

"You're calling her before Thursday. Don't wait any longer. If I don't hear from her that you've done something, I'll be back."

"But today's Tuesday."

"Uh huh. Two days to figure this out." Polly pointed at the counter and when Sky looked down to see what she was pointing at, she brought her bent forefinger up and lifted his chin with it so he had to look at her. "Two days, bud. If she's important to you, you'll let her know that."

"Yes, ma'am." He stepped back. "Really, really scary."

Polly laughed. "But I still love you."

As she walked outside, she thought about Sylvie and Eliseo. If only they were as easy to manipulate as young Skylar. It drove Henry crazy when she stuck her nose in other people's business, but sometimes it was so much fun. Especially when it worked out. Look at Doug and Anita. She'd gotten them started. For a long time, it felt like she'd failed miserably with that one. The best part about it was that though she'd introduced them, they would always feel as if their relationship was their own. Doug had actually gotten bold enough to move forward. Polly got into her truck and made sure that Sal's coffee was nestled in the cup holder. Unless Anita had asked Doug out. She laughed to herself. That would make more sense. Doug would be happy with things staying the way they were forever.

Doug was fine with Billy and Rachel living in the apartment for several months after they got married while the new apartments and duplexes were being built south of town. Nothing really bothered that boy.

Polly drove over to Sal's and opened her truck door to yapping and barking from the two dachshunds that lived in the house. Sal and Mark would never be surprised by unexpected visitors. She got out of the truck, and by the time she walked up to the front door, Sal had it open and was standing behind the screen. She hadn't been kidding. The girl looked like hell. Her hair was pulled back in a makeshift pony-tail, with hair strands flying all over the place. She was dressed in a t-shirt covered with one of Mark's work shirts and a pair of sloppy shorts that went down to her knees. Sal was wearing no makeup, which wasn't something that anyone outside of her closest friends and family ever saw.

"I'm not coming in," Polly said. "But I come bearing sanity." She held out the coffee cup and box of goodies.

"How do you know to do this kind of stuff for me?" Sal said weakly. "And today's your birthday, not my day."

Polly smiled. "Any day that you're sick and overwhelmed with a baby is your day. You guys looked so good Sunday night."

"It started after we got home. I took him in to see Doctor Mason yesterday. Just a cold. We'll live through it." Sal opened the screen door and held out a small wrapped package. "Not a big deal. Henry said we couldn't bring presents Sunday night, so I hoped maybe I could have coffee with you today. But then life fell apart and ..."

Polly took the gift and slipped the cup of coffee into Sal's hands. "Sniff that and imagine that you're at Sweet Beans with me. Can I put this on the table for you?" She brandished the box.

Sal backed up and Polly put the box of goodies down then stepped back. She held out the gift Sal had given her. "Can I open it?"

A squall from inside the house gave her the answer. "I'm sorry," Sal said. "I need to go. Open it later. I love you. For this," she gestured at the coffee, "and just because I love you. Talk later?"

"I love you, too." Polly headed back for her truck. It was close enough to lunch time that she headed straight for Bill and Marie Sturtz's home. When she felt a flutter in her gut, she realized she was nervous about seeing Bill. It was one thing to spend time with sick people in the hospital. You expected them to look pale and drawn. She wasn't prepared to sit at Marie's very familiar dinner table and look across to see Bill in his regular chair looking like death warmed over. Henry assured her that his dad was doing well, but it still made her nervous. The thought of losing him right now was more than she could bear. Of course they'd get through it if necessary, but my goodness she didn't want it to be necessary.

She drove slowly until she came to their street, trying to avoid the inevitable, and breathed a sigh of relief when she saw Henry's truck already there. Before getting out of her truck, she opened the package from Sal. It was a framed picture of the two of them from a formal they'd attended in college. Polly hadn't seen this in years. Sal in a short, skin-tight red dress that barely covered her bottom; Polly in a much more modest blue dress. She'd always felt like a frump next to her friend. This picture did nothing to dispel that feeling. If she'd been standing next to anyone other than Sal, she'd have just been a normal girl at a party. As much as her friend loved being the center of attention, she didn't make a big deal of it. Sal was who she was and refused to be anything else.

When Polly got to the back door of Bill and Marie's house, it was flung open by a little girl with her arms up.

"Polly!" Jessie's little girl, Molly, insisted on being picked up, so Polly bent over and lifted her onto a hip. Lonnie was taking plates from the cupboard and passed Henry, who was coming in from the dining room.

"Hi there, wife of mine," he said. He pulled Polly in for a hug and kissed her cheek.

"Me too," Molly said, bending her neck so Henry could kiss her cheek.

He obliged. "Word around town is that you solved the case last night and didn't even know it."

"You heard it too?" Polly asked.

"Everybody's talking about it," Lonnie said, coming back into the kitchen. "I ran up to the grocery store for a couple of things and heard the news. You're quite the celebrity."

"I didn't do anything." Polly put Molly back on the ground and the little girl ran out into the dining room. "Can I help here?"

"We've almost got it," Marie said, coming in to the room. "Go on out and find a seat. Bill's feeling good enough that we're going to have a bit of a crowd today. Jessie and Molly are joining us. Betty and Dick should be here in a few minutes. She called to say they were on their way."

Polly took Henry's hand as they walked through the door. "That's a lot of people," she whispered. "Is he okay?"

"He's fine. Everybody knows to keep it low key. Dad just wants to be part of the day. It's your day, you know." He walked into the living room with her. "Dad, are you decent?"

"I'm right here," Bill said grumpily, coming out from behind the Japanese screens. "I put my clothes on this morning just like every other morning of my life. Why wouldn't you think I was decent?"

"Sorry," Henry said.

Bill pulled Polly in for a strong bear hug as she dropped Henry's hand. "Happy Birthday, Polly. I'm glad you could make it for your party."

When he released her, she turned to Henry. "Party?"

"Just a little one."

"Did he tell you what they did to me this morning?" Polly asked Bill.

He linked his arm through hers and walked her back into the dining room.

"No," he said. "Tell me all about how my son treats his very special wife on her birthday."

Bill walked a little more slowly than usual and his face showed strain that she'd never seen before, but Polly was grateful he looked as good as he did. He gestured for her to sit beside him at the table and she did, telling him how Henry and the kids had messed with her earlier in the day.

In the middle of her story, the back door opened again and Bill's sister, Betty, and her husband, Dick, came inside. "We're finally here," Betty said. "That'll teach me to let this old man drive. He got behind a tractor and didn't want to pass it. Said it was a pretty color. The poor farmer was nearly off into the ditch trying to give us room to go around him."

Dick came into the dining room and winked at Polly. "She doesn't know it, but I like spending time with her. I take my time doing everything these days if my Betty is in the same place with me."

"Ya old nut," Betty said, swatting his backside. "Now move so I can hug my brother." She stepped around Dick, hugged Bill's neck, then put a package in front of Polly. "It's not a big deal. Just in case you didn't realize it by now, there's a theme."

Polly wasn't sure what the woman was talking about, but smiled just the same. "Can I open it?"

"No you can't, Missy," Henry said. "You have to wait for cake."

"There's cake?"

"There's always cake," Lonnie said. "You should know that by now. I made your favorite. At least Henry said it's your favorite."

"I have a lot of favorites," Polly replied. "Which one?"

"You'll see."

Lunch was a simple affair, a big tossed salad, roasted chicken, mashed potatoes and Brussels sprouts. To Polly's great surprise, Lonnie announced that they weren't actually eating potatoes, but mashed cauliflower.

Bill reached over and grabbed Polly's wrist. "Before they settle down about this heart attack, we're going to have tried every vegetable available. You have to save me."

"I think that's what they're trying to do," Polly said with a smile. "And these taste wonderful, so be good."

He set his jaw. "You're no help."

When the table was cleared, Marie and Lonnie disappeared into the kitchen and reappeared moments later. Lonnie carried a cake covered with lit candles and Marie had plates and fresh forks. Everyone sang Happy Birthday and waited as Polly blew out her candles.

"It's a carrot cake," Lonnie said. "Henry said you loved that."

"I do. Mary used to make a spice cake for me when I was young. She made chocolate cake all the time, but for my birthday, she pulled out my mother's spice cake recipe." Polly smiled. "Thank you."

Bill took her wrist again. "I can't even have cake without someone putting carrots in it."

"Hush," Marie said as she passed out the plates.

Polly cut the cake and before she knew it, Betty scooped it away from her and served her first, then everyone else. Marie opened a door in the hutch behind her, took out a gift and placed it in front of Polly.

"Go ahead," Marie said. "You can either eat or open."

"I'll open." Polly picked up Betty's gift first and tore the paper away from the shoebox. When she opened the lid, she looked at Henry before lifting out a crystal vase. "This is beautiful."

"It's not new," Betty said. "We grew up with that vase. It was always on the window over Mother's kitchen sink and it was always filled with flowers from her garden. In the winter, she filled it with flowers she'd dried over the summer. It's time that you fill it. Please don't put it away to keep it safe. It's meant to be used."

"Thank you so much," Polly said. "I will love using this. Over my kitchen sink?" she asked Henry.

"We'll make a big ledge for your treasures," he said, taking the vase from her. "I remember this."

Polly picked up the package that Marie had put in front of her and when she took too long to rip back the paper, Bill picked up his dinner knife and slit the tape off. "There you go," he said. "Now hurry."

"This is from my mother," Marie said. "When I was young and we traveled all the time, Mother thought that we should have something that was familiar. We used them at every celebration, whether it was a birthday or Easter or Christmas or even graduations."

Polly held up a pair of brass and ruby red glass candle sticks. "They're ..." She paused.

"As ugly as sin," Marie said, laughing out loud. "But we used them over and over and I treasure them. I want them to be in a happy home. If you choose to use them, that would be wonderful, but if you choose to hide them away and pass them off to Rebecca when she's older, I will understand."

"I will love using them," Polly said, clutching them to her chest.

"Now we told Jessie that she wasn't supposed to do anything," Marie started.

Jessie handed a messily wrapped package to Molly, who ran over and put it in Polly's lap. "Happy Birthday," the little girl said.

Polly reached over and kissed the top of Molly's head. "Thank you. Should I open this?"

"Yes!" Molly's eyes were bright with excitement as Polly pulled off tape and wrapping paper.

"These are fun," she said.

"The theme is a memory," Jessie said, leaning in front of Henry. "I took one of Molly's baby dresses and used the fabric for the top. Marie helped me sew them."

"Oh sweetie," Polly said. She reached down and pulled Molly close while gripping the pretty kitchen towels. Jessie had sewn the fabric to the top with a flap and button so Polly could hang it on an oven door. "Thank you."

Lonnie stood up. "Me next." She walked out into the living room and came back with an awkwardly shaped package. She lifted it over Jessie's head to Henry, who took it and held it.

He gave his sister a strange look. "Is this?"

She nodded. "Open it, Polly."

Polly tore the paper away to reveal a lamp made from a strangely shaped piece of wood.

"That's driftwood," Lonnie said. "I picked it up when we were at a lake somewhere and thought it was cool. What was I, Mom, ten?"

Marie smiled and nodded.

"Anyway, Henry and Dad said they could make a lamp out of it, so they did."

"It was one of my first projects in the shop," Henry said. "I'd totally forgotten about it."

"That's because it's been up in the attic," Lonnie replied. "I got a new shade for it this weekend and then spent time oiling it. The color is lots better now. Maybe you'd like to have it in your office at the new house?"

"I'd love that," Polly said. "Wow, thank you. I'm so glad to have part of your memories." Tears filled her eyes. She knew it was going to happen and just decided not to fight it.

Polly reached over to grip Bill's hand when she realized that he had tears in his eyes, too.

"Don't mind me," he said. "The doctor says that I'll outgrow these stupid things when my strength comes back and the drugs go away."

She laughed. "I'm just so glad you're here."

"Me too. Me too."

CHAPTER TWENTY-NINE

"Now we'll see who's better at this," Polly whispered to her dogs.

The front door opened and Rebecca, Kayla, and Andrew came in chattering after their day at school.

"Polly, are you mad about this morning?" Rebecca called out.

Polly got up from the desk she shared with Henry, slipped into the bathroom, and pushed the door closed. Then she realized the two dogs sitting outside the door were dead giveaways. She opened it and hurried them in with her.

"Polly? Where are you?" Rebecca yelled.

Andrew and Kayla joined her as they called Polly's name while running through the house.

"Stephanie said she's up here," Kayla said. "Where is she?"

The kids were in the media room right outside the door.

"Go knock on her bathroom door," Andrew said. "Maybe she got stuck or something."

Kayla piped up. "Maybe she's hiding in your bedroom with Wonder."

The three kids took off. Polly heard their feet running across the floor while they yelled and yelled for her.

"You guys," Andrew yelled. "The dogs are gone, too. She's probably out back with them. Let's go see."

The three kids ran down the back steps. The crash of doors told Polly they'd finally made it outside. She opened the bathroom door and went back to the desk after looking out the window to see the three kids running through the yard, yelling her name.

"Serves you right," she muttered.

The kids were gone longer than Polly expected, but that only meant she was able to get more work done. When Obiwan and Han jumped and ran to the front of the house, she grinned and waited.

"Polly!" Rebecca shouted.

"In the office," Polly called back.

The three kids ran into the room, huffing and puffing, their faces red with exertion.

"Where were you?" Andrew asked.

Polly tilted her head and peered at him. "Right here."

"No you weren't," he accused.

"I've been right here all the time," she said. "I swear."

Kayla planted her hands on her hips. "We looked for you. You weren't here."

"I've been here the whole time. Where were you?"

"We went outside and to the barn. You weren't anywhere."

Polly nodded. "That's because I've been here working."

Rebecca grinned. "So where were you? Because the dogs were in the same place."

"I don't know what you're talking about," Polly said. "You three must have been hallucinating."

"You're not going to tell us, are you?" Rebecca asked.

"Nothing to tell." Polly turned back to the computer. "Han and Obiwan probably need to go outside. Then it's time for you to get going on your homework. There are brownies and cookies in the fridge."

Andrew sighed as he headed for the back steps again. "Come on, dogs." He stopped and looked back at Polly. "Are you sure you didn't take them out?"

"No," she said, tipping her head at the stairway. "They're probably in desperate need."

"This house is strange," he muttered.

"You two girls should go out with him," Polly said.

Rebecca huffed. "We already had our exercise. Come on, Kayla. Let's find a cookie." She turned and stopped in front of the bathroom door. "You were in there, weren't you?"

"With two dogs?" Polly asked. "That seems silly, doesn't it?"

The girl blew out a loud breath and stalked out of the room.

"Mess with me, will ya?" Polly said under her breath.

~~~

Hayden, Heath, and Rebecca had kicked Polly and Henry out of the kitchen. While Polly spent time with Wonder and her kittens in Rebecca's room, Henry had gone into their bedroom to take a shower and sit in front of the television.

It amazed Polly to see the changes in the kittens even after just a few days. It was going to be hard to give any of them up, but Polly had no idea how they would manage seven cats and two dogs. She needed more humans in her house to balance this menagerie.

The kittens snuggled back around their mother and Polly rubbed Wonder's head. The cat purred and then bent to lick Flash's head. Polly got up and walked out into the living room, pulling the door closed.

Laughter and chatter came from the kitchen as she headed for her bedroom.

"How are the kittens doing?" Henry asked.

"Do you really care?"

He shrugged. "They're cute. I've come to accept that my life will be filled with strays and rescues. I might as well get into the spirit of things, don't you think?"

Polly flopped down on the bed beside him. "What do you think the kids are making for dinner?"

Henry grinned and took her hand. "Do you really care?"
~~~

She laughed. "You're right, I don't. How are things going at work this week?"

"It's been strange not having Dad there to talk to. I didn't realize how many times we talked during the day. I pick up my phone, then realize it isn't so important that I should bother him and move on."

Polly nodded. "It's not the same, but I remember that feeling after Dad died and then after Mary died. I talked to them all the time on the phone. One time I had the number dialed and just as it started to ring, I realized no one was there to answer my call, so I hung up fast."

"At least I can still talk to him," Henry said. "I don't want to think about the other."

"I'm so glad he pulled through this one. Is he going to slow down?"

"He says he won't. Mom's not talking about it." Henry looked toward the kitchen. "I wish Heath was a few years older. He'd be so great taking over that part of the work. Then I could really think about expanding into a full-blown cabinet shop."

"You don't need to hurry," Polly said. "Heath is going to be an adult and on his own much faster than either of us is ready for." She rolled over on her back. "All of them are. I look at Rebecca and see the young woman she's becoming. She still has plenty of kid left in her and these next five years will be a tossup between heaven and hell, but she'll be amazing as she grows into herself."

Henry smiled. "What do you dream she'll be when she grows up? Will she still live in Bellingwood? Do you really think she'll marry Andrew? Will we have lots of grandchildren?"

"I don't know." Polly rolled her head back and forth on the pillow. "She can be anything. She'd be a fantastic artist. As for marrying Andrew and living in Bellingwood, I don't know what I want for them. I'd love to have them together and live close to me because I want to be around her, but at the same time I want her to spread her wings and embrace the whole world. How do I reconcile those things?"

"How does any parent?" Henry asked.

"I feel like I gained so much experience and understanding of life by living in Boston," Polly said. "But at the same time, I lost so much time with Dad. I didn't expect him to die so young."

"You can't feel guilty."

She turned her head to look at him. "I don't. Dad would never have wanted that from me. But I miss him and wish life could be like a fantasy novel where death has little power. I'd give anything to talk to him and hear what he has to say about things like raising children." She chuckled. "Renovating a house, finding dead bodies, being married."

Henry reached out to take her hand. "I wish I could have known him."

"Me too." Polly's eyes filled with tears and she brought her other hand up to brush them away before sitting up. "This is silly. I'm being morose when it's my birthday and I have three wonderful kids making dinner for me."

They looked at the door when Rebecca pushed it open with a few taps. She walked in and handed them each a party hat. "It's a requirement if you want to eat dinner."

Henry rolled his eyes and laughed. "I have never been involved in so much silliness." He took one and put it on his head, stretching the elastic band down under his chin. Handing the other to Polly, he said, "Don't you dare make me go out there looking like a fool all by myself."

She took it and pulled it onto her head. "Better?"

Rebecca led them out and started singing, "Happy Birthday to you, Happy Birthday to you, Happy Birthday, dear Polly. Happy Birthday to you."

By the time they reached the dining room, everybody had chimed in.

The dining room table was set, complete with candles and a pretty basket of flowers in the center.

"I made appetizers," Rebecca said, "but we have to eat them with the meal." She pointed to a platter filled with stuffed mushrooms, something Polly loved but never made. "So sit down and take a few while we put everything else out on the table."

Henry held Polly's chair for her and then sat down beside her. Rebecca handed Polly the platter and went back into the kitchen to return with two glasses of wine for Henry and Polly. "We bought sparkling grape juice for us."

"That would have been fine for me, too," Polly said.

"It's your birthday," Hayden said. "Enjoy."

Heath brought out a basket of Sylvie's warmed crusty French rolls and put plates of salad down at everyone's place.

"Wow," Polly said. "This is pretty fancy."

The kids - mostly Hayden - had made chicken cordon bleu, mashed potatoes, and green beans with toasted almonds. Polly sat back and watched her family laugh together as they talked about the ins and outs of their day. Things were settling back down at school for Heath, especially after the arrest of the girls for cooking meth and the announcement of who the murderer was. It had taken the focus off him, even though people wanted to know how Polly had uncovered the plot.

Rebecca told about how a boy in her math class tried to crawl out of a window, but his belt had gotten stuck on the lock. Their principal, Miss Bickle, had threatened to call the police and accused him of being a runaway, but the math teacher talked her out of it by describing an intricate problem they were working on regarding spatial equations, mass and energy. Apparently, she'd not understood it any better than the class, so she just put a warning in the boy's record. Rebecca declared this made the math teacher her favorite ever.

Hayden spent the afternoon working at the Bell House. He was pushing pretty hard to get them in there before Christmas. Henry agreed that most of the rooms on the main level would be ready. He wasn't sure how they were going to finish everything in the kitchen, but floors and walls would be ready to go. The furnaces would be installed before the end of October.

It was hard to imagine they might finally move. Polly glanced around at all they'd absorbed into the apartment and gave an inward shudder. Packing and moving was going to be horrendous. But she supposed they didn't need to hurry.

"Earth to Polly," Rebecca said.

"What?"

"Are you ready for dessert?"

"I'm always ready for dessert," Polly replied. "What is it?"

Heath stood up and went into the kitchen and opened the refrigerator door. He took out a pie and shyly said, "I made this."

Polly was surprised. Heath rarely did much in the kitchen. "You did?"

"I had some help, but I wanted to. It's my mom's recipe for strawberry-rhubarb pie."

Polly could barely contain her tears. "I love that pie." She stood and hugged him as he came back to the table. Henry was good enough to take the pie from Heath's hands.

"It's my birthday present to you," Heath said. "And now that I know I can make it, I'll make it any time you want it. Hayden says I need to keep practicing the pie crust, but it's my first time."

"Thank you," Polly whispered. "This means everything to me."

"Presents," Rebecca said. "I'll be right back." She took off for her bedroom and Hayden got up to leave the room.

Polly turned to look expectantly at Henry. "Where's your present?"

He tapped his head. "Right here, baby. Don't worry. I've got what you want."

Heath sighed and went back into the kitchen to open the freezer door. "Ice cream?"

"Trying to ignore us?" Polly asked.

"All the time. So, ice cream?"

"Yes, please."

When the three kids were back at the table, Henry and Heath sliced pie and scooped ice cream.

"Open Hayden's first," Rebecca said.

"Really? That never happens."

"It's kind of special."

Polly opened the package Hayden had given to her. She looked at a photograph of two young boys in an ornate silver five by seven frame. "Is this you two?"

Hayden nodded. "I was ten and Heath was just four. This was Mom's favorite picture. It sat on the book shelf beside the piano.

Heath nodded. "She used to tell me that those two boys were good boys that day. When we were naughty, she could remember one day when we weren't. Then she'd laugh and hug me."

"This is so wonderful," Polly said. "Thank you for sharing it with me."

"Have you figured out the theme yet?" Rebecca asked.

Polly shook her head. She had, but wanted Rebecca to explain it in her own words.

"We know that you don't like it when we spend money on you, so I thought that if we gave you one of our memories it would, like, connect you better to the lives we had before you were in them. And everybody liked the idea because our memories would always have a place in your home."

"Oh, I love you," Polly said. "I think it's so cool that you trust me with these." She brushed her lips across the photograph. "Your mother would be proud of you boys. I'm so thankful you are in my life now."

"Here's mine," Rebecca said, handing Polly a package. "Mom and I didn't have a lot of stuff that we took every time we moved, but we had some things."

Polly knew that she was going to be wrecked again, so she took a deep breath before carefully lifting the tape away from the paper. "You're turning into quite a gift organizer, Rebecca. I'm lucky to be on this side of your creativity."

"People always wonder what to get for someone who has everything. I just give them ideas."

"They are great ideas." Polly extricated the small box from the wrapping paper and lifted the top off. "This is your music box," she said.

"And I want you to have it. Mom bought this for Christmas when I was five. She couldn't afford anything else and I saw it in a thrift store we shopped at. She went back the next day and bought it. Later she told me that she'd had to skip lunch that day to afford it for us. Open it up."

The glass encasement exposed the inner workings of the music box. Its wooden frame was worn from love, but Rebecca had polished and cleaned it. When Polly opened the lid, they listened as it played *You Are My Sunshine.*

"I played it all the time," Rebecca said. "Then I just put it on a shelf, but I remember how much I loved opening that up on Christmas morning. Mom sang along and told me stories about when I was a baby. I want it to always be important to someone."

Polly put her arms around Rebecca's shoulder and the two leaned against each other. "It is as important to me as you are, Rebecca. Thank you for sharing."

Rebecca held her for a moment, then sat back up and leaned forward to look at Henry. "We're all dying to know what you got Polly." She turned to look at Polly. "He wouldn't tell any of us."

"Well," Henry said, drawing out the word. "I'm a rebel. I didn't come up with a past memory because I've been so focused on us making future memories with whatever life has to give." He gestured to Heath and Hayden. "I appreciate the hard work you two have put into renovating the Bell House. You're helping us build a foundation for a lifetime of memories. We've talked about different things to do in that foyer and I spoke to my old buddy, Buck, about finding more wood for flooring. Once the ceiling and walls are back up, we have some beautiful wood coming in and my guys are going to help me put radiant heating in that floor." He grinned at Polly. "We're taking the fountain out."

She nodded. Someone had finally made a decision about that crazy thing.

"Next summer we'll decide whether we want to install it outside somewhere, but I've tagged a Christmas tree and you're going to have to make sure you have enough ornaments to fill it this Christmas. That foyer is big enough and I think we should invite everyone to our new house for a big New Year's Eve party. I'm sorry that I couldn't give you something tangible right now, but everything is paid for and on its way."

Polly couldn't breathe. "Thank you," she whispered. "Thank you."

The room had gone quiet as everyone waited for her to say something more.

"I guess I'm going to have to start working over there every afternoon," Rebecca said finally.

"What?" Polly asked.

"If they're ever going to finish all that work, I'm going to have to help. Anyway, I'm tired of cleaning the bathroom all the time. Maybe if I work over there, I'll be too tired to get into so much trouble. Kayla and Andrew will help, too."

"You don't have to do that," Hayden said. "We've got it."

"Because I'm a girl?" Rebecca challenged. "You don't think I can hit a nail?"

"Can you?"

She looked at the wall, then up at the ceiling. "Well, no. But you can teach me. I can do anything you can do. It's my house too."

"You're on," Henry said. "We'll teach you how to be a right-good carpenter. No reason not to, right boys?"

Hayden and Heath both shook their heads and then nodded. "Whatever she wants."

"That's right," Rebecca said. "Because girls rock." She took Polly's arm and leaned on her. "Don't we."

"We sure do."

"There are only three months between now and Christmas," Rebecca said. "Maybe we should start tonight."

Polly patted the smaller hand resting on her arm. "Tomorrow is soon enough. Let's stay home tonight and enjoy the pie."

"Did you have a good birthday?" Rebecca asked.

"It's been a terrific birthday. Best gift theme ever." Polly reached out, opened the lid of the music box again and picked up the photograph of Heath and Hayden. She could hardly wait to find new homes for these memories at the Bell House. This was only the beginning of what was to come.

THANK YOU FOR READING!

I'm so glad you enjoy these stories about Polly Giller and her friends. There are many ways to stay in touch with Diane and the Bellingwood community.

You can find more details about Sycamore House and Bellingwood at the website: http://nammynools.com/

Join the Bellingwood Facebook page:
https://www.facebook.com/pollygiller
for news about upcoming books, conversations while I'm writing and you're reading, and a continued look at life in a small town.

Diane Greenwood Muir's Amazon Author Page is a great place to watch for new releases.

Follow Diane on Twitter at twitter.com/nammynools for regular updates and notifications.

Recipes and decorating ideas found in the books can often be found on Pinterest at: http://pinterest.com/nammynools/

And, if you are looking for Sycamore House swag, check out Polly's CafePress store: http://www.cafepress.com/sycamorehouse

Turn the page for the Christmas short story – *All I Want for Christmas.*

ALL I WANT FOR CHRISTMAS

CHAPTER ONE

"That will be perfect in here," Polly said.

The twelve-foot Christmas tree now standing in the foyer of the Bell House had seemed immense when Henry brought it in on one of his flatbeds. Now that it was standing up, it didn't take up as much space as she'd expected.

"Do you like where I've placed it?" Henry called out from behind the tree. He'd spent the morning building a stand to hold it in place. They finally moved it close to the second-floor landing so he could wrap twine around the banister and the tree to hold it straight.

"I love it. It's almost evenly centered in the room." Polly had today and tomorrow morning to get the thing decorated for their staff Christmas party tomorrow night. Between her company and his, they had enough employees that bringing them all together for a celebration would be a great deal of fun.

Sycamore House's annual community Christmas party was last weekend. That event grew every year and everyone worked to make sure it was a fun event for the town. They were all thankful when it was over. The little party with food, a few decorations, and some extra Christmas trees a few years ago had transformed into quite an extravaganza. Even with no snow, Eliseo had the sleigh … on wheels … available for rides throughout the evening. Jason and his buddies had a grand time driving people around town to look at Christmas lights.

Tomorrow night's party was a combined event for employees and families of Sturtz Construction, Sycamore House and Sycamore Inn, as well as those hired by Sal and Sylvie at Sweet Beans. Every time Polly tried to tally a head count, she gave up. There would be over one hundred people. That was almost more than she could fathom. The only room that could hold everyone right now was the grand foyer. She wanted something different than the auditorium at Sycamore House. Polly certainly didn't want anyone over there to have to work to prepare for this party.

The lights of the chandelier sparkled along the walls. The dark wood of the stair treads and balusters stood in direct contrast to the pale color of the paint. Henry had put a multi-colored wooden floor down that filled her heart with its beauty. He'd carried the same wood patterns into the kitchen, the only other room in the house where they decided radiant heat made sense.

She'd already wrapped the banisters in greenery and white lights and an immense delivery of poinsettias was stashed in a corner. Dark green wreaths with bright red bows had been hung on each door. There was a set of double doors leading to the hallway of the second floor and a matching set below it on the first level. Two other sets of doors on each of the far walls led off to the kitchen on one end and what would someday be their living room and library on the other end.

The fountain was long gone. Well, it was hiding in the old garage, and there was no other furniture in the foyer. Later today, Hayden and Heath would bring over tables and chairs from Sycamore House that would remain until after Polly's New Year's Eve party.

Smaller Christmas trees were placed in other rooms throughout the house. Their family tree was in a corner of the kitchen. Rebecca and Polly had decorated it just after they started moving in at the first of the month. The kitchen was by no means finished. She hadn't decided what she wanted for cabinetry or appliances. They'd put her dining room table in there and were borrowing an extra refrigerator that Bill and Marie had in the garage. Henry found a cheap stove on craigslist.

Polly and Henry were living in the back corner of the house, in what would become the library. The worst part about that room was that the only working fireplace in the house so far made it a very comfortable room. The family ended up in there a lot with Polly having to kick them out at night so she could get some sleep.

Heath and Hayden took over the large living room at the northwest corner of the house. The sofas and chairs from the living room at Sycamore House had gone into that room and the boys did quite a lot of work to make it look like a nice studio apartment. There was a fireplace in that room as well, but Henry hadn't had it cleaned out yet. Things were barely finished by the time Polly had had enough and announced they were moving in. The living room still wasn't fully painted and the floor hadn't been refinished, but the walls were up and primed, the ceiling was finished, and it was good enough.

Rebecca's room *was* finished, but it was a lot smaller and she'd ended up painting the walls herself. There was no telling how long it would be until they'd move into the rooms upstairs, so Polly let her choose a paint color as long as she did the work. She'd gone with a pale yellow on the three walls that would see the morning sun and painted the back wall a deep blue. It was beautiful against the woodwork. She'd asked for a Christmas tree for her room. They'd gotten a small four-foot artificial tree and Rebecca wrapped it in colored lights and made her own ornaments. She'd been working steadily on different crafts and the tree was coming together.

The future parlor had become the media room. The family spent time in there, too. The floor wasn't finished, but Polly had covered it with rugs. It was a comfortable place to hang out when they were all there together. Blankets covered the furniture and were wrapped around its inhabitants most of the time. Kayla called it cozy. They'd purchased a second artificial tree for this room and everyone had gotten involved. One cold and dreary evening, Polly popped corn and the kids strung it onto thread for garland. Whenever she was outside with the dogs, she picked up pine cones and acorns and turned them into rustic ornaments. It might take her a few years to fully decorate all her trees, but she was going to have fun in the process.

Next to the parlor / media room was the dining room. They'd worked around the immense dining room table to finish this floor first. Polly had gotten her dark wainscoting and deep green walls.

There were so many windows on the east wall that it was a beautiful room. Since none of the big furniture was ready for use, the room was still empty. They hadn't used it yet, but she couldn't wait to have big family dinners around that table.

Henry came over to stand beside her and looked up at the tree. "Now you have to decorate it."

"I need the ladder."

He shook his head. "That still makes me nervous. Are you sure you won't wait for the boys?"

"I can go up a ladder."

"Please? At least let them wrap the lights and garland for you."

Polly laughed out loud. "That's all I'm putting on the tree."

"I'd feel a lot better if you'd just let them do it."

Heath, Hayden, and Rebecca had gone Christmas shopping together today. The boys weren't terribly excited about their excursion, but Rebecca's enthusiasm carried them out the door this morning in good spirits.

"We'll see where I'm at when they get home this afternoon," Polly said in grudging agreement.

A doorbell rang and Polly put her hand up to stop Henry. "Front or side door?" she asked.

"I vote for front door."

When they'd installed the doorbells, they discovered it was impossible to tell which one was chiming. Henry was going to fix it, but for now it was always a guessing game.

She took a few steps and opened the front door, then giggled. "Nope."

To get to the back door, she had to go through the kitchen and a back porch which was as big a room as any she'd had in her home in Story City. True to his word, Liam Hoffman had run water so she could have her laundry on the main floor.

Polly opened the door. "What are you doing here?" she asked Lydia, Andy and Beryl.

"We brought coffee." Beryl brandished a Sweet Beans coffee cup and snatched it back when Polly put her hand out. "That one's mine."

Andy laughed. "Here's yours."

Polly stepped back and gestured for them to come in. "Are you just visiting?"

Lydia scuffed her feet across the mat and went on into the kitchen. "Since Rebecca isn't having an art lesson with Beryl, we decided to spend the extra time together and wanted to see what you were doing with your foyer. None of us can imagine decorating a space that big. And you didn't ask for help."

Polly checked to see if her friend was scolding her.

Andy pushed the cup of coffee into Polly's hands. "We also brought treats, and really, we're just being snoopy. You told us that Henry bought a big tree for you and we wanted to see it."

The women had only been to the Bell House once since Polly moved in. She wanted to show it all off, but at the same time she hated that people were going to see it before things were finished. Polly had such big dreams for the house. She could imagine how each room looked, but they were still so far from those dreams becoming a reality. It had taken nine months for them to be this far. Sure, the biggies were finished, but there was so much yet to do.

"Come on, come on," Beryl said, pushing past all of them. "I want to see this monstrosity." She went through the doorway that led to the foyer and held it open. "Don't be wasting my time, girls. Move it."

"I love the greenery," Lydia said. She walked into the center of the room and looked up at the top of the tree. "My goodness. That's beautiful. And your wreaths on the doors? Perfection." Lydia dropped her purse on the floor, then walked over to the tree and moved a branch, then another.

"She's making it perfect," Beryl whispered.

"What will you do with the poinsettias?" Lydia asked.

Polly shook her head. "I don't know yet. I was thinking about putting them on the stairways and a few on the floor of the landing."

"What are you using for the top of the tree?"

"It's over here." Polly walked over to the corner of the room where she'd stowed the lights and garland. She'd found an immense white star, lit with a battery-operated LED light.

"That will be beautiful," Lydia affirmed. She rubbed her hands together. "Please let us help you."

" You want to help me?" Polly said with a laugh. "Don't you have your own decorating to do?"

"My house is done," Andy said. "Len and I put our decorations up the day after Thanksgiving."

"Me too," Lydia said. "The church decorations are finished. I have nothing more to do."

Polly turned to Beryl, who shrugged. "I'm not hosting parties at my house this year, so I put my cute little Charlie Brown Christmas tree on the kitchen table and my favorite Nativity set on the coffee table and I'm calling it Happy Holidays."

Henry came into the foyer from the back corner. "What are you ladies plotting?" he asked.

"They want to help me decorate this room," Polly said.

He took a deep breath. "Where are those boys when I need them?" After an extended sigh, he gave a wry laugh. "I'll go out to the garage and get the ladder. You can tell me how to string the lights and garland."

Beryl sat down in front of the boxes and pulled back the end flap on a box of lights. "Someone has to start this. It might as well be me." She waved her hand toward the kitchen. "Polly, be a good girl and get me a trash bag for the boxes."

Polly looked at her and put her hands on her hips. "What?"

"Sorry. *Please* be a good girl and get me a trash bag for the boxes." Beryl cackled. "And maybe a knife for the tape. This will kill my delicate fingers before I'm finished."

"It's a good thing I love you, Beryl Watson," Polly said.

"Should we have brought wine instead of coffee?" Beryl asked.

Polly stopped in front of the poinsettias where Andy was standing. "You don't have to carry those up the steps. I'll do that."

"I was just counting them. If you'd like, I think we could put one on every other step. That would leave enough for you to do something fun at the top."

"That sounds perfect." Polly shook her head. "I can't believe you're here. You always show up to help me when I need it the most."

"It's much more fun to do these things with friends," Lydia said. She slipped her shoes off and smiled. "I love these radiant heat floors." Then she nodded toward the kitchen and side yard. "Are we going to drive your husband crazy?"

"Probably," Polly said, nodding. "But he deserves it."

"Hey, Girlio," Beryl called out from the other side of the room. "Chop, chop."

"My master is calling." Polly went through the door into the kitchen. Decorating was going to be finished in no time at all.

CHAPTER TWO

Having everyone living on the first floor of the house was much more intimate than Polly had expected. One of the things that worried Polly the most about moving into the Bell House was that her family would spread out and they'd never see each other. So far, that wasn't the case at all. In fact, they spent more time in physical proximity to each other than ever before. The rooms were arranged so differently than at Sycamore House that they still hadn't figured out their favorite place to be. With no living room yet, they either ended up in the kitchen, the media room or Polly and Henry's bedroom.

And wherever there were people, that also meant there were piles of animals.

Kayla had taken the little gray kitten, but the other three - Flash, Batman, and Robin - as well as their mother, Wonder, had become permanent residents of the household.

Polly insisted that the doors to the upstairs remain closed so they didn't have to heat it and so none of the animals found their way up there. Of course, the second week they lived in the house, someone had gone upstairs and forgotten to close doors behind them. In the middle of dinner, they'd heard plaintive mewing. A quick head count of the felines in attendance revealed that Batman and Robin were absent.

Henry opened the door to the back staircase and sent Obiwan up first. He and Han followed and soon returned with the two kittens, none the worse for wear.

Since they weren't using the dining room, the original cat tree had been erected in front of the windows and a second had been purchased to sit beside it. The back yard with its trees offered a great number of daily visitors and entertainment for the cats.

Polly still insisted that someone go with Obiwan and Han when they were outside. While there was a back fence separating the property from the cemetery, the front was wide open to the city. Until they made decisions about how to enclose the yard, she expected the dogs to have supervision. Walking outside with the two dogs was already part of their lives, they just continued the practice. Polly enjoyed wandering the yard with them, learning about every bump and dip. The front yard hadn't recovered from the trauma of being dug up by Liam Hoffman in September, but the dirt was settling and it would come back to life next spring.

She was walking through the front yard with Han and Obiwan when the kids returned from their day out.

Lydia, Andy, and Beryl left after declaring that the foyer was gorgeous. Even Henry admitted that he hadn't expected it to be quite so beautiful. He'd expertly wrapped the tree in gold garland and white lights and then helped Polly top it with the brightly lit star. Andy and Lydia placed poinsettias up both staircases and put several in the window wells of the big front windows. The room still felt a little sterile, but Polly couldn't worry about it. They would fill it with tables for the party tomorrow night, and over the years, she'd continue to add to the room's beauty.

"We got presents!" Rebecca yelled, jumping out of the back seat of Heath's truck.

Obiwan barked and ran toward her.

"Did you have fun?"

Heath nodded. "That girl takes no prisoners when she's

shopping. It wasn't as bad as I thought it would be. We went into a store, bought what we needed and left. No wandering around, no browsing, no nothing."

"That's my girl," Polly said. "What did you get?"

"I can't show you," Rebecca said. "Well, I can show you some things, but not everything. Come on, guys. We're putting it all in my room."

"You can barely walk in there now," Polly said.

Rebecca gave her a happy grin. "It's the best."

"We'll unload and head over to Sycamore House for the tables," Hayden said. "Eliseo called to tell us where everything was. I guess Rachel put out tablecloths for us, too."

Polly nodded. "Great. We finished decorating. Once the tables are up, we'll be done until tomorrow."

"Should we bring anything else back?"

Hayden was asking about the never-ending piles of boxes and items still in the apartment. She and Henry were leaving their office there for now. They didn't have a place for it here yet. That was Rebecca's room right now. The kitchen hadn't been completely emptied at Sycamore House; they only brought over what they needed. There were no cabinets on the walls here, but the pantry kept the worst clutter out of the main kitchen area. Several small tables were still at the apartment and they'd left most everything on the walls. Baskets and boxes filled with items that were important but not necessary littered floors in every room. Her books were still on shelves; none had even been packed. The boxes and shelves in the garage hadn't been touched. Moving might kill her.

Once the holiday season was over and Polly didn't have to worry about entertaining people, she intended to completely empty Sycamore House and store things in the foyer until permanent homes could be found for their things.

"Don't worry about anything else," Polly said. "Unless there's something you want."

"Okay. Let me take these bags in to Miss Thing. She's having a blast."

Rebecca considered the whole thing to be a great adventure. She loved being in the Bell House.

Behind the foyer a six-foot-wide hallway spanned the length of the house from the kitchen, past the rooms to the library, where it turned a corner and went to the front of the house past what would one day be the living room. Polly refused to let the hallway become a storage area, but if push came to shove, she'd fill every nook and cranny on this first floor with their belongings.

She guessed that they were on an adventure. At least they were on it together.

With all that was going on, Rebecca hadn't had any time to venture out to her new studio. For that matter, Polly hadn't taken time to work in the whiskey room in the basement either. Time had just flown by.

When Henry announced at Polly's birthday that he was giving her the floor and radiant heat in the foyer and that they were going to have a New Year's Eve party here, it spurred everyone into action. Every hour of free time was spent in the house, finishing ceilings and walls. When they were stuck waiting for something else to happen, Polly and Rebecca packed like fiends. Trying to make decisions about what to bring with them in the first wave of moving had been difficult.

But it all started coming together, and when Hayden came home for fall break the week of Thanksgiving, furniture started moving from the apartment to the house. Rather than a big Thanksgiving meal, they celebrated with hamburgers and brats on the grill. There had been plenty of invitations for dinner, but just having the five of them together around their table in the new kitchen was something special.

Lonnie Sturtz had come home the week of Thanksgiving since she'd be in Greece for Christmas. She and her parents came over to the house on that Saturday. Most of the moving was completed and Polly was ready for her closest friends and family to see what they were doing.

Bill was nearly back to normal. His wife and son held him back from returning to work full-time, but he hadn't waited much longer than a week before he was in the shop. Len Specek promised to keep an eye on him and Ben Bowen had come to enjoy the steady work inside a warm building. Henry still hadn't found someone to work full-time there, but the work was slowing enough that everyone could take a breath.

Since Lonnie wasn't coming home for Christmas, Marie and Bill decided to go to Arizona. They were leaving Monday morning after the party and wouldn't be back until mid-March.

Han and Obiwan finally went up the steps to the side door and waited for Polly to open it and let them in. "You miss your horses, don't you, guys," she said. "We'll go over to visit soon. I promise."

Polly took her jacket off and hung it on a hook in the mudroom.

"We'll be back in a while," Hayden said as he and Heath passed her on their way out the door.

Polly tapped on Rebecca's closed door. "What goodies did you find?"

"You can't see." Rebecca stepped into the hallway, shutting the door behind her.

"Okay," Polly said with a laugh. "What are you doing now?"

"I don't know. Why?"

"I was thinking about going downtown. Maybe hit the antique shop and see if I can't find some pretty decorations for the tables."

Rebecca's eyes grew wide. "Yes! I love that store."

"I know," Polly replied. "We might wander into Bradford's Hardware and the drug store if we don't find what I'm looking for."

"More shopping. Best day ever."

"Did you lock the cats in your bedroom?" Polly asked.

"Oh. Yeah. But you can't look in there when I open the door."

"I promise."

Rebecca opened her bedroom door enough so the cats could move in and out, then followed Polly back to the mudroom where they put on their coats and headed for the truck.

Bellingwood's downtown was festive, with banners, lights, and greenery hanging from light posts.

When Polly turned into a parking space in front of Simon Gardner's antique shop, she felt her phone buzz and then ring. "Go on in," she said to Rebecca. "I'll see who this is."

She swiped the phone open and didn't recognize the number, but answered anyway. "Polly Giller."

"Hello Ms. Giller, this is Lester Dunlap at the Methodist Church."

"Hi there, Pastor. What can I do for you?"

"I have a bit of a situation, and after speaking with Mrs. Merritt, she recommended I contact you."

"Of course. How can I help?"

"We have a young family in need of a place to stay."

Polly wanted to laugh and tell him there was plenty of room in her inn, but she realized that she didn't even know. The hotel filled up during the holidays. If nothing else, though, she was certain there was room in the addition at Sycamore House.

"I can find room for them," she said. "I'm not certain whether it will be at the hotel or Sycamore House, but I definitely have room. How many people?"

"There are four children with their parents, as well as the mother's sister."

"I understand," she replied, her mind racing as she tried to decide on the best place for the family. "Where are they now?"

"At my house."

"Oh," Polly said. "This is an immediate issue."

"I'm so sorry."

"No. I'm actually better at those than anything else. Let me make a couple of phone calls and see which location will be best for them. I have your number now. I'll call you right back."

"Thank you. People in the church will help with most of their needs, but finding a place for them to stay until we can provide a home has been difficult."

"I'll call back in a few minutes." She swiped the call closed and tried to decide which location would be better for the family. She called Sycamore Inn first. If there were two rooms close together, she'd start there.

"Sycamore Inn, how may I help you?"

"Hi, this is Polly. Is Grey around?"

"He's out back at the ice rink with a class right now. Can I help? This is June."

Grey had hired a wonderful woman to work the front desk - June Livengood. She was friendly and enthusiastic about Bellingwood and Sycamore Inn. They'd received a lot of compliments about her the past few months. She lived down the street from Sylvie with her mother and her mother's older sister. The two older ladies were just a hoot and when the three of them were together, there was always laughter. June had never been married. She always said that when she kicked her mother and aunt off this earth, she'd travel around the world and find a young exotic gorgeous man to bring back to Bellingwood, just to stir the old biddies up.

"June, do you have any rooms available? This might be long term and I need at least two."

"Wow, that's a lot, but I think I do. Would you like them to be together?"

"If possible."

"I'd have to shuffle a few things around. Yes, hmmm. How long term?"

"I don't know yet. Pastor Dunlap has a family that needs a place to stay."

"Oh, I wonder if that's the family whose house burned down. I heard the church was helping them."

"I didn't hear about a house burning down," Polly said.

"Not in Bellingwood. It was in a little town north and west of here a couple of months ago. Pastor Dunlap was connected to them from a former church. They've been trying to make it, but couldn't get back on their feet," June replied. "Yes. I can move things around and we can put them together for as long as necessary. Tell the pastor to come over and I'll set them up."

"And no charge on this, June. If you have to bill it somewhere, put it to me."

"Got it. I'll let Grey know."

Polly waved at Rebecca when the girl stepped out of the door to the antique shop with a frown on her face.

"I appreciate your help, June."

"No problem. We're here to serve."

Polly held up a finger to tell Rebecca that it would be a few more minutes and waved for her to go back inside.

"Pastor Dunlap?" Polly asked when the call connected.

"Yes. Is this Polly?"

"It is and I have two rooms at the hotel. June Livengood is at the front desk and she'll help you get them settled. Please don't hesitate to call me if you need anything else. We're glad to help."

"Thank you so much for this," he replied. "I knew that Lydia would point me in the right direction, but I had no idea it would end up being this simple."

"Any time. Please let me know how I can help."

"Thank you, Ms. Giller."

"Polly."

"Thank you, Polly."

She sat back and realized Rebecca would continue to get more and more impatient, so Polly jumped out of the truck and headed into the warm and cozy antique shop.

"Good afternoon, Polly," Simon Gardner said. "Your daughter has been perusing my stock of Christmas decorations." He pointed at a stack of items on the counter in front of him. "I believe she's made some excellent choices."

Polly chuckled. "Oh dear. I really only wanted to decorate tables for our staff Christmas party. It looks as if Rebecca has other decorating plans in her head as well."

"Look at this Santa and sleigh," Rebecca said, coming up behind her. "Isn't it great?"

"It is. But where are we going to put it?"

"In the middle of a table, of course. A little greenery and it will be awesome."

"Okay," Polly agreed. "You're the boss."

Rebecca looked up at Simon. "It's taken a few years, but she's finally figured it out."

CHAPTER THREE

Everything was in chaos. Polly sat on the edge of her bed Sunday evening, tears of frustration brimming. She was absolutely certain that her blue pumps were here and not at Sycamore House. She'd doublechecked because this was the dress she planned to wear tonight. Polly already had to purchase new makeup. The things from her bathroom at home were hiding in a box somewhere.

Home. This place was supposed to be her new home, but right now it felt like it was the bane of her existence. Nothing was normal. Everything was in disarray. She couldn't find anything when she needed it, the caterers were here asking a million questions about things they'd decided two months ago, and now she couldn't find her damned shoes.

Henry stood in the doorway of their bedroom, or hell on earth, as Polly wanted to call it right now. Okay, she might be feeling a little over-dramatic.

"The caterers are back on track," he said. "It smells really good."

"Thanks," she said. "I was going to have to kill someone." Polly looked at him. "That'll teach me to rely on Sylvie. She just gets it."

He chuckled. "Like they aren't intimidated enough because they're cooking for her tonight."

Polly didn't want Sylvie or Rachel to have to work tonight. It was supposed to be a party for them, so she'd asked for help in finding someone to cater the party. Sylvie knew of a fellow classmate who was trying to get her business started down in Madrid and made the call. The truth was, Sylvie had been required to learn her business while in the line of fire at Sycamore House. That training had given her knowledge that others didn't have. During early discussions with this caterer, it had been patently obvious the woman hadn't had too many large jobs come her way, but she *was* willing to do the work.

The caterer's self-confidence eroded when she arrived at the house in the early afternoon having completely forgotten to plan for dishes and silverware. For some reason the woman thought the event was being held at Sycamore House where she'd have access to the entire kitchen. She also forgot to bring coffee pots and pitchers to serve drinks. Once Polly and the woman identified the things needed to pull off a successful party, Hayden, Heath, and Henry went back to Sycamore House with a list.

Whoever had packed the catering van had left butter for the rolls on a counter in Madrid. That wasn't discovered until later in the afternoon. A quick trip to the grocery store fixed it, but by that point Polly was a wreck.

Henry tried to tell her that the people who were attending were friends and family and she shouldn't worry. That wasn't helpful and he'd gone back to the kitchen to make sure things ran as smoothly as possible. Polly was waiting for yet another shoe to drop. Oh. Like her blue pumps. They could drop out of the sky at any moment and she'd be happy.

"You're looking pretty forlorn," he said. "Is there anything else I can do to help?"

Polly shook her head. "I can't find my shoes."

"I'm not sure what to do with that," he said, biting his lip. He stepped back out of the room and rapped on the door to the room next to theirs. "Rebecca? Polly needs your help."

He came back in and gave Polly a sheepish look. "I'm sorry. I can do a lot of things, but I really don't know what to do with this."

"It's okay. I can go barefoot. At least the floor is warm."

"Yes, it is," he agreed. "And the foyer looks beautiful. You did a wonderful job."

Rebecca had convinced Polly that the decorations on each table should be different. They were using gold, green, and yellow colored tablecloths, so it made sense to Polly. The two spent Saturday afternoon selecting some of the prettiest things from the antique shop and before she knew it, Polly had enough to decorate each of the twelve tables. From Santa and his sleigh to Christmas carolers, and ceramic Christmas trees to small wooden snowmen, the tables were filled with festive fun.

"What do you need?" Rebecca asked, coming up beside Henry.

"She can't find her shoes."

Rebecca looked at Polly. "Your blue ones? I know they're here somewhere." She closed her eyes in concentration. "I'll be right back."

She darted out of the room and Henry chuckled. "I'll make sure things are still going smoothly in the kitchen."

"Thank you." Polly picked her phone up to look at the time. "People will start arriving soon."

"And we'll be there to greet them," he said. "Maybe I'll stir Heath and Hayden up first."

"I have them," Rebecca called out from her room.

Polly jumped off her bed and wandered out into the hallway. She peeked into Rebecca's room. "Why are my shoes in here?"

Rebecca brandished the shoes and bent over to push a basket into the middle of her floor. "We put them in this basket when you remembered you were going to need them for tonight."

"Thank you," Polly said. She stepped into the room and hugged Rebecca. "You can never ever leave me. Promise?"

"Nope." Rebecca backed up and spun in a circle, the black skirt of her dress billowing out around her. "This is the coolest dress. I love it." The full skirt and its layers of black lace had tiny, sparkling rhinestones sewn in. The golden form-fitting bodice had long sleeves and was covered by a red and black vest. Jessie had come over after church and curled Rebecca's hair, building a pretty up-do for the evening.

"Now that I'm fully dressed, maybe I should go be cordial to the caterers," Polly said.

"I didn't realize that Sylvie was that good," Rebecca replied.

Polly nodded. "Yeah. We've really taken her for granted." She sighed. "Henry was right. It's just one evening and people will be fed. There's nothing that can fall apart so badly I can't get past it. Right?"

"Exactly." Rebecca took Polly's hand. "Maybe we avoid the kitchen for a few minutes, though."

Polly snapped her head to look at her daughter. "Do you know something?"

"No," Rebecca said with a laugh. "I was just thinking that you should look at the foyer and remember how pretty things are. The food will taste great and people will have fun with each other. And besides, aren't you giving everyone money tonight? They'll go home happy, no matter what."

"You're right." Polly and Henry had decided to do something extra on top of the year-end bonuses that had been planned into the budgets of their companies. It wasn't much, but at Christmas, sometimes a little extra went a long way toward making shopping easier.

Rebecca and Polly walked down the hallway to the foyer entrance across from the boys' room and went in.

She couldn't help it. This was going to be one of her favorite rooms. She hadn't considered that to be reality when they first bought the Springer House. Not only was the big fountain ugly in the center of the room, but the walls had been gold-flocked. After fifty years, the flocking had rotted away and what had once been white wainscoting was grey and stained. The stairs, while still in relatively good shape structurally, looked terrible and many of the balusters had been broken. Gutting a room top to bottom left a lot of options for renovation.

Polly had ended up painting most of this room herself and it had taken forever. She'd put down an ivory paint first and then washed gold over it. When she started, she had no idea if the effect would work, but it was gorgeous.

"Are you ready?" Hayden asked, coming up to stand beside her.

Polly nodded. He looked good tonight. All of her boys looked good. Henry was wearing a suit. He always looked good in a suit. The boys had resisted and she was fine with that. They were in black woolen slacks. Hayden wore a gold dress shirt while Heath wore dark blue. "We clean up good," Polly said.

"You look beautiful," Henry said, crossing the room. "I'm glad you found your shoes."

Polly lifted her right foot and waggled it. "Me too. Otherwise, I would have looked like a waif beside all of you pretty people." She pointed to the tables at the other end of the foyer. "Hors d'oeuvres are out?"

He nodded. "I think she's got this on the run now. All we need are guests."

As if on cue, the doorbell rang.

"I'll get it," Hayden said. He strode across the floor with Rebecca right behind him. As he put his hand on the doorknob of one door, she grabbed the other and the two stepped back as they pulled the doors open.

Polly chuckled at the grand reception for ... Jessie and Molly.

"Are we the first ones?" Jessie asked.

Polly rushed over to them. "You are, but that's great. I'm glad you're here."

"We can't stay long, but I wanted Molly to see your new house." Jessie looked up and around. "This is amazing. Isn't this amazing, Molly?"

The little girl's mouth was open as she took in the immensity of the room. Before Jessie could stop her, Molly took off, running as fast as her little legs would let her. She wove in and out of tables before coming to rest in front of the immense Christmas tree. "Mommy!" she yelled. "Look!"

The doorbell rang again and Rebecca was there to open the doors. This time, Bill and Marie Sturtz came in followed by Andy and Len Specek. Several families that Polly didn't recognize were right behind them. Henry, however, crossed over to shake their hands and welcome them.

"I love your table decorations," Andy said. "This all looks beautiful."

"Oh Polly," Marie gushed. "What a wonderful room. She pointed to the stairway. "Please tell me that you will insist on Rebecca having her wedding here. Can't you just imagine her coming down that beautiful staircase with a long train behind her?"

Polly nodded. "I'll do my best. That one's a little independent, though."

The three women watched as Rebecca greeted guests. She had something to say to everyone who came in.

"She's a natural," Andy whispered.

"Hayden tried to tell me this summer that she was good at this," Polly replied. "I didn't even ask her to greet people. She just stepped up to it tonight." Polly looked around for the rest of her family. Heath was talking to a group of young men and their wives or girlfriends. She assumed they were part of the construction crews that worked for Henry.

Sal and Mark came in together and Polly sighed. The woman was a stunner. Red was her favorite color and tonight she wore a long, red gown with a slit that came up to her mid-thigh. A white furry stole was wrapped around her shoulders. Polly knew it was fake; Sal couldn't bear to wear anything else. Her hair was pulled back into a tight bun and her lips were as red as her dress. As gorgeous as Mark was, tonight he definitely played second fiddle.

"Where's Alexander?" Polly asked.

Sal grinned. "Babysitter. I begged Joss for her lady. He doesn't need to be in the midst of all of this chaos."

"Uh huh. You just wanted to party."

Mark slid an arm around his wife's waist. "We are definitely partying tonight."

Camille came in with her roommate, Elise. Camille was dressed in a gorgeous white gown with a wavy gold pattern. Even Elise had gotten into the Christmas spirit with a pretty blue and green dress.

Noise at the front door caught Polly's attention. Kayla giggled beside Rebecca, excited to be here. Her sister, Stephanie, had come in with Skylar Morris, Polly's favorite barista. She was glad to see them in public together. Stephanie had wanted to keep the relationship from Kayla while she tested it out, but it hadn't taken long for that to fall apart. Kayla had known right away there was something up with her sister and the truth won out.

Rachel and Billy were here. Their wedding a month and a half ago had been a delight. Simple, sweet, a little kooky with the Halloween decorations around them, and perfect for the young couple. They were still living with Doug Randall in the apartment above Polly's garage at Sycamore House, but once construction was finished on the apartments south of town, they were ready to move into their first home together.

Henry had been guiding people to the hors d'oeuvres line and as more and more came in, the noise level in the room went up. It had been a great idea to bring the businesses together for this party.

Polly waved at Grey Greyson across the room. He'd slipped in at some point and she'd missed it. His entire staff was here this evening. He and Jeff had hired a temporary desk clerk for the several hours they'd be away from the hotel. She wondered where Jeff was. He was usually early to these events, but then, he usually was in charge of them.

Just as she started to wonder about Sylvie, Jason and Andrew came in the front door. Andrew stopped to talk to Kayla and Rebecca, and Jason looked around until he saw Heath. This made Polly curious. She walked over to the front door.

"Where's your mother?" she asked Andrew.

He looked around. "She's not here yet?"

"No. Should she be?"

He gave Polly a sly grin. "I guess not."

Polly grabbed his arm. "What does that mean?"

Andrew shrugged and smiled. "I don't know. You'll have to wait and see."

"You're a brat."

He nodded. "I know. But you love me anyway. Can I steal Rebecca so we can get something to eat?"

"Of course," Polly said. She touched Rebecca's shoulder. "Thank you for greeting tonight. You're terrific at this."

"It's my way of seeing everybody that comes in," Rebecca replied. "You know how I hate to miss things."

CHAPTER FOUR

"You can go now," Rebecca said from behind Polly. "I want to finish this tonight."

Rebecca and Andrew had only been away from the front door long enough for Polly to welcome Kristen, who spotted Stephanie and Rachel. Jeff Lyndsay had come in while Polly was at the door. She'd hoped his late arrival meant he was bringing someone, but he'd been fielding calls from home in Ohio.

"Are you sure?"

"Go. Work the room," Rebecca said. "We've got this."

Polly looked around and saw Henry, who looked up to catch her eye.

"Thanks, sweetie," Polly said and walked toward her husband.

"Polly, I'd like you to meet Denny Lindstrom and his wife Eva. He's one of my foremen."

Polly shook the man's hand and smiled at his wife. "I've seen you at the pharmacy," Polly said. "You work with Nate."

"He works with me," the woman retorted with a laugh. "I keep telling him that his wife is a saint, but his two little ones are cute as buttons. We're having dinner at their new home Thursday evening. Denny here is looking forward to seeing Nate's garage."

"You work on cars, too?" Polly asked.

"Not as much as I'd like," Denny replied. "When I was young, I was a real gearhead. Age and wisdom ..."

"And five daughters," his wife interrupted.

He laughed. "And five daughters made the hobby a little too expensive to maintain. I hope that once they're out on their own, I can get back to it."

"None of your daughters are interested in cars?" Henry asked.

"Sidney, maybe," he responded. "She's only eight. Maybe I'll bring a junker in and start tinkering on it with her. The other girls are only interested in having a car to drive."

Henry tapped Polly's shoulder and turned her toward the front door. "Look," he whispered.

She turned to see Eliseo and Sylvie come in the door together, Eliseo with his arm at Sylvie's waist. He wore a gray, loose-fitting suit with a dark blue mock-turtle sweater under the jacket. Sylvie's gown was green with a lacy gold overlay on the skirt. Her hair had been pulled up with floating curls and wisps around her face. She barely looked like the woman Polly knew so well.

Andrew and Jason joined her at the door and smiled when they saw Polly staring. Andrew nodded and waggled his eyebrows at Polly, grinning the entire time.

"Wow," Polly breathed. "When she makes an entrance, she makes an entrance."

Henry laughed. "Eliseo has to just be dying right now. He doesn't like any kind of attention."

"If he's taking Sylvie out and she looks like that, he can't avoid it." Polly turned back to the Lindstroms. "It was so nice to meet you. I need to say hello to my friend. Enjoy your evening." She squeezed Henry's hand and slipped away from him, moving through the growing crowd to find Sylvie.

"See, I told you," Andrew said.

"You told me nothing," Polly replied. "How long have you known?"

"About how good she looked?"

"Sure. We can start with that."

Sylvie smiled at Polly and gave Andrew a little push. "You go play with your friends. Thank you for standing with us. And you can go, too, Jason. I'll see you two at dinner."

The boys ran away as Andy and Len Specek joined them. "Sylvie Donovan, you're a dream," Andy said. "An absolute dream." She put her hand out to shake Eliseo's. "You're a lucky man this evening."

"I am," he said, his eyes twinkling.

Polly took his arm. "What did you do?"

His chest shook as he laughed. "I didn't want to come to one more event and wonder if you were going to turn me upside down because I didn't have the courage to ask Sylvie to come with me." He looked at the woman standing beside him. "So I asked."

"I don't know whether to laugh or cry," Polly said. She fingered the lapel of his suit. "This is wonderful. You look amazing."

"Elva picked it out for me. It's nothing I would have chosen, but she insisted."

"Doesn't he look great?" Sylvie asked. She took his arm and held it close to her. "Just great."

"Sylvie!" Sal cried out, grabbing her friend into a hug. "You're here." She stopped and backed up when she realized that Sylvie wasn't alone. "And you have a date."

"That's my wife," Mark Ogden interjected. "She knows exactly how to state the obvious." He put his hand out to Eliseo. "Good to see you, man. You're taking such good care of those horses, I don't get to spend much time with them." Mark pulled Sal close and kissed her forehead. "I'm trying to talk Sal into looking for a place in the country so we can have our own horses. She's not smitten with the idea."

Eliseo glanced at Polly, then Sal and then Sylvie. "We should talk, Doc. You know where I live, don't you?"

Mark nodded and grinned. "You're just down the road from Henry's aunt and uncle in the old Sturtz place?"

"Yes. We don't have near the animals I want to have out there yet. But I'd be interested in talking to you about ..."

Sal jumped in and grabbed Eliseo's arm. "Oh yes. Talk to him about that. Please talk to him." She turned to her husband. "Please listen to him. It's not that far away. You could have all the horses you wanted and when the kids get older, they could go out and ride with you. It would be perfect."

Mark laughed out loud. "I hadn't thought of it that way. I just always assumed I'd have a place ..." His voice drifted off as he looked at his wife's pleading face. "I hadn't thought of that option. But it's a good one." Mark walked behind Sylvie and took Eliseo's arm, moving them away. "You don't have any stables out there, though. Not even a barn?"

Eliseo turned back to Polly. "But I know someone who could build that. And I should really introduce you to my sister, Elva. She is better with horses than I am."

"That can't be," Mark said.

The two men walked away talking about stables and horses.

"What just happened?" Sylvie asked. "I was only with him for a few minutes and he ran away."

"Let him go," Sal said. "He's rescuing my future. I'll do whatever you need me to do so that will happen."

Polly and Andy took Sylvie's arms and with Sal, led her to another corner of the room.

"Tell me how he asked you," Polly said. "Don't leave anything out."

Sylvie laughed. "I feel like I'm in junior high."

"Stop blathering and tell us," Sal said, plopping down in a chair at the nearest table. "It has been too long since I've been in heels this high." She leaned over and slipped the first shoe off and rubbed her toes. "Is anyone looking? My mother would be humiliated at this behavior."

"No one's looking," Polly said.

"Sit with me, then."

When they sat down, Sal, using her bare toes, poked at Sylvie's leg. "Spill it. Tell us the whole story."

"It really was sweet," Sylvie said. "It was the Sunday after Thanksgiving."

Polly sat forward. "You've been holding out on us for that long?"

"A girl has to have a few secrets." Sylvie giggled. "Eliseo and I talked about it. We didn't want to tell anyone so we could surprise you." She batted her eyes. "We've actually had a few dates between then and now."

"Shut up," Polly said. "How did you get away with that?"

"We left town." She patted Polly's knee. "Once I hired and trained Marta, I was actually able to take a few hours off occasionally. We didn't want anyone to know, so we'd meet at Davey's, park my car, and go have lunch in Ames. It was kind of fun."

Andy sat forward. "That's how Len and I felt when we were dating. We wanted it to just be us before everyone else got involved and expected us to attend things as a couple."

"But how did he ask you to *this* event?" Polly asked again. "You still haven't told us."

"You know that was the weekend Rachel and Billy were gone for their honeymoon," Sylvie said. "I did the catering for the wedding on Saturday. And then there was that other little party on Sunday afternoon." She looked up to see that Jeff had joined them. "You were gone for that one. It was just me and Eliseo cleaning up afterwards. Finally, the place was empty. I was waiting for the dishwasher to finish and I'd gone back to sit at the table by the back window. He came in and sat down across from me. We talked about the boys and school. He told me about Elva's kids and how they were doing in school. We talked about Thanksgiving. Elva cooked for them. I think he loved having his family there for the holiday."

She took a breath and looked around.

"Okay, so?" Sal asked.

"So, we talked. And we kept talking. Neither of us wanted it to be over. We didn't want to stop talking." She chuckled. "But neither of us could invite the other one to our houses because there were people around. We just stayed in the kitchen. And then my stomach growled. Really loudly. I hadn't eaten anything all day. Eliseo got worried that he was keeping me from supper, so he stood up to say goodbye. I told him that I knew where food lived; I could find us something to eat. The next thing I knew we were digging through the refrigerator and together we put together a nice meal and sat back down at the table. It was just so natural and easy."

This time she stopped and looked at her audience with a wicked little smile on her lips.

Jeff, who was standing just off to her side, pushed her shoulder. "Don't you dare stop now."

"He just asked if I'd like to come to this with him. Of course I said yes. Then I asked why he hadn't asked me out on a date before. He said that I had so much going on and he didn't want to be a burden." Sylvie rolled her eyes and shook her head. "Like he could be a burden. He's always helping me with things. Well, I said *that* and told him we should go out to lunch. He asked if I wanted to go the next day. I couldn't because I hadn't scheduled it with Marta, but I agreed to Tuesday. And then we went again on Friday and a couple of times the next week and it's been really nice."

"When did you tell your boys?" Polly asked.

Sylvie smiled and took a breath. "Eliseo wanted to tell them himself so we had dinner at our house last night." She chuckled. "We didn't want to tell them before then because Andrew wouldn't be able to keep it a secret for very long. It nearly killed him to stay quiet about it today. Every time he picked up his phone, I thought he was going to text Rebecca. Eliseo told his sister last week because he needed her help finding a suit. She thinks it's cool. We're going to do separate Christmases, but then Christmas afternoon, everybody is coming to my house for dinner."

"You're kidding," Polly said. "You're having a family Christmas with him?"

"It's no big deal," Sylvie said. "Just dinner. And maybe a few presents. Eliseo has a couple of things he bought for the boys and it's easy for me to go out and buy gifts for Elva and her kids. They love everything." She shrugged. "Eliseo and I are going shopping on Tuesday for Elva anyway. He doesn't know what to get for her."

Polly sat back. "I'm just stunned. There was all this hullabaloo about getting you two together and now that you are, it's just like you always have been. And none of us were involved."

"You're the ones who created the hullabaloo," Sylvie said. "You just needed to be patient."

"That's a whole lot of patience," Polly replied. "But it all worked out, I guess. Can we call you a couple now?"

Sylvie shook her head in mock exasperation. "You can do whatever you like. I intend to enjoy this and not worry about labels."

CHAPTER FIVE

Rebecca and Polly sat at the table in the kitchen while they waited for Heath, Hayden, and Henry to finish carrying things to the caterer's van. They'd pack dishes and utensils over to Sycamore House tomorrow and Polly would drink coffee while running the dishwasher. She wasn't going to fuss about it anymore tonight. Things had gone well, everyone had a good time, and it was over.

She snapped a carrot in half and dipped it into a bowl of mashed potatoes.

"Ewww," Rebecca said. "That's gross."

"Have you ever tried it?"

"No. It's weird."

Polly pushed the container of carrots to Rebecca. "Try it before you judge. And what would you have me do? Use my finger as a scoop?"

Rebecca pushed it back. "I ate dinner with everyone else tonight. Why didn't you?"

"Too busy talking. It always happens to me." Polly scooped more potatoes with the other half of the carrot. "And by the way, you were awesome tonight. I had complete strangers tell me how terrific you were. I suppose you know all of their names."

"Yeah. Probably." Rebecca shrugged. "It was fun. That Jimmy Rio? He's cute."

Polly pursed her lips and lifted her eyebrows. "He's much too old for you."

"Duh. But he's still cute. And he's got a cute girlfriend, so there." Rebecca stuck her tongue out.

Henry and the boys came back in. He slipped his shoes off in the mudroom and came across the floor. "Post party meal again?" he asked.

"Just snacking."

"You could eat something and it wouldn't kill you."

"It might," Rebecca said. "Do you see what she's eating?"

Polly snapped another carrot stick in half and attacked the potatoes again. "She's so young."

Henry turned, headed back to the pantry and took out a stack of paper plates and brought them to the table. He pointed at the silverware tray on the homemade counter. They hadn't done anything in the kitchen yet except cobble together some wooden counters where everyone could work. January was when he planned to begin building out the kitchen. Polly could hardly wait. Every time she got one more room under control, the house felt more like home.

A sharp yap caught everyone's attention.

"The dogs," Polly said, jumping up and running down the hallway to the boys' room. Obiwan and Han were very glad to see her and talked as she let them out. "I should take you two for a long walk. You've been really good tonight." Polly opened the door to Rebecca's bedroom to let Wonder and her kittens out, then opened the door to her own room. Luke stretched out his front paws and yawned at her, while Leia snuggled deeper into the comforter. This was probably the coolest room in the house. Polly liked it that way. She slept better, but it made for some chilly mornings until the heat came up.

She quickly changed into a pair of jeans and a sweatshirt,

making sure to put on a warm pair of socks. Polly's mind was spinning with all that had happened tonight. It had been fun meeting and interacting with Henry's employees, something she'd not really spent much time doing before. They were scattered all over the region on different projects and it was rare that they ever came to town for anything.

"What are you doing?" Henry asked.

"Going to take the dogs for a long walk. I might wander over toward the hotel and the winery. We haven't been that way in a long time."

"The boys or I could do this."

"No. It's good. I have pent-up energy to burn." She tied her shoe and stood up.

"Let me come with you. I'll hurry."

"You don't have to," Polly protested.

Henry kissed the tip of her nose. "But I'd like to. We have to talk about what happened with Eliseo and Mark tonight."

Polly was caught off guard by his mention of Mark. She expected him to want to talk about Eliseo and Sylvie. "Mark?"

"I'll tell you when we get outside." Henry moved fast and was already in a pair of jeans and a thick, lined flannel shirt. He pulled a pair of old tennis shoes on and stood up. "I'm ready."

"Wow. You are. That was fast."

They headed back down the hallway to find Obiwan and Han sitting on the floor at the end of the table, looking piteously at the kids.

"We told them no," Rebecca said. "They don't believe us."

"Let's go, Obiwan," Polly said. "Outside for a walk."

Those last words got his attention and when Henry called Han's name and followed it with a click, the younger dog jumped to his feet to follow them out to the porch. Wearing leashes meant that it would be a long walk, not a trip around the yard. That sent both tails wagging.

Polly turned them south. They cut through the parking lot of the nursing home and then the yard of an empty lot, which brought them out into a cul-de-sac just off the highway.

"You're going to build a house for someone on that lot someday and we're going to have to take the long way around," she said.

"Or you could cut through the cemetery and come out by Andy's house," Henry replied.

Polly wasn't waiting any longer. "What's up with Mark and Eliseo?"

Henry stopped while Han marked his territory. "They want to build stables out on Uncle Loren's land."

"I heard them say something. Now it's serious?"

"Mark says that Sal is never moving to the country and he's waited too long to have horses. It's going to happen now." Henry laughed. "By the time we got to the end of the evening, they had an entire business plan and one that involves Elva running the stables and acting as a trainer."

"That's a great idea," Polly said. "You'll build the barns?"

He nodded. "It's a good location, but there's a lot of work to do before we start building. All of those outbuildings have to come down." Henry shook his head. "They're in bad shape anyway. It will be fine. I don't know if Eliseo knows what he's getting into with this project."

"Their father ran stables when they were growing up. If anyone knows," Polly said, "it's those two. I just hope Elva thinks it's a good idea. I'd hate to lose Eliseo." She sighed while she waited for Obiwan. "That's selfish of me. Eliseo should do what he wants with his life. I'm not going to hold him back. This would be a great future for him."

"You don't need to worry. It is going to be a long time before it's profitable enough to support too many people. However, maybe you might think about bringing in another employee to handle the work inside Sycamore House."

"I'll talk to Jeff after the first of the year. We won't do anything until they actually start moving forward."

"That sounds like it could happen after the first of the year, too. Mark doesn't want to wait. He said that he wants to get this going before he and Sal have more children. They'll be moving into a larger house and he'd like to deal with only one thing at a time."

"I wonder where they'd move," Polly mused.

They had crossed the highway and were approaching the hotel when she realized that she was seeing flashing lights in the driveway. "What happened?" she asked.

Both picked up the pace as they crossed the parking lot.

"I'll stay here with the dogs," Henry said.

It always amazed Polly that he let her get away with her raging curiosity. He had to be just as interested as she was, but he was patient.

Polly went into the hotel's lobby and was greeted by a wailing woman who was being comforted by another woman. Three children were sitting with them, all quietly crying.

Bert Bradford stood just away from them, talking to a man who kept glancing back at the little tableau.

"Polly," Grey said, coming up to her.

"What happened?"

"Their son is gone."

"Gone?"

"The parents put the older kids into the second room. The mother's sister planned to sleep in there with them tonight, but the adults were watching television in the parent's room. When the sister went in to prepare for bed, the oldest boy was gone."

"Did he run away? Was there an argument?"

Grey took her elbow and led her away from the conversations. "The boy is angry about leaving his friends. This is the family that just moved into town. You called June about finding room for them?"

"Oh. Sure." Polly frowned. "That's really too bad. What a horrible way to begin their Christmas holiday. They're certain he ran away?"

"They aren't certain of anything. She's already placed calls to people they know, but it's late and who knows where he's gone. We're just getting started tonight. Bert's called in help to start looking."

Polly nodded. "What's his name?"

"Cameron. Cameron Shaffer. He's eleven."

"Smart enough to figure out what he wants and how to get it."

Grey nodded. "They're nice people. Doug worked in a garage, but the business closed last year. He's been picking up some day work here and there. His wife, Julie, had a daycare in her home. Of course, that's gone now."

"And the sister?"

He shrugged. "I am unsure as to what she was doing. She lived with them and may have been a waitress. But little towns don't have many good jobs. They stayed with friends for a time, but the family is too large to continue as long-term guests."

"How did the fire start in their home, do you know?"

Grey smiled at her. "Old electrical wires in the basement overloaded. The fire started in the walls and before they knew it, the house was gone. They were lucky to get everyone out." His smile dropped. "They did lose a dog. The dad says that's one of the things that has Cameron all messed up. He misses his dog, his things, and his friends."

"I should get going," Polly said. "Henry's outside with the dogs. Please let me know if we can help."

"You threw a terrific party tonight," Grey said. "Thank you for the extra gift. I might have to buy some toys for my own dogs. Your home is going to be beautiful."

Polly gave him a quick hug and went back outside to find Henry. He was nowhere to be seen, so she figured that he had gotten cold and walked off with the dogs.

"Henry?" she called out quietly.

When he didn't respond, she walked into the parking lot in front of the hotel and looked around. No Henry. No dogs.

"Henry?"

Polly walked through the parking lot to the other side of the hotel and then into the street that led back to Secret Woods Winery. She could see their lights from here so a holiday party must be going on.

"Henry?" she called again, trying to be heard, yet quiet at the same time. It was nearly eleven o'clock and several homes along the street were dark. Tomorrow was another work day.

She went past Camille and Elise's home. The lights upstairs were all out, but the basement was still lit up. Elise was awake. Camille was asleep. There was something comforting about walking through Bellingwood and recognizing the homes of people she knew.

Another half block and she'd be in the parking lot of the winery. A wooded area separated it from the homes she passed. Trees were bare and she could see lights so she headed on in. "Henry, are you back here?"

"Polly," he called out.

She turned around, trying to place where his voice had come from. "Where are you?"

"Go west. I'll turn my phone's light on."

That was strange. Polly stopped for a moment in the parking lot, placing herself on a compass. She was confident with her directions, but every once in a while, she just had to think it through. With a laugh, she turned to the right.

"Are you back here somewhere?" Polly saw a light flashing in the trees and cut through. "What are you doing back here? Are the dogs okay?" Her voice drifted off as she realized what she was seeing. "Oh. Are you Cameron?"

The boy looked up at her in shock. "How did you know my name?"

"I was just at the hotel. The police are coming to look for you."

"I don't want to go back." He pointed at Henry. "He says I have to."

"Your parents are worried, I'm sure," Henry said. He stood up and handed Han's leash to Polly. The boy had hold of Obiwan's and was stroking her dog's neck.

Polly didn't know what it was about her dog, but he didn't strain to pull away from Cameron to get to her. He looked at her and then turned back and licked the boy's face.

"This is Polly's dog," Henry said.

"You named him Obiwan?"

Polly grinned. "It fits him, doesn't it? He kinda knows what's going on and takes care of people."

"And Han?"

Polly bent down and scratched the dog's ears. "He's a bold adventurer. Kessel Run. Twelve parsecs, you know. If our Han could find the right opportunity, he'd be a great smuggler."

Cameron started to laugh and then stopped himself. "I don't want to be in this stupid town. I want to go home."

"It sounds like your home isn't there any longer." Polly wasn't going to coddle him.

"My parents are losers. They screwed up their lives and now they're screwing up mine. That's what Benny says, too."

"Who's Benny?"

"My friend. His parents would never let his house burn down. And they'd make sure his cats got out, too."

"I'm sorry you lost your dog," Polly said. "What was his name?"

"*Her* name was Mocha. I didn't know where she was." He closed his eyes. "She had a broken leg and couldn't run. Dad was too busy getting everybody else out of the house. He wouldn't listen to me when I told him Mocha was still in there." Cameron's voice broke and Henry knelt beside him.

"I'm so sorry," Henry said.

"I loved her." Cameron choked on his words. "And now I don't have her and I don't have any friends and I don't have anything." He buried his face in Obiwan's side. "All of my clothes are hand-me-downs from somebody else because we're too poor to go buy new clothes. We've been waiting for the insurance check, but it's taking forever, Mom said. That's why we had to leave."

Polly shook her head. Kids didn't understand the big decisions their parents had to make. They only saw the pain that was dealt to them.

"You need to go back to the hotel," she said. "Your parents are worried sick."

"I don't want to," he said, his voice cracking as he cried.

Henry reached across the dog and put his hand on Cameron's shoulder. "Look at me, Cameron." He waited quietly until the boy looked up. "I'm going to make you a promise. I don't do this very often, but I'm going to do it right now. Things will get better and I promise that I will do everything I can to help your parents get back on their feet. You might not be able to go back to your old town, but you will meet new friends here. Your life is about to change for the better. I guarantee it."

"How can you do that?"

"Because I'm married to that woman over there. Polly Giller changes people's lives. Together, she and I will make this better for you."

Polly looked at her husband, astounded. He'd never done anything like this before.

"Pastor Dunlap is going to help, too," she said.

Henry shook his head. "It doesn't matter what Pastor Dunlap does. I'm making this guarantee. Personally. If you give Bellingwood, me, and Polly a chance, things will get better. Is it a deal?"

Cameron frowned as he looked at Henry, then Polly. "Are you sure?"

"I'm sure." Henry stood up and put his hand out to help Cameron come to his feet. "Deal?"

"I don't know." At least the kid was moving. Even if he didn't believe that Henry would make this better, they'd get him back to his family tonight.

Polly didn't know quite what to say. Her husband had taken this somewhere she would never have expected of him, but she quickly texted Grey and told him that they'd found Cameron and would be back in just a few minutes.

CHAPTER SIX

"Even I don't make crazy promises to kids. What were you thinking?" Polly asked as they headed home.

"I don't know," he said. "We'd been talking for a few minutes before you got there and it hit me that I could do something for this kid who was so tied up in knots."

They'd gotten Cameron back to the hotel. His mother had done the expected emotional weepy thing over him, while her disapproving sister and forlorn husband stood by trying to figure out whether to get involved. Henry introduced himself to the adults and spent a few minutes speaking with Doug Shaffer. It turned out the young man had some background in carpentry. He'd grown up with a father who had a home shop, but all of that had disappeared over the years. He'd come to Iowa from Wyoming to marry his wife. There weren't any jobs for him back in Wyoming either. He wasn't prepared to go home and admit failure and then have nothing to do.

"I'm calling Dad," Henry said as they walked.

"It's late. Your dad should be asleep. They're leaving for Arizona in the morning. Don't bother him," Polly scolded.

"I have to. He won't mind."

Polly shook her head and took Han's leash from Henry. The dog knew immediately that she was in control and pulled on it. Henry clicked his teeth and Han relaxed. That infuriated Polly, but she was just glad that the dog listened to Henry.

"Dad?" Henry said into his phone. "I know. I'm sorry. Were you really asleep?" He paused and laughed. "I didn't think so. I have a situation. Can you guys leave on Tuesday instead of tomorrow?"

Polly wandered off with the dogs while Henry talked to his father. They were nearly home and the dogs recognized the way. Once they hit their yard, she let them off their leashes and followed as they tore into the yard. Every day, Han ran for the fence beside the garage, then ran the entire perimeter of the yard. When he hit the end of the fence and arrived at the bushes out front, he turned around and sniffed his way back and forth through the grass. Obiwan just did as he pleased.

She called them back and opened the door to the mudroom. Polly had taken to giving them treats whenever they came in, ensuring that the boys always wanted to come back in when she was ready. As she took her shoes off, Henry walked inside.

"Well?" she asked.

"Dad's talking to Mom about leaving later in the week. He says if this guy is any good and wants the job, Len could train him for a couple of months. Ben would still stay at the shop until Dad's back."

"Len and Andy are going to Spain in January."

"I know," Henry said, nodding. "I'd like to get someone in there to help. We've slowed down and I haven't taken as many jobs, so this would be the perfect time for Doug to start. We'll see what Dad says when they meet tomorrow."

Polly grinned. "It would be nice to have another daycare provider in town. I can think of a bunch of people who would take advantage of that."

"We have to get them into a home. I'll call the pastor in the morning. See what he's thinking. Surely he doesn't expect them to stay in the hotel long-term."

"I don't know," Polly said. "All I knew was that I needed to say yes to giving them a place to stay for a while."

"You guys were gone a long time," Rebecca said, coming back down the hallway. "We put all the food away. That fridge is loaded." She huffed. "We're going to be eating leftovers forever."

"No complaining. And you should be in bed. You have school tomorrow."

"It's not fair. Hayden doesn't have to go."

"Hayden is a lot older than you. When you're in college, you'll get long winter breaks, too. Everything in its own time." Polly gave Rebecca a hug. "Now go to bed. And thank you again for all you did tonight. You were awesome."

"Just a few more days until Christmas vacation," Rebecca muttered, wandering down the hall. "You'd think they'd just let us start early. It isn't like we're going to be paying attention to anything this week."

Polly looked at Henry.

"I love that girl," he said.

"She's a character," Polly agreed. She opened the refrigerator and stood in front of it. "I'm still hungry but I don't want anything here." She turned to Henry. "I want pizza."

"Now?"

Polly sighed. "I'm being ridiculous. And you should go to bed. You have a lot going on tomorrow."

"Are you leaving the house to go get pizza?" he asked, coming over to stand beside her in front of the fridge.

She let the door swing shut. "No. That's silly." Polly opened the door again. "I'll find something here that shuts my tummy up. Go to bed. I'll talk to you in the morning."

Henry kissed her lips and headed down the hall. She smiled at Hayden as he came into the kitchen.

"I made Heath go to bed, but I'm still wired," he said. He pointed at the fridge. "And you're still hungry?"

"I never eat at these parties. Yeah, I'm starving."

"Sit down." Hayden pointed at the kitchen table. "I'll make something."

Polly poked her lower lip out. "I wanted pizza. We don't have any. I'm sad."

"Wow. You *are* Rebecca's mother," he said.

She laughed as she sat down. "What are you going to do with yourself until school starts back up?"

"Work around here. I'll finish painting the walls in that front room where Heath and I are sleeping. I thought I might refinish the window seat in there too. It needs work. I might have to replace a few boards in it."

"I want to snap my fingers and have this whole place finished," Polly said. "I'm already tired of living in chaos."

"Just think of all the fun you'd miss out on if it were done in a split second," Hayden said. "We're gonna make memories. Isn't that what you want?"

"I guess." She nodded. "You're right. I'm just being a whiner. It was so nice to have the foyer all done and be able to show it off to everyone tonight." Polly rubbed her hands together. "I can't wait to get started on this room."

"After the holidays, I'll be working in here, then," he said.

Polly watched as he moved back and forth from the refrigerator to the pantry and back to the makeshift counter top. She hadn't paid any attention to what he was doing. "What are you making?"

"Nothing. No big deal. You just sit there and wait." Hayden waved her back to her seat. "I've got this."

"Henry rescued a family tonight," Polly said.

Hayden chuckled, his back to her as he pulsed the mixer. "Of course he did. He's your husband."

"He thinks he found someone to work at the shop and he's making his dad wait a couple of days before leaving for Arizona."

Hayden turned around. "But Christmas is next week. They should just stay here until that's over. Then we can be a whole big family."

"You're right," Polly said, nodding. "I don't know what they'll do. Henry wants Bill to meet this guy and see if he might work out."

"I can't believe they're leaving anyway," Hayden said. "You know Marie has been helping Jessie do online classes."

"I didn't know that. In what?"

"Management. I think Marie has been having as much fun as Jessie." He turned so Polly couldn't see what he was doing. "Marie talks about education all the time. How it's so important. She's got a lot of strong ideas about it. We've been talking about Heath. He really doesn't want to go away to college."

"He should, though," Polly said.

"But in what?" Hayden put aside what he'd been working on and Polly realized that now he was chopping something on their cutting board.

"You're killing me with this secret meal," she said.

"It's no big deal."

"Why wouldn't Heath go into management? I know that he's talked about coming back to work with Henry when he's done."

Hayden glanced at her. "He'd be good at that. He loves Henry and he's really taken to carpentry and construction. Heath doesn't think college is important. I don't know how to tell him that he'll experience so much in college. You meet people you'd never encounter anywhere else. You're exposed to bigger ideas and books and thoughts and people. You have to take responsibility for yourself and it's still safe." He grinned at her. "Kind of."

"I believe all of those things," Polly said.

"Heath doesn't want to do grad school like me. He isn't interested in research or academics. I get that," Hayden said. "Our brains are wired differently. But he could learn so much. There's all that leadership and management stuff that he'd be great at. I'd be terrible at it. And he loves the numbers. He was figuring out cost per goods one day for something Henry was doing. He did it in his head. When I told him that it was cool, he looked at me like I had a third eye in my forehead. He couldn't understand why I didn't see it."

Hayden slipped something into the oven and turned around. "He sees numbers in front of him as plain as I see you right there. I watched him look at them one day. It freaked me out. But he thought everybody did that. I probably have a better grasp of all the concepts and equations because I've actually studied them, but if he ever put his heart into it, he'd waste me."

"You told him that?"

"Yeah. Probably not just like that. Don't want him getting a big head or anything. He's still my little brother."

Polly laughed. "What are you cooking over there?"

"Just a few more minutes and you'll see. Do you want something to drink? There's an open bottle of chardonnay."

"That sounds wonderful. Maybe it will shut my brain off so I can sleep. I keep thinking about that young family at the hotel. And when I try to turn that off, my mind is off and running with Eliseo and Sylvie's news tonight. Of course, that makes me think about Eliseo and Mark Ogden."

"What's that?" Hayden asked. He went over to the pantry and brought out two paper plates.

"They want to build stables up at Eliseo's place. Like renting space out for people to keep their horses. Those two men think Elva would be great at running it. Mark hardly knows Elva."

"You don't think she can do it?"

Polly shrugged. "She can probably do it, but I think Eliseo will have to be really involved and I'm being selfish. I'm not ready for him to leave Sycamore House."

"He'd never leave you in a lurch."

"I know," she said. "But he'd kill himself trying to take care of my horses and help his sister at the same time."

"And you'd never let him do that. I understand," Hayden said. He poured out two glasses of wine, put one in front of her and the other on the table across from her.

"I couldn't. He means too much to me."

"When are they planning to do this?"

"Mark wants to start right away. But he's like that. He gets an idea in his head and then plows forward to make it happen. He wants horses. Sal doesn't want to live in the country, so now he's working on another plan."

"Is he really that flakey?"

Polly huffed. "He's not flakey at all. He'll be all-in and totally on board. It will be successful and he'll stick with it forever. It's just that he moves really fast and it wears me out. He met Sal and before I knew it they were dating and then she moved out here and they were married and had a kid. When I discovered those horses at that farmer's place and they were in trouble, all I did was ask for help. The next thing I knew, he loaded them up and I barely had the barn built before he unloaded them. He was always right there to help me. And he'll always be with Sal. He's just one of those guys who makes a decision and then doesn't wait to bring it to reality." She took a drink of wine. "Like I said. He wears me out. I'm glad he's married to Sal."

Hayden laughed.

"What?"

"He sounds just like you."

"No he doesn't."

"Yes, Polly. He does."

"I took forever to hook up with Henry."

"Okay. That was the one thing that took forever. But everything else? You make a decision and then make it happen. You certainly didn't wait to buy this place and it hasn't even been a year and we're living here. You told Heath in one night that he was your son and before I realized what was happening, I was too. Best decisions you've ever made, but you didn't waste time."

"Maybe that's why Mark wears me out. I'm already exhausted from everything else."

Hayden opened the oven and with a hot pad, took a pan out, then brought it to the table. He placed it on a towel he'd folded over several times.

"You made pizza for me. How did you do that?"

"A little flour, some of the roast beef from tonight, a few veggies from the fridge, garlic, cheese and voila," he said.

"You're going to make a terrific husband." Polly held her plate up while Hayden cut the pizza into slices. "But until then, I'm begging for food from you more often."

CHAPTER SEVEN

Hayden helped Polly load her truck with the dishes and utensils to take back to Sycamore House the next morning. He offered to help while she ran things through the dishwasher and put them away, but it was his first day of Christmas break and he'd had a busy semester. He could enjoy one day.

However, by the time she'd unloaded the cartons into the storage room, she regretted refusing his help. Polly dragged the cartons to the threshold of the kitchen and then, one by one, carried them in and put them on the counter beside the dishwasher. Rachel wouldn't be in until later this morning and the office was empty. Jeff and Stephanie had slowly eliminated all Monday activities and closed the building; allowing the staff to have a day off. Even the after-school care had been eliminated after Joss convinced her board that the library should be open every day after school.

Polly loaded the dishwasher and felt out of place. It wouldn't take long for the dishwasher to run its course, but still, there was nothing for her to do here. The dishwasher cycle would finish in a few minutes anyway. She should have stopped at Sweet Beans, but she'd been so intent on finishing this task that when she came out of the neighborhood, she turned for the highway and Sycamore House.

She wandered out into the foyer and marveled at the beauty of the Christmas decorations they'd put up. White lights filled the windows. Small trees with brightly colored lights and garland were scattered throughout the foyer. One larger tree was lit up in the office and a large Santa, sleigh, and reindeer had been placed just inside the main windows of the office. The sleigh was filling with wrapped gifts. The Chamber of Commerce identified families throughout the year that could use extra help during the holidays and collected food and gifts to make it special for them.

Young Cameron had been so distressed last night. The one thing he clung to was Obiwan. How horrible it would be to feel that you'd failed your pet. She could barely think about losing any of her animals, much less due to something that awful. And then to lose everything else. That was unimaginable.

Polly went back into the kitchen and opened the dishwasher, stepping back as steam rose around her. Yeah. Not a fun job.

Her phone rang and she smiled when Henry's face popped up.

"Good morning, Yummy Face," she said.

He chuckled. "You stole my job. You aren't supposed to make up silly endearments for me."

"I'm your wuvable Wubbie Bubbie." she said.

"Okay. I'll try to remember that."

"What's up?"

"I'm just leaving the shop. Took Doug Shaffer over this morning. So far Dad likes him. Doug was a little nervous."

"Of course he was. New town, new people. He doesn't know if you're a good guy or not."

"Yeah. I know. Dad said I should just leave him with them today. That makes *me* nervous."

"He'll be fine. What do you think your dad's going to do? String him up and run him across the table saw?"

"I hope not," Henry said with a forced laugh. "That would be hard to explain."

"But he was ready to go when you got to the hotel?"

"Yeah. He told me he'd be in the lobby. I met him there. We had a cup of coffee first."

"Coffee," Polly moaned. "I haven't had enough."

"Where are you?"

"At Sycamore House doing dishes. I forgot to go to Sweet Beans first."

"There you are. I'm driving by. Wave at me."

Without thinking, Polly put her hand up and waved, then giggled and put it back down. "Have you talked to Pastor Dunlap yet this morning?"

"He's not in the office. I don't want to bother him on his day off. Especially this close to the holidays. He's got to be really busy."

"You should talk to him."

"I can't do that, Polly. He needs his day."

"He needs to know what's happening with these people. Does he know what Cameron did last night?"

"How would I know?" Henry sounded exasperated with her. She knew full well it was because she was asking him to do something outside of his comfort zone.

"Okay. I'll call him, then."

"Would you?"

"What?" Polly couldn't believe he'd let her make the call. He wouldn't bother the man on his day off, but she could?

"You offered."

"You owe me."

"Anything for my Wubbie ... " Henry paused. "Whatever."

"I'll get it out of the way. Talk to you later."

"I love you," he said quietly."

"I know." Polly chuckled as she hung up. She'd start another load in the dishwasher. Dang him, anyway.

She took her phone into the hallway and sat down on one of the benches. Flipping through her last calls, she landed on the one from Pastor Dunlap and called him back.

"Lester Dunlap here," he said.

"Hi, this is Polly."

"Hello there. How are you this morning?"

"I'm good. I'm sorry to bother you today, but I wanted to talk to you about the Shaffers."

"Is this about last night?" he asked.

"I'm glad you know about that. I think it was a tough night on them."

"Polly, this whole experience has been tough on them. People have no idea how close they are to homelessness. It can happen so fast and you're helpless to stop your world from caving in on you. Especially if you don't have family and friends around to support you until you can find your feet again."

"I'd never thought about that," she said softly. "That's scary."

"Yes, it is. And I've seen too much happen to good people to take security for granted."

"Do you see it even here in Bellingwood?" she asked.

"Every week. Families fall apart, life savings are lost to medical issues, foreclosures, job losses. It never stops." He took a breath. "But that's not yours to worry about. What can I help you with?"

"Except it *is* mine to worry about," she said. "How can I help this family?"

"You're helping right now by offering a place for the Shaffers to stay until we find them a home."

"Do you have any leads?"

"Not yet. But some of my best people are out looking. Bellingwood's been growing lately and there isn't much available housing. At least not until your husband finishes those apartments and some of the new homes on the south side."

"What about Christmas for the Shaffers?"

"We're working on that, too. We'll have food for them for the holiday and a few gifts for each of the children. The biggest thing is finding them a home and helping one or more of the adults become employed."

"Henry may have hired Doug this morning."

"He what?"

"He's taken Doug over to meet Bill and Len Specek at the shop. They desperately need another carpenter."

"Doug knows carpentry?"

"He has a little background, but Bill and Len are willing to teach him. Just having another worker in there will help. So, is Lydia working with whatever group is providing food and gifts to the family for Christmas?" Polly asked.

"No, it's several other women in the church. Lydia has her hands full."

"I see. Has anyone given any thought to how this family is supposed to feed themselves this week?"

The silence on the other end of the call told Polly he hadn't even considered it. She wondered what they'd eaten since Saturday. "I need to look into that," he said.

"Let me help," Polly said.

"It's okay, Polly. We can take care of this. Tell your husband thank you for helping Doug out with a job. That was a very kind thing to do."

"Thank you, Pastor Dunlap. I'll tell him."

Polly stared at her phone ending the call. She wished he wouldn't have refused her offer of help. If Lydia wasn't helping to organize things for the family, there was nothing more Polly could do now. It frustrated her that they thought some food and a few gifts would be plenty. The family had been devastated by loss. They were in a strange community with no support system and right now they were trapped in two small hotel rooms.

Maybe she'd call Lydia anyway. But first, another load of dishes needed to move in and out of the dishwasher.

The back door opened when she finished filling the rack of dishes.

"Hello?" she called out.

An arm reached into the kitchen, the hand holding a cup from Sweet Beans. "Am I forgiven?" Henry asked.

"Of course you are," she said, laughing. "Especially when you bring me coffee. Get in here."

He came on in to the kitchen and handed the coffee to her. He pointed at the last two cartons of dishes. "We're using paper at the New Year's Eve party. None of this dish washing nonsense."

"That sounds perfect." That party would be potluck. Polly was finished with hiring outside caterers. She didn't know what she would do for next year's company Christmas party, but she had to come up with a better plan. Or find a better caterer. Maybe one with a little more experience. The food was fantastic, but the rest of this was more than Polly wanted to deal with.

"Did you talk to the pastor?"

Polly nodded and flipped the switch to turn the dishwasher on again. If she'd stick to the task at hand, she'd finish in no time, but so far that wasn't happening.

"Nothing?" Henry asked.

She looked at him, confused. "Oh. Not really. He said thank you for helping Doug find a job."

"Okay. I guess. I didn't expect a thank you from him. I wasn't doing it for him."

"I know," Polly said, nodding. "The whole thing felt weird. I know he's responsible for a church full of people, but it was like he didn't want my help."

"Oh, come on," Henry said, sidling up to her. "Who wouldn't want your help?"

"They have a group of people who are in charge of the Shaffers and I'm not one of them." She shook her head. "I'm sorry. I'm being stupid, but I've never been turned down before when I offered to help. And after you made a connection with Cameron and then his dad, it just seemed natural that we might be more involved with the family. But maybe not."

"Let it go, honey. You have plenty of ways that you help people. The pastor probably thinks that they're already taking advantage of you with your offer of the hotel rooms. There aren't many people who give generously and then turn around and continue to do so over and over. When you interact with as many people as he does, you learn that there's a limit to what people will give. If he needs to ask for your help in the future, he doesn't want you to turn him down because you did too much this time."

Polly frowned. "Did too much? For a family who is hurting that badly? What's too much?"

"You're unique, Polly. He's spreading out the need so that no one feels overwhelmed. He doesn't understand that your limits are different than others." Henry chuckled. "Very few people understand that. I certainly didn't. I seem to remember a rather large ... " He looked down and away, bit his lip, and then grinned at her. " ... fight that we had because I didn't know what your capacity was to care for people." Henry tapped the coffee cup she was holding. "Take another drink, calm down and wait until later. We're going to have plenty of time to get to know the Shaffers."

"I hate it when you're right," she said, pouting. "It really stinks."

He stepped back. "It doesn't happen that often. I'm going to take a minute to enjoy it."

"You rat." Polly swatted at him. "You're always right. Most of the time you agree with me, so it's not noticeable."

The dishwasher finished its cycle and Polly opened the door again. "I hate this job," she said.

"Then I'm going to run away and go back to work."

Polly followed him out to the back hallway. "Thank you for bringing me coffee and telling me when I'm wrong." She wrapped her arms around his waist and kissed him. When he kissed her back, she held on, not wanting it to end. "I hope it's always like this," she whispered.

"It always will be."

CHAPTER EIGHT

Once the dishes were finished, Polly went back to the house. Two very happy dogs greeted her at the side door, which had become their main entrance. Someday they would build a new garage and erect a breezeway separating the back yard from the front yard on this side of the house, but that was on a very long list of things yet to happen. It was exciting to Polly that she had what seemed to be a lifetime of projects. She'd never be bored. At the same time, she wanted all the conveniences that would come with having every project finished.

"Let's go, boys," she said. "We're taking a ride. I was at Sycamore House today and you must be missing everyone. Eliseo was down in the barn with Khan and Kirk. All your friends are there."

"Go for a ride" was another phrase the dogs quickly learned after moving into the Bell House. It always meant a trip back to their old stomping grounds to visit the horses and donkeys and to re-mark their territory.

Polly pulled into the driveway behind Sycamore House and opened the door. Before she'd put her feet on the ground, Obiwan and Han were at the tree line of Sycamore Creek, sniffing and snuffling along.

"Come on, guys," she called out as she walked across the back lawn toward the barn. Nat was chasing Tom, the donkey, around the far end of the pasture, though he wasn't trying very hard. She wondered what Tom had done to get the horse riled up. Nat was pretty laid back.

The two dogs tore past her and pulled to a stop in front of the gate. She let them in, then wandered into the barn. "Eliseo, are you here?"

He came out of the tack room, carrying a child's helmet. "Just got some new equipment in. How are you this morning?"

"I'm good," she said with a grin. "How are you?"

Eliseo nodded. "Come on back. The party was a very nice event. The room where you hosted it was quite beautiful. You always do a nice job, Polly."

"Thank you," she said. He gestured to a wooden chair and Polly sat down. "I brought the dogs over. They love coming to see their friends."

"I know. Khan and Kirk heard them and ran outside to play. Those boys never run out of energy. I don't know where they get it." He turned and gave her one of his eye-lifts, which was as much of a smile as he could manage. "Same place little children get it, I suppose."

"Are Elva's kids excited about Christmas?"

"It's the most wonderful thing I've ever seen," he said. "I've never been around children as preparations are made. Every single thing is wondrous to them. They play with the decorations that we put out and it's almost as if it is real."

"I think their imaginations are closer to reality at that age," Polly agreed. "Don't you remember?"

"I don't. I know we had Christmas decorations, but I don't remember playing with them like this."

"Mom had a ceramic choir. The boys were in black robes and the girls were in red. She'd put them out on a table and let me arrange them. Some were soloists one day, while others took the forefront another day. Christmas songs would play in the background and I'd play with those choir members, moving them back and forth. And it was real to me," Polly said. "I can still see them in my mind's eye."

"Elva's kids are just like that. They tell each other stories while they play with the Nativity characters. It's the strangest mixture of the Christmas story and whatever other stories come into their little minds. We've watched all the Christmas shows and they're enraptured. You can almost see visions of sugarplums dancing in their heads. A couple of weeks ago, Matty asked his mother if Santa knew where they lived now that they lived in Bellingwood. He'd lived in the same house all of his life, so would Santa get lost?"

"What did she say?"

"Actually, it was Samuel who answered him. He told him that Santa didn't need addresses, he only needed to listen for the heart of each child to find them."

That choked her up. "Where did he get that? It's beautiful."

"I asked him," Eliseo said. "He just said that it was the right thing. He's always known that."

"What a good kid."

"Samuel will always be Elva's sensitive, sweet boy."

"They're still doing okay in school here?"

Eliseo nodded again. "They're children and they have their ups and downs, but so far, they're doing well."

Polly's phone rang and she drew it out of her pocket. When she didn't recognize the phone number, she stood up. "Excuse me. I'll be right back."

"This is Polly Giller," she said as she walked out into the main alley of the barn.

"Ms. Giller, this is Marian Tally. I don't know if you remember me."

"Of course I do, Mrs. Tally. You work for Child Protective Services, right?"

"That's right. I'd like to do a spot check before the end of the year. I understand you've moved into a new home?"

Polly took a deep breath. What was this about? "We have. It's still under a lot of construction, though. What is this about?"

"It's truly nothing. I just need to wrap up some paperwork on Heath Harvey. He'll turn eighteen next year and graduate from high school and we will no longer have any oversight with him. When would be a good time for me to stop by? I'll be in Bellingwood later this afternoon. Are you available?"

"Uh. Sure. But please understand there's a lot of chaos."

"Don't worry about a thing," Marian Tally said. "I'll just do a quick look, take some notes and be on my way. Say two o'clock?"

"Okay," Polly said. "I'll be there. You have the address?"

"The big house back on Beech Street, right?"

"Yes, that's it. Thank you."

"Thank you, Ms. Giller. I'll see you then."

Polly put the phone back in her pocket and felt her stomach lurch. This couldn't be good.

"Is everything okay, Polly?" Eliseo asked, coming out to check on her.

"I don't know. That was the woman from the state. She wants to see the Bell House. Something about paperwork for Heath before he turns eighteen. What if there's a problem because the building is still such a mess?"

Eliseo shook his head. "I wouldn't worry too much. You are making memories with the family as you re-build that home. She's not going to create any issues. Besides, why would she take Heath out of a safe environment this close to his becoming an adult? It's probably nothing more than she said it was."

"I need to get back and clean." Polly gave her head a quick shake. "I don't even know what I can clean up. The kitchen is a mess because there isn't any storage. The boys' room is clean but cluttered because there is so much furniture in there. Rebecca's room is ..." she shook her head. "... it's Rebecca's room. I need to go. I can barely think straight."

Polly headed for the other end of the barn, then stopped and turned around. "And now I'm mad because I don't have time to interrogate you about Sylvie."

His eyes twinkled with laughter. "Saved by a phone call."

"No," she said. "You're not. I'll take a few minutes. You two are rotten brats, hiding this dating thing from us."

"We've just decided to acknowledge that you're right about that," he replied. "It will be easier."

"So, how's it going?"

"We're enjoying our time together."

Polly scowled at him. "That's not what I was asking and you know it."

"It's going well. We have fun when we're together. It seems normal and comfortable." He stopped himself. "That's not the word I want to use there. Being with Sylvie isn't comfortable. It's exciting and fun. But it's like I waited my entire life to meet her and then I had to wait to spend time alone with her and now that we're finally together, the universe makes sense."

"That's beautiful," Polly said. "Almost poetic."

Eliseo waved his hand at the door. "Go clean your house. You wouldn't want things to be a mess when that woman shows up."

"Oh yeah," she said. "But don't think this conversation is over."

"I know that." Eliseo stood at the door while she went outside.

Obiwan and Han dashed over when she called and Eliseo took Khan and Kirk into the barn so it would be easier for her to leave with her dogs.

"I'm so sorry I cut that short, boys," Polly said, once she got them loaded back in the truck. "But I'm in a panic. How could this happen to me? I've been a good girl. She didn't do this last year. Is it really just about him aging out of the system?"

She pulled back into her driveway and before opening the door, called Henry.

"Hey Christmas-face. What's jingling?"

Polly chuckled. "You're such a nut. I'm in a panic."

"Why?"

"A woman from the state wants to go through our house before the end of the year. She says it's because Heath is aging out of the system and she needs information for his paperwork."

"Okay?"

"Not okay. What if she finds problems with the house and makes a scene about things? The place is a wreck."

"The place is not a wreck and she'll understand construction. If she says we should fix things, we will. They won't take Heath away. I promise. Trust the fact that this is just a formality. Don't worry. Do you need me to come home?"

"No. I'm going to go in and scrub every surface, though. Why didn't she give me some notice? Henry, this is crazy!"

"Calm down, Polly. Take a breath. Nothing bad is going to happen. Heath is healthy and happy. Rebecca is the same. You've given them a fantastic home."

"With you," she said.

"But they are in great shape. Just don't panic. I'm sure everything will be okay."

"It's on you, then, if it isn't."

"I'll take it," he replied.

"Thank you for talking me down again," Polly said. "You do that a lot, you know."

"It's your way of telling me that you aren't perfect. If you were, I couldn't keep up. Go do your thing. Call after she leaves."

Polly put her phone back into her pocket and went inside with the dogs. She stopped the two of them and, using a dirty towel from the laundry basket, wiped their feet before letting them into the rest of the house. She should sweep. And do laundry. Polly stood up and looked around. And clean toilets and wash dishes. She should have changed the sheets on the beds.

Polly stepped into the house and opened the door to the foyer and cringed. Linens were still on the tables, and everything was in complete disarray. They were going to take the time to clean the place up this week, but it hadn't happened yet. She wanted to cry.

There was only an hour before the woman came. Polly hadn't eaten lunch and there was no way to pull things together in time to make this place presentable enough. She had no idea where to even start. This was not what she needed in the middle of her Christmas season.

CHAPTER NINE

Moving through the house like a crazy woman, Polly had torn through the bathroom and the kitchen. She'd straightened up in Rebecca's room and then in her bedroom. She'd made sure things were clean in the media room and had doublechecked that Heath and Hayden's room was relatively neat. Fortunately, those two boys were both cleaner than Rebecca.

Now she was madly rushing through the foyer, trying to clean up from last night. She'd stuffed one trash bag full and had gathered the table linens into a corner.

When the doorbell rang, Polly nearly jumped out of her skin even though she'd been expecting it at any moment.

"Front door," she murmured to herself and crossed the room to pull the door open.

"Mrs. Tally," Polly said, stepping back. "Come in."

Marian Tally put her hand out to shake Polly's. "My goodness, this is a beautiful foyer. What an immense home this is."

"We have a lot of work to do on it. But thank you." Polly pushed the door shut. "We had our company party in here last night. I'm just starting to clean things up."

"I'm sorry if I've rushed you on that," Mrs. Tally said. "I didn't mean to place any additional stress on you. With the move that you made, I just need to make sure everything is in order. Would you mind showing me around?"

Polly took a deep breath. "We'll start in the half-finished kitchen. It's next on the project list, so please don't mind the chaos." She led the woman through the door into the kitchen.

"This is a little unfinished. Not what I expected to see." Mrs. Tally gave Polly a warm smile. "Your other home had such a wonderfully homey kitchen. I thought that would be the first thing you did here."

"We pushed pretty hard to move in. I was most interested in living and sleeping space. Henry and the boys will start building this out in January."

"The boys?"

"Heath and his older brother, Hayden. You know he's living with us as well."

Marian nodded slowly. "I did know that. It's wonderful that you've allowed them to remain together as a family."

"They are a family," Polly said. "And they're our family now." She walked past the dining room.

"What's this?" Mrs. Tally asked.

She'd stopped at the corner of the dining room. A serving counter had been built into the front corner with cupboards beneath it that opened into the kitchen on one side and into the dining room on the other. Tambor doors slid into the walls on either side. Polly opened one of the doors.

"We aren't using the dining room yet. I'm refinishing some other furniture that will go into this room. For now, it's just easier to gather in the kitchen.

"The colors are beautiful. All of this old, dark wood."

"Most of it needs to be refinished as well," Polly said. "Little by little these projects will happen. It seems a bit overwhelming, but I have a lifetime ahead of me."

"This looks like a comfortable room."

They'd stopped in front of the media room. Polly decided at

that moment she was finished with that cold, technical term. It was now the family room. There. That would help. "It's our family room. We spend a lot of time in here. When the second floor is finished and bedrooms are all moved up there, other rooms will serve different purposes down here, but for now, we like being together."

"This is Rebecca's room," Polly said, pushing the next door open. "The cats like living in here with her."

"You have a lot of animals."

"I do," Polly acknowledged. She pointed into the open doorway of her room. "Mine and Henry's room for now. It will be the library someday."

"That will be wonderful," the woman said. "And the boys?"

"Down here." Polly led her down the hallway to the door leading into the future living room. "The sofas from the living room at Sycamore House fit in here along with their beds, so it gives them plenty of room to work and relax. Hayden's working on his next degree at Iowa State. He needs the quiet."

"It looks like you've got quite a nice cozy home here. It won't always be that way, though, will it?"

"What do you mean?"

"If you spread out into the upstairs, you won't be quite as cozy and snug." Mrs. Tally grinned. "You'll have to have more children come along to fill this big old place up."

"I'd love that," Polly said. "But we'll take it as it comes."

"How many bedrooms do you have upstairs?"

Polly thought and quickly ticked them off in her head. "It's embarrassing to say."

"What do you mean?" Mrs. Tally asked with a laugh.

"Well, above the main area here, there are actually six bedrooms. We'll probably turn one into a game room or something. The thing is, over the other end of the house are the servants' quarters. There are four more bedrooms over there. I don't want to use those unless we must. They're pretty far away from the main part of the house."

"You definitely need more children to come into your life."

Polly shrugged. "Like I said. Whatever comes at us, I want to be able to handle. And if nothing else does and this is what we have, I'll find a way to use the house as much as possible."

"It's wonderfully fun. I'd love to come back when you have it all finished. Just to see what you've done with it."

"Maybe we'll have an open house."

Marian Tally smiled at her. "Or maybe I'll be checking on more and more kids that live here with you." She took out her phone and snapped a few pictures of Heath and Hayden's bedroom, then Polly followed her as the woman walked back to the family room. Marian took more pictures there and then as she brought up the phone to take pictures in the kitchen, Polly put her hand out.

"Do you have to?"

"It's okay. No one will see it but me and I'll have good notes with it. Really, Ms. Giller. There is nothing to worry about."

Polly nodded.

"Where are the bathrooms on this level?" Marian asked.

"There's one between our bedroom and the boys' room," Polly replied. "It will be perfect when it's the library and living room." She pointed toward the back of the kitchen. "And another back here."

Marian walked back that way and stopped as she looked around a corner. "Those stairs go upstairs?"

"This was the servant's area when the hotel was built. Storage, stairways, bathrooms. There's more storage in the rooms upstairs. And look at the steps. They are worn down. I'm sure people were up and down them throughout the day over and over."

"So much history in some of these old places."

Mrs. Tally took a few more pictures and Polly was so thankful she'd taken the time to clean and put out fresh towels.

"I really would love to see this as you bring it back to life. I don't think anyone realized what a treasure was hiding back here," she said as they walked toward the mud room. "What a great place for laundry. This will be convenient."

"I'm trying to figure out how to get a laundry chute from the upstairs level," Polly said, laughing as she finally relaxed. This hadn't taken long at all and Mrs. Tally was being quite gracious about things. "I can employ kids to carry their own clothes back upstairs, but I'm going to have to make it fun for their laundry to get down."

"Can I go out this way?"

"That's it?" Polly asked.

"That's all I needed. Because your husband is a contractor, I'm not too worried about the structure. I just wanted to see what Heath had going on here. It seems like you have a good place to raise kids. I hope you're able to dig into those extra rooms soon, though. You never know when you might need them."

"You're right," Polly said, as she held the door open. "My life turns upside down on a dime most of the time."

"Thank you for the tour." Mrs. Tally held onto the railing as she walked down the steps to the sidewalk. She gave Polly a little wave before getting into her car.

"Well that was a whole lot of nothing after all of my panic," Polly muttered to Obiwan, who had come up to sit beside her. "At last things are cleaner."

She went into the kitchen and made another pot of coffee, then put her mug beside it as she opened the refrigerator. They hadn't eaten all the pizza that Hayden made last night, so she took out the plate and contemplated heating it up in the microwave. Polly put the plate on the table, then headed for the pantry. Good heavens, she could hardly wait for cupboards in the kitchen so that she could find what she wanted without moving things around. The chips were on a shelf by themselves and she grabbed a half-empty bag, then went back to the table.

Polly made a quick call while waiting for the coffee to brew.

"Didja live through it, Jolly Polly?"

"Please never use that one again," she said.

Henry laughed. "How was the walk-through?"

"It was nothing. I cleaned and panicked for nothing. She just wanted to see what we had here."

"Didn't I tell you that it was no big deal?"

"I didn't believe you."

"Maybe you should start doing that. I'm always right."

"Uh huh."

"Are you all better now?"

"I am. I'm going to eat some leftovers and drink coffee and let my brain run loose until the kids come home from school."

"I love you. Can you go back to having a cheery Christmas now?"

"Yes sir," she said with a smile. "All better. I love you, too."

Polly put her phone down on the table and went back to the counter to pour a cup of coffee. She'd no sooner sat back down at the table when the doorbell rang again.

"Front door or side door?" she asked herself. Since she was close, she went to the side door.

"Merry Christmas," Lydia said.

"Hello there. What are you doing out and about?"

"I wanted to hear all about your party last night. Rumor is there was some excitement with Sylvie and Eliseo."

Polly stepped inside and held the door as Lydia came in. "Can you believe it?" She pointed to the table. "I just made a pot of coffee and was going to grab a quick bite of lunch before the kids came home. Can I get you anything?"

"No, dear. You eat your lunch. But you must tell me everything you know about Sylvie. Everything." Lydia took a mug from the rack where Polly kept them and poured herself a cup of coffee. She sat down across from Polly and pointed at the pizza. "I'm serious. Eat."

"Yes, ma'am." Polly brought the pizza to her mouth.

"Wait," Lydia said. "Talk first. No eat."

Polly took a quick bite and smiled as she chewed and swallowed. A little torture wouldn't hurt Lydia. "So, they came in together last night and both looked stunning. They'd already told Andrew and Jason, but not until Saturday night so the kids wouldn't spill. They've been going out for lunch together since Thanksgiving and none of us knew about it."

Lydia nodded and listened as Polly re-told the events of the night before. Then Polly said, "Didn't Andy tell you all of this?"

"Of course she did," Lydia said with a laugh. "I just wanted to hear your version and see your face while you told me. This is really happening. I'm so happy for our girl."

"Eliseo is so smitten. When I was over at the barn earlier today, he told me that he'd waited his whole life for her."

Lydia smiled. "I wonder where they'll live when they get married."

"Don't you dare," Polly said. "It was bad enough that you all had me and Henry all figured out. You can't do this to Sylvie, too."

"But we can. I'm serious, though. Where will they live? Sylvie loves her house. And if Eliseo's sister lives with him, it would be foolish to try to introduce a wife into that."

Polly swatted at her friend. "You're terrible. Maybe he'll move in with Sylvie and let Elva live out on the farm."

"She needs a man out there to help her take care of things."

"Sometimes you are such an old lady," Polly said. "Elva can live in the country without a man."

Lydia bobbed her head as she nodded. "You're right. I wouldn't want to, but Elva isn't me. You were perfectly fine living in that big old building by yourself. It would have scared the stuffing out of me to do that. I need to remember that my fears don't have to translate into everyone else's actions." She smiled. "I'm not going to guarantee that I'll ever remember that or that I'll even admit I just said that. Got it?"

"Got it."

CHAPTER TEN

Excitement resonated through the house. It had been building all week and now that Christmas Eve day was finally here, it was palpable. Hayden had gotten up early to make breakfast and by the time it was ready, Heath had turned on Christmas music. Humming and singing along to the carols added to the fun of the morning.

They'd brought in soccer chairs and put them around the tree in the foyer on Wednesday and Henry had cobbled together a few small tables. Evenings were spent there, the lights from the big Christmas tree enough to brighten the room. Hot cocoa and cookies were usually the last thing they shared before heading to bed. It had been a wonderful week together.

Presents were tucked around the tree. Polly had gone through them a couple of times and couldn't believe there was nothing there from Henry for her.

No one had any plans for today and yet, they were all vibrating with anticipation. Polly couldn't identify exactly what was happening, and as lunch approached, she knew something was up. Something that she wasn't involved in.

Henry left around eleven thirty to pick up pizza as she put ingredients for chili into the crock pot for dinner.

"Will you settle down?" Polly said to Rebecca, who had dashed into the kitchen once again. "Either that or tell me what's going on?"

"I'm just looking for the pizza," Rebecca said. "I'm starving."

"Seriously? You had a big breakfast."

"Got my metabolism started," Rebecca retorted. "Where is he?"

"I don't know, but you have to give him time to pick it up and drive back here."

Rebecca darted away again and Polly sighed. It drove her nuts when there were surprises around the corner. As much as she loved them, she hated them at the same time. She put the lid on top of the crock pot and set the temperature.

"Polly!" Rebecca called out. "Come back here and look at what Flash is doing."

Rebecca loved those kittens. Henry hadn't had it in him to force her to give any more up after Kayla had taken the first away. Rebecca had done well caring for them, which surprised Polly to no end. It hadn't made her keep her room any cleaner, but she ensured they were fed and watered and their litter was kept clean. That was all Polly could ask.

"What's going on?" Polly asked. The little orange tabby cat had buried himself in a basket of clothing and was leaping out of it onto the floor. "He's pretty cute."

"You should sit here and watch this for a while. They all have fun playing in my stuff."

Polly sat down on the edge of Rebecca's bed. She hadn't spent much time alone with Rebecca lately. It seemed like there was always a million things to do.

"It's hard to believe you're halfway through your eighth-grade year," Polly said. "Next year you'll be in high school. That hurts my head."

"Isn't it awesome, though?" Rebecca asked. "Pretty soon I'll be able to drive, too. Will you teach me how to drive a truck like yours or will I get a car?"

Polly laughed. "I don't know how to answer that. I haven't given it much thought."

"Well you should. It's going to happen. You have to be ready for it."

"You're right. I do have to be ready. But maybe not today." She rubbed Rebecca's shoulder. "I'm glad you brought it up, though. I'd hate for me to come up to your sixteenth birthday without ever considering what you'll possibly do for a vehicle."

"I know!" Rebecca said. She leaned against Polly's knee. "It is strange to think about all of the changes that are coming. Sometimes I wonder what it would have been like if Mom and me had never moved to Bellingwood."

"Mom and I," Polly corrected.

"Yeah, yeah, yeah. I was having a moment."

Polly laughed at her again, bent down and kissed Rebecca's forehead. "I'm glad you moved to town and met Andrew. I needed you in my life."

Rebecca's phone buzzed and she leaned away to read the text.

"What are you doing with your phone, young lady?" Polly asked. "It's supposed to be on the charger."

"Just this once, okay?"

"Okay. It's Christmas. What's going on?"

"I'm supposed to tell you to come with me and close your eyes. Will you do that?"

"Maybe. Where are we going?"

"Nowhere outside. You just have to close your eyes. Either that or I have to blindfold you."

"I'll close my eyes. But can I get out of your room first?"

Rebecca looked at the cluttered floor and laughed. "Okay. That's fair. I'll even let you get down to the foyer door. But you have to close them before I open it and lead you in."

"Deal."

Polly felt her own excitement build as butterflies launched themselves to flutter around in her stomach. When they got to the foyer door at the end of the hall, she stopped and shut her eyes, then let Rebecca take her hand and lead her through. The room was silent and she wondered what she could be walking into, but decided to trust her family.

"I've got you. Keep your eyes shut," Henry said, taking her hand. "For just another moment."

Rebecca dropped her hand and Polly leaned against her husband. "What's going on?" she whispered.

"You'll see." He wrapped his arm around her waist and said quietly. "Okay, open them."

Polly opened her eyes and it took a few moments for her to register what she saw in front of her.

It took no more than that moment, though, as two little boys ran to her. Polly knelt down and grabbed Noah and Elijah when they rushed into her arms.

"Merry Christmas!" the two boys yelled. "We're here!"

She smothered them with kisses. "What are you doing here? I'm so happy to see you." Polly looked up at Henry and he smiled and nodded.

"They're here to stay," he said. "Roy?"

Henry's friend, Roy Dunston, came into the foyer from the kitchen, carrying two suitcases. "How do you like your Christmas present, Polly?"

She hadn't let go of the two boys. "I can't believe this." Polly kissed each of them on the cheek again.

"You're getting sloppy," Elijah said. "Are you glad to see us?"

"Glad?" Polly asked. "I'm ready to burst, I'm so happy." She looked up at Hayden, Heath, and Rebecca who beamed at her. "Did you all know about this?"

Rebecca nodded and knelt down to hug Noah. "Look at you. Your leg is all better. And I swear you grew a whole foot."

"Just an inch," he said shyly. "But my leg is all fixed now."

Elijah took his brother's hand and looked solemnly at Polly. "Can we live with you forever?"

"Oh boys," Polly said, choking through tears. "Yes you can. I've missed you so much. I didn't know if I would ever see you again and now here you are in my house." She looked around. "In our house."

"It's a really big house," Noah said. "I might get lost."

"We won't let you get lost, little man," Hayden said. He reached down to take Noah's hand. "Let's find some pizza for you two. I suspect Polly wants to talk to Roy and Henry."

"Just a second," Polly said and pulled the boys back to her. She squeezed them both. "I can't believe you're here. This is the best Christmas ever."

Elijah smiled at her. "I say that."

"Yes you do," she said through tears. "We're going to have a lot of best-evers." Polly stood up. "Okay. You kids go eat pizza. I'll be right there."

After they'd gone through the doorway, she turned to Henry. "How long have you known about this?"

"A couple of weeks. Roy called and asked about the possibility of us adopting the boys. I've been talking to everyone to put this together as a surprise for you."

"Is that why Marian Tally was here?" Polly asked.

"We needed someone local to work with the agency in Chicago," Roy said. "Marian agreed to help. Fortunately, she could get away with telling you it was all about Heath."

Polly sat down in one of the soccer chairs. "What happened to the family you found for them?"

Roy shook his head. "Sandra is really sick with cancer. They didn't tell the boys right away. Hoped it wouldn't affect her as badly as it did. She just doesn't have the strength to take care of them and probably won't for quite a while. It was a terrible decision they had to make. They considered trying to incorporate the boys into it, just like any family would, but everything was so new and overwhelming. She called me one night about three weeks ago and asked me to come over. Polly, I felt awful for them. They are devastated at having to give the boys up, but it's going to take all they have to get her through this." He smiled. "And when I told them that I had the perfect home for Noah and Elijah, they broke down and sobbed, they were so grateful. They've heard all about you from the boys and have been part of the correspondence between you all. If she lives through this, they'll probably want to see the boys someday, but all of that will go through me."

"Whatever they want," Polly said, her heart heavy with pain for the poor woman. She wasn't sure how to manage the emotions that were dividing her right now. The sadness of this story threatened to overwhelm her joy at having Noah and Elijah back in her life.

"I called Henry the next morning," Roy said. "I told him to talk to you, but he said that wasn't necessary and that he had a plan."

"I talked to Rebecca, Heath, and Hayden right away," Henry interrupted. "We had a lot of work to do."

"Work?" Polly asked.

"We built a bed frame and bought the bed and bedding. It's washed and ready to go. Mom and Dad have been in on this, helping put it all together. The boys are going to sleep in Hayden and Heath's room until we come up with another plan. Dad and Len also built a divider for the room."

"It's Christmas," Polly said softly. "Do they still believe in Santa Claus?"

Roy grinned. "They sure do. I shipped all of the gifts that Sandra and Tony purchased to the Sycamore House."

"And we bought some things for them, too," Henry said. "After they go to bed tonight, we'll bring everything downstairs."

"Downstairs?"

He pointed up. "It's all in one of the bedrooms. I made Mrs. Tally promise she wouldn't ask to see those rooms. We'll show her later. As soon as we're finished with lunch, we'll bring down the bed and divider and rearrange the room for them. They know they'll be sleeping in the same room with Heath and Hayden."

Rebecca peeked in the door. "Is everything set?"

"We're getting there," Polly said. "You might be in trouble."

"Trouble, you-still-love-me trouble or trouble, I-have-to-clean-a-bathroom trouble?"

"I still love you," Polly replied. "A lot."

"Can you believe it? I have more brothers." Rebecca put her hand up above her head. "I have big brothers ..." She held her hand at her waist. "And little brothers. It's a brother sandwich." Rebecca threw both hands up in the air. "I'm going to be in so much trouble. That's a lot of boys in this house. You'd better go looking for girls next time. We're outnumbered."

Polly shook her head. "Where are you staying, Roy?"

"At the hotel. If you don't mind, I'll spend Christmas with you. Do you have room for me?"

"Of course we do," she said. "You brought my boys home. I'll always have room for you."

~~~

They'd brought the two sofas from Heath and Hayden's room out to the foyer and put them around the tree before setting up the bed for Noah and Elijah last night. Roy had stayed late and finally left when the little boys couldn't stop yawning. They'd had a huge day today. They fully understood what had happened with Sandra and Tony, and though they were scared for her, knew why it would be difficult for them to remain in Chicago.

For a while, the boys would have mixed feelings about leaving those two for Polly and Henry. There'd been a lot of love in that house, something the boys had needed after what they'd come from. But Noah and Elijah were excited to be in a big new house with people they knew well and already loved.

Polly sat back in the corner of the sofa with a cup of coffee in her hand. She was wearing the plush new robe and soft slippers that Heath had gotten for her.

The little boys were playing with toys. They'd been all over the foyer, running and yelling.

Heath was building something from a kit that his brother had gotten for him and Hayden was deep into a book. Rebecca had escaped to her room after receiving a text from Kayla. They just had to share all their stories from the morning.

She looked up as Noah came to stand in front of her. "Where is it?" he asked.

"Where's what?"
~~~

"The picture."

"The one Rebecca drew of you two?" Polly put her coffee down and stood up. "Follow me." She took his hand and turned to look for Elijah. "Elijah, come here. I want to show you something."

"What?" he asked.

"Come with me." Polly took the two boys into her bedroom and pointed to the wall above her headboard. "You're right there. You've always been close to me. And I'm going to put the picture Rebecca made of Heath and Hayden up there now, too. What do you think?"

Obiwan had followed them into the bedroom and jumped up on the bed. Noah reached over to hug the dog. "Were you waiting for us?"

"I think that's a good way to put it," Polly said. She helped him up onto the bed, then waited while Elijah climbed up beside his brother.

The two boys both stroked Obiwan's back.

"I'm sorry that Sandra got sick," she said.

They nodded. "She was nice to us."

"That's what Roy said. I'm glad you had a nice place to live. I worried about you. The saddest thing I ever did was let you drive away from Bellingwood."

"Did you cry?" Elijah asked.

"Oh honey, I cried that day and I cried other times, too, when I thought about you. Sometimes when I looked at this picture, I cried because I missed you so much."

"Roy told us that you would be glad we came to live here. Noah was scared you wouldn't want us anymore." Elijah patted his older brother's hand.

"Elijah, I hope you are always as honest as you are right now," Polly said. "You are a sweet and wonderful boy. But neither of you need to be scared that I don't want you. Last night you filled my heart with so much love. I never want it to go away."

"Obiwan slept with us all night," Noah said.

"Yes he did," she replied. "And he'll sleep with you whenever you want him to."

Elijah leaned forward. "Are we really going to be here forever?" he asked, almost in a whisper.

"Yes," Polly said firmly. She leaned forward to meet his face, then gave him a quick kiss on the forehead. "Forever."

"Sandra said we could call her anything we wanted. Tony called her Sandra, so that's what we called her. What should we call you?"

Polly shrugged. "What would you like to call me?"

The boys turned to face each other. Noah looked down at the bed and Elijah leaned forward again and spoke in that same whisper. "We talked about it. If we're going to be here forever, can we call you Mommy?"

Made in the USA
San Bernardino, CA
22 December 2019